The Art of the Turkish Tale

The Art of the Turkish Tale

Volume Two

Barbara K. Walker

Illustrated by Helen Siegl

Texas Tech University Press
The Republic of Turkey, Ministry of Culture

Volume Two

This book was set in Berkeley Old Style Book and printed on
acid-free paper that meets the guidelines for permanence and
durability of the Committee on Production Guidelines for Book
Longevity of the Council on Library Resources.

Cover art by Helen Siegl
Design by Cameron Poulter

Printed in the United States of America

Library of Congress Cataloging-in-Publication Data

Walker, Barbara K.
      The art of the Turkish tale.
      1. Folk literature, Turkish. I. Siegl, Helen.
   PL246.W35 1990   398.2'09561   90-39477
   ISBN 0-89672-228-7 (v. 1) — 0-89672-316-X (pbk.)
   ISBN 0-89672-265-1 (v. 2) — 0-89672-317-8 (pbk.)
   ISBN 0-89672-315-1 (set) — 0-89672-318-6 (pbk. set)

93 94 95 96 97 98 99 00 01 / 9 8 7 6 5 4 3 2 1

Texas Tech University Press
Lubbock, Texas 79409-1037 USA

Ministry of Culture Publications of the Republic of Turkey/1437

USA   Turkey
ISBN 0-89672-317-8 (pbk.)   ISBN 975-17-1141-X (pbk.)
ISBN 0-89672-318-6 (set)   ISBN 975-17-1139-8 (set)

In memory of Neriman Hızır,
our beloved Ayşe Abla,
radio storyteller to the Turkish nation

We are grateful to Kültür Bakanlığı
(The Ministry of Culture)
of the Republic of Türkiye,
whose funding has, in part,
made this publication possible.

Grateful acknowledgment is extended to The Friends, Texas Tech University Libraries/Southwest Collection, in Lubbock, Texas; The Institute of Turkish Studies, Inc., in Washington, D.C.; and Ziraat Bankası, New York Branch, for their substantial support toward the publication of this volume.

Contents

Foreword

The Heart of the Turkish Tale

A long, long time ago,
when the sieve was inside the straw,
when the donkey was the town crier
and the camel was the barber . . .
Once there was; once there wasn't.
God's creatures were as plentiful as grains
and talking too much was a sin . . .

A great many traditional Turkish tales were, and still are, introduced with this *tekerleme* (a formulaic jingle with numerous variants). In these lilting overtures, one finds the spirit and some of the essential features of the story: The vivid imagination, irreconcilable paradoxes, rhythmic structure (with built-in syllabic meters and internal rhymes), a comic sense bordering on the absurd, a sense of the mutability of the world, the aesthetic urge to avoid loquaciousness, the continuing presence of the past, and the predilection of the narrative to maintain freedom from time and place.

Turkish tales are nothing if they are not fanciful. Most of them have leaps of the imagination into the realm of phantasmagoria. Even in realistic and moralistic stories, there is usually an element of whimsy. Bizarre transformations abound. There are abrupt turns of events, inexplicable changes of identity. Even the anecdotes of Nasreddin Hoca, the thirteenth-century wit who came to embody much of popular Turkish humor, have a way of forcing the boundaries of logic although Hoca is the ultimate rationalist. It would not be incorrect to say that "the heart of the Turkish tale is fantasy."

The tales so ably collected in this volume by Dr. Barbara K. Walker come from the time-honored typology of Turkish oral narratives—wisdom stories, fables, heroic and historical narratives, love stories, legends, accounts of miraculous occurrences, humorous and satirical anecdotes.

The tradition goes back to the dawn of Turkish history in Central Asia more than fifteen centuries ago. In the early epochs of sedentary as well as nomadic culture, the "weightless genres" became paramount—poetry, music, dance, and the oral narrative. In later centuries, with the Turks migrating into Asia Minor and then holding sway in far-flung territories, a great synthesis of oral literature evolved (much of it was to be transcribed later). The synthesis comprised the autochthonous legacy of the Turks and the rich material they amassed from the Asian (mainly Chinese and Indian) tradition, from the Islamic lore, from the Middle East, Byzantium, the Balkans, and the rest of Europe.

That is why the Turkish repertoire is so vast and the diversity of tales so encompassing. Their shamans had, from the outset, relied on mesmerizing verses and instructive tales in shaping the spiritual life of the tribes. Tales were then talismans and thaumaturgical potions. During the process of conversion to Islam, missionaries and proselytizers used the legends and the historical accounts of the new faith to good advantage. Tales became tantalizing evangelical tools. Seljuk Anatolia and the Ottoman Empire nurtured storytelling as a prevalent form of entertainment and enlightenment: Professional storytellers, preachers and teachers, and comedians kept the tradition alive, developed new versions, and contributed fresh material. Mothers not only sang lullabies, but they also recounted familiar and unfamiliar bedtime stories. Everyday conversation was peppered with anecdotes, funny or instructive, religious or profane.

In a society where the rate of literacy remained below ten percent until the mid-1920s, oral narratives played a major role in cultural transmission. Hence the vast corpus of narrative material and the preponderance and success of the short story genre in recent decades.

The study of traditional Turkish culture will have to rely heavily on an analysis of oral literature to determine communal values and aspirations, to deal with aesthetic preferences, to establish sui generis characteristics. It is of course only one of the major components that will figure in a comprehensive survey. Oral literature, however, offers some significant prospects in the richness of its imaginative resources, its metaphorical systems, and its ethical precepts. It has also contributed in an important way to keeping folk culture alive and in preserving many aspects of pre-Islamic Turkic values during the Ottoman centuries that remained under Islamic and Arabo-Persian influences.

It is regrettable that, until now, very little work has been done on the substance and functions of Turkish tales in their cultural context. Aside from some pioneering work, mainly in the form of short articles, we have no meaningful study of their aesthetic strategies, narrative structures and devices, poetic elements, linguistic features, mythmaking processes, moral concepts, class relations, socioeconomic interactions, and so forth. Just as there has been no systematic analysis of the Turkish epics, the immense body of tales remains uncharted. Scholarship has not given us even a basic understanding of the themes and functions. We have yet to learn about the philosophical context, the cultural determinants, the mythological origins, the sense of good and evil, the aspirations and dream-fulfillment, the spirit of opposition and rebellion, and other features. We have no appreciation of how folktales are shaped by and how they reflect aspects of Turkish culture.

Impressive work has been done in the past few decades in collecting, recording, transcribing, and classifying a large number of tales. In a thirty-year period, Dr. Barbara K. Walker and her husband, Professor Warren Walker, have recorded some three thousand tales that are preserved at the Archive of Turkish Oral Narrative (Lubbock, Texas), of which they are the Curator and Director, respectively. In Turkey, too, many well-trained specialists have been quite energetic in collecting material from the oral tradition, and publication activity has gained momentum. It is conceivable that we now have the transcriptions of no fewer than five thousand tales and stories and that more than half of these have been published.

English translations, including both volumes of Barbara K. Walker's *The Art of the Turkish Tale*, have made several hundred of the best specimens accessible to the English-speaking world. The material in the present volume is remarkable for its enchantments: The originals display a vivid imagination and the translations are equal to the varieties of storytelling style. Dr. Walker's fidelity to authenticity is admirable: She does not adapt, recast, or anglicize the tales; she renders them into readable, enjoyable English without tampering with the original versions as recorded by experienced Turkish storytellers.

The diversity of the tales in this volume (as in the previous one) is quite impressive. Some have elaborate storylines and many layers of meaning; some are so streamlined as to seem puristic. A goodly number possess outright or subtle political criticism, whereas a few are straight love stories. The action varies from galloping to tame. There are cliff-hangers here as well as pussycats. Fatalism alternates with a defiant, almost revolutionary, spirit. Many belong to the pure "masal" (tale) genre told for pleasure while some are "mesel" (parables with a moral). Here are dragons, giants, witches, villains, weird creatures—but also innocent children, lovable characters, romantic lovers, guardian angels. Many tales strike the reader as complete in themselves, commanding quintessential power, but some might well be fragments of an epic or parts of a cycle. The demands on the reader's mind may be like the suspense of an Agatha Christie thriller, but often they can require you to suspend belief. The vision can change from perfect clarity to trompe l'oeil. Frequently one gets the impression that these are stories generated by a static society, but then one finds a dizzyingly dynamic tale of quest that reflects a nomadic culture and its disquietude. The collection oscillates between realism and surrealism. It is a panoply of the collective imagination that strives for both survival *and* sublimation—or perhaps survival *through* sublimation.

Brought together in a coherent fashion, these tales have started giving us new perceptions and perspectives for a better understanding of Turkish culture. In them, we find both a *realpolitik*, with depictions of cynical oppression and the need to make compromises, and an *idealpolitik*, with virtually utopian dreams of justice, equality, and prosperity. The tales constitute a vivid psychodrama. Being both mnemosyne and numinosum, they unfurl a lively panorama of cultural history. It would be fascinating, for example, to do a volume entitled *Ottoman Society and Culture as Revealed through Tales* or a major article entitled "Metamorphoses of the Hero in Turkish Tales" or "Paganism and Islam in Turkish Legends and Stories."

It is my sincere hope that the Walkers might undertake such studies. If not, other scholars, I hope, will produce substantive studies on the interaction between the lore of tales and Turkish culture. We now stand midway in the collection and classification of the tales: We have established most of the texts. The next stage should be a systematic analysis within the broad cultural context. This should include critical scrutiny and comparison with the oral narratives of other nations.

This collection should be read, first and foremost, for its inherent pleasure. Like all literary arts, the art of the tale is primarily a genre of joy. Traditional stories, modern storytelling, and the Walker versions cohere in giving us the pleasures of real life and imaginary events. These stories are full of delight. Although many of them go back several centuries, some perhaps more than a millennium, they sound fresh, almost contemporary. They should be savored for their optimism, because virtually every tale resolves a dilemma or saves the good person from a terrible plight. No wonder most of the tales culminate in the celebratory couplet:

"They have had their wish fulfilled;
"Let's go up to their bedstead."

Talat Sait Halman
Former Turkish Minister of
Culture and subsequently
Ambassador for Cultural Affairs

Acknowledgments

Without the assistance, cooperation, and moral support of colleagues dedicated to recording and preserving such tales, no presentation of field-collected Turkish folktales would be possible. To Drs. Ahmet Edip Uysal, Warren S. Walker, Tüncer Gülensoy, Saim Sakaoğlu, and Ahmet Ali Arslan, to Bn. Yurdanur Sakaoğlu, and to the late Bn. Neriman Hızır I am therefore heavily indebted. They have all contributed immeasurably to the variety and validity of the narratives in this volume.

In addition, no field collection could be achieved without the willingness of Turkish storytellers to share for our recording the narrative treasures so faithfully kept alive. Their joy in sharing these treasures is evidenced in the spirit and singing sounds of the present eighty tales. Acknowledged herewith—by name, Turkish province (as of September 1990), year of recording, and title(s) of tale(s) told—are the sixty-one tellers whose narratives appear here in volume 2 of *The Art of the Turkish Tale*:

Osman Akyel, Ankara, 1961: "The Quick-witted Rabbit" and "Why the Pine Tree Does Not Shed Its Needles"

Mehmet Arslan, Bursa, 1970: "Who Gets the Grain?"

Ömer Aslan, Elazığ, 1980: "Prophet İdris in Heaven"

Hâmit Atay, Sakarya, 1976: "Nasreddin Hoca and Tamerlane Go Hunting"

Mehmet Bilgin, Hatay, 1962: "Nasreddin Hoca and the 999 Liras"

Servet Bilir, Eskişehir, 1966: "What Would You Do Then?"

Abdurrahman Boyacı, Ankara, 1974: "The Farmer and the Bear"

Hasan Hüseyin Cilev, Bursa, 1972: "Hasan the Broom Maker"

Emine Coşkun, Bayburt, 1973: "Keloğlan and Köroğlu's Horse Kırat"

Niyâzi Çam, Bursa, 1970: "The Youngest Princess and Her Donkey-skull Husband"

Abdül Vahit Çelebi, Konya, 1977: "Mişon's Debt"

Aynı Çelik, Ordu, 1964: "The Prophetic Dream"

Nadır Çelik, Ankara, 1974: "The Cock, the Fox, and the Renewed Ablutions"

Mustafa Çırakoğlu, Muğla, 1972: "*A Bektaşi* and Allah As Partners"

Ali Çiftçi, Yozgat, 1981: "How the Vizier Won the Valuable Handkerchief," "The Law of the Land," "Mohammed Protects Man from Satan," and "The Snake and Prophet Mohammed"

Ali Çuga, Tokat, 1966: "Seven Brothers and a Sister"
Hacı Mehmet Deniz, İçel, 1962: "İfrit, His Uncle, and the *Ağa*"
Memduh Derin, Konya, 1989: "Fish Heads"
Veli Duman, Bursa, 1980: "How the Devil Entered the Ark" and "Ishmael As Intended Sacrifice"
Mahmut Nedim Epekyün, Bursa, 1970: "Hasan Plucks Three Geese" and "Why Heaven Lost the Lawsuit to Hell"
Filiz Erol, İstanbul, 1962: "Why Ahmet Earns More Than Mehmet"
Sadık Erol, Bolu, 1970: "Driving for Atatürk" and "The Tree That Bore Fruit on the Day It Was Planted"
Mehmet Kâsif Ertekin, Muğla, 1972: "The Cat and the Tiger"
Hacer Ertemli, Bursa, 1966: "That's the Place!"
Emine Fidan, Bursa, 1972: "The Padishah's Three Daughters and the Spindle Seller"
Hatice Genç, Hatay, 1962: "The Stepdaughter Who Married the Dervish"
Hatice Gölcük, Konya, 1989: "The Donkey, the Dog, the Cat, and the Cock"
Ülker Gölcük, Konya, 1989: "The Merchant's Youngest Daughter"
İbrahim Gürsoy, Ankara, 1970: "The Girl Rescued by Three Suitors"
Dikmen Gürün, Hatay, 1966: "The Boy Who Would Not Become a Decent Individual," "Timid Ali and the Giants," and (in 1986) "The Dragon-Prince and Banu"
Neriman Hızır, Ankara, 1961: "The Fisherman and the Little Fish," "It's So Simple, My Friend!" and "The Youngest Prince and the Unforgettable Girl" and (in 1962) "Bold Girl, Solver of Problems," "The Hoca and Tamerlane's Elephant," and "The Learned Turban"
Ali İpekçi, Amasya, 1973: "The Man Who Sought His Fate"
Ferhat Kalafatoğlu, Giresun, 1964: "Three Hunters: A *Tekerleme*"
Nurettin Kamışlıoğlu, Elazığ, 1977: "Keloğlan and Brother Fox"
Duralı Karakayı, Bilecik, 1976: "Arzu and Kamber"
Hulûsi Kargı, Sivas, 1988: "Why Shopkeepers Share Their Customers"
Nesim Zihni Karnat, Trabzon, 1962: "The Padishah, His Three Sons, and the Golden Apple"
Hülya Kırkıcı, Denizli, 1985: "The Mortality of a Caldron"
Nuri Konuralp, Hatay, 1962: "Inherited Behavior"
Mustafa Aydın Kopalak, Antalya, 1969: "The Legend of Muratpaşa Mosque"
Suzan Koraltürk, Trabzon, 1962: "The Prince and Pomegranate Seed"
Mehmet Kara Koruk, Eskişehir, 1975: "Nasreddin Hoca, the Door, and the Window"
Zekiye Kuş, Bursa, 1970: "The Black-haired Beloved"
Reşat Özbaş, Aydın, 1972: "The Black Sheep and Ahmet *Ağa*'s Daughter," "The Last Word," and "The Professor and the Boatman"

Hamiyet Özen, Trabzon, 1990: "A Ticket to Trabzon"
Hasan Özgürbüz, Manisa, 1962: "Separation Born of Suffering"
Enver Tahsin Pir, Erzincan, 1974: "Osman Effendi and the Train Ticket"
    and "Osman Kalkan and the Twice-shared Lemons"
Esat Söylü, Yozgat, 1974: "The Chastity Wager on a Faithful Wife"
İbrahim Şafak, Kastamonu, 1964: "The *Hoca* and the Dessert"
Bayram Şahin, İçel, 1974: "Nimrod, Abraham, and the Camel from the
    Rock" and "Nimrod and the Prophet Abraham"
Nadır Şahin, Kayseri, 1963: "The *Kadı*'s Canine Kinfolk"
Süleyman Sırrı Şahin, Sinop, 1964: "The Bilingual Boars of Sinop
    Province"
Osman Telli, Hatay, 1962: "The Peddler and the Kayseri Boy"
Ahmet Şerif Tragay, İstanbul, 1968: "Paradise or Hell?: A Choice Made"
İsmail Turunç, Erzincan, 1974: "The Ordeals of the White-bearded
    Young Man"
Süheyl Uçarer, İstanbul, 1974: "Who Is More Clever?"
Melek Uysal, Hatay, 1966: "The Industrious Woman and Her Lazy
    Husband"
Şükrü Velioğlu, Ankara, 1989: "It Can't Be Mine!"
Kara Yakup, Ankara, 1970: "From *Felek* to *Elek*"
Osman Yılmaz, Yozgat, 1966: "Azrail and the Forty-day Furlough" and
    "The Substitute Bride"
Finally, an unidentified man in his sixties told in Bursa in 1973 the tale
    "Nasreddin Hoca and the Oven."

Too, as was true for volume 1, there are several persons whose discerning translations of the field-collected tales made the compilation of this second volume pleasurable as well as possible. Among those translators, the most faithful and outstanding were Drs. Ahmet Edip Uysal and Dikmen Gürün Uçarer, Bn. Necibe Ertaş, and the late Bn. Neriman Hızır and Zafer Çetinkaya Sükan.

Once again, also, Helen Siegl in her sensitive and painstaking dry-point etchings and collagraphs has captured both the character and the spirit of the culture giving rise to these tales, enriching immeasurably the dimension of this second look at the art of the Turkish tale.

To all these contributors toward a fuller understanding and appreciation of Turkish oral narrative I extend my warmest thanks.

The Art of the Turkish Tale

Introduction

Through volume 1 of *The Art of the Turkish Tale,* readers were introduced to the oral tale as a form and were offered selected Turkish tales as a rich sampling of that form. The fifty-one tales included in the first volume, drawn from more than three thousand field-collected tales in the Archive of Turkish Oral Narrative, gave at least a small taste of the delights still available today in Turkish oral tradition.

The eighty tales in volume 2, also drawn from the Turkish Archive, carry the reader more deeply into Turkey's cultural holdings. They create a veritable Turkish carpet of such varied strands as legends, dilemma tales, riddling tales, fables, tales of the supernatural, *cantes fables,* romances, Biblical remnants, Islamic saints' legends, historical reminiscences, and humorous anecdotes. In addition to the widely known folk figure Nasreddin Hoca, such folk types as the trickster, the fool, the *keloğlan,* the *Bektaşi,* the *ifrit,* the *kadı,* the *hoca,* Köroğlu, the Kayseri resident, the supposedly stupid Laz, and even the Erzincan Province local folk hero Osman Kalkan people these tales.

Because these tales were recorded in Turkish on magnetic tape and faithfully translated, one can catch the voices of the tellers and can sense the ambience of the telling. The sixty-one narrators varied widely in age, geographic location, degree of formal education, and preference for narrative subjects and forms. Each had his or her own storytelling style, and each was stimulated to maximum achievement by the obvious and attentive interest of the field collectors.

These tales, gathered over three decades, represent most of the years between 1961 and 1990, providing evidence that the oral narrative in Turkey is still alive and well despite the lure of radio and television. Although the number of narrators in urban settings willing to record tales lasting more than three or four hours at a sitting has dwindled, there are rich sources to be found today in eastern Turkey and in the mountainous areas elsewhere in the Republic. Good narrators are not limited, either, to remote spots; all of the cities and major towns in Turkey offer fruitful fields for harvesting folktales, especially Nasreddin Hoca, Kayseri, and Laz anecdotes and *keloğlan* tales. And Turks themselves are increasingly identifying and salvaging specimens of what may be the richest store of oral narratives among western or westernized nations.

I trust that this taste of Turkish storytelling will prompt at least a few readers to tell some of the tales themselves, for such tales are meant to be shared. They are at once universal and refreshingly different, and fortunately they are still being told in the country where they were found. They deserve to be told around the world.

Basic Elements of the Art of the Turkish Tale

As was demonstrated at considerable length in the Introduction to volume 1, the oral tale in Turkey—aside from several short forms to be discussed later—accommodates admirably the three distinctive yet interlocking elements in the art of a living tale: the functional element, the narrative element, and the performance element. (The term *living tale* is here understood to mean a tale that has been told, with personal variations, from one generation to another in the same culture and that can still be found on the lips of storytellers today. To persist in the oral tradition, such a tale must incorporate features of continuing interest and significance to that particular culture.)

The tale functions as moral guide and cultural reminder, bonding both individual and community in preservation of long-standing values, customs, and relationships. Among the values most clearly reinforced in the tales collected here are persistence, soundness of character, concern for others, initiative, trust in Allah, obedience, courage, cleverness, and patience. Cultural reminders abound in dress, military service, Islamic practices, historical figures, and family and social customs. They are present, as well, in relationships between authority figures and their subjects, parents and children, siblings, peers, and lovers.

In the tale, too, are found most or all of the earmarks of sound oral narrative: beginning and ending formulas, restriction to a single main plot, simplicity of characterization, the presence of two strongly contrasted major characters, persistent use of repetition, and ultimate success of the character initially perceived as weakest, youngest, or most despised. Use of the *tekerleme* (a traditional opening) by its nonsense and humor prepares listeners to move into the world of the narrative; one version or another of the traditional closing both concludes the narrative satisfactorily and returns the listeners refreshed to their everyday lives. And between the *tekerleme* and the closing lies a tale well worth remembering.

Finally, the *manner* of telling—the performance of the tale—bears distinctively individual marks. Although the core of any given tale is present in any telling of that tale, the use of such stylistic touches as alliteration, onomatopoeia, proverbial expressions, inclusion of potent numbers (three, seven, forty), lively conversation, rhetorical questions or exclamations, use of songs or poems traditionally associated with the tale being told, marked repetition, and either cleverly personal or solidly traditional techniques of opening and closing differ considerably from narrator to narrator. Thus is brought to the reader the full flavor of any particular telling, the "voice" that gives each tale its Turkishness, its freshness, its vitality.

Principles for Selection of Tales

With such a wide range of tales from which to choose, what principles guided the selection of tales to include? For this volume, four major considerations prompted the choices made. Variety in subject, form, and length was an important factor. Too, a wide range of narrators in terms of age, geographic location, extent of formal education, and storytelling style was sought. Then, representation across the span of thirty years of field recording in Turkey was needed. Finally, tales reflecting Turkey's rich historical and religious heritage were essential. The threefold desire to please, inform, and entertain, as well as the imperative to provide ample occasions for Helen Siegl's sensitive artistic presentation of the characters, the setting, and the culture, undergirded all four of the major considerations and proved to be the deciding test for the final selection.

Variety seemed essential in order to convey the richness of Turkey's narrative stock. In addition to variant treatments of the subjects introduced in volume 1, it was necessary to incorporate anecdotes involving the *Bektaşi*, the Laz, the Kayseri resident, the Jew (since 1492 welcomed and protected by the Turks), and at least one local folk character (in this volume, Erzincan Province's clever Osman Kalkan). Too, both Nasreddin Hoca and the *keloğlan* required emphasis because of their continuing predominance in Turkish oral tradition. An effort was made to include Turkish variants of such well-known tale types as Animals in Night Quarters (The Bremen Town Musicians), The Anger Bargain, Bluebeard, The Brave Little Tailor, Cinderella, The Dragon Slayer, Polyphemus, Puss in Boots, and The Seven Brothers, universal tales whose long-standing Turkish versions are still heard in Turkey today (these versions may very well outdate the more familiar ones). Tales including grateful animals and extraordinary companions were also needed. As for variety in form, in addition to variants of the forms supplied in volume 1, the *nükte* (see "From *Felek* to *Elek*"), the *kıssa* (see "The Law of the Land"), and the *pourquoi* (see "The Cat and the Tiger" and "Why the Pine Tree Does Not Shed Its Needles") needed to be represented as well as the dilemma tale (see "The Girl Rescued by Three Suitors") and the riddling tale (see "Hasan Plucks Three Geese" and "The Prophetic Dream"). In terms of length, at least one tale requiring well over an hour in the Turkish telling (see "Hasan the Broom Maker") and several requiring less than a minute (see "The Quick-witted Rabbit," for example) served to suggest a fair range in length of current Turkish tales.

It was not difficult to identify tales representing a wide range of narrators. The narrators of these eighty tales ranged in age from a 13-year-old girl (Hatice Gölcük of Konya Province) to a 77-year-old man (Hâmit Atay of Sakarya Province). Every decade of life between these two extremes was fully represented. Geographically, the narrators represented every sector of Turkey except the far northwest (Eastern Thrace) and the far east (the easternmost location represented in this volume is the recently formed province of Bayburt). As for extent of formal education, at least a dozen narrators (chiefly elderly women and men) were totally illiterate; most had had at least some primary schooling; half had completed middle school; a smaller number had finished high school, and half a dozen had had university or medical training. The narrators with the smallest amount of formal education proved most strongly committed to preserving the oral tradition and most willing to tell tales of considerable length and complexity; those with the highest degree of formal schooling tended to relate a *fıkra,* or anecdote, rather than a fully developed tale. Variety in storytelling style was determined partly by the tape recordings and partly by our notes and recollections of the tale-telling events. The liveliest tellings were secured when the audience included friends or neighbors or relatives of the narrators in addition to the collector or collectors. Since for this volume, as for volume 1, I chose insofar as possible tales that either my husband, Warren S. Walker, or I had collected, it proved relatively easy to identify narrators to represent many styles of storytelling. These styles can be detected even in the English versions because the "voice" of each narrator has been preserved.

For this volume, the years 1962, 1966, 1970, 1972, 1974, and 1989 proved most productive, though more than two-thirds of the years from 1961 through 1990 are represented by at least one narrative. The primary purpose of securing a cross-section of years was to determine the state of health and viability of the folktale in Turkey. It would appear from the dates of these Archive recordings that Turkey's rapid urbanization, westernization, and sophistication of communication have combined to make oral narrative there an increasingly endangered species.

Aside from the legend "How the Siege of Van Was Lifted," volume 1 took no notice of oral reflection of Turkey's rich history. Nor did that volume incorporate more than slanting suggestions of the immensely varied religious heritage carried in the Turkish folk memory. In volume 2 these omissions have been to a small degree rectified. Herein are found such figures as Tamerlane (the fourteenth-century Mongol conqueror who swept westward to the Black Sea), Fatih Sultan Mehmet (Mehmet the Conqueror, who led his troops in the capture of Constantinople in 1453), and Harun Reshid (probably the most colorful and powerful of Abbassid caliphs as well as a notable military leader, so well known that he was the caliph in *The Arabian Nights*). Here, too, appears a moving personal account of Mustafa Kemal Atatürk, leader of the Turkish War of Independence following World War I and founder of the Republic of Turkey. As for oral narrative images of figures common to all three monotheistic religions long associated with Turkey—Judaism, Christianity, and Islam—a sampling includes Abraham, the Devil, Gabriel, Ishmael, Jonah, Nimrod, and Noah. The Prophet Mohammed and several early caliphs represent Islam, as do countless uses of Islamic terminology (for example, *haram* and *helâl*), greetings, and practices. It is interesting to note that more can be found about Nimrod in Turkish oral tradition today than was revealed in any of the scriptures sacred to the three major monotheistic religions.

In satisfying the needs for variety, for a wide range of narrators, for a balanced representation of a full three decades of field-collected tales, and for inclusion of narrative reflections of Turkey's rich historical and religious background, this volume serves as both complement and supplement to volume 1. Both in the tales provided and in the approach to tales and tale telling, then, this volume fleshes out the image of Turkish oral narrative sketched in the first volume.

Anecdotes as a Folk Narrative Art Form

Because anecdotes are usually short, pithy, and entertaining and because they are readily absorbed and transmitted, they are often overlooked as an art form and as an index to folk culture. Even the major study of Turkish oral narrative, Eberhard and Boratav's *Typen Türkischer Volksmärchen,* takes no notice of this form. But the Turkish anecdote provides an excellent window on Turkish folk narrative. Through this small window can be viewed the values, attitudes, and broad sense of humor of Turks in all walks of life. Furthermore, a well-told anecdote demands a marked degree of narrative skill, and its economical form leaves no room for loose ends. Many can tell jokes, but few can deliver well-turned anecdotes worthy of repeated transmission. The anecdotes in this volume provide a small sampling of a widely used but underrated art form.

Two kinds of Turkish anecdotes invite initial notice: the *nükte* and the *kıssa.* An anecdote dependent for its effect on a terminal play on words—words frequently rhymed, as well—is called in Turkish a *nükte.* Such anecdotes are particularly difficult to translate and even more difficult for a non-Turk to find either entertaining or laugh provoking. But the Turks relish such anecdotes, and one, "From *Felek* to *Elek,*" is therefore included here. The explanation of *felek* and *elek* is not properly part of the anecdote. The other listeners were laughing and slapping their thighs at the snapper ending when the narrator, Kara Yakup, realized that Warren had not caught the humor of the ending. His explanation has been included as an example of concern of a narrator that a non-Turkish listener appreciate the full flavor and art of the short tale.

Another anecdotal form, the *kıssa*, appears in "The Law of the Land." Again, the narrator, this time Ali Çiftçi, was determined to communicate the full import of the narrative, and he therefore identified the tale as a *kıssa* and clarified the function of such items in the Turkish cultural setting. Clearly, the narrator saw, beyond the content of the anecdote, its usefulness as a cautionary tale long past the times of religious courts into late twentieth-century secular courts and legislative bodies.

The *nükte* and the *kıssa* are specialized forms within the broad range of the Turkish anecdote, or *fıkra*, a short narrative that can serve any number of purposes. A *fıkra* may entertain; it may reproach; it may inform; it may function as a put-down; it may emphasize the supposed cleverness or stupidity of residents of a particular place or members of a distinct ethnic group; it may point up the cupidity of a *kadı*, a judge in an Ottoman court (loosely applied to all judges), or the lasciviousness of a *hoca* (Muslim preacher). Seemingly, a *fıkra* is over almost as soon as it has begun, but it has made a telling point. It is effective in great measure because it presents a large message in a small package.

Hundreds, perhaps thousands, of Turkish anecdotes center on the beloved folk character Nasreddin Hoca, said by many to have lived in the central Anatolian town of Akşehir during the time of the dreaded conqueror Tamerlane. Sometimes foolish, sometimes wise, but always unmistakably human, Nasreddin Hoca served in his community as Muslim preacher and teacher and, on occasion, as judge. But the anecdotes in which he figures are by no means confined to his official functions, nor is the setting of the anecdotes limited to Akşehir. A narrator beginning "Once the Hoca . . ." or "One day the Hoca . . ." or "One winter evening the Hoca . . ." is certain to draw an appreciative audience, an audience well aware that the subject of this *fıkra* is no ordinary *hoca*, but Nasreddin Hoca himself. The nine Nasreddin Hoca anecdotes herein provide a flavorsome taste of Turkey's best-known folk character. As is true with other folk heroes, the Hoca has become the focus of many hundreds of anecdotes derived from other sources but adapted to him. One of such anecdotes clearly is "Who Is More Clever?" which appears in a lengthier version and a considerably more turgid style as "The Ass Carrying Salt" in Thomas James's *Aesop* (1848). Whether the Hoca version preceded or followed the one attributed to Aesop (himself believed to have lived in central Anatolia many centuries ago), the Hoca version is certain to outlast the Aesopian one because of the sprightliness of its telling and the personality of the donkey's owner. Too, the question with which the narrator closes the Hoca version is more artful and more winning than the moral appended to the fable.

Among other anecdotes in this volume, "Mişon's Debt," told in broad Jewish dialect to an appreciative mixed Turkish and Jewish audience, and

"The Last Word" feature Jews, a group represented in various anecdotes and longer narratives and in the Karagöz shadow-puppet plays of Turkish oral tradition. Four anecdotes herein focus on the Laz (a distinct ethnic group located along the eastern Black Sea coast): "The Bilingual Boars of Sinop Province," "It Can't Be Mine!" "A Ticket to Trabzon," and "What Would You Do Then?" Although in most Laz-centered *fıkra*, the Laz (quite often named Temel or Dursun or Hızır) is pictured as rather stupid, he is in his own oral tradition presented as cleverer than the man from Kayseri, long reputed to be the wiliest of Turks. It is said that though one may not read or write, if he comes from Kayseri he is certain to outwit even the Devil. This observation is amply borne out by innumerable anecdotes about Kayseri residents. See, for example, "Fish Heads" and "The Peddler and the Kayseri Boy."

In Turkey the *fıkra* has long been used to highlight the failings of religious and secular figures—not unlike western anticlerical and antijudicial anecdotes. The assumed greediness of the *hoca,* the blind "justice" of the *kadı,* the immorality of the *Bektaşi,* the superior attitude of the professor, and the absence of lawyers in Heaven are held up for close inspection in various anecdotes in this volume. These provide just the tip of an iceberg of entertaining short tales that could readily be adapted to fit any culture around the world, for they mirror universal frailties. Still, these anecdotes and various others in volume 2—for example, "That's the Place!" and the two about the Erzincan Province trickster Osman Kalkan—have a distinctively Turkish flavor and bear telling in their present forms as evidence of the art of the Turkish tale.

Historical and Religious Tales and a Legend

T hanks to its geographic location as the bridge between Europe and Asia, Turkey carries in its oral tradition bits and pieces of almost four thousand years of historical and religious episodes. Invasions from both west and east, the rise and fall of empires, and the birth and growth of the three major monotheistic religions have all left marks on the repertoires of tale tellers. But unlike accounts frozen in print, the tales that have survived throughout dozens of generations bear a curious relevance to life and culture in Turkey today. Episodes from the Gilgamesh Epic (told by illiterate narrators unfamiliar even with the name Gilgamesh) and tales of encounters with one-eyed giants (related by raconteurs unacquainted with Homer's *Odyssey*) rub shoulders in the Archive with episodes involving Tamerlane, Mehmet the Conqueror, and the twentieth-century hero Atatürk.

Too, today's narrators tell of Noah and the ark, the Creation, Joseph's rejection of temptation by the pharaoh's wife, Abraham's promised sacrifice of his first-born son, confrontations between Abraham and Nimrod, and events in the life of Mohammed—all with fine disregard for chronology but with conviction that their tales provide guidance and assurance for twentieth-century listeners.

And so they do. In the brief account "Why Shopkeepers Share Their Customers," Mehmet the Conqueror is pleased to find that his people are concerned for one another. That concern, witnessed by Fatih Sultan Mehmet just after the middle of the fifteenth century, is still evidenced today in late twentieth-century Turkey. Both Warren and I have, on separate occasions, experienced precisely the same nudge to buy further items from other shopkeepers—"so they, too, might have good luck today"—that the Conqueror encountered five centuries ago.

On first reading, "The Tree That Bore Fruit on the Day It Was Planted" seems merely a relic, a folk memory of largess dispensed by Caliph Harun Reshid in response to an old man's investing his feeble efforts in a future he would not live to see. But again the tale is functional: it reinforces the traits of generosity and concern for others, values that continue to be central among Turks.

The names of such historical figures have gone into the collective unconscious of those maintaining the oral tradition, to be inserted wherever their inclusion will lend authority to the teaching. Whether a given incident occurred during the reign of Caliph Harun Reshid or of Fatih Sultan Mehmet or during the oppressive rule of Tamerlane is immaterial; the primary purpose is to retain and reinforce the values stressed in the tale. It is Turkish narrators' good fortune to have these names at their disposal as part of their own heritage, to relish and to share.

Where, you may ask, does Polyphemus, the one-eyed giant, have occasion to enter the Turkish oral stream? Among other tales in the Archive, he appears under the name *Tepegöz* in the narrative titled "The Ordeals of the White-bearded Young Man." He appears also, at much greater length, in an account in the Turkish oral epic "The Book of Dede Korkut," several episodes of which have been collected from narrators in what is now Bayburt Province. Like Tepegöz, various other characters—Bamsi Beyrek, for example—are still afloat in Turkish oral narratives. And, as in the Tepegöz episode, one value or another—courage, initiative, persistence, cleverness—is reinforced among twentieth-century Turks by these tales, relics from an earlier time made relevant today. Moreover, what keeps the tales alive is the artistry of their telling, an artistry that continues to compete successfully with the offerings of cinema, radio, and television.

Since approximately 99 percent of the Turks are Muslims, it is not surprising to find among current oral narratives accounts of Biblical figures—Abraham, Gabriel, Joseph, Nimrod, and Noah, for instance—as well as those of the Prophet Mohammed and his colleagues and a host of Muslim saints. Curiously, most of such Archive-housed accounts never made their way into the Old Testament, the Torah, or the Koran. They reflect instead a folk Islam, one to which even today's Turkish Muslims can relate. "The Snake and Prophet Mohammed" and "Mohammed Protects Man from Satan" circulate fairly widely in one variant or another. They certainly do not derive from the Koran. Yet each affords a fresh and congenial way of visualizing Mohammed, and each provides its own particular brand of support for the humble believer. Too, there is decided homely charm in "How the Devil Entered the Ark." The tale proceeds from tribal insurrections "many hundreds of years ago" that prompt Allah to send the Flood, to Noah's being encouraged by the old woman with the daily jug of cow's milk, to the balkiness of the Devil-inhabited donkey that provokes Noah's exasperated "Get in there, cursed one!" to the narrator's admission at the close: "I cannot remember how long that great flood lasted."

Concern with the afterlife and especially concern with Judgment Day inform a number of religiously oriented narratives in the Archive, concerns certainly not limited either to Muslims or to Turkish listeners. In "Azrail and the Forty-day Furlough," the young bride both suggests a plea to the Angel of Death and prays fervently for at least a short reprieve from death for her husband; thus the groom wins forty extra days of life. "Nimrod and the Prophet Abraham" provides the folk believer with a reassuring view of Allah's power and mercy. The good Muslim in "Paradise or Hell?: A Choice Made" chooses the known mortal friendship—another important value—rather than the place in Paradise he has earned. (The narrator left this collector wondering whether that return ticket was honored in Paradise, a bonus in a tale well told.) And Prophet İdris, the soul of honor, cleverly manages to ensure his own afterlife in "Prophet İdris in Heaven." These tales and many others in the Archive reflect an anthropomorphism that probably derives not from study of the Koran but from the tellers' own desire to pass on to their hearers colorful accounts that had in earlier years comforted or pleased the tellers themselves.

"The Legend of Muratpaşa Mosque," a variant of Aarne-Thompson Type 745A—The Predestined Treasure, offers an extra element in the faithful Muslim's using his unexpected fortune not only to have a mosque built but to endow its replacement if it should fall into ruin. The same power that had predestined the treasure, it is assumed, continued to protect what remained of that treasure from those not entitled to it long after the predestined owner had died. A sense of eternal justice is artfully conveyed in this legend.

To approach Turkish history, Islam, and faithful Muslims through the medium of the gifted storyteller is to find a deeper dimension than can be gained by the study of documents. And as long as a single hearer is willing to listen to such a storyteller, that deeper dimension can be preserved.

Other Distinctive Narrative Forms

Two of the tales in the present volume fit the *cante fable* classification: "Arzu and Kamber," a romance doomed almost from the start, and "Keloğlan and Köroğlu's Horse Kırat," a combination of the trickster and hero tales. In these two tales, the most significant portions of dialogue between major characters were presented in four-line rhymed stanzas. Although in earlier versions the poetic passages were probably sung—perhaps to the accompaniment of a folk instrument called the *saz* or *bağlama*—in the versions recorded for the Archive the passages were half-chanted and half-recited, leaving no doubt that they differed from the prose narrative. In both of these tales, a thoroughly Turkish character, the *keloğlan* (a boy or man bald from a scalp disease but both clever and lucky), plays the role of trickster. In "Arzu and Kamber," Keloğlan initiates the action, drives a hard bargain for possession of the foundling Kamber, and then leaves the scene with the winnings from his bargain. In "Keloğlan and Köroğlu's Horse Kırat," Keloğlan remains on the scene throughout most of the action, and the action is precipitated and then enhanced by his trickery. In neither of the tales does the *keloğlan* speak in verse, an indication that he is not deemed by the storyteller one of the two major characters. Both the use of versified dialogue and the presence of tricky Keloğlan make these two tales distinctive.

Several of the tales in this volume stand out because they are clearly variants of stories long familiar from other cultures. "The Padishah's Three Daughters and the Spindle Seller" resembles the story of Bluebeard. In "Timid Ali and the Giants" we have a variant of The Brave Little Tailor. "Keloğlan and Brother Fox" has many similarities to the Puss in Boots tale. In "The Padishah, His Three Sons, and the Golden Apple" we find many parallels to the dragon-slayer story. "Seven Brothers and a Sister" is a markedly Turkish version of The Seven Brothers. The Anger Bargain is represented by "İfrit, His Uncle, and the *Ağa*." And "The Stepdaughter Who Married the Dervish" is one of many Archive variants of the Cinderella story. An episode from the Polyphemus tale, as mentioned earlier, is found in "The Ordeals of the White-bearded Young Man." Since a variant of The Calumniated Wife, "Cengidilaver," was included in volume 1, a variant, "The Wager on the Wife's Chastity," has been included here. That variant and the Turkish version of Animals in Night Quarters (The Bremen Town Musicians) are discussed below. In each instance, there is no way of determining which of the two—the familiar form or the Turkish one—came first, nor is such a determination needed. Each form is peculiarly relevant to the culture in which it is passed down from one generation to the next. No culture holds a monopoly on any universal tale type. Furthermore, it is the cultural differences that make them of interest to storytellers and readers alike.

The Turkish variant of the Bremen Town Musicians, "The Donkey, the Dog, the Cat, and the Cock," deserves separate notice because it was exceptionally well told. The devices used by the narrator illustrate the art that marks a Turkish tale. The teller, a thirteen-year-old girl in Konya, had been reared by a family of accomplished storytellers and was already well on her way to becoming an outstanding narrator herself. By strategic use of repetition and by personalizing the four animals as Brother Donkey, Brother Dog, Brother Cat, and Brother Cock, she had her entire adult audience concerned about the quartet's welfare. The offer of transportation by Brother Donkey was entirely in keeping with the Turkish values of friendship and of concern for others. In identifying forty thieves as the obstacle to be overcome, she incorporated a thoroughly Turkish feature. Her imitation of the respective animal sounds without resorting to the notion that they fancied themselves as singers was entirely in keeping with animal character, as were the animals' responses to the intrusion of the brave thief. The crowning touch of the telling, however, came in the animals' reporting the thieves the following morning to the gendarmes in the next village, to ensure that the thieves received the attention required by law and order. The reward—allowing the four animals to live in comfort thereafter—tied up the loose ends neatly and left the audience fully satisfied. I was among the audience that evening, and I rejoiced for the future of Turkish tale telling.

Too, the narrator of "The Chastity Wager on a Faithful Wife" used certain techniques that require special comment. Since Esat Söylü, the storyteller, knew that before he could get to the crux of this particular tale, he needed to provide some background that offered little opportunity for drama, he engaged the full attention of the coffeehouse audience by using a narrative hook: in the very first minute, he introduced the notorious bully boy Bekri Mustafa. Now, any tale that includes Bekri Mustafa is certain to have plenty of action, and none of the listeners wanted to miss a word of it. Actually, the narrator was twenty-one minutes into the thirty-one-minute tale before Bekri Mustafa entered the plot, but long before that, the listeners had become deeply involved in the fate of the supposedly deceived husband. The device had worked just as the narrator had planned. Other devices used by this narrator to hold interest and build suspense included lively conversation, a violent clash of characters, the employment of a witch by the villain, the success of the deception, the determination of the falsely accused wife to clear her name, the assumption of a disguise, Bekri Mustafa's action as bully, the branding of the villain, and the court trial. From that point on, the listeners were confident that the villain would receive his just deserts. To bring the tale full circle, Bekri Mustafa was given a place in the palace, and happiness for the principals was assured. It would be difficult to find a point at which this narrative could be improved.

Noteworthy Performance Details

Although each of the sixty-one narrators had his or her individual manner of tale telling, certain performance details were held in common as part of Turkish oral tradition. A look at some of these details may be helpful in identifying characteristic marks of Turkish storytelling. Onomatopoeia, the use of potent numbers, traditional formulaic openings and closings, the extended use of repetition, descriptions and proverbial comparisons, and the rhetorical question, discussed briefly below, are just a handful of such details.

The use of onomatopoeia (sound suggestive of action or motion) is common in the narratives. Among onomatopoeic expressions, these ten occur frequently: *Tak! Tak! Tak!* (for the knocking at a door), *Çik-a-dak* (for the galloping of a horse), *Tukkır-tukkır* (for the cantering of a horse), *tıngır mıngır* (for the sound of a rocking cradle), *horol, horol* or *HOROL, HOROL* (for light or heavy snoring), *Hav! Hav!* (for a dog's barking), *Miav! Miav!* (for the meowing of a cat), *tıpış tıpış* (for ladylike walking), *tıpır tıpır* (for tiptoeing), and *prrrrt!* (for the sound of birds' wings in flight).

Found frequently is the use of potent numbers such as three and forty. The hero is given three tasks to accomplish; a girl has three suitors; a horse gives three magic hairs, an ant three hairs from her foreleg, a fish three scales; a hero has three extraordinary companions or three milk brothers; there are three brothers or three sisters in a family—in short, use of the number three can be found throughout the present tales. Use of the number forty in narration is equally common: forty days and forty nights to complete a quest; forty *batmans* of meat and forty *batmans* of wine; forty slave girls; forty days and forty nights of wedding festivities; forty thieves. These and many other uses of forty are found throughout Turkish narration, just as they are in Turkish everyday life.

Some treatment or another of the traditional formulaic opening "Once there was and once there wasn't" or "Once there was and twice there wasn't"—or, if the narrator chooses, no formulaic opening at all—distinguishes one tale-telling performance from another. So, too, a formulaic closing may or may not be used, as the teller chooses. Here are two samples of such formulaic closings, the second one followed by its Turkish original to show the near rhyme that marks many closings: "Three apples fell from the sky, one for the teller of this tale, one for the listener, and one for whoever will pass this tale along" and "They had their wish fulfilled;/Let us go up and sit in their seats" (*"Onlar ermiş muradına;/Biz çıkalım kerevetine"*).

The extended use of repetition—an element thoroughly relished by listeners—marks several of the tales in this volume. Such repetition may involve duplication of encounters with three giants (as in "The Black-haired

Beloved") or with three helpless creatures (as in "The Prince and Pomegranate Seed") or with three extraordinary companions (as in "The Prophetic Dream"); it may involve recounting the entire action of a tale or an episode (as in "The Padishah, His Three Sons, and the Golden Apple" and "The Youngest Prince and the Unforgettable Girl"), or it may merely involve the passing on of instructions for tasks (as in "The Youngest Princess and Her Donkey-skull Husband"). A narrator we know who had omitted repetition in a tale familiar to his audience was cautioned by a listener, "Tell it *right*, Sergeant!"

Descriptions and proverbial comparisons also distinguish the tellings of artful narrators. At times, these descriptions seem to fly in the face of logic: "a very, very thin youth, thin as a crescent moon" (in "Bold Girl, Solver of Problems") and "three gorgeously dressed girls, each one more beautiful than the others" would seem close to nonsensical. But those and similar turns of phrase are very much a part of the Turkish narrator's style, and their use is expected by the hearers.

A device used effectively in relating the narrator to the listeners and the listeners to the tale is the rhetorical question or comment. "(What *don't* they know, those fairies!)" in "Bold Girl, Solver of Problems" and "Who knows how long that lock of hair was?" (in "The Black-haired Beloved") are but two examples of this device to be found among the present tales. Closely associated with the rhetorical question and also intended to draw audience and teller together is the narrator's own comment inserted in the narrative—often just a word or a phrase—such as the one used early in "The Black-haired Beloved": "One day an old woman (like me) was passing along the street." Those two words, "like me," orient the listeners to one of the crucial characters in the tale and indicate that the narrator is comfortable with her story, her audience, and herself.

The treasury of Turkish tales is rich and many dimensioned, and no introduction can do it full justice. Still, the perceptive reader can browse these eighty tales and savor personally the multifaceted art of the Turkish tale.

The Ordeals of the White-bearded Young Man

Once there were and once there were not two friends who went together on a journey. One evening along their way they were accepted as guests in a home where they had two hosts, one a black-bearded man and the other a white-bearded man. When the time for the evening meal arrived, the black-bearded man sat and ate with the guests while the white-bearded man served them.

At one point in the evening when both hosts were out of the room, the guests discussed this strange situation. "The white-bearded man seems quite obviously to be the older of the two, yet he was the one who did all of the work. How can this be?"

The second guest said, "I don't know, but let us ask one or the other of them about this curious thing."

When the white-bearded man returned, one of the guests said, "O kind host, I should like to ask you a question about yourself, if you will give me permission to do so."

"Go right ahead and ask whatever you wish," said the host.

"Well, we could not help observing that you, with your white beard, were the one who provided all the service at dinner. Why was it you, rather than he, who served us?"

He said, "I shall tell you the reason for this, my guests. Now listen. Several years ago, twelve of us from this village decided to go to a certain city to find work. Much to our surprise, when we reached that city, we found that it was completely deserted. We could not find a single human being anywhere in that city. This alarmed us somewhat, and so when we retired that night, we agreed that one of us would stand guard to protect the others. When morning came and we awoke, we discovered that our friend who had served as guard had disappeared. He was nowhere to be found. That night a second guard was posted, and he too disappeared. What had happened to these two guards? We could discover no answer to this puzzling question. Night after night one more of our number would stand guard and the next morning be gone, until eleven of my friends had disappeared. I was the only one left, and I was sure that I too would now disappear.

"As I was thinking about this, I strolled in the empty city. When I came to a lake, I sat down on the bank and looked at the water. Before long, two fairy girls came along, left their clothes on the opposite bank, and entered the water. I had learned from my father some of the ways of fairy girls, and so I went carefully around to the other side of the lake and stole the clothes of one of these girls. When the two came out of the water, only one was able to fly away, for I had taken the fairy clothes of the other. When she saw me, she said, 'O Son of Adam, through the will of Allah I shall marry you. But we must be very wary of a monster who lives in this place. He has already devoured all of the people in this city. If we do not kill him, then he will devour us too.'

"I said, 'Very well, but how are we to go about killing him?'

"She said, 'In such and such a building there are several barrels of gunpowder stored. We should roll them to the mouth of the cave in which the monster lives, explode them, and thus kill him. Then the two of us can live here in peace.'"

At that point in his story, the white-bearded host asked, "Are you listening, O my guests?"

"We are listening," they said.

Satisfied, he continued. "We did just as the fairy girl had suggested, and we killed the monster with the gunpowder. The fairy girl and I lived there in that city for some time together, and she bore me two children. Unfortunately, both of these children died, and after we had lost the second child, the fairy girl grieved deeply.

"One day soon after that, the fairy girl said, 'Let us stroll through the city and walk along the edges of the lake where we met.' We did just what she had suggested, but when we came to the lake, she jumped into the water and disappeared.

"I grew so lonely by myself in that deserted city that after a while I could not remain there any longer. Leaving that place, I traveled until I reached the seashore. As I was walking along the beach, a very large wave rolled in, knocked me off my feet, and carried me out to sea. I swam and struggled for a long while in the sea to keep from drowning, and after many hours had passed, I was washed up on some rocks. After I had rested for a while, I realized that I was hungry.

"I arose and began walking again, but I did not know where to go in the strange land to which I had been carried by the sea. After walking a great distance, I came upon a flock of sheep. I said to myself, 'If there is a flock of sheep, then there must also be a shepherd, and if there is a shepherd, then I may be able to get some bread from him.'

"It did not take me long to find the shepherd, but when I found him, I was greatly surprised to discover that he was a *tepegöz* [a one-eyed giant]. I called out to him, '*Selâmünaleyküm*,' but he did not accept my greeting. Instead, he treated me like one of his animals, took me home with him in the evening, and placed me in the sheepfold with his flock. Then he rolled a large rock against the door of the sheepfold. After making a fire in the fireplace, he slaughtered two of the sheep, cooked them, and ate them. But these two sheep did not fill him, and he said, 'I am still hungry.' He placed two iron skewers on the fire and lay down to wait for them to heat.

"I said to myself, 'He is now going to kill me and cook me on those skewers.' But when the skewers were red hot, I grabbed one and plunged it into his eye, blinding the *tepegöz* completely. He tried to catch me, but I hid in the center of the flock of sheep.

"In the morning when it was time to take the sheep out to graze, Tepegöz stood at the door of the sheepfold and let the sheep pass out only two or three at a time. I covered myself with the skin of one of the sheep he had eaten the night before. Waiting for the last two sheep to leave the fold, I pressed myself closely between them so that he could feel only my sheepskin-covered back, and in this way I managed to leave the sheepfold safely. But Tepegöz now began to shout loudly to other one-eyed giants in the area, who quickly came to help him. They all began to search for me. But I fled in the direction opposite the one from which the others had come, and in this way I escaped.

"After I had walked some distance, I saw another shepherd along the way. I looked at him very closely and observed that this one was not a *tepegöz*. I called, '*Selâmünaleyküm.*'

"'*Aleykümselâm,*' he answered.

"I asked him for some bread, and he gave me part of the bread he had with him. In the evening he took me back to the village with him. He said, 'There is an *ağa* in this village. Why don't we go to him and offer him your services, perhaps as a shepherd to pasture his flock. In that way you would have a place to live, and you would earn your daily bread and cheese.'

"He helped me to make this arrangement, and I became a servant of the *ağa*. This *ağa* had a daughter to whom I was soon engaged to be married. As a poor man then, I could not afford to pay the bride price for this girl. I was, therefore, to herd the *ağa*'s flock for seven years to pay for this. Well, I began living there in that way, and I continued to pasture the flock for three or five years. Then, one day when I returned home with the flock, they told me, 'The *muhtar* and the village council wish to see you.'

"It seemed that my wife had died during the day. In that village they had a custom of placing a dead body in an underground vault and placing the corpse's spouse there too. They gave the spouse food and light for forty days and locked him or her in the burial dungeon. They gave me the usual supply of food and light and threw me into a dungeon full of dead bodies, locking the iron door behind me. On the thirty-ninth day the iron door was opened again and another person was thrown into the burial dungeon with her dead spouse. The live one was a woman whose husband had died."

At this point the white-bearded host asked, "Are you listening, O my guests?"

3

"Yes, yes! We are listening," the guests said.

Satisfied, the white-bearded host then continued his account. "That woman had been given the same supply of food and light that I had been given. The two of us managed to survive on it for several days, but as it was beginning to be used up, I said, 'Let me examine this building more closely. Isn't there any part of it through which we may break out and escape?' Going back and forth along every wall, I finally came to a place where a thin ray of light was shining through a slight crack in the wall like a gleam from a mirror. I called to the woman, 'Come here! There is light shining through here!' We dug and dug and bored and bored to widen that crack, and after a while we had opened it enough so that we could crawl through it and escape.

"The two of us traveled and traveled, and after a while we reached a village one evening. We asked each other, 'Is there or is there not a cemetery in this village? If there is not, then let us not stop here.' We looked about for a cemetery, and after we found one, we spent the night there. In the morning we started out toward a seaport that we had been told about, and there we bought tickets for passage on an outward-bound ship.

"Soon after the ship set sail, the captain said of me, 'Where did that worthless fellow ever get such a beautiful woman? Seize him and throw him overboard!' They grabbed me and were about to obey his order when a fierce storm suddenly arose.

"Out of the storm came a loud voice that said, 'Don't you dare to throw him overboard or we shall totally demolish your ship!' The crew was frightened by this loud voice, and as a result they set me free.

"But after the storm had calmed and we had sailed a good distance, the captain said, 'Whoever it was who threatened us must now have been left a long way behind. Seize that man and throw him overboard!' But once again the storm descended upon the ship, and once again the loud voice warned them not to harm me. Again I was released. And in this way I finally crossed over to our side of the sea with the woman.

"After we had reached safety, the fairy girl reappeared to me. She said, 'O Son of Adam, I have done many things to assist you, and for this help I want you to release me of all obligation to you.' (She had been my first wife, and she had deserted me at the lake where I had first found her.)

"'When you fell into the turbulent sea,' she said, 'it was I who rescued you and carried you onto the rocks. That was one service. When Tepegöz called all his giant kinsmen to hunt for you, you would have been captured and eaten if I had not blocked their way. That was a second service to you. When you were in the death dungeon, it was I who opened up the hole that you widened in order to escape. That was a third service. Then when you were twice about to be cast overboard from the ship, it was I who frightened the crew into releasing you. That was a fourth service. Now give up your rightful claim against me and make my obligation to you *helâl*.'

5

"I said to her, 'I absolve you of all obligation and indebtedness to me. I make it all *helâl.*' "

Then he addressed us more directly and said, "My guests, that is why I am white-bearded at a very early age. The black-bearded man is my older brother."

The Legend of Muratpaşa Mosque

In the Şarampol district of Antalya is the largest mosque in Antalya, the Muratpaşa Mosque. The area where it now stands was once occupied by a business in secondhand goods operated by a man named Murat Usta. This Murat Usta worked very hard, but he earned little more than enough to live on. He was a strictly honest man, however, and he never envied the wealth of others.

One night Murat Usta had a dream in which he was approached by a group of angels who said to him, "Murat Usta, you have a good thing waiting for you in the desert of Arabia. Go there and get it." After the morning prayers of the next day, Murat Usta started to travel. He traveled little; he traveled far. And after a while he reached a place where there was a single grapevine growing, and on that grapevine there was a single bunch of grapes.

When he saw that bunch of grapes, he said, "This may be the good thing waiting for me. O Allah, thank you!" He picked the bunch of grapes and ate it. As he looked about him, he saw a town in the distance, and he walked on to that town.

When he reached the town, he was surprised to meet some old friends of his. "What are you doing here, Murat Usta?" they asked him.

"I was told in a dream that there was a good thing waiting here for me. I received that, and now I shall return home."

His old friends laughed and made fun of him. One of them said, "Well, now, look at this fellow who came all the way here because of a dream he had. Back home I once had a dream that there was a secondhand dealer living at Şarampol who had a pot of gold hidden under the stairway in his house, but I did not even pursue that, close as it was!"

After hearing this, Murat Usta bade his old friends farewell and returned to Şarampol. When he reached his own house, he immediately dug beneath the stairway, and there he found buried two pots of gold coins. With some of the money from these coins, he had a mosque built. In one corner of the mosque—but no one else knew which corner—he buried a quantity of gold large enough to build a second mosque when time had demolished the first one. As years went on, both that mosque and the surrounding area became known as Muratpaşa in honor of the man who had had the mosque built.

Much later, people who had heard rumors of the gold buried in the mosque tried to find it. One night they secretly tore out one whole corner of the mosque, but all they found was a note in a jar. The note said, "It's not with me but with the other." And so the buried gold of Murat Usta was never found.

The Law of the Land

I heard once of a country where every man was required to attend every prayer service in the mosque. Anyone who missed even one prayer service was given three wishes on three successive days, and then he was hanged.

A strong, handsome young man arrived in that country, and he was both successful and well liked there. But one day he missed the afternoon prayer service, and that fact was reported at once to the authorities. The public prosecutor ordered him to appear in court, where the judge said to him, "Son, we have been advised that you did not attend the afternoon prayer service yesterday in the mosque. According to the law of this country, whoever misses a prayer service will be given three wishes, and then he will be hanged. You should know this so that you can act accordingly. Tomorrow is your first day."

The young man left the court and began walking the streets deep in thought. He met a girl on the street who happened to be the judge's daughter. She said, "Brother, you look very troubled. What are you thinking about?"

"Why should *you* care? It is *my* problem."

"Just let me know what your problem is."

"Well, here in your country there is a law providing the granting of three wishes to the man who misses a prayer service in the mosque; then on the third day, he is hanged. I missed the afternoon prayer service yesterday, and as a result I have been tried and condemned to die in three days."

The girl said, "Do not despair. If you will marry me, I shall save you from death."

"How could you save me?"

"That part of it is *my* business," she said. "Just be willing to marry me, and—believe me!—I shall save you."

"All right. I promise to marry you."

7

"Then this is what you must do," she said. "Listen carefully, and do exactly as I say. Tomorrow when you go to court, state your wish that you be permitted to marry the judge's daughter. The judge may try to deny you this wish, but the prosecutor will uphold it. The law is the law, and the law applies to this. The prosecutor will probably say, 'If a condemned man wishes to marry a girl—even if he is to live with her for only two days—he has the right, by law, to do so.' They will then give me to you.

"On the second day, you will enter the courtroom with a peddler's *küp*. When they ask for your second wish, say, 'I want three *küp*s of gold.' They may say, 'But, son, you will die tomorrow. What could you do with three *küp*s of gold?' Then you say, 'Is your law really law? If it is, then that is what I want.'

"On the third day, you will enter the courtroom with a large iron club on your shoulder. When they say, 'Son, what is your third wish?' you will say, 'I wish to hit the judge and the prosecutor on the head with this club.' Then you will be acquitted."

On the first day of reporting to the court to make his wish, the young man said, "I wish to marry the judge's daughter."

The judge said, "Son, you will die two days from now. What will you do with my daughter?"

"Father, is your law really law? If so, I demand your daughter, and you must grant my wish."

The prosecutor then said, "Sir, the young man is right. The law decrees that his wish be granted."

On the second day, the young man entered the courtroom with a large peddler's *küp* on his back. "Make your second wish, young man," said the judge.

"I wish three *küp*s of gold."

"But, son, you will die tomorrow. What good will gold be to you?"

"Your law is law. I will do what I wish with the gold." And his second wish was granted. He was given the three *küp*s of gold.

On the third day, he entered the courtroom with a large iron club on his shoulder. "Make your third wish, young man," said the judge.

"This is what I want," he said. "I wish to hit the heads of the judge and the prosecutor with this club."

When the young man had said this, the judge looked at the prosecutor, and the prosecutor looked at the judge. Then the judge said, "You know, it seems to me—uh, uh, uh—as if this young man must already have performed his afternoon prayers."

The prosecutor added quickly, "It is *definitely* true that he performed his prayers."

Rising, the judge declared, "This young man is acquitted of any charge against him. The court is adjourned."

This kind of tale is known as a *kissa*, a parable or moral fable, with the moral being that people should not make laws that violate common sense. Such laws may well circle back and hit the lawmakers.

Inherited Behavior

There was once a widow who used to carry her daily supply of water from the fountain in a skin bag. She would make a trip each morning to the fountain, and the water that she brought back would last her until the next day.

One day a boy in that village decided to play a trick on the widow. As she was returning from the fountain with her bag of water, the boy sneaked up behind her and pierced the skin bag several times with a needle. The woman's home was rather far from the fountain, and by the time she reached home almost all of the water had run out of the bag. She emptied the little that was left into an earthenware pot and returned once more to the fountain to refill her bag. But once again the boy punctured her bag, and this time she saw him. After he had played this trick for several days, she finally decided to go and complain to the boy's father.

The widow went to the boy's home when the father had just returned from his day's work. She said to him, "Uncle Hasan, this son of yours is making my life miserable, and I cannot stand his pranks any longer."

"What has he done?" asked the man.

"I carry water from the fountain every day," she said, "and he sneaks up behind me and punctures my skin bag with a needle and lets the water run out. He has already done this too often to me."

"I see," said the father. "Well, you go along home, and I shall see to it that this does not happen again."

When she had left, the father at first planned to call the boy to him and order him to stop annoying the poor woman, but then he decided against this and began to think about the problem. "Have I ever fed my son with any food that has been stolen or otherwise illegally obtained?" he asked himself. He thought and thought, but as far as he could remember, he had never fed his son even a mouthful of food so obtained.

He then went to the boy's mother and said, "If this boy is mine and if he was reared in this house, then he should not conduct himself in this way. I have searched my mind and yet I cannot remember having given him any food that was *haram* [forbidden, unethical]. Now you think and see if you can recall having given the child any food of this sort."

The woman sat down and thought for a while, and then she said to her husband, "Oh, yes, I remember now. After he was born I never fed the child with anything *haram*, but early in my pregnancy with him I did. There was once a man who brought a basket of pomegranates to be delivered to our neighbor. The neighbor was not at home when he arrived, and so he left the basket in our home to be delivered when the neighbor returned. I was very thirsty that day and I thought about stealing one of the pomegranates from the basket. But instead of doing this, I took one from the basket, pricked it several times with a needle, and sucked it to quench my thirst. I then put the fruit back into the basket and said nothing about it."

"Well, then, go at once to that neighbor and ask him to make that pomegranate juice *helâl* [lawful, absolved]."

She went to the home of their neighbor and did as her husband had directed her. As soon as she was absolved of her sin by the forgiveness of that neighbor, the boy's behavior improved and he no longer teased the poor old widow. His father never mentioned this to him, but he did not have to, for the boy was cured as soon as the mother's deed had been made *helâl*.

The Substitute Bride

Once there was and once there wasn't, when the sieve was in the straw, when Allah's creatures were many, and it was a sin to talk too much—well, in those times there were two married sisters who lived as neighbors. As Allah would have it, both of these brides became pregnant on the same day. Nine months, nine days, and nine hours later, they both began to have labor pains. As their labor pains were increasing, an old man appeared, around sixty or seventy years of age. On his back he had a bag hung from a string that passed around his neck.

This grandfather knocked—*Tak! Tak! Tak!*—on the door of one of the sisters and asked for alms, but she said, "Look at this old man! Here I am in labor, trying to give birth to a boy, and you come asking for alms. Get out!"

In answer to this the old man said, "May you give birth not to a boy but to a girl, and may one of her lips be so big that it drags on the ground, and may the other be so big that it touches the sky. I hope that you will never get a buyer nor sell her!" Now, the old man who spoke in this way was the Blessed Hızır.

He went to the next door and knocked—*Tak! Tak! Tak!* His knock was answered by the second sister, whose labor was also at a very critical stage. She answered the old man's plea by going to the pantry and there filling a bag with food for him.

In response to her kindness, the old man said, "May you have a daughter whose hands will cause water to spring forth from any place that they touch, a girl whose face will cause roses to bloom wherever she looks. Instead of lice, may liras fall from her hair. I have made this prayer in your behalf, and I now request your permission to depart." But before he actually left, a girl—one of the most beautiful girls in the world—was born to this second sister.

The other sister bore a girl whose one lip dragged on the ground and whose other lip swept the sky. Her face was so ugly that it caused terror to anyone who happened to look at her.

The first girl grew even more beautiful as weeks and months and years passed. From the time that she was five, her beauty began to be known everywhere. And wherever she touched the ground, water sprang forth; wherever she looked, roses bloomed; and when she combed her hair, not lice but liras fell from her locks. A few years later, the son of the padishah sent a matchmaker to her family, saying, "If they do not give her to me, I shall never marry at all. I want no one but her."

When this beauty was about to leave her home to go to the palace to become the prince's bride, the ugly girl insisted that she wanted to go along with her. No one objected to this, for the two girls were, after all, cousins. "Let her go along," they all said.

Before the girls set off for the palace, the mother of the ugly cousin gave her daughter some *çöreks* and a little bottle of water. These the ugly cousin carried in her bosom. After they had traveled a short distance in their carriage, the ugly girl said, "You were too excited to eat any breakfast. Now eat some of this bread."

"All right. I shall take a small piece." But when she had taken one bite of the *çörek*, oh, how it burned her mouth! It was so salty! She cried out, "Oh, Cousin, I am thirsty. Please give me some water!"

"I shall give you some water for your right eye."

"Please do not be so cruel!"

At that, the ugly girl poked her finger into the beautiful girl's right eye and plucked it out. Then she gave her cousin just a sip of water.

"Oh, my mouth is burning! Please give me some more water!"

"I shall give you more water for your other eye." After she had plucked out the other eye, she put both eyes in her pocket and gave her cousin some more water. Later, when they were going along a road so curvy that it made the carriage sway back and forth, she pushed the beautiful girl out of the carriage. She then put on some of the clothes and the head scarf of her beautiful

cousin and proceeded (with one lip dragging on the ground and the other sweeping the sky) to the palace as the bride of the son of the padishah.

When the son of the padishah saw her, he could not believe that it was the same girl he had wished to marry. "You are not the girl I arranged to wed! You have one lip on the ground and the other in the sky. What happened to you? You used to be so beautiful!"

"Well, since a great mishap befell me, I counted the days, and they aged me so much that I look like this." What the girl said made little sense to the prince. But he reluctantly accepted it, and the wedding preparations continued.

In the meantime, a shepherd of that region found the beautiful girl in a ditch by the side of the road. Hungry and miserable for the want of water, she was moaning so weakly that the shepherd thought at first that it was one of his flock. Then he saw that it was a very beautiful girl—but without eyes! Carrying her on his back, the shepherd took her home to his own house and gave her into the care of his wife.

When the other villagers learned of this, they taunted the shepherd and his wife, saying, "You have hardly enough to take care of yourselves, and now you bring this girl into your household!" Hearing that, the shepherd's wife also began to reproach him: "Why did you ever bring a blind girl to your home? You are only a shepherd who eats dry bread!"

"Oh, Wife, do not speak that way! She is a blind girl, one of Allah's creatures, and there may be people who will give her a loaf of bread that we can all share."

A few days later the beautiful girl said to the shepherd's wife, "Grandmother, please give me a comb and a pan of water. I have some lice in my hair and I want to comb them out."

"Oh, blind girl, what a thing to ask for! Where am I to find a pan and a comb for you?"

"Well, anything of the sort will do for me."

The wife of the shepherd looked around and finally found a dirty and broken bowl that had been used as a dog's dish. She asked, "Will this do?"

"Oh, yes." And after the shepherd's wife had also found her a piece of an old comb, the beautiful girl began to comb her hair. Every time that the comb passed through her hair, there was a *tik* sound in the bowl.

"Blind girl!"

"Yes, grandmother?"

"What fell from your hair into the bowl?"

"Nothing, grandmother."

But when the shepherd's wife went and looked into the bowl, she could hardly believe her eyes, for she saw two gold liras glittering there. As the gold coins continued to fall from the girl's hair, the shepherd's wife became more and more pleased. When she showed her husband these coins that evening, the two of them placed a large kettle beneath the beautiful girl's head and then combed and combed her hair until the kettle was full of gold liras. With the money they bought some fine clothes for themselves and for the blind girl.

At that time, there had been a great drought in the land, and the padishah announced through town criers that he had seventy colts to be fed and kept over the winter. Anyone who was willing to take care of one of those colts was to come to the palace, take a colt, and provide for it until the following summer, when it was to be returned.

As soon as the beautiful girl heard about this, she said to the shepherd, "Grandfather, go and ask for one of those colts from the padishah. We can take care of one for him."

"But, daughter, we are poor people. We have neither a good enough stable to house such a colt nor hay with which to feed him."

"Never mind all that. Just go and ask for one of the colts."

When the shepherd went to the palace to ask for a colt, he was given a very sickly animal. It was weak and mangy. The girl took this colt and tied it in their old stable. Every place touched by the girl's hand had water gush from it, and everywhere she turned her face, roses bloomed and grain grew. With so much good water to drink and with such an abundance of grain to eat, the colt became taller and stronger every day, and by spring he had become an unusually fine horse.

14

When summer came around, the padishah had criers announce that the time had come for the return of the colts. If any colt had died over the winter, its caretaker was to return its hide. After this message had reached the home of the shepherd, grooms of the padishah arrived to reclaim the colt. But the blind girl said to them, "He will not come out of the stable unless the padishah sends his son for him." The grooms noticed that the colt had grown so large that it could hardly pass through the stable door.

After they had gone, the girl said to the colt, "When the son of the padishah comes for you, you just lie here and refuse to get up until I say the lines that I am going to whisper to you now." Then she whispered,

> "What good came to me from your master?
> No good came to me from your master—
> So, what good can I hope for from you?"

She said, "When you hear me saying these lines, then you should get up on your feet."

The padishah's grooms returned to the palace and reported, "Our padishah, one of your colts has grown into an exceptionally fine horse over the winter. He has grown as tall as the stable itself at such and such a shepherd's house. But this powerful horse will not come out of the stable unless your son comes in person to get him."

When the son of the padishah arrived at the stable, he was surprised

15

at what he saw there. He was surprised at the size of the horse. He was surprised by the ample supply of water that gushed from the ground in fountains. He was surprised by the rich pastures all around the stable. "Why doesn't the colt get up?" he asked.

The shepherd said, "He will not arise unless our sultan *hanım* comes to him."

When the beautiful girl came, her face covered with a veil, she said, "Stand up, O horse!" But the colt did not move. Then she spoke again:

"What good came to me from your master?
No good came to me from your master.
So, what good can I hope for from you?"

As soon as it heard these words, the colt sprang up. As it did so, its head just grazed the ceiling of the stable. The son of the padishah stared in amazement. He found it difficult to believe that the sickly colt had been transformed into a horse so tall and strong.

After he had ridden the colt back to the palace, the son of the padishah called his wife to him and said to her, "Today you will grind bulgur here in the palace. You will call all of the women in the neighborhood to come to the palace to help you grind this bulgur. At the home of such and such a shepherd there lives a blind woman. I want you to include her among those that you call to the palace."

A servant was sent to the home of that shepherd. He said to the shepherd, "The women of the palace are grinding bulgur today. Other women of the neighborhood have been invited to come and help them. We have heard that there is a blind girl living here. Let her come and grind bulgur with the others."

The shepherd replied, "She can come only if the son of the padishah comes and stretches his father's silken sash on the ground for her to walk upon."

When the servant returned to the son of the padishah, he reported, "The blind girl at the home of the shepherd will not come unless you stretch your father's silken sash on the ground for her to walk upon."

The sash that the girl requested was provided, but now she had another requirement to be met before she would go to the palace to grind bulgur: "I have two eyes missing. Unless they are returned to me, I shall not go."

When the son of the padishah heard this, he had criers announce everywhere, "Anyone who has two eyes to sell will be paid well for them."

Upon learning of this, the wife of the son of the padishah called a servant and said to him, "Here. Take these two eyes and sell them for as much as you can get for them, and I shall divide the money with you."

When the servant took the eyes to the padishah's son to sell them, the prince asked, "How much do you want for them?"

"I want five thousand gold liras."

"Very well," said the prince, and he paid the man that amount.

When the eyes were delivered to the blind girl, she said, "Ya, Allah! *Bismillâh!*" Placing the eyes in their sockets, she recited two prayers, rubbed her hands over her eyes, and was able to see as clear as a mirror. Both eyes saw as well as if they had been newly created. She once again became as beautiful as she had been in the past, for she had received the blessing of Hızır.

She went to the palace and after looking around, she found fifty women all working away grinding bulgur and telling each other their life stories. "What has happened to *you* in this world?" And, "What adventures have *you* had?" "And *you?*"

"Well, such and such happened to me." And, "This was my fortune." And, "I once did this and that."

When it was the turn of the beautiful girl to tell her life story, the ugly girl (with one lip on the ground and the other in the sky) realized the danger of her own position and so she tried to prevent her cousin from talking. "Don't try to compel her to talk. She would not care to discuss such things with you."

But the others all said, "No, no! We want to hear her story, too!"

All the while this was going on, the son of the padishah was hiding behind a curtain listening. He listened to the stories of all the women because he wanted to learn if the beautiful girl was, as he suspected, his former fiancée.

The beauty said to the other women, "How can I tell you my experiences? What has happened to me is worse than the fate of a cooked hen! I suffered a great deal."

One of the women asked, "What was it? Please tell us!"

Another said, "I shall be your slave if you will only tell it to us."

Still another said, "I shall be your dog if you will tell us."

(They said all these things to urge her to tell her story because, after all, they were women!)

Her cousin tried once more to prevent her from talking by saying, "What could she tell you? What is so remarkable about her story?"

But when the others all continued to insist that she tell her story, the beautiful girl decided to do so. "Once there were two sisters who became pregnant on the same day. When they were about to deliver their children, the Blessed Hızır visited them separately, asking each for alms. My aunt refused to give, but my mother gave him alms and pleased him. Because my aunt had rudely rejected Hızır, he cursed with ugliness the girl she was about bear. Because my mother had treated him respectfully, he blessed with beauty and special powers the girl she was to bear.

"When it was time for me to go to the palace to wed the son of the padishah, my cousin insisted upon accompanying me. On the way to the

17

palace she gave me some *çörek* that burned my mouth because it was so salty. When I cried out for water to drink, she would give it to me only in exchange for my two eyes. A little farther along the route, she pushed me out of the carriage and left me in a ditch in the wilderness. There a shepherd found me and carried me to his home, where he and his wife reared me. And that is the story of my life."

Right at that point the son of the padishah stepped out from behind the curtain. Putting his arm around the beautiful girl, he said, "This was my fiancée. This was the girl I intended to wed." Turning then to the girl with one lip on the ground and the other in the sky, he asked, "Would you like to return to the home of your father, or would you be carried away by Kırat?"

When the ugly girl preferred the horse, he took her to the village cemetery, tied her to the tail of a horse, and whipped the animal into a gallop. She was, as a result, bounced to pieces against the gravestones. That is the end of the girl and of my tale.

Why Heaven Lost the Lawsuit to Hell

There was once a boundary dispute between the residents of Heaven and the residents of Hell. Those living in Heaven said that the wall dividing the two regions belonged to them, while those living in Hell insisted that the wall belonged to them.

As each side was presenting its evidence, the case seemed to be favoring the residents of Hell. Their arguments seemed the more convincing, partly because they had a very clever lawyer. When the judge handed down his decision, it gave the victory to the dwellers in Hell.

That evening, a leading member of the community in Heaven asked several of his friends, "Why are you all so depressed?"

"Well," said one, "we lost a very important lawsuit today that we should have won."

"Why did you lose, then?"

"Because our opponents had a very clever lawyer," said another.

"Why didn't you have an equally clever lawyer?"

"Well, we wanted very badly to hire a lawyer," said a third, "but after searching Heaven from one end to the other, we could not find even one lawyer!"

The Industrious Woman and Her Lazy Husband

In a village near our town there lived a very industrious widow, and in that same village there was a very lazy man. The widow used to sell milk during the morning, work as a maid in a wealthy household in the afternoon, and scrub the backs of women during the evening at the *hamam*.

The lazy man, on the other hand, did nothing but lie in the courtyard of the mosque all day long. One day, some of the villagers said to him, "Why don't you get married, and stop this lazy sort of life? There is that widow who is so industrious. She would take care of you."

Finally, the lazy man was persuaded to marry the widow, and when she agreed to this proposal, they were indeed married. Now the man did nothing but lie around the house all day. This widow was a clever one, and one morning she said to her husband, "It must be dull to stay around this house all day. You are a strong and healthy man. You might enjoy carrying a few of my milk cans to nearby houses and in that way get to see a few people besides me."

The husband didn't think much of her idea, but he decided to try it, anyway. He carried milk cans to two of the closest houses, chatted a bit with the neighbors, and then went back home to his bed. The next day, his wife said, "My, you look more cheerful already, and you did a fine job yesterday. Could you also carry milk cans to the two houses farther along the road today?"

Her husband agreed to do just that. Of course, when he delivered the milk cans, he stopped a bit to chat, so he was later than usual in going back to bed. And, little by little, his wife kept adding more houses to his list, until finally he was delivering all of the milk cans. Thus the widow solved the problem of delivering the milk, and the husband saw little of his bed during the morning.

After that matter was settled, one day the widow said, "My husband, you are doing so well with the milk delivery and you're looking so pleased with your life that you might enjoy sweeping the courtyard of the mosque in the afternoon, when you have nothing else to do. And the *hoca* might even let you carry his *ibrik* for the ritual ablutions. I understand that he is paying someone else a few kuruş every day to do that service for him."

19

The husband grumbled a bit about this idea, but he tried it once or twice, and after he had become accustomed to it, he did not mind the work at all. She said to him, "You see, it is not so bad! You are doing very well, and you are earning money. As you know, I go at night to the women's *hamam* to scrub backs. You might enjoy going to the men's *hamam* and scrubbing backs there." Finding the idea interesting, he *did* go to the men's *hamam*, not once, but night after night, and he enjoyed the work. Besides, it gave him some coins to tuck into his sash.

Meanwhile, the other villagers were amazed at the change that had come over this fellow. He had become such a hard worker that he seemed not to stop day or night. Moreover, his wife, once the hardest-working woman in the village, now remained at home most of the day. When some of the villagers mentioned this curious change to him, he agreed. "Yes, that is true," he said.

Then one villager suggested that he divorce this woman because she was overworking him. "You could live better without her," they said. "You now work day and night!"

"Yes, you are right," he answered. "I probably *should* divorce her, but I have no time to waste in court!"

The Kadı's Canine Kinfolk

There was once a man who had a black dog with which he hunted wolves. He was such a good dog that the man would sometimes give him a sheep as a reward for his faithful service. In time, this dog had a small flock of sheep. When the dog finally died, his flock numbered fifteen.

Following the death of his dog, the man went to the local *kadı* and said, "*Kadı* effendi, I had a dog who has just died. This dog owned a flock of fifteen sheep. Who should inherit his property?"

Seeing a fine opportunity to benefit himself, the *kadı* said, "I am his heir. Go and bring the sheep here."

The man left the *kadı's* office, but on his way to fetch the sheep, he decided to return and ask the *kadı* an important question. He returned, entered the judge's office again, and said, "*Kadı* effendi, in case anyone questions the legality of this inheritance, I need to know this: Are you related to my black dog on your father's side of the family or on your mother's side?"

The Black-haired Beloved

O nce there was and twice there wasn't a padishah who had a single
child, a son. In order to protect this boy, his parents kept him in a
golden cage. They used to take him outdoors on sunny days, setting his golden cage before their house near the street, and then later they
would carry the cage inside again.

One day an old woman (like me) was passing along the street carrying
two pitchers full of water. Picking up one of the two golden balls with which
he played, the boy threw one at the old woman. But she did not catch it.
Instead, it broke one of her pitchers.

She said, "*Aman!* You are the padishah's only son, and so what can I say
to you? I say only this: May you suffer from passion for Zülfisiyah." When the
boy heard the word *Zülfisiyah,* he did not understand what it meant. He had
never heard such a word before. Still, his heart began to burn within him for
this Zülfisiyah.

The next day, that same old woman went to the fountain for water with
a single pitcher. The young man threw his other golden ball at her, and he
broke that second pitcher too. Again, she said, "Oh, you boy! May you suffer
from black love." And later, when he broke a third pitcher of hers, the old
woman cursed him a third time.

21

With this third curse, the padishah's son could think of nothing else but Zülfisiyah, Zülfisiyah, Zülfisiyah. From thinking and thinking of Zülfisiyah, he grew pale and thin. He couldn't eat; he couldn't sleep for thinking and wondering about Zülfisiyah. Doctors were called in to examine him, and these doctors reported to the padishah, "Our padishah, the prince is suffering from black love."

"But for whom does he have such love? He has never seen anyone for whom he could have any such passion. What sort of melancholy love *is* this?"

"Our padishah, if you will hide yourself somewhere in his room and listen to what he says to himself when he thinks he is alone, you will discover the cause of his sickness." The padishah did exactly that. He hid and he listened, but what he heard made no sense at all to him.

The next day, the padishah said, "Oh, he is really suffering from Zülfisiyah!" But nobody seemed to understand just exactly what Zülfisiyah was.

When the padishah's son grew older and became a young man, he said one day to his parents, "I am going to go in search of Zülfisiyah!" They did not want to let him go, but they finally consented, thinking that he would probably return by the time he had completed only half the search. So the young man kissed his parents' hands and set out on his journey, traveling a great distance. He traveled little, he traveled much, and when he looked back, he saw that he had gone a distance no greater than the length of a needle.

Soon after that, he entered another country. Looking around there, he realized that he had come into a land of giants. He saw a giant sitting before an oven preparing bread dough to be baked. Not knowing whether this giant was male or female, he crept closer. When he saw that the giant had breasts thrown over the shoulders, he knew that this was a female giant. He ran up quietly behind her and began nursing from one of her huge breasts.

The giantess said, "*Aman!* Who taught you to nurse from my breast? If you had not sucked my breast, I would have eaten you, but now that you have done that, you are my milk son and I cannot harm you. Soon my giant son will be coming home, and so I must hide you from him." Saying this, she slapped him once, turning him into an apple, and placed him on a shelf.

As soon as her son arrived home, he began sniffing around and saying, "I smell the flesh of a son of Adam here."

"Son, do not call him a son of Adam," she said. "He is your milk brother now. If you will swear that you will not harm him, I will show him to you."

The giant son said, "I shall not harm him." When the giantess slapped the apple and turned it back into a young man, the giant son started playing with his little human brother, tossing him up into the air and stroking him gently. "What are you seeking here, my brother?" he asked.

"I am searching for Zülfisiyah," said the young man.

22

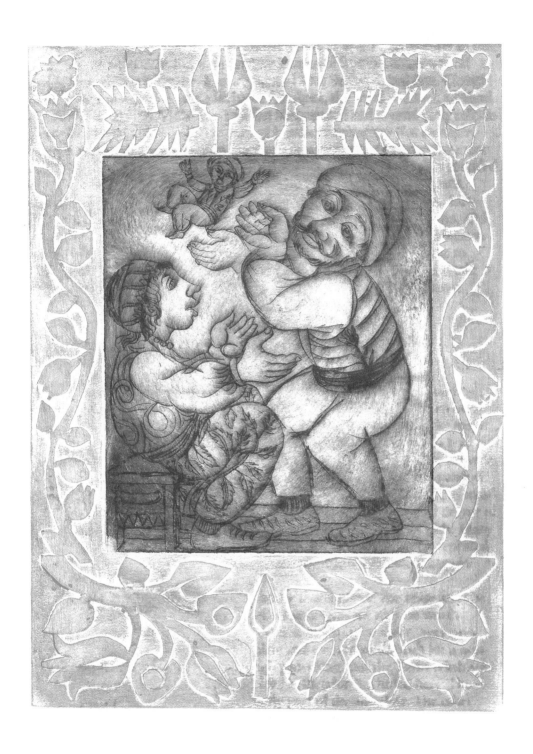

23

Thinking about this for a moment, the giant son said, "We have not heard of anything like that. But if there is anyone at all who knows about it, it would be my aunt, who lives a great distance from here. I do not know about this thing, but she may well know. In the morning I shall see you off to her home. There you should first do to her what you have already done to my mother."

This giant brother was named Mountain Destroyer. When he was seeing off the son of the padishah the next morning, the young man said to this giant, "Brother, here is my handkerchief. If you should ever see blood dripping from it, know by that sign that I am in serious trouble." The giant son hung the handkerchief on the wall and then wished his human brother a good journey.

The son of the padishah then went to the home of the aunt of his giant brother. She was firing an oven in preparation for baking bread. Running up quietly behind her, he grabbed one of her huge breasts and began to nurse from it.

The giantess said, "*Aman!* Who taught you to nurse from my breast? If you had not sucked my breast, I would have eaten you, but now that you have done that, you are my milk son, and I cannot harm you. My giant son, named Ocean Sucker, will soon come home. What shall I do with you?" She slapped the young man once and turned him into a pitcher, and she set that pitcher on the table.

When Ocean Sucker arrived home, he began sniffing here and there and saying, "Mother, I smell here the flesh of a son of Adam."

She said, "Do not call him a son of Adam. He has become my milk son by nursing from my breast. He is now your milk brother, and if you will swear not to eat him, I shall bring him out where you can see him."

When her son agreed to accept him as his milk brother, the mother slapped the pitcher and turned it back into a young man again. The giant son began playing with his little human brother, tossing him up into the air and stroking him gently. "What are you seeking here, my brother?" he asked.

"I came here searching for Zülfisiyah."

"Zülfisiyah? What is Zülfisiyah? We have never heard of such a word. Our oldest aunt lives a great distance from here. Perhaps either she or her son will know about this."

Before leaving the next morning, the son of the padishah said to Ocean Sucker, "Here is my armband. If I should ever be in very serious trouble, this armband will drip blood." The giant son hung the armband on the wall and then he wished his human brother a good journey.

When the son of the padishah reached the home of the oldest aunt of his giant brothers, she was firing an oven in which to bake bread. Slipping up quietly behind her, he began to nurse from one of her huge breasts.

The giantess said, "*Aman!* Who taught you to nurse from my breast? If you had not sucked my breast, I would have eaten you, but now that you have done that, you are my milk son and I cannot harm you. Very soon my son, Wind and Hurricane, will come home. What shall I do with you?" She slapped the young man once and turned him into a drinking glass and set it on the table.

When Wind and Hurricane arrived home, he began sniffing here and there, saying, "Mother, I smell the flesh of a son of Adam. Where is he?"

"Son, he is no longer a son of Adam, for he sucked my breast and became your milk brother. If you will swear not to harm him, I shall show him to you." After he had sworn not to harm his milk brother, the giantess slapped the drinking glass and turned it back into the son of the padishah.

The giant son began playing with his little human brother, tossing him up into the air and stroking him gently. Then he asked his little brother, "Why did you come here?"

"I have come all this distance in search of Zülfisiyah."

The giant son then said to him, "Oh, my brother, Zülfisiyah is a girl who lives on an island in the middle of such and such a sea. It is very difficult to see her, for she lives in a tower on that island and never comes out of it. In the morning I shall see you off and tell you exactly how to get there."

Before leaving the next morning, the son of the padishah took a signet ring from his finger and gave it to Wind and Hurricane. "Here is my ring," he said. "If I should ever be in very serious trouble, this signet ring will drip blood." The giant son hung the ring on a nail in the wall, and then he gave his human brother careful instructions about the route to follow in seeking Zülfisiyah. He wished his human brother a good journey, and the son of the padishah went on his way.

Following exactly the instructions given to him by Wind and Hurricane, the prince went and found that very sea. He searched that sea until he found the right island, and at last he came to the tower in which the girl lived.

She had not seen him when he arrived at the tower. She was combing her beautiful black hair at the window, and occasionally a hair would fall from her head into the sea below. The son of the padishah sang,

"I have wandered the earth to find you here.
Now let me in, Zülfisiyah dear."

When Zülfisiyah heard this, she drew the curtain across her window and said, "Oh, some son of Adam has come here!"

The young man sang again,

"Don't draw the curtain before your lovely face
And cover those eyebrows dyed so black!
I have wandered the earth and traced you here.
Now let me in, Zülfisiyah dear."

25

To this the girl responded,

"I have drawn the curtain across my face
And covered my eyebrows dyed so black,
But since you have traveled and traced me here,
I cannot refuse to allow you near."

The girl lowered a small boat, and in this she drew the young man up to the top of the tower. After the two had sat and talked for a while, the prince said, "Zülfisiyah, down at the foot of this tower there is a beautiful garden. Let us go down and walk here and there in that garden."

"O son of the padishah," she said, "I cannot leave this tower. You are a son of Adam and may do so. You go down and walk for a while in the garden and then come back."

"I could not bear being away from you," he said.

"I shall give you a lock of my hair to take with you. If you miss me, you can take it out and look at it. But take care not to lose my hair."

When she gave him a lock of her beautiful black hair, he tied it very carefully to the end of his silken sash. Going down the winding stairway to the garden below, he began to walk here and there in it. Whenever he began to miss the beautiful black-haired Zülfisiyah, he took out the lock of her hair and gazed at it. After wandering about for some time in the garden and looking now and then at that lock of hair, he decided to return to Zülfisiyah. As he was looking one last time at the lock of hair, however, a strong gust of wind snatched it out of his hand and carried it away.

This lock of hair blew a very great distance in the wind and landed in a cabbage patch in another country, where it coiled itself within the leaves of a head of cabbage. Who knows how long that lock of hair was? When that cabbage was taken to market, someone bought it, took it home, and there discovered the hair. It was very beautiful, and no one was able to determine what kind of hair it was and to whom it had belonged. It was therefore taken as a treasure to the padishah of that land.

The padishah assembled all the wise old men of his kingdom, hoping to find among them someone who would know where that lock of beautiful black hair had come from. It was shown to many people before anyone could identify it. Finally an old woman looked at it and said, "This is the hair of Zülfisiyah, a beautiful girl who lives in a tower on an island in such and such a sea."

"Can you bring her here?" asked the padishah.

"Yes. I shall take my magic urn (*küp*) and my magic whip and fly to that island. Somehow, I shall manage to bring her here to you, my padishah."

True enough, the old woman went to her home, climbed on her magic *küp*, beat the *küp* with her magic whip, and in good time landed in Zülfisiyah's garden. She hid the *küp* and the magic whip in a clump of bushes and then she began rolling about on the ground as one in desperate condition.

On that same day, the son of the padishah said to Zülfısiyah, "Come. Let us go down for a while and walk in the garden."

"You will have to go alone," she said. "I cannot leave the tower to go with you."

"Well, if you cannot go, you cannot go. But at least give me a lock of your hair to take along with me."

"No. I cannot do that, either. The last time you went down there I gave you a lock of my hair and you lost it. This may bring great trouble upon me. You just go ahead and stroll about in the garden."

The young man went down the stairs to the garden. As he was walking here and there, he saw the old woman rolling on the ground. "How did you get here, grandmother?" he asked. He had no fear of her, for she was obviously one of his own kind, a human being.

"Oh, son, a storm carried me here, throwing me upon this island. I have been left alone here. Please take me in as the guest of Allah, son."

Although the son of the padishah knew that Zülfısiyah might not like this, he consented, saying, "All right. Come along with me." When he returned to the top of the tower with the old woman, he said to Zülfısiyah, "See whom I have brought!"

But Zülfısiyah said, "I do not want any of Adam's kind except you."

The young man tried to persuade her to permit the old woman to remain with them, saying, "Please! She is a poor and lonely old woman with no one to look after her." Finally they agreed that the old woman could stay, but only on the ground level of the tower.

One day, however, the old woman moved part way up the stairs of the tower to a point where she could visit with the girl and influence her. She said, "Zülfısiyah, my girl, you must surely realize that your prince does not really love you."

"Oh, yes, he does! Would he have come such a great distance if he had not loved me?"

"If he really loved you, he would have told you about his talisman. Has he ever told you what his talisman is?"

"No. But what is a talisman?"

"There is some object that controls his life. That is his talisman. You need to find out what it is so that you alone can control his life."

"How can I find out from him what his talisman is?"

The old woman said, "Wrap your head in a cloth this evening and tell him that you are ill. When your prince asks, 'What is the matter, Zülfısiyah?' you must answer, 'You have never told me what your talisman is. That is why I am ill.'"

When the son of the padishah returned from the garden that evening, he saw that his black-haired beauty had her head wrapped. He said, "Zülfısiyah,

27

why do you have your head wrapped like that? And why did you kiss me so coldly?"

"Well, I am hurt because you have never told me about your talisman. That is what has made me ill."

"Why do you want to know about my talisman?" the young man asked. After they had talked this way and that about it, he finally said, "Well, my tobacco case is my talisman."

As soon as she had an opportunity, Zülfisiyah told the old woman, "His talisman is his tobacco case, grandmother." That night while the young man slept, the old woman crept upstairs to his room and stole the tobacco case. She then took it down to the garden and threw it into the sea.

In the morning the young man arose but he did not notice anything unusual. After he had gone down to walk again, the old woman said, "Zülfisiyah, I *told* you that your prince does not really love you."

"Oh, yes. He loves me very much."

"No, he doesn't. If he did, he would tell you what his talisman is."

"He did tell me! It is his tobacco case."

"He may say that, but it is not really his talisman."

That evening Zülfisiyah again bound her head with a cloth and said that she felt ill. When her prince asked her what was the matter, she said, "I am ill because you did not really tell me what your talisman is."

"Talisman, talisman!" the young man said. "What is it that you want to do with my talisman?" They talked again this way and that about it, and finally the prince said, "My talisman is my cigarette holder."

Learning of this, the old woman entered his room that night and stole his cigarette holder while he lay sound asleep. Going quietly down the winding stairs to the garden, she threw the cigarette holder into the sea. Still, nothing happened to the young man.

The next morning, the old woman said again to Zülfisiyah, "I am certain now that your prince does not love you. He never tells you the truth about his talisman. The cigarette holder is not his talisman at all."

That evening, Zülfisiyah pretended to be very cross. She said to the son of the padishah, "You do not really love me, for if you did, you would tell me truthfully what your talisman is."

"Zülfisiyah, why is it that you keep asking and asking about my talisman? You never asked me about it before that old woman came. Is *she* the one who really wants to know so that she can take my life?"

"Oh, no, no!" said Zülfisiyah. "*I* am the one who wants to know." And again they talked this way and that about it.

Finally he said, "Zülfisiyah, I *do* love you very much. You know that. And if you *must* know my talisman, it is my bow string."

That night the old woman, who had been listening on the stairway, crept into the prince's room and searched it up and down, here and there.

But where was the prince's bow string? Suspecting the old woman, he had unstrung his bow and put the bow string into his pocket. Just before dawn, the old woman found it, and she hurried down the stairway and out into the garden and threw the bow string into the sea.

In the morning, the son of the padishah could not be awakened. Zülfisiyah called him and called him, but he did not even move in answer to her calls. She stared at him, puzzled and sad, and then she went to the old woman. "Grandmother," she said, "something bad has happened to my prince. I have called him and called him, but he cannot be awakened."

"Do not worry, my girl. I think I saw in your garden a special plant that will revive him. But you will need to come down to the garden with me and pick that plant yourself. It is the only way that plant will work."

"But, grandmother, I do not ever leave the tower. I cannot go down into the garden."

"If you love your prince you will," said the old woman. And finally she persuaded Zülfisiyah to go down the winding stairs into the garden.

"My dear," said the old woman, "just think what you have been missing by staying all the time in that tower. This garden is just *filled* with beautiful flowers and trees and bushes. Come over this way and see this lovely bush!"

"Grandmother, the only thing I am looking for is the plant that will awaken my prince," the girl said. "Where is it?"

"I think I saw it over here," said the old woman, and she led Zülfisiyah straight to the bushes where she had hidden her *küp* and her whip. "Come a little closer, my dear. It's just beyond the *küp*."

As soon as Zülfisiyah had come to the side of the *küp*, the old woman picked her up by her heels and dropped her headfirst into the *küp*. Mounting the *küp* herself, the old woman whipped it, and it rose into the air and flew right to the roof of the palace of that other padishah.

When Zülfisiyah was taken down into the palace and told that she would become the bride of that padishah, she ordered that the windows of her room be covered with black curtains. "I have forty days of mourning to observe," she said.

Let's leave her mourning while we see what the giant sons are doing. At exactly the moment when the prince's bow string had been thrown into the sea, drops of blood had begun to fall from the handkerchief, the armband, and the signet ring that the prince had left with his giant brothers. "*Aman!*" said one. "Our little human brother is in serious trouble. I must get my cousins, and we'll go together to help him." So the three met and went with great long steps to that sea where the prince had gone to seek Zülfisiyah. When they arrived at the tower on the island, they climbed the stairs and found the prince lying lifeless on his bed. Searching here and there, they noticed that his bow was unstrung. "His bow string!" one said. "Where is his bow string?" They looked and looked, but they could find it nowhere in the tower.

29

"Ocean Sucker, come and do your work," said Wind and Hurricane. "Perhaps we'll find the bow string in the sea." So Ocean Sucker sucked up the sea around the island, and, true enough, they found not only the bow string but the tobacco case and the cigarette holder, as well.

When they had hurried up the stairs and laid these objects on the prince's chest, he began to stir and half awaken from his deathlike sleep. When he finally awoke enough to sit up, he asked, "Where is Zülfisiyah?"

The giant sons said, "We have seen nothing of Zülfisiyah."

"Where is the old woman?"

"*What* old woman? We have seen no old woman. There is no one here at all except you and your giant brothers. Come. We'll return to the home of the youngest of us. From there you can search for Zülfisiyah." So Mountain Destroyer hoisted the son of the padishah onto his shoulders and the three giant sons went with great long steps to the house of that first giant mother. They all spent the night there, and in the morning the giant sons saw their little human brother off on his quest for Zülfisiyah.

Setting out at once, the son of the padishah traveled many days and nights until he came to a city where a padishah lived. But what was this? Everyone was dressed in black, and the houses were draped in black. "Why are you wearing black?" he asked an old man.

"Well, son, the most beautiful girl in the world lives here now, and *she* is in mourning so *we* are all in mourning."

"Ah!" the prince said to himself. "Perhaps that beautiful girl is Zülfisi-yah!" He searched until he found the padishah's palace and went beneath the windows that were most heavily draped. He sang,

"A jasmine stick within your hand,
A new bride you must be.
But mount my horse and let us flee!
Zülfisiyah, fly with me!"

Opening her curtains, Zülfisiyah sang,

"A jasmine stick's within my hand,
But I am no new bride today.
Oh, end my mourning as you say
'Now mount, my love, and fly away!' "

The son of the padishah then threw a rope up to Zülfisiyah's window. She tied it firmly to the bedstead and then lowered herself by it to the ground. Silently they fled together.

At last they had all of their wishes fulfilled, and may all of us be as happy as they!

The Youngest Prince and the Unforgettable Girl

O nce there was and once there wasn't, when God's creatures were many, and it was a sin to talk too much—well, in those days there were three sisters, and all day long and all night long they used to spin thread out of cotton. In the morning, the youngest sister would take the spun thread to the market and exchange it for some more cotton and three candles and three pieces of bread and would come back again. They were very poor, and they had no one to provide for them, for their parents were dead.

One day they had much thread spun, and they gave it to the youngest sister. "Hurry to the market," they said, "and exchange this thread for cotton and bring candles and bread back to us."

And she started toward the market. She was young, that one, and when she was on her way she saw a person selling live chickens and she liked those chickens very much. Without a second thought, she exchanged all the spun thread for one chicken. When she took the chicken home, her sisters said,

"What is this? Where is our cotton? And where are our candles and our bread?"

"Well," she said, "I couldn't bring you those. Instead, I brought you a live chicken."

They said, "Have you gone mad? What shall we do without bread and without cotton? How shall we work tonight without our candles? Get out of here!" And they drove her away.

She left, and she walked and she walked. And when darkness came, she lay down with the chicken at her breast, and they slept together. When dawn came, the chicken left the girl's breast and flew away into the forest. The chicken went, and the girl went after it. When it flew into the heart of the forest, the girl lost sight of it. She looked to her left and she looked to her right, and there was no chicken anywhere. She looked around, and instead of a chicken she found trees full of fruits. Oh, she felt so hungry! She picked some apples and some pears and some plums, and she just *stuffed* herself with food. Then she sat down to rest a little.

As she was resting, she looked around and she saw three tents, each one more beautiful than the others, and all shining in the light. The first was covered with diamonds, the second was covered with rubies, and the third was covered with pearls. She waited to see if there was anyone there, and she saw no motion at all. So she went nearer and nearer, and went into the tents, one after another. Inside, the tents were in great disorder, with pajamas all around and the beds not made. It looked as if some hunters had left a row of birds on the floors. So she tidied the tents and made the beds and folded the pajamas, and she plucked the birds and roasted them. She even made the coffee and set it near the fire. She ate a little bit herself, and then she went and hid herself in the forest and kept watch over the tents.

It seems there was a padishah in that land who had three sons. There was a war, and the padishah had sent his three sons to fight in that war. But things didn't go well for their side in the war, so they decided to come back and live in their three tents in the forest until the war was over. They hunted in the daytime and lived in their tents at night.

When the three brothers came back from hunting that day, they didn't know who had done all these good things for them, and they were curious to find out. The eldest brother said, "I'll stay home tomorrow and watch to see if that person will come again," and so he did. The other brothers went hunting, but the eldest brother put a chair outside his diamond-covered tent and sat there, waiting. He waited and waited, but the girl saw him sitting there and she didn't come near the tents. After a while, he became very sleepy, so he went inside his tent and lay down and fell sound asleep.

As soon as he was asleep, the girl tidied the tents and made the other two beds and folded all the pajamas, and she plucked the birds and roasted them. After she had eaten a little bit, she went and hid herself in the forest and kept watch over the tents.

When the other two brothers came back in the evening, they asked, "Who was it that came and fixed everything so nicely?" But the eldest brother said he hadn't seen anyone because he had fallen asleep.

The middle brother said, "Then *I'll* stay tomorrow, but I will sit up and watch and wait until I find out who has been caring for our tents." But it happened with him just as it had with the eldest brother. After the other two had gone off to hunt, he put a chair out in front of his tent and he sat there, waiting. He waited and waited, but the girl saw him there, and she didn't come near the tents. After a while, he became very sleepy, so he went inside his ruby-covered tent and lay down and fell sound asleep.

As soon as he was asleep, the girl tidied up the tents and made the other two beds and folded all the pajamas, and she plucked the birds she found on the floors and roasted them. After she had eaten a little bit, she went and hid herself in the forest and kept watch over the tents.

When the other two brothers came back in the evening, they asked, "Who was it that came and fixed everything so nicely?" But the middle brother said he hadn't seen anyone because he had fallen asleep.

Then the youngest brother said, "I'll watch tomorrow. I know I can find out who it is." So the next morning while the two older brothers rode off to hunt, the youngest one stayed behind. To make sure that he would stay awake, he cut his finger deeply, and then he rubbed a great deal of salt into the cut. It hurt so much that he wouldn't be able to go to sleep even if he became sleepy. He wrapped his finger tightly, and then he lay down on the bed in his pearl-covered tent.

The girl looked and saw that the youngest brother was lying still, so still, on his bed. Quietly she tidied his tent and picked up the birds that she found on the floor. Then she tidied the other tents and made up the other two beds and folded the pajamas. She picked up the rest of the birds and plucked them all and roasted them. After she had fed herself a little, she started away to hide. But just as she was passing the pearl-covered tent, the youngest brother jumped to his feet and caught her. "Who are you?" he said. "Are you a human being or are you a jinn?"

"I am not a jinn. I am a human being like you," she said.

"Who are you?" the youngest one asked.

And she told her whole story, from first to last—how she and her sisters were very poor, living alone, without parents, and how they worked all day and all night spinning thread out of cotton. Each morning, she said, she would take the spun thread to the market and exchange it for some more cotton and three candles and three pieces of bread and would come back again. But one day, instead of buying candles and bread, she had bought a live chicken and taken it home. Her sisters, she said, were very angry and drove her away. So she and the chicken slept together that night, and then they went into the forest, where she lost the chicken. While she was looking for the chicken, she found a place in the forest where there were fruit trees of all kinds, and she ate and ate until she was satisfied. After she had rested, she said, she noticed three shining tents, one covered with diamonds, one covered with rubies, and the other covered with pearls. No one was in the tents. But the tents were in great disorder, so she had tidied them up. She found birds on the floor, she said, so she plucked and roasted the birds and ate a little of the food. Then she hid, to see who would come. That evening, three young men came to the tents, and they were all surprised to find the tents tidied and the birds plucked and roasted. The next day, the oldest young man had stayed home to watch, but he had fallen asleep. After he was asleep, she had done her work and had hidden herself again, to watch. Again, they were surprised to find the tents tidied and the food cooked. The next day, the second young man had stayed home to watch, but he, too, had fallen asleep. So she had tidied the tents and roasted the birds and then had hidden to watch. The third day, the youngest one had stayed to watch, but after she had done her work he had caught her, she said, so now she had no place to go.

"You can live in my pearl-covered tent," the youngest one said.

But, "What about your brothers?" she said. "What will you tell them?"

"Well, my brothers don't have to know anything about it," he said.

So they stayed together in the youngest brother's tent, and every morning after the three hunters rode away she would tidy up the tents and make the beds and fold the pajamas. Then she would pick up the birds from the floors and pluck them and roast them and feed herself. And who but jinns could be doing such work? At night, nobody but the youngest brother saw her.

After a while, the war came to an end, and the padishah decided to call his sons back. They were all three engaged to be married, and the father thought it was time for their weddings. This was good news for the two older brothers, but the youngest one was less pleased. The two older brothers were determined to go back at once, but as for the youngest one, the blood was frozen in his veins. He scarcely knew what to do. While the other two were packing up their belongings, he said he wasn't going to take his tent back with him. He said, "I'm going to leave mine here."

When the girl was asleep at night and his brothers were ready to leave, the youngest brother went to the edge of the forest and picked roses and roses, and he put the roses all around the girl's bed. He wrote a note on a piece of paper telling the girl who he was and where he was going and why he was going. Then he left, riding away on his horse.

In the morning when she woke up, the girl saw that he wasn't there and that the other tents weren't there. She was left all alone, and she felt very sad about it. Then she saw the message on the piece of paper and she read it.

Now that she knew what had happened, she decided to set out to find the prince.

On her way early that morning, she saw a hermit monk. The girl stopped him and she said, "Please, Father Monk, could you give me your robes and your hood in exchange for my pearl-covered tent over there and all that goes with it?"

The monk agreed to exchange his robes and his hood for the tent and its contents, and the girl dressed herself in his robes and gathered all her hair into the hermit monk's pointed hood. After she had finished dressing herself, she asked the monk if he had seen three young men traveling together, and the monk said yes, that he had seen three horsemen going in a certain direction, with two headed forward eagerly and the third always stopping to look behind him.

She started on her way in the direction the horsemen had gone. She went and went, and finally she saw the three riders, with the first two riding joyfully and the third one turning and looking back at every other step, very unhappy.

As the monk approached, the third young man started talking with him. "What have you seen, Father Monk?" he asked.

And the monk (really the girl) answered,

"I saw a sweetheart lying,
And red, red roses dying,
The mark of a true love's forsaking,
And, ah, but my own heart was breaking."

"Oh!" said the prince. And he thought the monk had seen the girl he had left behind, and he was talking about her. They walked along together, and every other minute he would ask, "What have you seen, Father Monk?"

And the monk (really the girl) would answer,

"I saw a sweetheart lying,
And red, red roses dying,
The mark of a true love's forsaking,
And, ah, but my own heart was breaking."

After a while, this repeated conversation annoyed his brothers. They said, "Stop talking with this monk. Why do you have to be busy with him when we are trying to get along home?"

But when they stopped to have lunch under a tree, he invited the monk to sit with them, and there again he asked the same question, "What have you seen, Father Monk?"

And the monk (really the girl) answered,

"I saw a sweetheart lying,
And red, red roses dying,

35

The mark of a true love's forsaking,
And, ah, but my own heart was breaking."

He asked what the monk would do when they came to the city, and the monk said he didn't have anybody except his mother and a sister. He asked where the monk came from, and the girl gave the name of the place where she had lived with her sisters. The prince said, "What about my starting a shop for you, to sell rugs and carpets, so that I could come and see you very often?" And thus it was settled.

The very next day, the shop was prepared. And it was filled with goods to be sold, and the monk was to sell these things. And the prince started coming to him very often. Every time he came, he would ask, "Father Monk, what have you seen?"

And the monk (really the girl) would answer,

"I saw a sweetheart lying,
And red, red roses dying,
The mark of a true love's forsaking,
And, ah, but my own heart was breaking."

Finally it was time for the brothers to get married, and the two older ones had their weddings. When it was time for the youngest one to be married, he came to the monk and said, "Tomorrow I am going to the *hamam* for my wedding bath and I want you to come along with me."

The monk said no, no, that he couldn't go. He wasn't in the habit of going into a very hot *hamam*.

But the prince insisted very much on his going along with him, so he said, "All right. I'll come along with you as far as the *hamam*."

The next morning, the musicians and the whole procession came to take the bridegroom and his friend the monk to the *hamam*. The monk went along with them willingly enough. But when they insisted that he should go in together with the bridegroom, he said, no, he wouldn't go. But he finally agreed to go into the *hamam* with his robes on. "I can't take my robes off," he said. So he did go inside.

As the soap was being washed from his eyes, the prince would open his eyes and say, "Oh, Father Monk, what have you seen?"

And the monk (really the girl) would answer,

"I saw a sweetheart lying,
And red, red roses dying,
The mark of a true love's forsaking,
And, ah, but my own heart was breaking."

And while he was being bathed, the prince asked, "What have you seen, Father Monk?"

And the monk (really the girl) would answer,

"I saw a sweetheart lying,
And red, red roses dying,
The mark of a true love's forsaking,
And, ah, but my own heart was breaking."

By the time the wedding preparations were on, however, the monk started answering the prince by saying, "Please try to forget about this girl. It's a shame you should mention it when your own wedding is so close."

But, "No," answered the prince all the time. "She burns my heart with the hottest fire, and I shall never forget her until I die."

One day, as the wedding was very soon to be held, the prince said to the monk, "You have a mother and sister. I'm inviting them to my wedding." The monk (really the girl) found a kind old woman and said to that woman, "Grandmother, you are going to act as my mother, and I am going to pretend that I am the monk's sister." So the next day, she prepared herself to go to the wedding. She looked really very, very beautiful and so nicely dressed. And she went with the old woman to the wedding.

On the other hand, the prince let the people know that the mother and sister of his best friend, the monk, were coming and that they should be treated with honor. True enough, they were welcomed to the wedding and offered the best seats. The girl was so beautiful and so nicely dressed that everyone turned around and looked at her. But when the prince asked, "Where is your brother, the monk?" the girl answered, "He said to tell you that he must perform a wedding service and will therefore be unable to come. He will talk with you tomorrow about it. He wishes you and your bride great happiness." And the prince had to be satisfied with that.

The mother of the bridegroom and the mother of the bride, too, thought the girl was very beautiful. Now, the bride herself was not beautiful at all. The two mothers thought that if they could only see to it that the bridegroom had the beautiful girl for the first night, he would see his true bride with the same eyes after that. So they said, "If we are able to keep this girl here for the first night, we'll give her to the prince as his bride, and then we can send her back tomorrow."

When it was time for everyone to go home, they said to the girl's mother, "The young folks are going to have fun now. Why should she go? Couldn't you go home, and let your daughter stay overnight for the wedding entertainment?"

So the old woman went on home, and the girl stayed. They took her to a room and took the wedding gown off the bride and dressed the girl in it. Then they gave her to the bridegroom instead of the bride.

When he had returned from the mosque, the bridegroom knelt to pray in the nuptial room and then he went to open the veil of the bride. And what he saw was something like the second half of the same apple as the girl in the pearl-covered tent.

He gave her a pear to peel, and while she was peeling the pear, she cut her finger. To stop the blood, the prince gave her a handkerchief embroidered with pearls and wrapped it around her finger. He also gave her a ring that only the padishahs and their family could wear, and he slipped it on her finger.

The next morning, the mothers-in-law sent the girl away, and the real bride came to take her place. The girl went home and put on her monk's robes and her hood and went to the shop. The prince came to the shop to talk with him, and told him that his bride was an exact copy of the girl he loved. "Oh, tell me, Father Monk, what have you seen?"

And this time the monk just revolted. "Not any more, not any more!" he said. "You should be ashamed of remembering the other girl."

But the prince said, "She is just like that other girl, almost a second half of the same apple."

When the prince said that, the monk felt very unhappy, and tears began to drop from his eyes. To wipe his eyes, he raised his hand, one finger of which was wrapped in the handkerchief the prince had given his bride the night before. When the prince saw that, he said, "What is this? That is my handkerchief, the handkerchief I have given to my wife. Was it stolen and given to you?"

"No," the monk said, "it wasn't stolen. I have nothing to do with theft."

As the tears continued to fall, the monk used the other hand to wipe his eyes, and on one finger of that hand was the royal ring. And the prince said, "How can this ring I gave my wife last night be on your finger? Was it stolen?"

"No," the monk said, "there is no theft about it. I am not a thief."

But the prince wasn't listening to the monk any more. "Please take your hood off your head," he said.

"Oh," replied the monk, "if I took off this hood, all the secrets of the world would be out."

At that, the prince jumped up and took off the monk's hood. Immediately the girl's beautiful hair fell down around her shoulders, and she looked as lovely as she really was. So he took her back to the palace with him, and sent the other bride away. They had another wedding that lasted for forty days and forty nights, and then they lived happily forever after.

Three apples fell from the sky, one for the teller of this tale, one for the listener, and one for whoever will pass this tale along.

Keloğlan and Brother Fox

O nce there was and once there wasn't a fox who used to steal grapes at night from the small vineyard of Keloğlan. Keloğlan had been too sleepy at night to catch the thief, but one night he cut his finger deeply and poured salt into the wound in order to keep awake. Because of the pain in his finger, he was able to stay awake this time, and so in the middle of the night he caught the fox eating grapes in his vineyard.

The fox pleaded for his life: "Please, Keloğlan, do not kill me. Let us become close friends, like brothers, and I shall help you."

Keloğlan laughed. "My friend? My *brother*? I do not see how that can be possible, but we can try."

Time passed until one day the fox caught two partridges. Carrying the partridges in his teeth, he took them and dropped them beside Keloğlan's mat. "Keloğlan, my brother, get up! I have brought you two partridges. Clean them and eat them!" Keloğlan arose from his sleeping mat and did as Brother Fox had directed.

Time again passed along until one day the fox, walking along the bank of a stream, came upon the daughters of the padishah doing their laundry in the stream. They were all only half dressed, for they had left their outer garments in a bundle. Inside that bundle of clothing they had placed their rings and other jewelry. The fox very quietly crept closer and closer to the bundle until he could grab it. Holding the bundle tightly with his teeth, the fox fled. When they saw him running away, the daughters of the padishah began shouting, "Help! Help! A thieving fox has stolen our clothes and our jewelry!" But nobody was able to catch the thief.

Going to Keloğlan's house, the fox called, "Wake up! Wake up, Brother Keloğlan! Look here at the jewels I have brought for you!"

Keloğlan looked and then asked, "Brother Fox, where did you get these jewels?"

The fox said, "Do not ask such a question. That is none of your business."

After another day or two had passed, the fox said to Keloğlan, "Brother Keloğlan, get up! Get up! Go and take a good bath, for I intend to get a daughter of the padishah as a bride for you."

Keloğlan stared at him. "Brother Fox, are you crazy?" he said. "Think now of who I am and where I am, and then think of who the daughter of the padishah is and where *she* is! How can you say such a thing?"

The fox said, "Brother, don't interfere with my work! If I say I will do that, then I will do that! Go and scrub yourself well. I swear to you that I shall get a daughter of the padishah for you."

When Brother Fox left Keloğlan, he went straight to the palace of the padishah and knocked on the door—*Tak! Tak! Tak!*

Those inside asked, "Who is it?"

The fox answered, "Open the door! It is I, Brother Fox, the servant of Şakşakı Bey. Şakşakı Bey sends you his greetings and asks that you lend him a set of scales on which he can weigh some of his gold."

Within the palace there was confusion. They said, "*Aman, aman,* Allah! Can there be such a thing as weighing *gold?*" But to the fox they said, "All right. You may borrow the scales," and they handed the scales to him.

The fox took the scales and returned to Keloğlan's house with them. There he stuck to the bottom of the cannister two pieces of gold from the padishah's daughters' bundle. He wanted to give the impression that his master had simply overlooked them while he was weighing his gold. Then after three or five hours he returned the scales to the palace.

When the padishah's wife found the gold pieces at the bottom of the scale, she went at once to her husband and said, "My padishah, they returned the scales, but when they did, there were two pieces of gold left in the bottom of the scale cannister. They apparently forgot them or did not bother to examine the cannister."

The padishah said, "*Aman, aman,* Allah! Şakşakı Bey must be richer than I am!"

41

The fox allowed fifteen days to pass, and then he went to the palace again and requested to borrow the scales once more in order to weigh more of the gold of Şakşakı Bey. When he returned the scales, he played the same trick that he had earlier: he deliberately left two pieces of gold in the cannister.

Three or five days later, the fox said to Keloğlan, "Brother, the time has come for me to go to the palace and say that I want a daughter of the padishah for you."

Keloğlan looked up from his sleeping mat. "Oh, Brother Fox," he said, "how will you ever be able to do that? How can you want a padishah's daughter for me as wife? I am only a poor *keloğlan*. To what will the padishah's daughter come? I don't even have one decent room!"

The fox said, "Keloğlan, mind your own business! If I said that I can do it, then I can do it!"

Then Brother Fox went to the padishah's palace. In those days, there were gold and silver chairs for guests to sit upon. If one chose to sit on the silver chair, the host understood from this that he had come to ask for his daughter as wife to someone. Upon being shown to the padishah's presence, the fox went at once and sat in the silver chair. He said, "My padishah, I chose this chair because I wish to ask for the hand of one of your daughters for Şakşakı Bey. He wants to marry one of your daughters."

The padishah went to his wife's room and consulted with her about this matter. He said, "Wife, what do you think about this? Şakşakı Bey sent his assistant to say that he wishes to marry one of our daughters."

The wife of the padishah said, "Yes." (There was the same kind of thinking in the old days that there is now. If the bridegroom is rich enough, then the other things don't seem to be important. Nobody seems to care about the bridegroom's character or his family line.) The wife of the padishah said, "We should say yes. It seems that he is a very wealthy man."

The padishah returned from his wife's room and said to the fox, "Yes, we shall accept this offer. His parents may come and ask for one of our daughters as a wife for their son."

The fox said, "But, my padishah, his land is a very great distance away, and his parents are both very old. Surely the wedding feast can be held without them."

"*Now?*" the padishah asked.

"Yes, yes, now! Let us go shopping together for the things that will be needed."

The padishah, his wife, and Brother Fox went together to the various stores to do the shopping necessary to prepare for the wedding. Among other places, they went to a jewelry shop, but after they had made three or five selections, the jeweler asked for money for these purchases. The fox shamed him by saying, "How could you demand payment now, right in the presence of the padishah? You will get your money later. Do not worry about that!"

The fox used the same strategy in all the stores where they shopped, and he managed not to pay a single lira during their whole purchasing trip. Brother Fox had a tailor make a magnificent suit, and when it was finished, he took it home. There he found Keloğlan sleeping, as usual. He said, "Hey, Keloğlan, wake up! Wake up! The bride will soon be coming!" Dazed, Keloğlan arose, took a good bath, and put on his new suit.

Now, before the final events of the wedding festivities had arrived, when the bride would be taken to the groom's home, the fox had acquired a real mansion for Keloğlan. The mansion that he got had belonged to a family of seven-headed giants. The fox had gone there with Keloğlan, and the giants had been pleased to see them coming, for they expected to use them for their dinner that night. The fox knew what they were thinking, and he said to them, "O Brother Giants, you are thinking of eating us, but there is another matter that should be of greater concern to you. In three or five hours, you will see a great procession coming. They will be the padishah's soldiers, coming under order to destroy all of the giants in this land. I think that you should hide immediately!"

Badly frightened, the giants asked the fox, "Where can we hide? It will not be safe to hide inside our mansion!"

The fox said, "I believe you have on your property a certain deep dry well. Hurry! Hurry! Get in there and hide! When the padishah's soldiers have passed by, I shall tell you, and then you can come out again. They will not think to look in the well."

The seven-headed giants descended to the very bottom of that dry well. Then Brother Fox and Keloğlan tumbled into the well all of the large boulders that they could find. They also sealed the mouth of the well with an especially large boulder. In this way, all of the giants were killed.

The fox had given the bridal procession exact directions for the route they were to follow to reach the bridegroom's home: "Take this road and then turn onto that road, and after that keep going straight ahead. Do not turn off that road anywhere, and at the end of it you will come to the mansion of Şakşakı Bey. It is very large."

When the procession had started on its way, the fox said to Keloğlan, "Go to the roof of this mansion, and wait for the bride there." (In older times it was a custom for the bridegroom to await the bride on the roof of his house.) Keloğlan did as Brother Fox had directed and waited on the roof of the mansion for the coming of the bride. After the procession had arrived with the bride, the wedding was complete, and Keloğlan and the middle daughter of the padishah were married.

As you know, Keloğlan was Şakşakı Bey by now. He grew richer all the time. Only a few days after the wedding, thousands of sheep had arrived to pasture on his land. The fox had said to all of the shepherds in the area, "You

43

are supposed to take your flocks to such and such a place. If you fail to comply with this order, the padishah will have your heads cut off."

Everyone passing by said, "Look at all those sheep! To whom do they all belong? They must belong to some very rich man!"

When people asked such questions, Brother Fox was there to answer them. "All these sheep and those cows and horses belong to Şakşakı Bey!"

After some time had passed, the fox said to himself, "I think I shall test Brother Keloğlan's friendship and loyalty. I wonder if he realizes how much I have done for him. Does he appreciate the things I have arranged for him? I can find out by pretending to die." So one day when Keloğlan had gone hunting, the fox lay down on his mat and groaned and groaned, and finally shut his eyes and lay as if dead.

Now, the middle daughter of the padishah, the one who was the chosen wife of Şakşakı Bey, was a very compassionate woman, and she was deeply grieved at the death of her brother-in-law. She began to cry, and she was still crying when Keloğlan arrived home. When Keloğlan saw that his wife was greatly upset, he said to her, "My dear, why are you crying?"

"Brother Fox has died," she said. "That is why I am crying."

"Well, my dear, crying will not bring Brother Fox back to life. Dry your eyes and be of good cheer. A fox is a fox, and we have a good life together. Why should you grieve about a fox? Just throw his body into the trash."

Brother Fox heard very clearly everything that Keloğlan had said. He arose at once and said to Keloğlan, "Shame on you! I did a great many things for you. It was I who made you a bey. It was I who arranged to have the padishah's compassionate daughter become your wife. You were just a *keloğlan,* and you had nothing. Now, what a pity! You are ready to throw my body onto the trash heap! Ha!"

Frightened and ashamed, Keloğlan began to plead: "Please, Brother Fox, forgive me. In trying to comfort my grieving wife, I have made a very great mistake. In truth, I thought that you were dead, or I would not have spoken so about my brother!"

Brother Fox did forgive him, and the days began to pass again just as they had before. After some time, the fox really did die. This time, Keloğlan had a beautiful funeral procession arranged, and the fox was buried as the brother of Şakşakı Bey, as indeed he deserved.

May we ourselves find friends as loyal and faithful and forgiving, and may we and they live long!

Bold Girl, Solver of Problems

Once there was and once there wasn't, when Allah's creatures were many, and it was a sin to talk too much, time in time—well, in those times, there were two sisters. These sisters had neither father nor mother but lived by themselves, and they were poor. They had almost no food to eat, they were so poor.

One day Bold Girl, the elder of these two sisters, said to the younger one, "This won't do at all. At least let me get you married to someone, and then I can live on what you may have."

So she put on her *çarşaf* and went out. She looked here and there, but she could not find anybody fit to marry her sister. Finally she came to a great big house with a black door. The door was black, and the curtains were black, and everything else in sight was black. It was a very strange sort of place.

There were some children playing there, and Bold Girl asked, "Whose house is this?"

They said, "It belongs to the padishah, of course."

"Why is it all black?" she asked.

"Oh," said a child, "they are mourning because they had a son and he is lost, so they are mourning for him."

As Bold Girl opened the door and walked into the house, one of the servants stopped her, saying, "Where are you going?"

Bold Girl said, "I want to see the lady of the house."

"How can you go in without asking permission? You wait here, and I'll ask the lady."

The servant asked the lady, and the lady said, "All right. Let her come in, and let's see what she has to say. Don't break her heart. Let her come in."

So Bold Girl was admitted and taken to the lady's room, a room all black—the walls were black, the bedstead was black, the door was black, the curtains were black, the covers were black—and the woman was wearing black and crying into a black handkerchief. "*Selâmünaleyküm!*" said the woman.

And "*Aleykümselâm!*" the girl answered.

"Who are you?"

Bold Girl said, "Well, we are two sisters and live together as orphans, and we are very, very poor. So I decided to find someone to own us. I have

45

come out and looked around on my left and on my right, and I haven't been able to find anyone. And what is *your* problem, my lady? Why do you cry, and why do you mourn, all dressed in black?"

"Don't open my wounds," said the woman. "Let's forget all about it. Nothing can be done about it."

"Oh, no," said Bold Girl. "Maybe we can do something about it. Tell me, please."

"Well, all right," she said. "This is my story. I had a son, eighteen or nineteen years of age. He was the apple of my eye, and he got sick. We cared for him, we did everything for him, and he was still sick. We had the palace doctor, who took care of him, and one morning we woke up and he wasn't there. We don't even know whether he died or whether he just disappeared. We don't know what happened. How would *you* take it?"

"Well," said Bold Girl, "suppose I find your son for you. Would you marry my young sister to your son?"

"Oh," said the lady of the house, "how I wish you could! Of course I would. I promise that I would take her into the palace and I would marry her to my son. I wish you could find my son for me!"

Bold Girl said, "Allah is great. Let us see what He'll show us."

The lady of the house gave her some money to help them a little, and then Bold Girl left the palace. She went home and talked to her sister. She was a very, very clever one, this Bold Girl. She said to her sister, "Listen to me. I have a plan. If it works, it is going to be very, very happy for you in the end. This is what you are going to do. I'm taking you to the cemetery tonight just after dusk. There's a great big tree there. You are going to climb high up in that tree, and you'll watch everything that happens down below. Take care not to fall asleep, because if you fall asleep, then you'll fall out of the tree and nothing will come of our plan except that you may die. So you'll be very careful not to go to sleep, and you'll be very careful to look out, to watch what happens, all night long. And in the morning you'll come down and tell me all that happened during the night."

The younger sister was no child anymore; she was at a marrying age. Bold Girl took her just after dusk to the cemetery and helped her up into the tree and once again told her to be careful not to fall asleep. Bold Girl went back home, but the younger sister stayed up in the tree and watched carefully to see what was happening.

After midnight, while she was sitting there, she heard the footsteps of a horse coming—*tukkır-tukkır, tukkır-tukkır*—and there was a man on the horse with a torch in his hand. He came right to the foot of the tree in which the girl was hiding, and he got off the horse and began to dig at the grave right under the tree. And out of the grave came a young man. The man who had come on the horse had some dinner leftovers, and he poured them on the ground in front of the young man. The youth ate—as eat he must—and

46

47

then the man said, "Will you be with me?"

The young man said, "No." So the horseman took his whip and beat and beat the poor boy. Then he pushed him into the grave again and covered it and rode away on his horse.

In the morning, the younger sister came down from the tree and told Bold Girl everything she had seen and heard. "Do you think this youth is their son?" asked the younger one.

Bold Girl said, "Perhaps. I'll go and talk to the lady about it." So she went to the palace to see the lady, and told her the whole story. "I put my sister up in the tree, and I told her not to fall asleep. After midnight there came a horseman, riding—*tukkır-tukkır, tukkır-tukkır.* He was a tall blond man, and he had a torch in his hand. He came and dug the grave with his hands, and a very, very thin youth, thin as a crescent moon and dark of skin, came out of the grave. The horseman poured out some leftover food—pieces of bread and scrapings from plates—and ordered him to eat. He ate as he could, and then he was asked whether he would be with him. When the answer was no, he was beaten and beaten and beaten with a whip and pushed into the grave again, and the horseman went away, *tukkır-tukkır, tukkır-tukkır,* on his horse again. Do you think the youth in that grave could be your son? Don't you want to come along with us tonight and see for yourself?"

"Oh, yes!" said the mother. "I will do that."

That night, every precaution was taken. Soldiers were stationed in the direction the horseman was to come, the younger sister was up in the tree, and everyone was waiting. After midnight the horseman came again, with a torch in his hand because it was dark in the graveyard, and what did they see? The horseman was the palace doctor! He came and stuck the torch into the ground and dug and dug and dug at the earth and opened the grave. Out came the young man, dressed as the son of the padishah. They watched him, and as the horseman poured the leftovers—pieces of meat and pieces of bone and pieces of bread—and the padishah saw his own son eating those leftover pieces of food, his heart bled for his son. When it came the right time, they began to whistle, and all the soldiers closed in on the horseman and captured him. They took the sick boy to the hospital, and they took good care of him. Every day, Bold Girl came and asked about the health of the boy, and the mother kept on saying, "I remember my promise. Don't worry."

Finally, the boy got well, and the promise was fulfilled. The younger sister and the son of the padishah were married. "Now," said Bold Girl to the younger one, "I've found a fat tail for you. You can lick on it, and eat and live on it, and forget about me. Don't even ask about me."

Now Bold Girl started out to seek her own fortune. She went and went, straight over hills and over dales, picking hyacinths and tulips all the way. She walked—how she walked!—until at last she came to another city with a mansion large enough for a padishah. "Oh," she said, "perhaps I can work here as a servant and earn my bread and cheese." So she asked there for work. "I can work here if they want me," she said.

The servants inside said, "There are already many servants here. We don't think they would want any more. But let's ask."

"All right," said the cook, "let her in. She may help me by peeling onions and potatoes and stringing beans." So she was taken to the kitchen, and she worked all day long. She peeled potatoes and onions and cut them, and she cut the other vegetables, and she washed the dishes and she scrubbed the bottoms of the cooking pots, and she put the shelves in order. Well, she worked hard all day long!

It seems it was the habit of the padishah's wife to come down to the kitchen once a week. One day when she got down to the kitchen, she saw everything spotlessly clean. She wasn't used to seeing the kitchen so nicely arranged and cleaned. "Look, look," she said. "Who has done this? Who is responsible for this?"

And they said, "This new girl who is taking care of the kitchen has done it."

"Oh, she must be very good," the wife of the padishah said. "She's not going to work in the kitchen anymore. She's going to come upstairs and be in my service. She will light the stoves and sweep the floors and clean the lamps." So Bold Girl left the kitchen, and she worked in the lady's rooms. She lighted her stoves and made her bed and cleaned the floors and did every sort of work upstairs.

Now, this padishah and his wife had a son, but he was bewitched. He wouldn't eat anything; he wouldn't talk to anyone; he wouldn't do anything. He would just sit in his room and stare. He hadn't talked to a single person for years.

One day the padishah said to his wife, "Listen, Wife, this girl is very active and she's very clever. She seems to be a very able person. Why don't we put our son's room in her charge, so she will work in there? Perhaps she'll be helpful."

One day she was carrying water upstairs in two buckets, and right at that moment the padishah's son happened to be coming out of his room. When Bold Girl saw him coming out of his room, she pretended to slip, and she let herself fall down the stairs with her legs up and the water pouring all over her. She made a very funny sight, but all on purpose. And the prince, who hadn't laughed for years, couldn't help himself. He began to laugh. The good news was carried to the padishah and his wife: "The prince has laughed! The prince has laughed!"

"Well," said the padishah's wife, "maybe you were right. Let's put her in his service. That may do some good for our son."

They told the girl that from that day on, she would be in charge of the

prince's room, to light his stove and make his bed and attend to his orders or whatever else was to be done for him. She was to sleep in the same room, too. She liked her new work. "It's much better this way," she said.

And she started caring for that room. She cleaned it every day. She worked and worked, and when it was nighttime, she went to bed. They put a poor little mattress for her there on the floor, and she slept on it.

The prince talked to himself, saying, "Now, in addition to all else, I have to suffer this girl in here. How did this Bold Girl come into my life?" In truth, the prince was in love with the daughter of the padishah of fairies. There was a secret way out of his room, and every night he would go to his sweetheart after everyone else had gone to sleep. But from the day Bold Girl began to sleep in his room, he was unable to go to visit his sweetheart.

At last he couldn't bear it any longer, and he decided to go and visit the daughter of the padishah of fairies anyway. To make sure that Bold Girl was asleep, he took a big needle and stuck it into her flesh. She just gritted her teeth and never made a sound, pretending she was asleep.

After the prince had made sure she was asleep, he left. He lifted up one corner of the carpet and opened a trapdoor in the floor, and there was a stairway going down. He went *tıpır tıpır tıpır tıpır* down the steps. The girl lifted up her head and saw where he had gone.

Now, the fairy padishah's daughter was going to have a child. "Where have you been all this time?" said she.

And he said, "Oh, don't ask me! I have Bold Girl with me. This is how it happened. She was working in the palace, and one day I saw her fall down the stairs with two buckets of water pouring over her and her feet sticking up in the air. It was a funny sight, and I wish I hadn't done so, but I laughed. They thought that she pleased me, and they ordered her to sleep in my room. And ever since, she has been sleeping there."

50

The fairy padishah's daughter said, "I am about to have our baby, and I need help. Somehow, we must find a midwife to help me."

Bold Girl was listening, and when she heard this, she made herself look hunchbacked and ugly and old. She wrapped herself in heavy clothes and took a lantern in her hand and a stick, and she went around the palace to the entrance of the fairy padishah's house. Just then, the padishah's son came out of the house and saw this old woman. "Where are you going, old woman?" he said to her.

And she said, "Oh, I'm in a hurry. I have to deliver a baby. I'm a midwife, and this lantern is not bright enough for me to find my way there, and yet they're in a hurry. I have to get there."

"Oh, you are a *midwife?*" said the prince. "My wife is going to have a baby, too. Please come and deliver mine first."

"How can I do it? They are waiting for me," she said.

"Oh, *please* do come in and take mine first. I'll give you more money. Please come!" Because she was all wrapped up in clothes, he could not recognize the old woman as Bold Girl and took her in.

He didn't know her, but the fairy padishah's daughter knew her. (What *don't* they know, those fairies!) She gave birth to a very, very blond, golden-haired baby son. And then she said, "My father and mother don't know anything about this baby, so I can't keep him here. *You* take this baby and let him be yours."

"All right," said the old woman. "I have a younger sister, and she'll take care of this baby."

She took the baby and went upstairs, putting the baby in her loose baggy trousers [şalvar]. She stretched her legs by the doorsill and she began screaming, "Help! Help! What sort of padishah's house *is* this? The baby's already born, and nobody knows anything about it! Help! Help!"

And they all ran. They dashed to the doorsill and there, true enough, caught in the şalvar was a beautiful newborn baby boy. "Oh, how nice!" they said. "Our prince has a baby son. What a happy event!" So they made a good bed for Bold Girl, and they put her in bed with the baby next to her.

The fairy padishah's daughter heard all this excitement, and (What *don't* they know!) she understood what was happening. She said to the prince, "That girl has saved me from a very hard spot. From now on, you must be my brother, and nothing more. Now, go and get married to that girl. I give what is mine to her, and may it be *helâl,* like my mother's milk, to her. Go, then, and marry the girl."

So, whether he liked it or not, he came back and, in a wedding that lasted forty days and forty nights, he and Bold Girl were married. They ate and drank and had their wishes fulfilled. May we likewise have good fortune come from bad.

51

The Padishah, His Three Sons, and the Golden Apple

Once there was and once there wasn't a padishah who had three sons. In the garden of the padishah's palace there grew a single apple tree that each year bore a single golden apple. However, the padishah had never been able to pick this golden apple, for on the night that it appeared, a two-headed giant would come to the palace garden, take the apple, and disappear with it.

One year the oldest of the padishah's sons said, "Father, I shall wait for the golden apple to appear tonight, and I shall bring it to you." He took a sword from his father's vast collection and went to wait for the golden apple to appear. *Aman!* The eldest son fell asleep during the night, and when the golden apple appeared, the two-headed giant came and took it away with him.

The next year when it was time for the golden apple to appear, the padishah's second son said, "Father, I shall wait for the golden apple to appear tonight, and I shall pick it and bring it to you." So the second son armed himself and went to the palace garden, but he, too, fell asleep before the apple had appeared, and the two-headed giant came and took it away with him.

The third year, the youngest son went to his father and said, "Father, I shall wait for the golden apple to appear tonight, and I shall pick it and bring it to you." During the night, the youngest son became very sleepy, but he was careful not to fall asleep. When the golden apple appeared on the tree, the two-headed giant also appeared in the palace garden by the tree.

The youngest son was prepared for the giant's appearance, and he swung his sword and cut off one of the giant's heads. He then quickly picked the golden apple from the tree, and as the creature stumbled out of the palace garden with blood flowing all over him, the youngest son took the apple to his father. "Here is the apple, my father," he said, "but I was able to cut off only one of the giant's heads. I want to pursue him and kill him."

"My son," said his father, "you are too young to undertake such a task by yourself, but you may go if your brothers are willing to go with you. Ask them, if you wish."

His older brothers agreed to go with him, so all three went to find the giant, following the trail of blood that he had left behind. After following the

53

trail for three or five hours, they came to a well. The bloody trail went all the way down into that well. Besides being very deep, the well had a fire burning at the very bottom of it. "I'll go down first," said the oldest brother, so they lowered him into the well. But when he came close to the fire, he shouted, "I am burning! I am burning! Pull me up!" And the other two brothers pulled him up.

The second son then said, "Let me go down now. I can stand the fire." So the other two lowered him carefully into the well. But when he came close to the fire, he shouted, "Oh, I cannot stand it! I am burning! I am burning! Pull me up!" And the other two brothers pulled him up.

As soon as the second son was safely up, the youngest son said, "Now *I* shall go down, but if I shout, 'Pull me up! Pull me up! I am *burning*,' do not pull me up. Just lower me farther." This they did. When the youngest son came close to the fire and felt that he could not stand the heat, he shouted, "Pull me up!" But his brothers, remembering what he had said, just lowered him farther into the well. The youngest son suddenly found himself touching ground in an underworld palace with three huge iron doors.

After the youngest son had rested for a little while, he opened one of the iron doors and found behind it a very pretty girl. It seems that in the two-headed giant's palace there were three young girls who lived in three separate rooms. The two-headed giant had captured them and brought them to the palace as his wives, but none knew about the others. The giant also had his own private room. Because he had just had one head cut off, he had gone to his room and lain down with his eyes wide open.

The girl was as surprised to see the prince as the prince was to see the girl. "What are you doing here?" the girl asked. "You must hide quickly, because the giant will devour you if he sees you."

"I am not afraid of the giant," said the prince, and he opened the second iron door. Behind that door was another pretty girl. And when the prince opened the third door, he found a girl even prettier than the other two. As for the girls, they were astonished to discover each other. While the girls were talking of this and that, the prince asked, "Where is the giant?"

The prettiest girl said, "I heard him entering his own room." They all went to the door of the giant's room, and they could all hear him sleeping, HOROL, HOROL! "Please do not enter his room," said that prettiest one, "or he will devour you."

"I am not afraid of that giant," said the prince. "I have already cut off one of his heads, and I mean to cut off the other one."

"Then," said the prettiest one, "please look carefully at his eyes when you go in. If his eyes are open, that will mean that he is asleep. If they are closed, you had better beware, for that will mean that the giant is awake."

The youngest son of the padishah went quietly into the giant's room and saw that his eyes were open. "Ah! He is indeed asleep!" the prince said to himself. Quickly he stepped toward the giant and cut off his other head. Then he took the three girls and hurried to the opening where he had entered the underground palace. He tied the rope to the first girl's waist and told his brothers to pull on the rope. "My oldest brother," he said, "I am sending you your kismet." The other two brothers pulled that first girl to the surface and then lowered the rope again. The youngest prince then tied the rope to the waist of the second girl and called, "My second brother, I am sending you your kismet. Pull on the rope." The brothers pulled the second girl from the well.

As the brothers were lowering the rope for the third time, the prettiest girl said, "Your brothers may well deceive you and leave you here when they see me. Here is a lock of my hair. If you have any difficulty in leaving the underground palace, rub this lock of hair and you will receive help. But hear this warning: two rams will appear, one white and one black. If you mount the white ram, you will be carried up to the surface of the earth. If you mount the black ram, you will be carried down seven levels below where you are now. Do not mount the black ram."

Putting the girl's words in his pocket [remembering them], the prince tied the rope around the waist of the third and prettiest girl and called to his brothers, "You can pull now. I am sending up my own kismet." And the two brothers pulled the third girl to the surface.

But when his brothers saw that third girl, they both felt angry at the youngest son for saving for himself the youngest and prettiest girl. Therefore, when they had pulled him up halfway to the top, they cut the rope, and he plunged back down to the bottom of the well. As for the two older brothers, they took the three girls and left for their father's palace.

The youngest son, finding himself once more at the bottom of the well, prayed, "O Allah, please send me help!" Soon two rams appeared, one white and the other black. While he was thinking he should mount the white ram and thus be carried up to the earth, the black ram rushed between his legs and he was carried seven levels below the level of the well floor.

When he arrived there, he said to himself, "Oh, how hot and tired I am! I'll lie down for a little while under a tree in that valley." And so he did. As he looked above him, he saw on a high branch a hawk's nest with three baby hawks in it. He also saw a snake going up the tree to eat the baby hawks. But when the snake looked down and saw a human being, it dropped from the tree in order to seize and devour the youngest son instead of the baby hawks. The youngest son quickly drew his sword and killed the snake. Feeling even more tired after that, he lay down and fell asleep at once. Meanwhile, the baby hawks' mother flew back to the tree. When she saw a human being, she prepared to attack and kill him, but the baby hawks cried out, "No, no, Mother! He saved us from the snake that was about to devour us!" The mother, grateful then for the help that had been given to her children, spread her wings over the prince to protect him from the sun so that he could sleep.

When the youngest son awoke, he was startled to see that huge hawk

above him. But the hawk spoke to him: "Tell me what your greatest wish is and I shall grant it."

"My hawk, you cannot grant me my greatest wish, but thank you anyway," he said. "I could not see your chicks destroyed."

"Remember, though," said the hawk, "if you should ever need my help, come and find me." And she flew to join her brood.

The prince took the road toward a town that he could see in the distance and finally he came to an old woman's home. "I am thirsty, grandmother," he said. "Have you some water that I can drink?"

The old woman brought him a glass of water, but as he looked at it, he could see worms in it. "Grandmother," he said, "why are there worms in this water?"

She answered, "Son, there is a two-headed giant that lives at the source of our water. He appears each year, chooses the youngest and prettiest girl of our town, eats her, and leaves our water supply open to us for just two hours. The townspeople get as much water as they can during that time and store it in large earthen jars. But our water often gets worms in it during the year. Tomorrow is the day on which the giant will receive the padishah's daughter as this year's victim. It is the only way by which the town can get water. If she is not delivered to him, he will not let us have any water. Many of our brave young men have fought with the giant, but none could vanquish him. Instead, they were all devoured by him."

"Grandmother," the prince said, "please take me to the place where the daughter of the padishah is to be given to the giant." When they arrived at that place, all the townspeople were gathered there. Some were crying for joy about fresh water, and others were crying out of compassion for the padishah's daughter. Still, they knew she must be sacrificed if they were to have their yearly ration of water.

57

The youngest son sprang forward and declared, "I shall fight the giant." The townspeople tried to persuade him that others larger and stronger than he had also tried, only to be eaten up by the giant. Still, the youngest son was determined to fight.

There was a huge tree near the place where the giant would appear, and the girl had been tied to it. The prince said to the girl, "Hold onto my waist." He then drew his sword and challenged the giant.

The giant became angry at this delay in his anticipated meal. He inhaled deeply, thinking that he would eat the youngest son also with relish. When the giant exhaled, even the roots of the huge tree shook. The prince fought the giant bravely. He was able to chop off one of his heads, and he continued to fight the wounded giant valiantly. Finally he succeeded in chopping off his second head.

The people of the town could not believe their eyes. They rejoiced at the victory over the giant and at the release of their water supply. The padishah of this land asked to have the prince brought to his golden palace and placed in a room. He was brought to the padishah's presence, and the padishah asked, "What can I do to reward you for saving the life of my daughter and for freeing our water supply?"

"My padishah," said the prince, "I ask only your good health."

"My health is for *me*," the padishah answered. "What can I give to you?"

"Nothing, my padishah, except your good health," said the prince.

"Well, then, would you wish to have my daughter as your bride? Or would you prefer that I surrender my throne to you?"

"My padishah, I know of nothing that is needed. Please allow me to walk about for a bit and then return." With the padishah's permission, the prince left the palace and wandered off to the valley. There he found the hawk whose young he had saved from certain death, and he said to her, "Please take me up from this depth and carry me up to the world above."

The hawk agreed to take the boy up, but she said, "In order to do that great task, I shall need forty *batman*s of meat and forty *batman*s of wine."

Hearing this, the prince returned to the golden palace and asked the padishah to provide forty *batman*s of meat and forty *batman*s of wine for him. The padishah immediately took measures to fill the prince's request. When the meat and the wine were ready, they brought the supplies to the valley. This hawk's wings were each forty meters in length. The padishah's men arranged the containers of food and wine under each wing of the hawk.

"Now," said the hawk to the prince, "mount on my back. When I say *kald*, give me a *batman* of wine, and when I say *kok*, give me a *batman* of meat. In that way, I shall have strength enough for the journey." The prince then mounted himself on the hawk's back, and they flew out of the valley. Each time the hawk said "*Kald*," the prince gave her wine, and each time she said "*Kok*," he gave her meat. Thus their journey continued for thirty-nine

58

days. On the fortieth day, the supply of meat was exhausted. The hawk became aware of this fact, but still she said "*Kok.*" Thereupon, the prince cut a piece of flesh from his foot and gave it to the hawk. The hawk realized that the meat was human flesh, and slipped it under her tongue. She continued to fly, advancing two meters and slipping back one because of her need for meat.

When they arrived at the upper world, the hawk said, "Get off now and start walking toward your home."

"Ah," said the prince, "but I would rather wait until I have seen you fly off toward your young ones."

But, "Walk," said the hawk, and the prince began to walk. But as he walked, he limped because of the pain in his foot. "Come back," said the hawk. "I know why you are limping. When the supplies were finished and I said '*Kok,*' you cut a piece of flesh from your foot and gave it to me." She then took the piece of flesh she had slipped under her tongue and, carefully placing it back on the boy's foot, sealed the flesh with her saliva. The prince's foot was immediately healed. The hawk then spread her wings and started on her journey back down to the world below.

At that very time there were wedding preparations going on at the padishah's palace. The two older brothers who had brought back the girls from the mouth of the well were now preparing to wed them. One of the chief viziers was to perform the wedding ceremony. The second son was to wed the youngest and prettiest of the girls. The eldest was preparing to marry the second-youngest girl that the two-headed giant of the golden apples had captured. In this land, wedding preparations and festivities lasted for three years.

Meanwhile, the youngest son was a long way from his father's palace. He started to walk on his journey home. After a while he came across a baker. His father had ordered the bakers of the land to bake the very best bread ever to be baked on earth. And the padishah had decreed that he would have all the bakers' heads chopped off if they could not produce among them the superior bread requested. The bakers were pondering on how to achieve that feat when the youngest son went into a baker's shop and asked to be hired as a helper. At first, the baker said, "Get out! Here we are trying to decide how to produce the most wonderful bread on earth, which the padishah has ordered, and you come in wanting to be an apprentice!"

"But," said the prince, "I can bake the required bread."

"Ha!" exclaimed the baker. "Here every baker in the land stands in danger of losing his head over this task, and you, a mere boy, claim that you can do it yourself. Get along with you!"

"But, sir, I *can* bake the bread that the padishah requires. Just lock me in a room with a sack of flour, yeast, and water. And, of course, provide me with my daily food. I promise that I shall produce the bread that has been demanded."

59

Since no one else could promise anything of the kind, the baker consented, and the prince was locked in a room with the required baking ingredients and food. The baker, however, found a hole in the door and watched the prince the whole time. For thirty-nine days, the prince ate and slept and did nothing else. On the fortieth day he mixed the ingredients, made dough, and then rubbed the lock of hair that the youngest girl of the underground palace had given him. The bread he baked was the most delicious bread ever to be baked in the world. The baker was beside himself with joy, and he gave the youngest son many gifts. The boy took them and continued on his way, and the baker took the bread to the padishah's palace.

Meanwhile, the prince met a *helva* maker along the way. He asked the *helva* maker if he would hire him as a helper. At first, the *helva* maker said, "Get out! Here we are trying to decide how to make the most delicious *helva* ever made in the world, and you come in wanting to be a helper! The padishah has said he will have all the confectioners' heads chopped off if among them they cannot produce the best *helva* ever. You are no more than a boy! How can you help us in such a serious situation?"

"But, sir, I *can* make the *helva* that the padishah requires," said the prince. "Just give me the ingredients and my daily food and lock me in a room, and I promise to produce exactly the *helva* the padishah desires."

Thinking that he had nothing to lose, the *helva* maker hired the prince and locked him inside a room with everything that was needed to supply his food and to make *helva*. Again, for the first thirty-nine days, the prince did nothing but eat and sleep. On the fortieth day, he put the ingredients together and, in truth, produced by means of that lock of hair the most delicious *helva* ever made by man. The *helva* maker was overjoyed with the results of the prince's work, and he took the *helva* to the palace of the padishah.

The youngest son continued on his way, and after a while he came upon a jeweler. He asked the jeweler if he would hire him as a helper. At first, the jeweler said, "Get out! Here we are trying to decide how to produce the golden tray that the padishah has ordered, with a golden rooster walking about, a golden hen laying eggs, and golden baby chicks feeding and moving around. With an order like that—and our heads to pay if we fail—how can you expect any jeweler to be interested in hiring a helper?"

"But, sir, I can make exactly the kind of tray that the padishah has demanded," said the prince. "Just lock me in a room with gold to work with, a sack of hazelnuts, and a sack of raisins. I promise that in forty days you will have the tray that is required."

With no other hope at hand, the jeweler did as the prince had asked, and the necessary supplies were locked inside the room with the new helper. Again, the youngest son just ate and slept for the first thirty-nine days. On the fortieth day, he molded the golden rooster, hen, and baby chicks as well as the golden tray. Then he rubbed the girl's lock of hair over them. The rooster walked about, the hen laid eggs, and the baby chicks fed themselves. The jeweler rejoiced to see the work of his new helper, and he ran to the palace of the padishah with exactly the tray that the padishah had ordered.

The prince then approached his father's palace. The youngest and prettiest girl he had rescued from the well was at the middle window of the seven-story golden palace. She looked out smiling, for she knew that her destined husband was approaching. He in turn knew that his destined bride would not wed anyone else, but he did not yet reveal himself.

The palace grounds were very, very large. All the people of the land were gathered there for the celebrations, for there were to be bullfights and spear fights in which men who had never been defeated were going to compete. The padishah sat on a golden throne among his viziers. When the competitions were over, there were five champions in five different fields. Three of the contests were won by the padishah's older sons. The youngest son went to the grand vizier and said, "I can defeat the champions in each of those five fields, for I am an expert in every field."

"My boy," said the grand vizier, "you cannot possibly compete with these champions. They are the very best in the world. If they were ever to grip you, they would break every bone in your body."

"But, sir, I *can* defeat all five of the champions," said the prince. "Please take me to the presence of the padishah so that I can state my case." When he was taken before the padishah, he bowed down and asked to wrestle with the champion wrestler.

The padishah looked down on the young man with good humor and said, "Son, you cannot compete with the champion wrestler, for he is the strongest man on earth. He would break you with no effort."

"Sir," said the young man, "I should still like to try, for I am sure I can defeat him, even if he be the oldest son of the padishah." Of course, the prince was relying on the lock of hair given to him by the prettiest girl. The two wrestlers then came forth to the middle of the arena, and the youngest son brought his brother down with the first grapple. Then the youngest son called out, "Now, my padishah, I want the bull."

They brought the bull into the ring and the youngest son grabbed the bull by one horn with his left hand and forced it to the ground. Next he asked to compete with the champion *cirit* player, and he defeated his other brother at the *cirit* game. He next asked to compete with the champion of the sword game, asking the padishah for permission.

By this time, the padishah's eyes were as big as fists, and he looked annoyed. "Know, young man," he said, "that the sword competition has no restrictions, no regulations, and no penalties. You will surely be killed by the champion."

"My padishah, I accept those conditions. Both our lives will be in jeopardy, which seems quite fair to me." He then dueled with his brother and broke his brother's sword, then threw him on the ground. Just as he was about to plunge his sword into his brother's heart, he turned toward the padishah and said, "What is your wish, my padishah?"

The padishah called him to his side and asked him who he was and where he had come from. The prince said that he would tell his story to the padishah, and he recounted the many adventures that had befallen him.

"Once there was a padishah who had three sons. He also had a beautiful garden with an apple tree that each year bore a golden apple. But the padishah was never able to pick the golden apple because a two-headed giant would pluck it the very night that it appeared. The oldest son went out to the garden to keep watch and get the golden apple for the padishah, but he fell asleep and the giant got the golden apple again that year. The next year his second son stood guard by the apple tree, but he too fell asleep and the golden apple was snatched away by the giant. The third year the youngest son kept watch, and when the giant appeared he cut one of his two heads off and brought the golden apple to his father. When the youngest son wanted to pursue the wounded giant, his father, the padishah, sent his two brothers along with him.

"They all came to a well where the giant's tracks disappeared. Both of the older sons tried to go into the well after the giant, but the fire at the bottom of the well was too hot for them. The youngest son bore the fire and found the giant's underground castle protected by iron gates. He went in, killed the giant, and brought out the giant's three brides for himself and his brothers. He sent the women up one at a time, and the two elder brothers pulled each one up to the surface. When they saw the youngest son's intended wife, they became envious, and while the youngest one was holding on to the rope to come out of the well, instead of pulling him up, they cut the rope and let him fall back to the bottom. They took the brides and went home and left their brother down below. They betrayed their youngest brother. The girl looking out of the middle window of the palace is my intended wife, the champions I defeated are my two older brothers, and you are my father."

The padishah was astounded and overjoyed to be reunited with his youngest and bravest son. He renounced his authority, and placed his youngest son on the throne. He had a magnificent wedding for all three of his sons, with the oldest marrying his kismet, the second-oldest marrying his kismet, and the youngest marrying the youngest and prettiest girl, just as the youngest son had planned when he first sent them up out of the well.

When all of this was over, the two elder sons and their brides were sent to far, far parts of the kingdom. As for the youngest son and his bride, they had their wishes fulfilled. Let's go up and sit in their seats!

Prophet İdris in Heaven

Prophet İdris wanted to enter heaven in order to see what it was like. The angels at the gate refused to let him in at first. They said, "Once you get inside, you will not want to leave."

İdris answered, "I promise that if you let me in to look around, I shall leave again." After he had made this promise, the angels allowed him to enter. He looked here and there for some time, and he liked everything that he saw. He left, as he had said he would, but before going, he left his scissors on a doorstep quite a distance from the gate.

Shortly after he had departed, he returned again and said to the angels at the gate, "I'm sorry, but I laid my scissors down inside and forgot to take them with me." They allowed him inside to get his scissors.

Once he was inside for a second time, however, he refused to leave. He said, "I left after entering heaven for the first time because I promised to do so. The second time I entered, I made no such promise, and so I refuse to leave." And he stayed there.

Tailors all believe this story, and they consider him their patron saint because he was the first to sew garments and wear them.

The Cat and the Tiger

They say that the cat is the uncle of the tiger. Anyhow, one day a strong tiger saw her uncle the cat and asked him, "Oh, my uncle, why are you so small?"

The cat said, "If you were in the hands of human beings you would know why I am so small."

Then the tiger said, "Show me a human being, will you, Uncle?"

"Follow me!" said the cat.

While they were going along, they saw cows grazing. "What are those, Uncle?" asked the tiger. "Are they human beings?"

"Huh! A very young one of the human beings can gather a hundred of them before him and can bring them to these fields," said the cat.

They continued walking and saw ten horses grazing. Again the tiger asked if these were human beings. "They are nothing when compared to human beings. Human beings can ride on them," said the cat bitterly.

After some time they saw camels. The tiger asked, "Uncle, are those human beings?"

"No," answered the cat. "A child can gather fifteen of them and can graze them."

They went on and met a woodcutter. The cat told of their mission. When the woodcutter heard this, he asked the tiger to put her forefeet between the two huge pieces of wood and hold them apart. When the tiger did this, the rail which was holding the two pieces apart fell down, and the forefeet of the tiger were pressed tightly between them.

The woodcutter laid down his ax and came to watch the tiger. The cat climbed up into a tree. The tiger began to ask, "What do you think, Uncle? Will they set me free when I am as small as you are?"

"I do not know—mew," said the cat whenever the tiger asked this question.

They say that the mewing of the cat began with this happening.

Driving for Atatürk

One day Atatürk, accompanied by İsmet Pasha and Fevzi Pasha, left Ankara to inspect the front lines, which were near Polatlı. There were three cars in the group, one car for each general. This was during the last part of the War of Independence, quite close to the end of that war. As we were approaching Polatlı, we had to cross a small stream. While we were trying to cross that stream, our automobile became stuck in the mud. It was an old, low-horsepower Adler. Fevzi Pasha's car tried to cross below ours, and his became stuck. And still farther down, İsmet Pasha's car was also stuck. It was only a small stream, but the place along the road to it where we wanted to cross was marshy. And so all three cars were stuck.

We had to get the cars out of the mud. All the aides had gotten out of the cars. Salih Omurtak was Atatürk's aide, a lieutenant at the time. While we were trying to get the cars out of the mud, six peasants appeared from behind a hill. It was obvious from their clothes and behavior that they were from some nearby village. İsmet Pasha started shouting to them, "Hey! Quick! Come here!" He called them to his own car and forced them to get it out of the mud. All the rest of us—Atatürk's aide, Fevzi Pasha's aide, and I—were trying to get Atatürk's car out first. Atatürk himself was behind his car with the others, pushing from behind, and I was at the wheel. As the wheels of the car spun around, mud flew up and covered Atatürk from head to foot. Salih Omurtak took his handkerchief from his pocket and tried to wipe the mud off Atatürk's face, but Atatürk stopped him, saying, "Never mind, Salih. It is the soil of my country. Let us continue trying to free the car."

I shall never forget his words. It was a great expression.

When Atatürk saw how İsmet Pasha was forcing the peasants to pull his car out, using threatening words to make them work harder, he said, "Salih, go quickly and tell him not to scold these men. We shall get the other cars out just as we have this one."

Later, when İsmet İnönü came to Atatürk, Atatürk said to him, "İsmet, what are you doing to those men? Leave them alone. They are wounded at heart. Their families and children and property have all been left in enemy territory. They managed to save themselves by fleeing to our side, where they are wandering about. I met these fellows here yesterday and several times before that, and I tried to console them, saying, 'We shall soon save your families and children from the enemy.' And now you are scolding them. Don't scold them!"

We finally got all three cars free from the mud, and when we got a little closer to the front lines, the generals walked the rest of the way while we waited with the cars at the rear. They returned to the cars about three hours later, and then we returned by car to Ankara.

These are my memories.

Who Is More Clever?

Nasreddin Hoca had a very clever donkey. Sometimes the Hoca was pleased by his donkey's cleverness, but at other times he was annoyed by it.

For several years of his life, Nasreddin Hoca made money by supplying grocery stores with salt. He would fill bags with large chunks of salt, load them on his donkey, and take the salt to the mill to be ground. Then he would take the ground salt to various grocery stores and sell it.

This salt was very heavy, and after carrying it for some time, his donkey became tired of this procedure. The donkey finally decided upon a way of lightening his heavy burden. Both going to and coming from the mill, the donkey lay down in the shallow water at the edge of a river along the way. While he was lying in the water, some of the salt melted away.

When Nasreddin Hoca realized what the donkey was doing, he said to himself, "I'll show that donkey something!" On the following day, he filled the salt bags not with salt but with sponges. On the way to the mill, the donkey, as usual, lay down in the river. This time, however, his load grew heavier instead of lighter, for the sponges filled with water. The sponges became so heavy, in fact, that the donkey could not stand up with them on his back.

Going to the donkey, the Hoca said, "What do you think about that? Is it you or I who could be called more clever?"

A Bektaşi *and Allah as Partners*

Once a *Bektaşi* plowed and sowed his field, but he did not harvest any crop that year. "Allah did not give me a crop this year," he said, "but I am sure He will be more generous next year."

He plowed and sowed his field the following year, but he still had no crop to harvest. The *Bektaşi* said, "O Allah, next year you and I shall be partners."

That year, the *Bektaşi* had a very good crop. After he had cut and harvested the crop, he put the wheat and the straw into four equal heaps, two for Allah and two for himself. When the work was finished, he proudly looked at the heaps and said, "O Allah, thank you for a good harvest. Half of it belongs to you."

Then he started thinking, "Allah is all alone, so half of the crop will be too much for Him." He raked part of the wheat and the straw from Allah's piles over to his own heaps. He looked again at Allah's share and at his own, and, "Even this amount will be too much for Allah," he decided, and again he raked some of Allah's wheat and straw over to his own heaps. "It's really hard to believe that Allah needs *any* of this crop," he muttered to himself.

Just as he was about to rake the rest of Allah's share onto his own heaps, the wind came up, and rain began to fall. Soon the wind blew with great fury, and the rain grew into a cloudburst. The *Bektaşi* took shelter in a cave near his field. From there, he could watch his straw blown away by the wind, and his wheat swept away by the torrent.

Then a streak of lightning came right past his cave, followed immediately by a very loud roll of thunder. "O Allah!" he said, shaking with fear, "it was You who gave the crop to me. It was also You who took it away. Now that the matter is settled, why are you still so angry at me?"

Fish Heads

They say that the cleverest men in Turkey come from Kayseri, and that even *boys* from Kayseri have been able to outwit the Devil. Of course, everyone wants to know what makes Kayseri men so clever.

For that reason, a country fellow was excited when he discovered that his seatmate on the train to İstanbul was from Kayseri. Like a proper countryman, he did not ask his question at once, but talked of this and that with the Kayseri man until the two were quite comfortable with each other.

Then the country fellow said, "Sir, you come from Kayseri. Can you tell me what makes Kayseri men so clever?"

"Of course!" said the Kayseri man. "We eat fish heads."

"*Fish heads?*"

"*Fish heads.*"

Well, that answer puzzled the country fellow, but he asked no more questions until he saw the Kayseri man open his lunch sack. Inside, there were a loaf of bread and ten small fish. *Chut! Chut! Chut!* The Kayseri man chopped off the heads of the fish with his pocket knife and pushed them to one side.

"Sir, aren't you going to eat the *heads?*" the fellow asked.

"No," answered the Kayseri man. "I already come from Kayseri."

"How much would you charge me for one fish head?"

The Kayseri man thought. Then, "One lira," he said.

"And for all ten fish heads?"

"Ten liras."

Immediately, the country fellow took his worn purse from his sash and counted out ten liras. "There!" he said. And he began to eat the fish heads, one after another—CRUNCH, CRUNCH, CRUNCH!—with not so much as a crumb of bread to help them down.

When he had finished every bone, the country fellow asked, "Sir, how much did you pay for each of those fish?"

"One lira," said the Kayseri man.

"*What?* You charged me one lira apiece for each fish head, and you paid only one lira apiece for each fish?"

"Aha!" said the Kayseri man. "You see? It's working *already!*"

Arzu and Kamber

Once there was and once there was not an *ağa* whose camel herder was a *keloğlan*. This *keloğlan* had been taking care of the *ağa's* camels for some time when he said to his master one day, "Oh, my *ağa*, why do we just sit around here and do nothing all the time? We have forty camels. Why don't we use them? Everyone else seems continually going to and returning from Yemen on some kind of business. Why don't we also go to Yemen?"

"All right, Keloğlan. *İnşallah!* your words of advice will be auspicious."

The two of them set about preparing their forty camels and themselves for traveling such a great distance, and when all was ready, they set out on their journey. After traveling for seven days and seven nights, they came to a mountain pasture on a high plateau where they decided to camp for the night. Keloğlan climbed up on top of one of the camels to scan the area, and as he looked in every direction, he saw a short distance ahead of them a palace. He climbed down and walked to that palace, which seemed entirely deserted. Entering the palace, he found forty rooms inside. He opened the doors of thirty-nine of these rooms and looked within. They were filled, just filled, with treasures of all kinds, but there was not a living soul in any of them. He did not open the fortieth door.

Returning to his master, he said, "Oh, my *ağa*, there is a deserted palace quite close to us containing all sorts of things, many of which I have never seen before. There are forty rooms in that palace. I opened the doors of the first thirty-nine rooms but not the door of the fortieth. What lies behind that fortieth door I do not know. If it is material riches of some sort, they are yours. If it is a living creature, it is mine." They went together to the deserted palace and loaded onto the forty camels all of the valuable goods that were in the first thirty-nine rooms. Then they went to the fortieth room and opened the door. Inside they found a baby boy sucking its thumb.

"Praise Allah for this!" said the *ağa*. "I have always wanted very much to have a son, and now Allah has given me one."

"But he is mine!" said Keloğlan.

"Keloğlan, I shall give you a camel with all the goods loaded on it for this baby boy."

"No!"

"I'll give you two camels."

"No!"

"I'll give you three or five."

"No, no!"

"Keloğlan, you may take twenty camels for this child, but let us keep this whole venture a secret. I don't want any of the people of our village to know about this."

"All right, then. It is agreed upon."

Instead of continuing on to Yemen, they turned back toward home with their camel caravan. When they reached the edge of their village, they were met by a messenger who announced, "Good news, *Ağa!* Your wife gave birth to a daughter while you were away."

"Praise be to Allah," he said, "who first gave me a son and then a daughter." The *ağa* stopped right there to recite a prayer.

They then proceeded to the *ağa's* garden, where they divided the forty camels loaded with goods. While they were doing this, the *ağa's* wife appeared and asked, "What has happened? Where did all of these goods come from?"

The *ağa* explained to his wife everything that had happened from the time they had left the village. He concluded by saying, "I told Keloğlan that I would give him twenty loaded camels in exchange for the baby boy. He accepted this proposal, and we are now dividing the camels and all these goods."

Keloğlan took his share of the camel caravan and left the village. The *ağa*, for his part, was entirely satisfied with the bargain he had made with Keloğlan.

Years passed, and the boy and girl in the *ağa*'s home grew up together happily. The girl was named Arzu, and the boy was named Kamber. When they were old enough, they entered school, and went there every day together. One day when they were on their way to school an old woman stopped them and said, "Why do you go to school every day? I know a nice, quiet place where you could go and play instead of going to school. No one else ever goes there, and so you would not be noticed."

So the children went to that secret place and played that day instead of attending school. But the evil old woman went to their mother and said, "Where is your daughter? Where does she go all the time instead of going to school? I saw her today at Ahmet Bey's straw rick, and the two of them were wrestling."

The mother said to herself, "*Aman, aman*, Allah! Who is this boy? Is he perhaps a Gypsy? We know nothing of his origin, of his parents, or of his ancestors. And now he is teaching bad things to my daughter." She went to Ahmet Bey's straw rick and found the two children playing there. Angrily, she whipped the boy severely and took the girl home with her. Kamber, who was left alone, felt sad and puzzled.

A little while later, Kamber gave Arzu a bracelet which bore a statement that she and Kamber were engaged. One day when Arzu went to the fountain to wash her hands and face, she took off the bracelet and laid it beside the fountain. When she was finished at the fountain, she forgot entirely about the bracelet and left it lying there. Shortly afterwards, Kamber went to the fountain for a drink and found the bracelet. Recognizing it from the inscription it bore, he put it into his pocket and went home.

There, Arzu said to him,

"My bracelet you found at the fountain today,
Left there when I washed my hands and face.
Thus, Kamber, you served in my two eyes' place.
I know that you found it there today."

Kamber answered her lines:

"I did not go to the fountain today,
Nor did I wash my hands and face.
How could I serve in your two eyes' place?
I did not find it there today.

"Plum trees now in the garden grow,
But the winter's snow is dull and gray.

70

For him who finds your bracelet, say
The reward to be his if your bracelet he show."

Arzu answered:

"Medlars too in the garden grow,
But the winter's snow is dull and gray.
To him who finds my bracelet, say
My breasts will be his if the treasure he show."

Then Kamber admitted that he had her bracelet and showed it to her. He said, "I shall take this bracelet and show its inscription to the *muhtar* and his Council of Elders. Then I shall request them to go to your father and, by the will of Allah and the consent of the Prophet, ask for your hand in marriage to me."

"Very well," said Arzu. "You may take the bracelet and keep it."

In time, the *muhtar* and his Council of Elders did appear at the home of the *ağa*. Because the *ağa* was not there, they spoke instead to his wife: "We come by the will of Allah and with the consent of the Prophet to ask for the hand of Arzu in marriage to Kamber."

But they were able to say no more, for the mother shouted, "Donkeys and sons of donkeys! Away with your marriage proposals!" And she drove them off her doorstep.

Greatly upset by this treatment, the Council of Elders went back to Kamber and said, "Oh, Kamber, we went there. We asked for the hand of Arzu, but the mother spoke very rudely to us and drove us away."

Kamber said only, "I understand. Thank you for attempting to do this." Inwardly, however, he was hurt and offended.

The father, on the other hand, thought that such a marriage would be fitting, and he tried to persuade his wife of it. "My wife, it would be a good thing for us to go ahead and have these two children married."

"No," said his wife firmly.

Upset and angered by his wife's refusal to listen to reason, the father said, "Wife, I have learned that Kamber's uncle is a padishah. If he learns of this affront to his kinsman, he may come here and kill us in revenge!"

But the wife's answer still was "No!"

As it happened, Arzu overheard this discussion between her parents, and as soon as they had stopped arguing, she went to see Kamber. "Kamber, I have heard that you have an uncle who is a padishah. He is called Sultan and his wife is named Fadık. They live several days' traveling distance from here. If you could go and find them, they might be able to help us."

In the meantime, Arzu's hand had been requested in marriage by a wealthy *ağa* of a neighboring village. Arzu's mother had accepted this proposal immediately. When her parents asked Arzu for her response to this proposal, she said, "I want forty days in which to consider it." Afterward, she took seven loaves of bread to Kamber and said, "Here is some food for your travel in search of your padishah uncle. Take these loaves with you."

Then Kamber set out on his journey. He went day after day, night after night, without eating anything at all. After the seventh night, he came to a grassy plain where he saw a great many soldiers practicing the skills of warfare while their padishah observed their movements. As Kamber came along, he was singing:

"Grazing together on the grassy plain
Are chestnut-colored colts and white,
But, lonely, I taste no delight.
My sweetheart's lost to an *ağa* for gain."

When the padishah on the plain heard this, he said, "Listen! Someone is singing! Bring whoever that is to me." The guards caught Kamber and took him into the presence of the padishah. The padishah said to Kamber, "If you can tell me my name and my wife's name, I shall give you your freedom, but if you cannot, I shall have the executioner behead you."

Then Kamber sang:

"Grazing together on the grassy plain
Are chestnut-colored colts and white,
But, lonely, I taste no delight.
My sweetheart's lost to an *ağa* for gain.

"I hold my Aunt Fadık in one strong hand;
The other holds Kamber, the minstrel lone.
Now one of my hands holds a minstrel grown,
And Sultan, my uncle, has the other strong hand.

"In one of my hands is a minstrel pearl;
Aunt Fadık is held by the other hand.
Does Sultan, my uncle, hold this strong hand?
The other is held by my Arzu, my girl."

Hearing this, the padishah exclaimed excitedly, "I have searched for you for years, and now *you* have found *me!*" Saying this, the padishah embraced Kamber, and the two of them were filled with joy over their discovery of one another. "How are you? What have you been doing? And who is Arzu?" the padishah asked.

"Arzu is my beloved, but they are taking her away from me. That is the reason I have come here. They are going to have her married to a rich man, an *ağa*."

The padishah uncle of Kamber said to one of his officers, "Send a hundred troops there right away! Order them to behead those people responsible for Kamber's mistreatment and to bring the girl here alive, if at all possible."

The soldiers set out at once for the village where Arzu lived, and Kamber remained with his padishah uncle. But he was not at ease in his heart, for all the while he worried about how Arzu's parents would respond.

In Arzu's and Kamber's village the treacherous old woman heard about the approach of the troops and the reason for their coming. She hastened to Arzu's parents and said, "The soldiers of Sultan are on their way to get Arzu for Kamber. Do you know what they will do to all of us? They will destroy us. But I know a way to deceive the soldiers. Get me an earthenware jug of water and two yellow onions."

When she had received these things, she took them and went to a newly filled grave along the road the soldiers would pass as they came to the village. As the troops came past, they saw her pouring water on the grave. Holding the onions to her eyes, she wept profusely, sat down on the ground, and began to beat her knees in grief.

Seeing her in such pitiable condition, the commander of the troops went to her and said, "Oh, mother, what is wrong?"

"What else could it be? There was a girl here named Arzu who killed herself when she was deserted by her lover, Kamber. She could not live without him, and so she took her own life. I am weeping on her behalf and weeping at the thought of her bad fortune. If I did not weep for her, who would?"

The soldiers listened to the old woman's story; they observed her condition, and they believed her. But now what should they do? They could not decide whether to take the body back with them or leave it there. They knew that if they did not return with the girl, dead or alive, the padishah would execute them; but they also knew that it was forbidden in their faith to dig up a body from its grave. They finally decided that there was no way in which they could act correctly and survive. Their best course, therefore, was to take no action at all. "Let us all separate," they said, "and let each return quietly to his own village and never report to the padishah at all. In this way we may escape his wrath."

As all of this was going on, Kamber grew more and more anxious about Arzu's destiny. Going to the padishah to secure his permission to leave, Kamber said, "My dear uncle, I am deeply distressed. I cannot remain here inactive any longer. Please give me permission to go and see what is the matter."

The padishah summoned his viziers and ordered, "Bring here at once my great horse Düldül, the one horse I always keep in the underground stable." Quickly the viziers' servants brought Düldül and gave his reins to Kamber.

Mounting Düldül, Kamber said to the horse, "Take me at once to the cemetery of my home village." The magic horse flew there in the blink of an eye. At the edge of the cemetery Kamber found a shepherd. "O shepherd,

73

I have been seven days without a morsel of food. Please milk one of your sheep and give me the milk and a piece of bread."

The shepherd milked one of his sheep, as Kamber had requested, and gave Kamber the milk and a piece of bread. As he began to eat the food, they heard the distant beating of a drum. *Güm-bi-di! Güm-bi-di! Güm!*"

"What is that?" asked Kamber. "It sounds like a drum beat."

"Of course it is! They are celebrating the wedding of a girl named Arzu, and the wedding is almost over."

"May Allah grant you a blessed increase, shepherd! Here! Quick! Take these new clothes of mine and give me your old ones."

"Are you trying to make a fool of me? No one would exchange fine clothes like yours for the rags that I am wearing." But when Kamber insisted, the shepherd finally agreed, and the two men exchanged their clothes.

Wearing the old clothes of the shepherd, Kamber went to the wedding. When Arzu saw him, she recognized him at once. Kamber went to where a large caldron of rice was cooking and began to eat some of the rice. Arzu called to him:

"O man who comes from the opposite way,
Where are the troops you were sent to get?
Straight to your uncle's home you went, yet
Had he no troops he could spare today?"

Kamber replied:

"It is I who came from the opposite way.
Can you still see, or have tears made you blind?
O Arzu, I came with your rescue in mind.
For that reason I came; for that reason I stay."

Arzu then asked:

"What is it now you're pretending to be,
Clad as you are, and playing a role?
Are you a fisherman? Where is your pole?
If shepherd you are, not a sheep do I see."

Kamber then said:

"Not as shepherd or fisherman came I today.
When you're staring at me, even I am in doubt
As to what I've become, and the role I play out.
Allah grant you good fortune, my Arzu, I pray."

After saying this, Kamber went to the home of Arzu's parents.

When she saw him coming, Arzu's mother said, "Oh, welcome, son. Welcome! Perhaps it is for the best that things have worked out the way they

74

have. Perhaps even you will benefit in fortune from it, so please do not be upset about it." Yes, this is what she said to Kamber, but within her own group she said, "Let us try to detain him here until evening so that we will have an opportunity to kill him."

They slaughtered a lamb and poisoned its meat. Arzu saw them killing the lamb, and she suspected at once that they had some evil reason for this sudden action. When the meat was cooked, she took one look at it and frowned, for she realized at once that it had been poisoned. Arzu's parents invited Kamber to stay for dinner, and after he was seated, they served him some of the poisoned lamb. As they were doing so, Kamber spoke to Arzu:

"I noticed your frown upon seeing this meat;
I noticed your frown as you looked at the lamb.
Not a bite I shall eat, although hungry I am,
For the poison inside makes it deadly to eat."

Arzu answered:

"I may frown if I wish, with my reason unknown.
Is it poisoned? I think so. My lover, beware!
Eat from the foods that beside it are there,
But taste not the meat, Kamber. Leave it alone!"

"May Allah increase all of your blessings!" said Kamber. He carefully avoided all of the meat.

Arzu's mother was observing all this. She said to herself, "I shall make them brother and sister." Taking milk from her own breast, she mixed it with some plant juices and made a drink that she thought would forbid them to marry. But Arzu detected her mother's plan and said:

"Now the cook has added her own milk, I think,
And milk brother he who tastes of that fare
Will become, so my lover, take care! Oh, take care,
Or brother and sister we'll be with that drink!"

Again Kamber said, "May Allah increase all your blessings!" He did not even touch the milk drink.

When the meal was finished, Arzu said, "Kamber, let us go into the rose garden. There let us walk together for the last time."

They entered the rose garden, where Kamber picked a rose and presented it to her. She smelled the rose and gave it back again to Kamber.

As they were walking in the garden, they were being watched by that evil old woman. She went to Arzu's mother and reported what she had seen. Very angry, the mother started toward the rose garden.

At that very moment, Kamber was saying, "Arzu, if your mother should see us together here like this, she would become almost blind with fury.

Then what should we do?"

"If she comes," said Arzu, "then let her come!" Even as she was saying this, her mother appeared in the garden, shouting and gesturing. Ignoring her wrath, Arzu said:

"O dearest mother, there's milk in your teat,
The breast that so tenderly fed me before.
Kamber's hand has been pierced by a thorn. Are you sure
A cure for that wound you can make and thus treat?"

Her mother said, "My daughter, don't you realize that people will know about this tryst of yours? They will kill you. They will place you in a close, dark prison with Kamber."
To this Arzu responded:

"The black oaken stick that I hold in my hand
Strikes again and again that immovable stone
As at love and lovesickness you rail and you moan.
If a woman you be, my true love understand.

"Yes, Mother, how clearly the danger I see!
Let them come, then, and kill us, for we are both brave.
Let them lay us together in one narrow grave,
And leave us together, my Kamber and me."

Arzu's mother left the garden, saying, "I am tired of your stubbornness. Talk! Talk! Talk! And much good may it do you!"

Arzu said to her lover, "Kamber, in the end by force they will give me away. Still, let us hope for the best."

Now, Kamber had left his padishah uncle's horse with a friend. "O Allah, I pray that with the help of my great white horse I may prevent my Arzu from being taken away to someone else."

Meanwhile, the *ağa* whose marriage to Arzu was being celebrated said, "I have heard that there is a man at such and such a place in this village who has an exceptionally fine horse. I wonder if he would sell it to me?" He went to take a look at the horse, and Kamber placed a very high price on it.

When the man paid the one hundred gold liras that he had quoted, Kamber said, "I cannot actually sell my horse to anyone before I have groomed it." Going to the white horse then, he groomed it well and said to it, "O Düldül, do me a great service. When I give you a signal at the home of this man, where the last of the wedding is held, bite off his head!"

To carry Arzu to the village of her bridegroom, they brought a horse to her parents' home. But somehow, the horse's leg was broken. They then brought a cart to carry her in, but the wheel of the cart collapsed. Finally they decided to go and get the horse which the *ağa* had just bought and have him carry the bride. Those who observed all these things said, "The hand of Allah is against this marriage. That poor, unfortunate girl!"

When Kamber looked at Arzu, he saw that her eyes were red from weeping. "O Allah," he said, "it is not her fault." And his heart ached with pity for her. Then to the great white horse he said:

"Oh, Düldül, the time has now come to arise.
My Arzu, my love, who should be by my side,
Is going to become another man's bride.
Oh, Düldül, bend down for the flower of my eyes."

Hearing this, the horse first rose to his feet and then stooped down to permit the girl to mount. They placed the bride on the horse's back.

Kamber then sang out:

"Oh, the sparks will fly! How the sparks will fly!
Let the women come now and follow the bride.
My Arzu, may Allah grant you a safe ride.
Oh, stirrups, be gentle. Squeeze not, lest she cry."

And Arzu sang back:

"Oh, the sparks will fly! How the sparks will fly!
Let the women come here and follow me there.
But may the stirrups break and tear
The feet over which my Kamber would sigh."

77

Those who heard this exchange now realized that the young man must be Kamber. Angry at his interference in this affair, they caught the young man, beat him badly, and then cast him aside. Disheartened by all that was happening, Kamber sang:

> "The thickets along the banks of the streams
> Shelter partridges here where they choose to hide,
> But my Arzu is helplessly borne as a bride
> To a burden in life that is less than her dreams."

Again the bystanders heard this. "Hey!" they said. "This is Kamber. He is still here." And again they beat him.

Injured and angry, Kamber said to those who abused him, "May Allah curse you! I leave the girl to you." Saying this, Kamber took a different path, a shortcut to the same village. Farther on, the two paths joined, and Kamber reached that point first. He saw there three or five ravens circling about above a dead goat. As he waited for the others to reach that intersection, he decided to call to Arzu as she passed and talk with her again. To himself he said, "This may be the last time that I can do so. Perhaps she does not want me any more." Then he sang:

> "Now the ravens that come at the end are here;
> Circling the carcass, they shriek as they yearn.
> May her hands not feel the reins as they burn,
> The reins that are held as my Arzu comes near."

As she came along on the horse, Arzu heard this and responded to it:

> "Oh, the ravens that always come from above
> Circle about as they fly o'er the land.
> Let the reins, if they will, break open that hand,
> The hand that can never belong to my love."

She then continued, saying, "Oh, Kamber, this evil old woman was the one who would not allow us to be reunited. Curse her!"

Kamber sang in response:

> "O evil woman who stood in love's way,
> May you bite your fingers clear to the bone
> As your five sons die and leave you alone.
> And loud as a stallion may you neigh!"

This old woman did have five sons, and when Kamber had cursed them in this way, all five of them dropped dead as stones. When this happened, the *muhtar* and the imam could keep silent no longer. They said, "Did you suppose it your duty to prevent the marriage of these two young people? You have paid for your error with the lives of your five sons."

Then Arzu said, "Kamber, I have one more thing I must say."
"Very well, then; say it."
She then sang these lines:

"Though thickets along the banks of the streams
Shelter partridges here where they choose to hide,
May the man who is taking me now as a bride
Never reach home to fulfill his dreams."

Almost as soon as she had finished this song, messengers arrived to announce the sudden death of the bridegroom.

When this news was announced, the groom's family lamented, saying,
"Oh, we have spent so much money on this wedding! We shall wait now for
three or five days, and then we shall return and take the bride to our home.
She is ours."

Kamber started to speak, but said only "Oh!" when flame burst forth
from his mouth and completely consumed him. Nothing of him remained
but a heap of ashes.

Shocked at this sight, Arzu quickly dismounted from the horse. Snatch-
ing the veil from her head, she began to sweep his ashes together. But then
she stopped, saying, "Kamber sacrificed himself for me. This veil is not good
enough to touch him. I shall sweep up his ashes with my own hair." While
she was doing this, her hair caught fire, and she too was consumed in flames.
Thus in death were united the two who had in life loved so long. May Allah
give them peace.

The Professor and the Boatman

One day a professor and a boatman were sailing in the same boat. The professor asked, "Boatman, do you know anything about the sciences?"

"No, sir," the boatman answered.

"That's a pity," the professor said. "You have lost one tenth of your life needlessly."

They went a little farther, and the professor asked, "Boatman, do you know anything about mathematics?"

"No, sir," the boatman answered.

"That's a shame," the professor said. "You have lost one ninth of your life needlessly."

A little while later, the professor asked, "Boatman, do you know anything about grammar?"

"No, sir," the boatman answered.

"I'm sorry to hear that," the professor said. "You have lost one eighth of your life needlessly."

Suddenly a terrible storm began. The boatman asked, "Professor, do you know how to swim?"

"No, I don't," said the professor.

"That's too bad," the boatman replied. "In that case, the rest of your life will be lost needlessly."

The Hoca and Tamerlane's Elephant

When Tamerlane invaded Akşehir, the town where Nasreddin Hoca lived, he gave an elephant to the townspeople as a special treat to amuse them. Well, it was a present from Tamerlane, and they had to take good care of the elephant. Meanwhile, the elephant roamed around at will, eating the vegetables out of the gardens and breaking branches off the trees and doing all the harm that a big elephant could do in a small town.

The residents were very much troubled about this, and they wanted to complain. But who would dare to go to Tamerlane and tell him that the townspeople didn't want that elephant? They thought and thought, and they finally decided that only Nasreddin Hoca could find his way around this problem. So they asked the Hoca to go to Tamerlane and tell him that they were very happy with the elephant but he was just too much for them, and to ask if Tamerlane would please take the elephant back.

Nasreddin Hoca said, "All right. I'll do so if you'll come along with me."

All the townsfolk started on the way behind the Hoca, but as they neared the place where Tamerlane was, the crowd dropped off one by one. Nasreddin Hoca didn't know this because he was thinking about what he could say.

When he was brought before Tamerlane, the Hoca started his carefully prepared speech about not wanting the elephant. "Your Honor," he began, "I and all my townspeople—" He turned around, swinging his arms to show Tamerlane all the friends from his town. Then he saw that not one of the people of Akşehir had come with him as far as the court of Tamerlane. He was all alone with the powerful conqueror. He swallowed hard and went on with his speech, saying, "I and all my townspeople are greatly honored by the elephant you gave us. We love him so! There is just one thing that troubles us about him. He's a very *lonely* elephant. Won't you please give us another one to be his mate so that he won't be so unhappy?"

81

A broad smile spread over Tamerlane's face. "You are right, Hoca. It is not good for that elephant to be alone. I'll send for a female elephant at this moment, and you may take her back with my greetings to the people of Akşehir."

When the people of Akşehir saw Nasreddin Hoca coming into the town with *another* elephant, they said, "Hoca Effendi, what have you done? *One* elephant was one too many!"

And Nasreddin Hoca said, "Well, my friends, where were you when I stood before Tamerlane? With this new elephant, I bring you his greetings. We may be thankful that he sent us no more!"

Nasreddin Hoca and the Oven

One day Nasreddin Hoca decided to build his wife a new oven in their backyard. He searched until he had found enough stones to make the oven. Then he worked for days and days, stone on stone, building exactly the kind of oven his wife needed.

When he had finished his work, the Hoca called all of his neighbors to look at it. "Neighbors," he said, "I have built this oven myself. Please take a good look at it and tell me if I have made any mistakes in the construction."

The neighbors examined the oven very carefully from this side to that side and from top to bottom. Then they gathered to discuss the Hoca's oven. Finally, one neighbor spoke up. "Ah, Hoca, this oven is very well built. It does, however, have one weakness. The door of the oven faces the north, and you know that in the winter we have a good deal of wind from that direction. In such winds, your oven will smoke badly."

The Hoca considered the matter. "Yes, you are right," he said. "I am glad you called the matter to my attention. I shall attend to it properly."

On the following day, Nasreddin Hoca took his new oven apart, stone by stone, and began to build a new one. Several days later, he had completed his work, and again he called all of his neighbors to examine it. They studied it from this side to that side and from top to bottom. Finally, one of the neighbors said, "Ah, Hoca, this oven is very well built. It does, however, have one weakness. The door of the oven faces south. It probably will not heat very well, and when the south wind blows, it may smoke rather badly."

Nasreddin Hoca considered this problem and then he said, "Neighbor, you are right. I should have thought of that myself. Thank you for your advice."

The following morning, the Hoca took the oven apart, stone by stone, and began to build a new one. For days and days he worked, until at last the oven was finished. "There!" he said. "The door doesn't face north and it doesn't face south. *Now* let's see what the neighbors will say about it." And he called all of his neighbors to hear their opinions.

The neighbors studied the oven from this side to that side and from top to bottom. Finally the oldest of them said, "Ah, Hoca, again you have built a fine oven. We couldn't have done better ourselves. There is just one small fault I need to point out to you. The opening of the oven faces east, and when the east wind blows, the smoke from your oven will go right to your house."

The Hoca sighed. "Yes, you are probably right," he said. "And my wife wouldn't like that at all, nor would I. I see that I must rebuild the oven to correct that fault. Thank you."

By this time, the Hoca had had almost enough of building ovens. Still, he was determined to complete what he had begun. As he took the oven apart, stone by stone, he had a splendid idea. Surely, *this* time the oven would have no flaws.

Going to the market, he searched until he had found a set of very strong oxcart wheels mounted firmly on their axle. After paying for the wheels, he rolled them home, with the wheels creaking and groaning all the way. Setting the wheels and their axle on a level spot in his backyard, the Hoca then began, stone by stone, to rebuild the oven. When he had finished, the oven rested snugly on the axle between the wheels. Yes, indeed, it was a fine oven. "*Now* let my neighbors find a flaw in it!" he said. And he called all of his neighbors to look.

"Wheels! Hoca Effendi, what can you be thinking of?" asked one of his friends.

"Ah, it's very simple," replied the Hoca. "Let's say the wind is from the north, and my oven opens to the north. Now, watch!" And the Hoca turned the oven and the wheels so that the opening faced away from the north. "No matter *which* way the wind blows, my oven will not smoke," said the Hoca. "All I need to do is to turn it on these wheels, and my wife can bake the finest bread with the least smoke in all of Akşehir!"

And the neighbors had to agree that Nasreddin Hoca was right.

Why Shopkeepers Share Their Customers

After Fatih Sultan Mehmet had conquered İstanbul, he used to disguise himself and visit different groups of people in the city to see what kinds of lives they led. One morning quite early he went disguised into a marketplace to discover how the tradesmen there treated one another.

Fatih Mehmet went into a shop and bought several of the things that he needed, but when he asked to buy other things, the shopkeeper refused to sell them to him. He said, "I have already sold you some things today, so I shall have a good day in my business. But the shopkeeper next door has not sold anything yet today. Please go to him to buy those other things you need."

The padishah went to the second shop to buy the rest of what he needed, but the same thing happened again. After he had bought three items, the shopkeeper refused to sell him the other things he asked for. He said, "I have already sold you some things this morning, so I shall have a good day in my business. But the merchant down the street has been open as long as I have today, and he has sold nothing yet. Please go to his shop to buy the rest of the things you need." So Fatih Mehmet had to go to a third shop.

Fatih Sultan Mehmet went back to his palace well pleased with what he had seen in the marketplace. "Truly, my people are concerned for one another," he said. And so they were.

Who Gets the Grain?

Once a turtle, a porcupine, a crab, and a fox went into partnership as farmers. They all worked together to plow the field. They all worked together to plant the wheat. And when the wheat was ripe, they all worked together to harvest their crop. When they had finished threshing and winnowing, there was a large heap of golden grain on the threshing floor.

Now it was time to divide the grain. But how should it be divided? The fox had a suggestion: "Partners," he said, "let's have a race from this end of our field to the heap of grain. Whoever reaches the grain first, jumps on the heap, and says "*Herrop!*" [Hurrah!] will win all the grain. What do you say, partners?"

Now, the crab was standing alongside the fox as he asked that question. As soon as they all had agreed to race, the crab secretly fastened himself to the fox's bushy tail.

"*Haydi!*" [Let's go!] shouted the fox, and the turtle, the porcupine, and the fox all started running toward the threshing floor. As for the crab, he hung on tightly as the fox ran with great leaps clear across the field. Thinking that he had surely won the race by reaching the threshing floor, the fox looked back and laughed to see his slower partners plodding along.

As the fox was laughing, the crab let go of the fox's tail, scuttled onto the heap of grain, and, "*Herrop!*" he shouted. Thus the crab won the whole harvest.

Why the Pine Tree Does Not Shed Its Needles

One year long, long ago, a hard winter had been predicted. All of the migratory birds were preparing to fly away to warmer lands. But there was among them a small bird that had broken its wing and thus was unable to fly south with the others.

The mother of this small injured bird went from one tree to another—the maple, the oak, the cherry, the olive, the peach, the pistachio—begging each to shelter her young one during the bitter winter. They all refused.

A pine tree, pitying the mother and the small one, opened up its branches and allowed the baby bird to hide among them. The needles of the pine tree did not fall that year, and the tiny bird was protected by them all during the cold winter.

Since that time, the needles of the pine tree have never fallen, no matter how hard the winter might be. As for the trees that had refused the mother bird's plea, their leaves have fallen with the approach of winter, and they have been left with bare boughs to shiver and shake in the icy blasts.

The Man Who Sought His Fate

Once there was and once there wasn't a man who seemed to have no talent for any kind of work. No matter what field he tried, he reaped only failure. At last he said to his wife, "My dear, this kind of life will never do. There must be some answer to my problem. I shall go to find Fate and tell it my situation. Allah willing, it will tell me how to put an end to my problems."

After his wife had prepared provisions for his travel, the man set out on a long journey. Where, then, does one look for Fate? After traveling for some distance, he came to the top of a mountain. There, sitting by the side of the road, was a wolf.

The wolf said, "Where are you going, my friend?"

"I am searching for Fate," said the man. "I am going to explain to Fate the difficulties that I have in my life. If Allah wills, Fate will give me an answer that will end my hopeless days."

The wolf said, "I always have a terrible headache. Will you please ask Fate about this for me? Ask Fate how I can put an end to my headache. Please don't forget to ask this."

The man said, "All right. If I can remember to do so, I shall ask Fate about your problem."

After the man had gone along farther, he passed a vineyard guarded by a watchman. The watchman greeted him, "*Selâmünaleyküm.*"

"*Aleykümselâm,*" answered the traveler.

"Where are you going, my brother?" asked the watchman.

The traveler answered, "I have no talent for any kind of work. No matter what field I try, I reap only failure. I am searching for Fate to tell it my difficulties. If I find it, Allah willing, it will tell me how to put an end to my troubles."

The watchman said, "Brother, I, too, was unable to succeed at anything I tried. At last, I took this work as watchman, but I have not found it a very comfortable way to live. Please ask Fate about my problem, too. Ask Fate how I can find the things in life that I really want."

"All right, my brother," said the traveler. "If I don't forget about it, I shall ask Fate about *your* problem, too." He walked on as he said this. He walked and walked, and then in a little valley he came to a river.

From the surface of the river a fish spoke to him. "Where are you going, my brother?" it asked.

"I am searching for Fate in order to tell it my problems in life, but I may have trouble getting across this river to continue my journey."

The fish said, "If you will agree to ask Fate about *my* problem, too, I shall carry you across this river on my back."

"All right," said the man. "What is your problem?"

The fish said, "The river that you see here flows through my mouth because I have been unable to shut my mouth throughout my entire life thus far. Please tell Fate my problem and learn from Fate what can be done about this problem."

After the man had been carried across the river by the fish, he said good-bye and continued walking. He finally reached Fate's house. Fate sat before its house with a wheel before it.

"*Selâmünaleyküm*," said the traveler.

And, "*Aleykümselâm*," Fate answered.

"I came looking for Fate, but I found you instead," said the man.

"I am Fate. What is your difficulty?"

"Because I have no talent for any kind of work, I am very poor. I therefore decided to come here and ask you about it. What can I do to bring my troubles to an end?"

Fate spun the wheel around once and then asked, "My friend, were there any others who had difficulties they wanted to have solved?"

"Oh, yes," said the man. "I met a wolf who complained of having a continuous headache. That wolf sent his greetings to you and asked to know what the remedy was for his headache."

Fate said, "There is only one remedy for such a headache. He must eat the head of the most stupid man he can find, and then his own head will become well."

The traveler continued, "A little farther along I came upon a man who was a watchman at a vineyard. He said to me, 'I have served as a watchman in this vineyard, but I have not found it a very comfortable way to live. Please ask Fate how I can find the things in life that I really want.'"

Fate said, "Buried in that vineyard are two jars filled with gold pieces. Go there, and let the two of you work together to find that gold. There will be enough to take care of you both for the rest of your lives."

The traveler then said, "A little farther along upon my way here I came upon a fish that complained that the water of that river ran continuously through its mouth. This happened because the fish had never during its whole life been able to shut its mouth."

Fate said, "Its mouth remains open because there are two valuable stones in it. On your way back, take out those stones, and it will be able to close its mouth at once."

"All right," said the man. "Thank you, and good-bye."

87

When the traveler reached the river on his way home, he found the fish eagerly awaiting him. "What did Fate tell you about my problem?" asked the fish.

"Fate said that there were two valuable stones in your mouth and that if I took them out, you would be able to close your mouth." Saying this, he removed the two stones.

The fish looked at the stones. "Ahhh, those are diamonds," he said. "Keep them. You will be able to use them better than I."

"Fate turned the Wheel of Fortune for me," said the traveler. "What do I need of those stones?" And he left them there on the shore and went along on his journey.

Not long afterwards, he came to the vineyard. The watchman had been waiting for him. "Did you ever find Fate, my friend?" he asked.

"Yes, I found Fate."

"What did Fate say about my situation?" asked the watchman.

"Fate said to tell you that buried in this vineyard are two jars of gold coins. If you find them, they will make you comfortable for the rest of your life."

The watchman said, "But I do not know where they are. Let us work together to find the jars, and then we can each take one."

"Fate gave a turn to the Wheel of Fortune for me, and so I do not need any of your gold." Saying this, he continued on his way.

When he reached the wolf, that animal asked him, "Did you see Fate? What did Fate tell you was a remedy for my headache?"

"Yes, I saw Fate. Fate said to tell you that if you ate the head of a stupid man, your own head would be cured."

"But Fate did not tell how I might know which man was stupid?" asked the wolf. "I shall have to think about that. As for you, what did Fate tell you?"

"Fate told me nothing. It just gave a turn to the Wheel of Fortune for me, and that is all that I needed. But Fate did answer the questions of the watchman and the fish." And the man told the wolf every detail of his journey, from first to last.

"Ahhh," said the wolf when the man had finished talking. "Your own story has given me the answer that I needed. There is surely no man who could be more stupid than you. You refused two diamonds which you took from the mouth of the fish. Then, although the watchman agreed to give you one of the jars of gold pieces buried in the vineyard, you refused that, too. Each time these opportunities were offered to you, you said, 'Fate gave a turn to the Wheel of Fortune for me, and so I do not need anything else.' A man who fails to take advantage of such opportunities is not only stupid; he has had the answer he sought from Fate about how he can put an end to his problems. On that matter, my friend, I can both help you and cure my own headache."

And with that, the wolf ate the head and ended his headache.

How the Vizier Won the Valuable Handkerchief

There were once a padishah and a vizier who were good friends. When that padishah died, his son became padishah. Still, he kept his father's vizier at his side. One day the new padishah and this vizier went for a ride on their horses, and along the road they came upon a beautiful and valuable handkerchief.

The padishah thought, "If I take this handkerchief as my own, my old vizier may be offended."

As for the vizier, he thought, "If I take this handkerchief as my own, my padishah may be offended."

The two talked about the matter. After all, weren't they friends? At last, the vizier said, "My padishah, let us each tell an adventure that we have experienced. Whichever one has had the more remarkable adventure will become the owner of that valuable handkerchief."

Agreeing with this suggestion, the padishah began his tale. "O my vizier, after I became padishah, I placed in the treasury each day a large quantity of liras, but by the following morning, the liras had disappeared. "How could this happen?" I wondered. "Neither the doors nor the windows nor the walls have been damaged."

"After this had been going on for quite a while, I went walking one day in disguise. I walked and walked, and at last I saw three dervishes who had little bells on their shoes. '*Selâmünaleyküm!*' I said to them.

"And, '*Aleykümselâm!*' they answered.

"'Fathers,' I said, 'I am curious about those bells. Can you tell me why you wear them?'

"'Friend,' said one, 'as you know, we are holy men, and we do not wish to harm a single one of Allah's creatures. To step on even an ant would be a sin for us.'

"'True,' the second one agreed. 'These bells warn ants and other small creatures to beware of our feet.'

"'Ah! They are indeed holy men,' I thought. And I continued to walk with them.

"As night drew near, we sought shelter for a little while in a cave. To pass the time, we talked. Finally, one of the dervishes said, 'Each man must have a special skill. We are all friends here. Let us tell each other our special skills.'

"The first dervish said, 'My special skill is very useful. I can open the iron gates of the padishah's palace with no effort not just in seven places but in seventy places.'

"The second dervish said, 'With my special skill, I can understand the language of dogs.'

"The third dervish said, 'My skill is quite different. Once I have seen a man, I can always recognize him again, no matter how he is dressed—even if he is wearing the clothes of a woman.'

"Then the dervishes turned to me and asked me what my special skill was. 'Ah!' I said. 'By moving my hand this way, I can condemn a man to be hanged. By moving my hand that way, I can save him from the executioner.'

"'That is indeed a useful skill,' they all said.

"Then the first dervish said, 'Come, my friends. It is dark outside, and we have work to do.' And since they were going, I went, too.

"As we walked along, we heard a dog barking, '*Hav! Hav! Hav!*'

"The dervish who could understand the language of dogs said, 'Aha! That dog said, "Hey, where are you going with the padishah?"'

"I said, 'Padishah! What would the padishah be doing among people like us?'

"When we reached the palace treasury, the dervish who could open iron gates just *touched* the gates, and they swung open—*Tangır! Tangır!* We took

90

the liras that had been put in the treasury that day and returned to the cave and hid them. We stayed there that night.

"The next morning, we all went to the marketplace. While we were among the crowds of people, I quietly slipped away from the three dervishes. Going to the palace, I had a messenger notify the gendarmes. They soon found the three thieves and arrested them.

"The three were placed on trial, found guilty by the court, and condemned to be hanged. Gallows were prepared, and the nooses of the ropes were oiled and made ready for their necks.

"Before going down to the courtyard myself, I dressed in women's clothes and placed a heavy veil over my face. As I passed the condemned men, the dervish who had claimed he could recognize a person no matter how he disguised himself called to me, 'Get along! Get along! No wonder we find ourselves in such trouble! What fools we were to befriend an unreliable fellow like you! Use *your* skill now, and save us!'

"At that very moment, I moved my hand that way and saved all three of them from the executioner. That was my most remarkable adventure," said the padishah.

Then it was the vizier's turn to tell his tale. He said, "My padishah, back in the earlier time, when I was serving as your father's grand vizier, I got a haircut late one afternoon while I was sitting in front of a coffeehouse drinking coffee. As two ladies passed along the street, one of them tall and one of middle height, I said to the barber, 'That tall woman is all right, but I think I'd rather spend a night with that woman of middle height.'

"Well, the barber heard me, and so did the women. The woman of middle height said, 'If it's that way, then come along with me.'

"I followed her. We finally arrived at a tall building and climbed up the stairs several stories. It was evening by then, so we ate and drank for a while. When it was time to go to bed, a pair of pajamas was brought for me. I took off my clothes and hung them on a hook and then put on the pajamas.

"'Sir,' the woman said, 'you go down to the toilet, and then we shall go to bed.'

"As I was going downstairs to the toilet, carrying an *ibrik* of water in one hand and a lamp in the other, the woman followed me down to the landing. There she struck me with a stick. 'Çüş!' she said, and I was transformed at once into a red donkey. She then called out the window to a groom, 'Hey, groom! Put this beast in the stable. Make him carry wood, and show him no mercy. Let him lie wherever he collapses from exhaustion.'

"The groom came, hit me twice—once on the left side and once on the right—took me to the stable, and tied me there. When he placed hay and barley before me, I managed to eat the barley, but I could not eat the hay. I could hear and understand what people said, but I could not speak to them except, 'Hee har! Hee har!'

91

"Well, I worked for a week carrying wood on my back. One day when there was no strength left in my legs, I had fallen some distance behind the rest of the donkeys, and my foot struck a stone in the path. I stumbled and fell. The load of wood on my back was so heavy that I could not get up again. The groom showed me no mercy at all. He would not even lift the wood from my back. Instead, he looked for an ax with which to cut off my head. Luckily, the ax was not part of my load, so the groom had to go ahead some distance after it.

"While he was gone, two workers took pity on me. 'How cruel to treat an animal that way!' one said. When they had removed the load of wood from my back, I was able to get up on my feet again, and I ran off.

"After a while, I wandered into the courtyard of a house. When I had been there for just a few minutes, a small girl came out of the house and shouted, 'Look, Mother! There is a red donkey in our courtyard!'

"The mother answered, 'My daughter, that is not really a donkey. Actually, it is a man.' Coming close to me, she asked, 'Aren't you a man? Didn't such and such a woman living in such and such a house turn you into this shape? Would you take your revenge upon this woman if I restored you to your former condition?'

"My eyes filled with tears. I could not speak, but the mother understood my feeling. She brought a small stick and struck me lightly with it several times. All of a sudden, I found myself restored to the form of a man wearing pajamas.

"During this time, the padishah, your father, had sent people out searching everywhere for me, but I could not be found. After I had been restored to my true self, I went into the padishah's presence, even though I was still in miserable condition.

"The padishah greeted me by saying, 'Where have you been for a whole week, you vagabond?'

"'Please do not ask me, Your Majesty! I have had a terrible experience!' I said.

"The woman who had restored me to my true shape had told me how to get my revenge. She had said, 'You will go back to that evil woman. Again she will tell you to undress, and she will bring you an *ibrik* and tell you to go down to the toilet. Tell her that you do not know the way to the toilet and that she must lead you to it. Then as you descend, strike her with a stick when you reach the same place at the bottom of the stairs where she transformed you into a donkey.'

"After I had recovered my strength, I went again late in the afternoon to the same barber. While having my hair cut, I sat outside drinking coffee. Soon the same two women came walking along the street. As before, I said to the barber, 'That tall woman is all right, but I think I'd rather spend a night with that woman of middle height.'

"Well, the barber heard me, and so did the women. The woman of middle height said, 'If it's that way, then come along with me.'

"I followed her. We finally arrived at that same tall building and climbed up the same stairs several stories. It was evening by then, so we ate and drank for a while. When it was time to go to bed, a pair of pajamas was brought for me. 'Get up and undress, sir, and put on these pajamas,' she said. Then, handing me an *ibrik* of water and a lamp, she said, 'Here. Take these and go down to the toilet, and then we shall go to bed.'

"'But I do not know the way to the toilet,' I said. 'Take the lamp and show me the way, and I'll follow you.'

"The woman went on ahead, and I followed. When we reached the place where I had been transformed into a red donkey, I struck her with a stick and said, '*Çüş!*' and she was transformed into a yellow donkey. And I have enjoyed her ever since. Is that not so, my yellow donkey?'

"My yellow donkey bowed her head in assent."

Three Hunters: A Tekerleme

There were three of us hunters, Ese, Musa, and Köse. One day we went out hunting with all of us carrying old-fashioned guns, breechless, flintless muzzleloaders.

While we were out hunting, we saw an unborn rabbit by an ungrown hemlock plant. All three famous hunters grabbed their muzzleloading guns. "Let *me* shoot first," said Ese.

"*I* want to shoot first," said Musa.

But Köse interfered and solved the problem. "Ese shoots first. If he misses, Musa shoots."

Ese shot, and missed the unborn rabbit. Then Musa shot, and missed the unborn rabbit. When it was Köse's turn, he shot that unborn rabbit with his breechless, flintless gun.

We took the rabbit and continued on our way. Just before we reached a plain, we came to a village in which there were only three houses. Two of them were completely crumbled, and the third one had no roof. We entered

the house that had no roof.

There were three women in that house, two dead and the third without life. We asked the one without life for a kettle in which to cook our rabbit. She said, "Young men, I have three kettles here. Look at them, see which one you like best, and take that one." We looked at the three kettles. Two were smashed in at the sides, and the third had no bottom. After talking this way and that, we chose the third one.

Taking the bottomless kettle, we went on down to the plain, where we came upon three streams. Two of the streams were dry, and the third had no water. The hunters said, "We are tired, and this is a good place to rest. Let's stay here and cook our rabbit."

We filled our bottomless kettle with water from the waterless stream. Then we cleaned our unborn rabbit, and after lighting a fire, we put it on to cook. When it had cooked thoroughly, we started eating it. We ate and ate and ate, but nothing came into our mouths. And how could we ask for more? Our eyes could not see any more, nor could our stomachs get enough.

Then Köse stood up and said, "Did you see your friend when before was before, and when before was the time when the hen was the imam and the cock a town crier?"

I was the hunter who shot the unborn rabbit with the breechless, flintless gun by the ungrown hemlock plant, and that was the end of our hunting trip.

The Quick-witted Rabbit

One day a rabbit crept out of his burrow to fetch something to eat. He had hopped only a few steps from his burrow, however, when he met a wolf. "I shall eat you," said the wolf.

The rabbit was frightened, but he kept his wits about him. "Alas, Mr. Wolf, you will not live to eat me, for three hunters are close behind you."

Fearing the hunters, the wolf turned to look for them. While the wolf was looking away, the rabbit took three great leaps and snuggled down into his burrow.

Indeed, it is true that small creatures with large brains are more than equal to large creatures with small brains!

Why Ahmet Earns More Than Mehmet

One day a man went to visit a friend of his. After they had talked for a while, the visitor said to his host, "There is one thing that puzzles me about your household. You have two servants, Ahmet and Mehmet. They both work for you, yet I understand that you pay Ahmet one hundred liras a month while you pay Mehmet only fifty liras a month. That doesn't seem quite fair, does it?"

The host smiled. "Yes, it is true that I pay Ahmet twice as much as I pay Mehmet, but I have my reasons. See—I'll show you why. Ahmet!" he called.

"Yes, sir!" Ahmet said, and he quickly appeared before his master.

"Ahmet," said his master, "here is some money. Please go to the store down on the next corner and buy me some tobacco."

"Yes, sir. Right away, sir," said Ahmet, and he took the money his master gave him and went out upon the errand.

"Well," said the host, "now Ahmet is taking off his slippers and putting on his shoes."

A moment later, he said, "Now Ahmet has reached the first corner and is going around the corner."

A moment later, he said, "Now Ahmet is going past the bakery."

A moment later, he said, "Now Ahmet is in the store, buying the tobacco and getting the change."

Then, "Now Ahmet is coming past the bakery."

Again, "Now Ahmet is coming around the corner."

Then, "Now Ahmet is coming inside, to take off his shoes and put on his slippers. Ahmet!" he called.

"Yes, sir!" Ahmet answered, and he came into the room wearing his slippers and carrying the tobacco and the change, which he gave to his master.

"Thank you, Ahmet. You may go," said the master. And Ahmet left.

"Mehmet!" called the host.

"Yes, sir!" Mehmet said, and he quickly appeared before his master.

"Mehmet," said his master, "here is some money. Please go to the store down on the next corner and buy me some tobacco."

"Yes, sir! Right away, sir!" said Mehmet, and he took the money his master gave him and went upon the errand.

"Well," said the host, "Mehmet should be taking off his slippers and putting on his shoes."

A moment later, he said, "Now Mehmet should have reached the first corner and be going around the corner."

A moment later, he said, "Now Mehmet should be going past the bakery."

A moment later, he said, "Now Mehmet should be in the store buying the tobacco and getting the change."

Then, "Now Mehmet should be coming past the bakery."

Again, "Now Mehmet should be coming around the corner."

And, "Now Mehmet should be coming inside, to take off his shoes and put on his slippers. Mehmet!" he called.

"Yes, sir!" Mehmet said, and he quickly appeared before his master.

"Where is the tobacco?" asked his master.

"Oh, I don't have the tobacco yet. I am just putting on my shoes to go out," answered Mehmet.

"There!" said the host. "*Now* do you see why I pay Ahmet one hundred liras a month and Mehmet only fifty liras?"

Nasreddin Hoca, the Door, and the Window

Nasreddin Hoca once had a new house built here, close to the center of the village. After the front door had been put in place and properly hung, he mounted a secure lock on it. Near this door he had a large window installed, but instead of putting a lock on the window, he left it open at all times.

His neighbors were curious about this. "Hoca," they said, "you have placed a strong door on the house and locked it securely. That will keep thieves out. But you have an open window alongside it through which thieves could enter very easily. What is the reason for this?"

"Ah," said Nasreddin Hoca, "the locked door is to keep my friends out while I am saying my prayers. But I keep the window open in case a thief comes along. He will enter and take what he wants, whether the window is open or closed. I leave it open so that he will not break the glass."

That's the Place!

There was an old woman in İstanbul who wanted to take a ferryboat to a village along the Bosporus. By the time she got to the ticket counter to pay for her passage, however, she could not remember the name of that village. The ticket agent asked, "Where are you going?"

"Oh, son," she said, "old age has made me so forgetful that I cannot even remember what I had for dinner last night. Now I can't remember the name of the place I am supposed to be going."

While she was talking to the ticket agent, a long line of people was forming behind her, all waiting to buy their own tickets. Their grumbling made the ticket agent impatient. "Come on, now! Say where you are going so that all these other people may buy their ferryboat tickets also. The boat is almost ready to leave!"

But the old woman still could not remember. "Son," she said, "can't you understand that I am an old woman? They invited me somewhere for dinner tonight, and I want to go. *I* know. I'll tell you about them, and perhaps you

will know where they live. There is a customs official, Ali Riza Effendi, who lives near them, and surely you must know *him*. Hacer *Hanım* lives on the right side of my hosts' home, and Hikmet *Hanım* lives on the left. Above my friends' apartment lives Colonel Ali Bey, who has two daughters, Handan and Candan. Below them lives Major Osman Bey, who has two sons, Metin and Çetin. My friend who lives among these people has invited me to come to dinner tonight. During the rest of the year they live in Sariyer, but during the summer they rent an apartment at this other place to get a change of air. Where did they rent this apartment?"

"How should I know?" said the ticket agent.

A rowdy fellow behind her in line shouted, "*Ölüsü kandilli!* Buy your ticket so that we can buy ours!"

When she heard this oath, the old woman exclaimed, "May Allah bless your tongue, son! Kandilli is the place where I am going!" And she bought her ticket, of course.

The Peddler
and the Kayseri Boy

A peddler arrived in Kayseri one day, and as he was walking about through the city he saw a boy with an antique object that had been dug up from the earth. "Are you selling that thing, son?" he asked. "Well, I might," said the boy.

"How much do you want for it?" asked the peddler.

"I won't sell it for money," said the boy, "but I shall give it to you in trade for that donkey of yours."

"All right. I'll trade you the donkey for it."

"There is one condition. Before we complete the bargain, you must bray loudly like a donkey."

The peddler brayed several times like a donkey, and then he said, "All right. Now let me have the antique piece."

"I have thought further about it," said the boy, "and I have changed my mind. If a donkey like you knows how valuable this thing is, why shouldn't I, a human being from Kayseri, know as much? Keep your donkey, and I'll keep this antique piece."

Keloğlan and Köroğlu's Horse Kırat

Once there was and once there wasn't a *keloğlan*. This *keloğlan* was poor, so poor that he said daily, "O Allah, what is to become of me? I have had no chance at all in life!"

Then one day he heard a town crier shouting, "Whoever will steal Köroğlu's horse Kırat and bring that horse to Hasan Pasha will be made the pasha's vizier!"

"Ah," said Keloğlan, "at last good fortune has come my way. Who else would try that dangerous task? All I can lose is this bald head if I should fail." And he went into Hasan Pasha's presence. "My pasha," he said, "I shall bring you the horse you seek."

Hasan Pasha looked at that ragged runt of a *keloğlan* and laughed. Still, he *did* want Köroğlu's magic horse, and no one else had offered to seek it for him. "Very well, then, Keloğlan. Go, and may your way be open."

Keloğlan set out, walking, walking, walking, until he came to Köroğlu's stronghold at Çamlibel. He sat down just outside the gate. When Köroğlu came home, he found Keloğlan there, still sitting. "Son, what are you doing here? Where did you come from, and where are you going?"

"Oh, sir," Keloğlan said, "I am poor and I have nowhere else to go. For the love of Allah, take care of me."

"Very well," Köroğlu said. "I am known for my charity to the poor. I'll have you washed and well dressed, and give you food and a place to sleep."

"Charity is not what I ask," Keloğlan said. "I ask only a chance to work for my bread and cheese. Fine clothes are not for me. And I can sleep in the stable. Only give me some useful work to do."

"If that is what you ask, let it be so," said Köroğlu. Then, turning to one of his men, he said, "Give this *keloğlan* a horse to take care of. We'll see what he can do."

Keloğlan went with the man to Köroğlu's stables. At the very end of the third stable was a thin, weak horse barely able to stand on its four feet. "Now, *there's* a horse for you," said the man. "Let's see what you can do with *this* one!" And he left Keloğlan with that sickly steed.

But Keloğlan was determined, and stubborn, besides. Week after week after week he fed that horse and watered him and curried him. And at night, after all the other grooms had fallen asleep, Keloğlan went from stall to stall gathering the barley given to the rest of the horses and taking it for his own

100

horse to eat. Week by week by week, his horse grew stronger and healthier, until it was the best-looking, strongest horse in the stable.

Now, Köroğlu used to wander through his three stables, saying nothing but looking carefully at the condition of all the horses. When Keloğlan's horse became so strong and healthy, Köroğlu observed it, but still he said nothing. The other grooms noticed the change, too, and they grumbled among themselves. "He was given the worst horse in the stables, but now look at it!" one said. "What can we do to him?"

"And he will surely make *our* work look bad," said another. "We must do something about that *keloğlan!*"

Köroğlu overheard this talk, and he went to Keloğlan. "Son," he said, "don't let the other grooms know about it, but take this money and buy some good foods and drinks and prepare a feast for all the grooms. Buy some lambs to roast, and give the grooms plenty to eat and drink."

Keloğlan had the food and the drinks prepared, and they all feasted in a field well away from the stables. The rest of the grooms ate and ate and drank and drank, and even Ayvaz, hero that he was, joined in the merrymaking. As for Keloğlan, he ate a bit of lamb, but he touched not a drop of the drink. He just kept filling the mugs of the rest until they were all so drunk that they fell sound asleep, *horol, horol.*

"Ayvaz! Ayvaz!" called Keloğlan, but Ayvaz, too, was beyond waking. "Ah," Keloğlan said to himself, "here is the opportunity I have been waiting for!" Reaching into Ayvaz's sash, he took from it the keys to the stables. Hurrying to the first stable, he opened it and went directly to Kırat's stall. He tried and tried to unlock the gate of the stall, but the key would not turn.

"*Aman!*" he said. "I've come just this close to winning what I came for!" Then he saw Durat in the next stall, with the gate unlocked. "How will Hasan Pasha know the difference between Kırat and Durat?" he said. "I'll take Durat, instead." And, saddling and mounting Durat, he rode away from the stable and well along on his way home.

Let's leave him riding along and return to Ayvaz and the rest of the grooms. After their sound sleep, they awoke and looked for Keloğlan. But where was he? He was gone! Ayvaz felt here and there in his sash for the keys to the stables, but they, too, were gone. "*Eyvah!*" he shouted. "The keys are gone. That *keloğlan* has probably stolen Kırat!"

Running to the first stable, Ayvaz found the key to Kırat's stall still stuck useless in the lock. "Allah be praised!" he said. "Kırat is still safe!" Then, looking for Durat, he found that one gone. "*Aman, aman,* Allah! Where is Durat?" he said. He searched all three stables, but Durat was nowhere to be found.

Troubled, he went to Köroğlu. "That *keloğlan* you liked so much has run off with Durat. He tried to take Kırat, but he couldn't open the lock on that stall."

"Oh, my Ayvaz, that's nothing to worry about. Kırat, the darling of my eyes, is still safe, Allah be thanked! Go back now to your regular work."

But Ayvaz was still angry about the loss of Durat, and he said, "You made such a favorite of Keloğlan. See now what he has done to us!"

"Go back to your work, my son, and fret no more," said Köroğlu. But Ayvaz still stood there, and this made Köroğlu himself think more seriously about the loss. After three or five minutes of thought, he ordered, "Bring Kırat to me!"

Mounting Kırat, Köroğlu galloped in pursuit of Keloğlan and the stolen horse. As was always true when Kırat galloped, a huge cloud of dust rose behind him. Seeing that cloud of dust, Keloğlan said, "*Aman, aman,* Allah! Köroğlu himself is coming! What can I do? He will surely kill me for abusing his trust!"

As he fled, Keloğlan saw a mill nearby. Galloping to the mill, he dismounted and said to the miller, "Köroğlu has heard that you have been cheating farmers who bring grain to be ground, and he is coming after you! You have a wife and children. Give me your clothes in exchange for mine and then run to your house and hide. Let him cut off my worthless head if he is going to kill anybody."

Quickly, the miller and Keloğlan exchanged clothes and dressed, and then the miller ran to his house. As for Keloğlan, he smeared flour over his face and over the miller's cap.

Just then, Köroğlu rode up to the mill and called out, "Miller! Miller!

There was a *keloğlan* who came here. See! Here is the horse he was riding! But where is Keloğlan?" When Keloğlan pointed to the house, Köroğlu dismounted. "Here, miller. Hold my horse while I go after that *keloğlan!*" Then he ran to the house and roared, "Come out! Come out!"

The miller was terrified. He came running out of the house, saying, "Believe me! I didn't take too much of the wheat! I took only what was right."

"What are you talking about?" said Köroğlu. "I care nothing about your *wheat.* Aren't you a *keloğlan?*"

"No, I'm not. That *keloğlan* traded clothes with me and then ordered me to run to my house. He is probably still at the mill."

Köroğlu rushed back to the mill, but when he got there, he saw Keloğlan riding back and forth on Kırat. Keloğlan called to him, "Köroğlu, I have made a promise which I hope you will understand."

"What is it?"

"I cannot tell you at this time, but trust me. I have a certain promise which I have to keep. After that, I promise to return Kırat to you with my own hands."

"Don't take Kırat, Keloğlan! You have eaten my bread. Remember your obligation!"

"I have an earlier obligation which I must keep. Köroğlu, depend upon me. I shall not forget either your bread or my promise to you." Then, spurring Kırat, Keloğlan rode off.

Quickly, Köroğlu mounted Durat. He could have stopped Kırat if he had tried hard enough. Kırat was flying through the air, but Keloğlan did not know that Durat, though younger, could also fly. Köroğlu decided, however, not to catch Kırat. He would instead find another means of recovering his horse. He called out, "Hey, Keloğlan! I have the power to catch you, but I shall not, for Kırat has his pride, too. I shall not let anyone say that Durat caught Kırat!"

Keloğlan spurred Kırat to fly even faster, and they passed out of that place. So that he would know the place toward which Keloğlan was taking Kırat, Köroğlu rode along on the ground beneath Kırat, and he kept up with them until they had entered the mountains. But then how could he follow them? Was he a bird? He dismounted and walked back some distance toward Çamlibel. Then, seeing that Durat was badly winded, Köroğlu took off Durat's saddle and carried it on his own back.

Meanwhile, what had become of Ayvaz? He had been pacing back and forth, watching for Köroğlu's return. "Where has Köroğlu been all this time?" he asked himself. Suddenly he noticed a peddler coming along the road with his pack on his back. Calling to Köroğlu's wife, Ayvaz said, "Nigâr, come out! A peddler is coming. He's the first peddler to come our way in seven years. You can probably buy three or five things from him."

"Yes, I shall. You are right, Ayvaz. No peddler has come this way in seven years."

But when they looked more closely, they saw that the person was not a peddler at all. It was Köroğlu, leading a horse by its bridle and carrying its saddle upon his own back.

Köroğlu arrived at last, and sat down on the doorstep. "Ayvaz, bring me a cup of coffee. I am greatly upset." Ayvaz just stood there, amazed that Durat, not Kırat, had come with Köroğlu. Köroğlu spoke again. "My son, don't just stand there! Get me some coffee. I am feeling depressed."

Ayvaz went on inside and laid out the cups and began to boil the coffee. Once more, Köroğlu spoke. "My son, bring me my coffee. I feel depressed." Then Ayvaz poured the coffee and took it to him.

As Köroğlu drank his coffee, he said to himself, "What can I do to restore both my horse and my honor?" Not only then, but all night long he lay awake, thinking and planning. By dawn, he had decided what to do. "Ayvaz!" he called. "You know where I keep my seven different disguises. Bring me my dervish costume and my white false beard. Prepare everything I need, including my pen and my pen case." All these things were brought to him.

Then, putting on his dervish costume and attaching his white beard, Köroğlu started walking down the road toward the place he had last seen Keloğlan and Kırat. He walked and walked and walked, across plains and through valleys, over mountains and along plateaus, until he came to the territory of Hasan Pasha.

Just inside the border he saw a farmer plowing. Going to this farmer, he said, "My son, do you have a piece of bread you could give me? I have not eaten in three or five days, and I am hungry."

"Don't bother me now!" said the farmer. "I want to finish my plowing so that I can go to look at Köroğlu's horse. A *keloğlan* has stolen that horse and brought it for Hasan Pasha."

"Does that horse belong to Hasan Pasha or to Köroğlu?"

"It belongs to Hasan Pasha! After all, who is that Köroğlu? He is a nobody!"

"Oh, is that so? My son, I feel sorry for you. You are eager to go, but you have all this plowing to do. Why don't you go and change your clothes and leave me to do the plowing for you?"

The farmer left the plowing to that dervish and hurried to his house. After the farmer had left the field, Köroğlu plowed for a few minutes and then unfastened the plow from the oxen and walked slowly with them along the road.

Very soon he was overtaken by a lame man limping along as fast as he could go. Köroğlu said to him, "My son, where are you going in such a hurry?"

"Don't ask me, father! A cursed *keloğlan* has stolen Köroğlu's horse and brought it for Hasan Pasha. I am not going to see that coward Hasan Pasha. I am going because I am embarrassed for Köroğlu." After saying this, the cripple began to cry.

"Son, is that horse suitable for Hasan Pasha or for Köroğlu?"

"It is not at all suitable for a coward like Hasan Pasha. It is the very eyes of the hero Köroğlu."

"All right, son," said Köroğlu. "These oxen are yours. I give them to you freely. Accept me tonight as the guest of Allah and then spread the word tomorrow that a dervish, a *hoca* with holy healing powers, has come to the village. Say that this *hoca* can cure illnesses, can give peace to people with troubled minds, and can restore the insane to sanity. Do this, and do not worry about anything else."

In the morning the lame man went directly to Hasan Pasha and said, "Hasan Pasha, may you live long! The grooms have given your new horse food and water, but it will neither eat nor drink. All it does is to urinate here and there and paw the earth in its stall. The grooms have become afraid of it."

"Well, what can be done?"

"A very wise *hoca*, a healing *hoca*, has come to the village. He is able to cure all kinds of illnesses," the lame man said.

"Bring that *hoca* here," ordered the pasha. When the lame man returned with Köroğlu, Hasan Pasha said, "*Hoca*, can you restore sanity to the insane?"

"Oh, that is the kind of healing I do best!"

"Well, if it is within your power, restore sanity to my mad new horse. I shall pay you whatever you ask for this important work. Come with me to the stable."

When they had arrived at the stable, Köroğlu took his pen and his pen holder and a small square piece of paper from his sash and began to write something down on the paper. Then he said, "Bring me a caldron of water." When this caldron had been brought, he recited something to the water, he

106

blew upon it, and then he began to write down something about it. He then said, "All right, now. The cure has begun. Don't try to come close to the mad horse. I'll be able now to move closer to him by reciting and blowing."

"All right, *hoca*."

As the *hoca* slowly moved closer to the stable door, Hasan Pasha called to the *keloğlan,* who by now had become a vizier. "Come and watch the way this *hoca* heals the horse you brought."

Keloğlan recognized Köroğlu immediately, despite the dervish disguise. He well remembered the promise that he had made to Köroğlu at the mill, and he resolved to keep that promise. "Ah," he said. "How fine that you have found a healing *hoca!*" And he gave no sign of recognition.

They opened the stable door, and the horse, already excited at catching the scent of Köroğlu, became even wilder when he saw him. "Beware, *hoca!*" they shouted. "He will knock you down!"

"Let him knock me down if he wishes," said Köroğlu. "As for you, stay well away for your own safety." Then, approaching the horse, he took off Kırat's saddle and bridle. "Bring five measures of barley," he said as he groomed Kırat as no one else could possibly do. When the barley was brought, Köroğlu said, "Now bring a large quantity of water." Thus he fed and watered his horse well. And all the while, he was speaking softly to Kırat.

"May Allah bless you, *hoca!*" the people called. "Now may we come nearer?"

"No, you must not risk coming any closer. I can recite lines to keep him calm, but you do not know how to do that. And only I can get him through the stable door. I'll mount him and ride him back and forth a little so that he will become accustomed to it. Then your pasha will also be able to mount him."

The *hoca* resaddled and rebridled Kırat, with all the people watching through the stable door. But some of them began talking among themselves about this *hoca.* One said, "How is it that the mad horse has suddenly become so calm? That *hoca* must be Köroğlu himself!"

But Keloğlan, standing nearby, overheard them and said, "Who are you to know Köroğlu? I stayed with him for three or five weeks before I was able to steal the horse, and I would know him if I saw him. I see no Köroğlu; I see only a healing *hoca.*" And the rest fell silent.

Köroğlu now mounted the horse, but he purposely mounted Kırat backward, for he had great confidence now. When Hasan Pasha saw this, he called, "Aha! You are Köroğlu himself. We all know that now, so you might as well mount the horse properly." But Köroğlu, joyous at being once more on Kırat's back, just tossed his head and continued to ride as he was.

"Bring out soldiers to surround him, for he may try to take the horse away!" Hasan Pasha ordered. As the soldiers came out, Köroğlu began singing to the horse:

"Kırat, my life, my eyes, my pride!
He who can mount you is a bey.
Your double wings on either side
Lift you until you fly away.

"You wear your six years well. Aha!
Your legs are strong; your head is fine.
Your brother bears the Persian shah.
Glitter, Kırat! Let's see you shine!"

Hasan Pasha called, "Köroğlu, we recognize you now. You are no healing *hoca* at all! And we know the Persian shah owns Kırat's brother. Now mount the horse properly."

Köroğlu dismounted, bowed, and remounted. Then he said, "*Haydi!* Try to stop us now! We are going, Kırat and I!" He looked this way and that way, and then the horse began to rise, flying straight into the skies.

"Stop him! Stop him!" shouted Hasan Pasha, but his shouting was useless. He could do nothing but gather his soldiers again.

Now, Hasan Pasha was engaged to be married, and the wedding was soon to start. Köroğlu had one more trick to play before he left, so as soon as he had left Hasan Pasha behind, he had Kırat descend to the street. "From which house will the bride come?" he asked some boys, and they pointed out the house. Köroğlu rode Kırat right to that door, and—*Tak! Tak! Tak!*—he knocked.

When the girl came to the door, Köroğlu held out his hand. "For the love of Allah, give me a piece of bread," he said. The girl brought the bread, but as she was handing it to him, he said, "Step a little closer, my daughter. I can't quite reach it." When she came closer, he grabbed her by the arm and carried her off.

Her neighbor ran at once to Hasan Pasha with the news. "Hear, now, my pasha! While you have been thinking about your horse, you've lost your bride! Your engagement has been broken."

Hasan Pasha lined up his soldiers in ranks to trap the horse and its riders. Furthermore, he had his *hoca*s recite prayers and blow curses after Kırat. Their power was so great that it succeeded in blinding the eyes of Kırat.

When Köroğlu and the girl reached a stream, that stream seemed a sea to Kırat, and he stepped back in confusion. Understanding Kırat's condition, Köroğlu talked and sang to the horse:

"Downhill as prompt as a partridge you run;
Uphill as rapid as rabbits you race.
Now like a new-wed bride in the sun
Go, my Kırat, with that light in your face."

Again, Kırat stepped toward the stream, and again those incantations of the *hoca*s drew him back. Despairing, Köroğlu cried, "O Allah, they have somehow blinded the eyes of my horse. Open his eyes again, I pray!" Allah heard this prayer and opened Kırat's eyes. He crossed the water and ascended a steep rock on the other side.

By now, however, the soldiers were right behind them, and they crossed the stream and surrounded the rock. Once Kırat had come down from the rock, both Köroğlu and the girl would become Hasan Pasha's prisoners.

But Köroğlu was unafraid. "See!" he said to the girl. "There comes your groom."

"Yes, I see him," said the girl, "but you are worth three or five of that one!" For she had fallen in love with this hero.

"Shall we take his *pilav* away from him?" asked Köroğlu.

"No. Instead, let us save our lives now."

"What lives? What do you have in mind?" Köroğlu said.

"Nothing. Oh, nothing."

"I am a brave man."

"Then what can I say? If you are a brave man, do whatever you will."

Köroğlu now began to sing, threatening Hasan Pasha and his troops:

"Thirty-two heroes have come from the stream,
Thirty-two heroes with swords drawn to fight.
Those who remain will be naught but a dream;
Those who flee now will sleep safely tonight."

Hasan Pasha and his soldiers retreated before the attack of Köroğlu's thirty-two warriors, who had just arrived. As for Köroğlu, he climbed down from the rock, snatched Hasan Pasha's dish of *pilav*, and took it to the girl. After she had eaten her fill, the whole group started out for Çamlibel.

When they arrived at the gate of the stronghold, Ayvaz saw the girl with

Köroğlu and he thought, "Oh-h-h, how beautiful!" And he watched as they entered the courtyard.

Noticing Ayvaz's attention to the girl, Köroğlu began to sing again:

"Oh, Ayvaz, this girl is a beauty, 'tis true.
Unmatched are her eyes and her slender waist.
But she's sweetheart neither for me nor for you.
Her flavors can no one at Çamlibel taste."

"Do you bring her here as our sister, then?" asked Ayvaz. "From where has she come?"

"Oh, Ayvaz, my son, I understand your feelings, and that is why I sang as I did. I am a brave man, and I do not lie. Nor does any man steal my horse without losing a member of his family. Hasan Pasha stole my Kırat, and, in return, I stole his fiancée. But Kırat has been recovered unharmed, and this girl will likewise be restored unharmed. She is my sister and yours, both in this world and in the next. Ayvaz, you are to take her to the stream and leave her there."

Then turning to the girl, Köroğlu said, "I shall return you in the same condition in which I found you. To steal a family member from one who steals my horse is a matter of principle for me, but I go no farther. For me to behave otherwise would be unfitting to my dignity."

Though the girl herself did not want to leave, she had no choice but to go. Thus Köroğlu had fair and honorable revenge for the theft of his faithful Kırat.

The Fisherman and the Little Fish

There was once a fisherman who had worked all day without any success. He had cast his nets and cast his nets, but he had caught nothing. Finally, when he was almost ready to go home, he caught one small fish.

"Please let me go," begged the fish. "I am so small now that I would not even fill a hole in one of your teeth. If you let me go now, I shall grow larger in the sea, and then the next time you catch me, I shall be of some real use to you."

"Oh, no, little fish," said the fisherman, holding it tightly. "If I let you go now, I may never see you again. After all, a small fish in my hand is better than a large fish in my imagination!"

The Tree That Bore Fruit on the Day It Was Planted

One day Sultan Harun Reshid went on a tour of his country with his grand vizier to learn how his subjects lived. Along the way, he saw a poor old man leaning on a stick as he tried to plant a tree. He was so weak and frail that he could scarcely stand.

This puzzled the sultan. "Why do you suppose, my grand vizier, that a man at death's door would plant a tree?"

"I suppose, Your Majesty, that the man likes trees. There could be no reason other than that," answered the grand vizier.

"I want to hear the reason from the old man himself," said Harun Reshid. "Go and ask him what he is doing."

In answer to this question, the old man replied, "Sir, I am planting a tree."

"But *why* are you planting it?"

"I am planting it for the sake of Allah," said the old man.

"But you are already so very old. Do you think you will live to enjoy the fruit from this tree?"

"Only Allah knows," replied the old man. "Perhaps I shall."

Harun Reshid was pleased with the old man's answers, and he directed the grand vizier to give the old man a golden lira.

The grand vizier went to the old man and said, "Father, take this gold coin."

The old man took the gold coin and held it up, saying, "Look! My tree began bearing fruit even while it was being planted."

This, too, pleased Harun Reshid, and he directed his grand vizier to give the old man another coin. When the grand vizier gave him another gold coin, the old man held up both of his coins and said, "You see! The tree I am planting has borne two pieces of fruit."

Harun Reshid ordered still another piece of gold for the old man. When he received it, the old man held up the three golden coins and said, "What more could one expect from a tree than that it bear three pieces of fruit on its first day?"

Hasan the Broom Maker

Once there was and twice there wasn't, when jinns played *cirit* in the old *hamam*—well, in those times, there were a man and a woman who had just one child, a son. When this son, Hasan, was still a small boy, his father suddenly became ill and died. Time came, time went, and Hasan became a young man. One day he said, "My mother, I do nothing but waste my time. I should at least learn some kind of trade at which I could work. At least, I could earn three or five kuruş a day."

"Well, if this is the way you feel, then you may work."

"Tell me, then, Mother. What was my father's business? I can do what he did."

"Your father was a farmer," she said. And since they had a neighbor who was an *ağa*, the mother said to that neighbor, "My son, Hasan, wishes to learn some kind of trade. Would you put him to work in your fields? As for pay, three or five kuruş a day would be fine. I'm happy that he wants to work!"

"All right," said the *ağa*, and he took Hasan to a field where a man was sowing grain. "Son," the man said, "you drive the oxen and plow for me, and I'll sow." They worked together in this way for a little while and then the man said, "You go on plowing now while I take a little nap beside the river."

Hasan continued working by himself, but he did not notice how tired the oxen were becoming. Finally one ox dropped dead of exhaustion, and the other soon followed. Now that both oxen were dead, Hasan put the yoke on his own back and went home. "Mother," he said, "I am not meant to be a farmer. And my father wasn't a farmer, either, or there would be some farm tools somewhere around the house. *You* know what my father's business was. Tell me! I want to know."

Well, the woman finally told him, "Your father was a broom maker. The tools for his broom making are up in the attic—just a vineyard knife and a *kıskaç* with which to tie the brooms."

Immediately, Hasan climbed up into the attic and came back with the vineyard knife and the *kıskaç*. Leaving the house with his tools, he went to a stream and walked along it until he came to a bed of reeds. He worked—how he worked!—cutting the reeds and tying them to make sturdy brooms. For three or five days he worked, not eating, not sleeping, until he had made a large heap of brooms. Satisfied, he lay down to sleep for a while.

Now, it happened that at that time, such brooms were in great demand around İstanbul. To look for brooms like these, men had been sent in boats

112

along the streams to places where brooms might be being made. All at once, some of these men saw that great heap of good brooms. They rowed alongside that place, looking to left and to right for the broom maker. They saw no one, but their calls and their noise wakened Hasan from his sleep.

"Whose brooms are these?" they asked.

"They are mine," Hasan said. "I made them."

"Well, how much money do you want for them?"

"I'll take the regular price," he said. The buyers accepted this bargain and they bought all of his brooms. After Hasan had loaded the brooms into the boats, he was paid exactly what had been promised: thirty liras, a great amount of money in the old days.

Putting this money into his sash, Hasan picked up his vineyard knife and his *kıskaç* and went straight to the marketplace in his *kaza*. There for three liras he bought a horse. He also bought a pair of shoes, a cap, a pair of baggy trousers, and a shirt, as well as some things for his mother. After buying some *helva*, too, he went home. "Mother," he said, "do you see what happened? Since broom making was my family craft, I succeeded at it and earned a great deal of money. I have bought a horse, some clothes, and some food, and I still have money in my sash."

After they had eaten their meal and were satisfied, Hasan got up and began to strut around, puffed up with pride. After a while, he said, "Mother, it's time for me to marry. Do go and ask the padishah for the hand of his daughter for me."

113

"My son, would they give the daughter of a padishah to a *broom maker?*"

"Could they find anyone more worthy?" asked Hasan. He continued to strut here and there, so what could his mother do but go?

She went to the padishah's palace, all right, but when she reached the door she was ashamed to knock. The padishah was looking out of the window and he saw the woman come and then turn away, without saying anything to anyone, and go along home.

"What happened, Mother? Did you ask?" said Hasan.

"Wait, Son," she said. "Just think. Would they give their daughter to people like us? I was too embarrassed to ask."

"Quick, Mother! Go back and ask. It can do no harm to *ask*," Hasan said. And he walked with his mother to the door.

"Well, Son, I'll sacrifice my head for you," she said, and back she went to the padishah's palace.

The padishah saw that same woman coming again, and he said to his servant, "Go and see if she is without bread or other food. She may be hungry. At least give her a piece of bread and some cheese so that her stomach can be comfortable."

The servant at once took out some bread and cheese and gave it to the woman. What could the woman do now? She returned home without saying a word.

"What happened, Mother?" Hasan asked.

"*Aman, aman,* Allah! I went there and knocked at the door. They gave me a piece of bread and some cheese. They thought that I was a beggar."

"Well, then, go back at once and ask the question."

Again, for the third time, the woman went. She knocked at the door and a servant answered. "Auntie, what do you want?"

"With your permission, I want to enter the presence of the padishah."

They went to the padishah and reported this to him. "All right. Let her come in," said the padishah. When she came in, he said, "Auntie, I hope it is good news that you bring! You have come here and then left this place two or three times already today."

"My padishah, I have a son, Hasan the broom maker. With the will of Allah and the consent of the Prophet, I have come to ask the hand of your daughter for him."

"Since it is asked with the will of Allah," said the padishah, "I shall give her to him in marriage. But I have one condition. I own thirty thousand gold liras that are now held by a foreign state. If he goes and gets those thirty thousand gold liras and brings them back to me, I shall give him my daughter."

"Very well," said the woman, and she left for home.

When she reached home, Hasan asked, "What happened, Mother?"

"My son, I spoke to him in the name of Allah and he accepted the proposal, but he set a certain condition. He has thirty thousand gold liras that are being held by a foreign state. He said that if you could get that money and bring it back to him, he would be willing to give you his daughter."

"All right. If that is the condition, ask him for a saddlebag in which to carry the money back. Ask him, too, in which direction I must ride to find that other state."

The woman returned once more to the padishah. "My padishah," she said, "our Hasan the broom maker will go after your money, but he wants from you a saddlebag in which he can carry the money back. He also needs to know the direction in which he should ride to find that state that has your gold liras."

To himself, the padishah said, "I have tried so hard with no success to get that money back. How can this woman's son possibly regain it?" Still, he said to a servant, "Give this woman a saddlebag and also seven liras with which to buy any food she might need while Hasan is gone." And to the woman he said, "Tell Hasan he must ride to the northeast."

Hasan's mother gave the saddlebag to her son and said, "Ride northeast to find that state. Oh, my son, may Allah be with you."

Hasan groomed his three-lira horse. Then he kissed his mother's hands, and taking the vineyard knife left by his father, he started on his way. He rode a little, he rode far, until at last he came to that other state. By then, it was midnight, and he could see the capital of that state down in a hollow valley. He went to the top of a hill overlooking this valley and started shouting, "O padishah! O padishah of this state! I have come here from Turkey. If you will return my padishah's thirty thousand gold liras tonight, all will be well, but if you do not return them, I shall completely destroy your country. I have with me a great many soldiers, and I have been the victor in many battles."

His voice rang from one side to the other of that hollow valley. Well pleased, he continued to shout.

"What *is* this voice?" "Where does it come from?" "Who can be shouting these threats?" The people rushed out of their houses in panic.

The padishah ordered one man after another to go and investigate the voice, but no one would go. Finally, the very last man, a blind man, agreed to go. Following the voice, which kept on shouting, the blind man came to Hasan. "Instead of shouting here at midnight, come and say these things to our padishah. He will give the money back."

Hasan saw that the man was blind. "Could they not find a whole man to send? Think of it! A blind one as a messenger!" He took the blind man up behind him on his three-lira horse, and together they rode to the padishah's palace. There Hasan said, "I have come from Turkey to get my padishah's gold liras and take them home to him. I want them *now*. If you do not give them to me this very night, your fate will be controlled by my signals. My men have surrounded your capital, and you have no power against them."

115

"My son," said the padishah, "it is scarcely past midnight now, and my people need their sleep. In the morning I shall give you the liras."

"No. You must give them to me *now*. If you wait until tomorrow, you are doomed."

"Very well," said the padishah. After all, what could he do against such force? So he and his viziers counted out the thirty thousand gold liras into the saddlebag. After that, Hasan was given a room in the padishah's palace. "Stay here the rest of the night, and you can leave in the morning," the padishah said. But Hasan did not go to sleep. Instead, he listened.

Soon he heard a *Tak! Tak! Tak!* It seems that the padishah's daughter was in the next room, and the lover she wanted to marry was knocking at her window. "Come," said the lover. "Let's run away together. No one will notice, for a hero has come from Turkey, and your father is planning to kill him. Come quickly!"

The padishah's daughter said, "Come back in an hour, and I'll be ready to go with you."

Hasan heard all this, and then he looked through the keyhole of his door. Outside, there were two guards with huge swords ready to kill him while he was asleep. The sentries were not changed, however, and at last the two guards became so tired that they fell asleep—*horol, horol.*

Quietly Hasan opened his door by lifting it from its hinges. He put the saddlebag on his back and went straight to the courtyard. When he found the stable locked, he lifted that door from its hinges. He found his three-lira horse and, after wrapping its hoofs in felt to keep them from making any noise, he put the saddlebag on its back and led it into the courtyard. He knocked—*Tak! Tak! Tak!*—at the window of the princess.

"Have you come already?" asked the girl.

"I have come. Be quick, now!"

Since she was eager to join her lover, she picked up her bundle and followed him. They went to the horse and mounted it and away they went, fleeing through the rest of the night. Since she was seated behind him, how could she know that he was not her lover but instead that hero from Turkey?

Well, to make a long story shorter, after traveling—*Çik-a-dak! Çik-a-dak! Çik-a-dak!*—until dawn, they crossed the border into Turkey. They were very tired by then, so they dismounted in a grassy place near a fountain to rest. As he helped her to dismount, she discovered that he was not her lover at all but that young hero from Turkey. At that moment, Hasan said, "You must accept my religion, or I shall take your life."

What could the girl do? She said, "This must be my kismet. Tell me, then, what I must do to accept your faith, and I shall become a Muslim." So she repeated the testimonial statement Hasan gave her and thus accepted his faith.

He removed the saddlebag from the horse and allowed the horse to graze while they were resting. Just then, a band of forty thieves passed along the road near the fountain, and the thieves noticed the boy and the girl there. But one of them also noticed something shining in an open saddlebag, though he could not see clearly what it was. He said, "There is something golden in that saddlebag. I wonder what it can be?"

"Whatever it is," said another, "it is not going to come to us. Since we have horses under us, let us go to take a look."

When they came closer, they saw that the saddlebag was filled with gold. First they took the saddlebag and then they took the girl. Finally they stripped Hasan as naked as when he had been delivered by his mother. "Mount the boy's horse," the leader said to the girl, and the girl mounted Hasan's three-lira horse. Then they all rode away toward a forest, taking the girl with them.

Hasan ran after them, but one of the thieves turned around and saw him. "Do not follow us," said one of them, "or we shall kill you."

By this time they had come to a road that ran through the forest, and Hasan had lost his sense of direction. He said to the thieves, "Since you have taken my gold and my girl and my garments, how can I even return to my own *kaza*? At least give me back my vineyard knife so that I can cut dock leaves to cover the front and the back of my body."

The leader of the thieves said, "Very well. Give him his knife." They threw the knife to him and then rode away.

Hasan took the knife and started walking, but he was entirely lost. He

followed a footpath at first, but when that crossed a road, he took that larger way. After a while he came to a stream with a bridge across it. As he stood on that bridge, it began to sway from side to side. "*Aman!* What kind of bridge *is* this?" he said. When he came to the center of the bridge, he saw a trapdoor in the floor of the bridge. Opening the trapdoor, he saw that it led to a room built right into the bridge. It was late by then, and Hasan said to himself, "Perhaps I should stay here for the night. Tomorrow I'll look for my way home."

So he went down into the room and looked around. There he found a grindstone, and he started grinding and sharpening the blade of his vineyard knife so that the next day he could cut branches more easily. "I could at least make a decent covering for myself," he said.

Now, it happened that that bridge belonged to the forty thieves. It was arranged in such a way that when a caravan crossed it, the swaying of the bridge would provide a signal to the thieves. The thieves did not know that Hasan had found the bridge. They thought instead that a caravan had started to cross it. The leader of the thieves said to twenty of his men, "That must be a caravan crossing our bridge. Go and bring them and all their goods here."

Twenty of the thieves went and searched, looking this way and that way, but they could see no one. "Perhaps that boy came this way and climbed upon the bridge," said one, as they opened the trapdoor. One of them bent down to look inside.

But Hasan had heard them, and he moved to one side of the trapdoor and waited. When the first brigand bent down to look, Hasan grabbed him by the hair and—*Slish!*—cut off his head with his sharp vineyard knife.

Then another one of the thieves said, "Our friend descended very quickly," and he himself looked down inside the room. Hasan cut off his head in the same way, and then, one after another, he cut off the heads of the

rest of the twenty thieves, piling up the bodies like so many sacks. Happy at having killed all those thieves, Hasan took the clothes of the last one and put them on to cover his nakedness. Then he took his vineyard knife and climbed up to the surface of the bridge. Again the bridge began to sway, so Hasan went back down through the trapdoor and pulled the trapdoor shut.

Meanwhile, the leader of the thieves said to the remaining nineteen, "I sent twenty men, and still they have not brought back that caravan. Hurry along! All the rest of you go, too."

So they also went, looking first to this side and then to that side, but they saw no caravan. "Then where are our friends?" said one.

"Perhaps they went down into the secret room," said another, and he opened the trapdoor and bent down to look inside. At once, Hasan pulled him down and—*Slish!*—cut off his head. In this same way, Hasan killed all nineteen of them.

Now there was no one left but the leader. "Great Allah!" he said to himself. "I sent twenty men and nothing happened. Then I sent nineteen men and still nothing happened. Did the caravan get away? I must see." He went, too, and looked to this side and to that side without seeing anyone. Like the others, he opened the trapdoor, bending down to look inside, and—*Slish!*—Hasan cut off his head.

To discover whether or not there was anyone left in the band of thieves, Hasan went outside and shook the bridge. When no one came, he shook it again, and still no one came. "Well, at last I have killed them all," he said. "This bridge must have given them some kind of signal. But what is the signal? How does it work?" He looked along this side of the bridge and he looked along that side of the bridge, and then he discovered a wire fastened to the very end of the bridge. Following that wire where it led into the forest, Hasan came to the mouth of a cave where there was a bell with a hole in it. "Ha!" he said. "So *that* is the signal!"

Hasan entered the cave and found that it was very large, with many rooms inside. He opened the door of one room and saw that it was filled with fine carpets. He opened the door of the next room and found it filled with *kilims*. He opened the door of another room filled with pearls and still another room filled with gold. He went along and went along, opening door after door, and found that every room was filled with some kind of valuable thing. When he opened the thirty-ninth door, he saw a girl as beautiful as the fourteenth of the moon. He closed that door at once and went on to the fortieth room, where he found the girl he had brought. "Come!" he said. "Be quick!"

"How did you manage to get here?"

"I have killed all of them," he said, "and they have found their kismet. Where are my own clothes?" The girl brought him his clothes, and after he had put them on he said, "And where is my three-lira horse? And the saddlebag?"

The girl showed him where the horse and the saddlebag had been put, and he took them out of the cave. He took nothing but the horse, the saddlebag, and the girl. After he had put the saddlebag on his three-lira horse, Hasan and the girl mounted and were ready to leave.

But the beautiful girl in the thirty-ninth room could restrain herself no longer. She came out just as they were going to ride away and said, "Young man, where are you going?"

"I am going to my own *kaza*," he said.

"To whom will you leave me? I was taken as the sister of the forty thieves, and I heard you say that you had killed them all. This is a world in which you are held responsible for everything you do. My forty brothers have paid with their lives for what they did. But now if you leave me here alone, I shall starve to death. The least you can do is to take me along with you."

"Come along with us, then," said Hasan, "but my three-lira horse will not carry all of us."

"There is a very special horse in the stable, a horse fit for a hero like you," she said. "We must take Blackbird for you to ride. But let us not forget all of the wealth that is collected here. Take at least some of these things."

Going back inside the cave, the three loaded all the gold into eighty sacks, and these sacks they loaded onto the backs of the thieves' forty mules. Then Hasan went to the stable to get Blackbird. But when he tried to bridle the horse, it reared and bit, and would not let him come near. The sister of the forty thieves spoke then to the horse. "Blackbird, listen to what I say. This is a world in which each one is held responsible for what he does. My forty brothers have robbed and killed many people, and now they have paid with their lives for their evil deeds. I am going, and there will no longer be anyone here to look after you. Hasan will be your new master. Surrender to him, because from this day forward he will be the one to look after you."

After she had spoken in this way to the horse, Blackbird surrendered. The two girls mounted the three-lira horse, and Hasan mounted Blackbird. But, "Be careful, Hasan," warned the beautiful girl. "Do not pull on Blackbird's reins."

They rode off together, with the caravan of forty loaded mules ahead of them. As Hasan looked at the two girls and at the mules, he said, "How amazing is the hand of Allah! Is all this wealth now mine?" And in his pride, he pulled suddenly on Blackbird's reins. At once, Blackbird began to fly. "*Aman!*" said Hasan. "She warned me about the reins!" And he looked down at the sister of the forty thieves. She signaled to him to pull the reins down, and after he had done this, Blackbird returned to the earth with the rest. Hasan then left the reins lying loose.

After a long journey, they finally arrived in Hasan's *kaza* and went on to his town. As soon as they had arrived at his mother's house, they unloaded the mules. Since his mother's house had only one room besides the kitchen,

120

there was no space for all those sacks of gold, so they were stacked behind the house in the garden. Hasan then said to his mother, "Mother, we are hungry. Go and take a piece of what is in those sacks, and with it get us plenty of food from a store. Let us satisfy our appetites."

The old woman went and looked at the things in the sacks, but she did not recognize them as gold coins, for never in her whole life in that town had she seen such things. "My son," she said, "why did you bring home all those onion skins? When the northeast wind blows, you may burn down the forest with the fire these will make."

"Mother, don't worry about that. Just take one of them and go to the store with it. Get some food from the owner of the store and pay him with that piece. Then bring the food home."

The woman took one piece from a sack and went to the food store. She said to the owner, "Give me some bread and give me some cheese and give me some *helva,* and give me this and that." But when she gave the gold coin to the man, he said, "Auntie, I do not have enough money to give you your change from that coin."

She left the foods there and went to another storekeeper, but he, too, said, "I do not have enough money here to exchange for that coin." And the third storekeeper said the same thing, so finally she came home without any food at all.

"What happened, Mother? Where is the food?"

"My son, I went to this storekeeper and that storekeeper, and none of them had enough change to give me. I don't understand it."

"My mother, Allah has given me much wealth. You should have taken the food and given the man this piece of gold without accepting any change." So Hasan went to the store himself and said to the storekeeper, "Give me this and that," ordering all of the things he wanted to buy. Then he gave the storekeeper a piece of gold.

"My son," said the storekeeper, "I do not have enough money to give you the correct change for this piece of gold."

"Take it and keep what is left as a gift from me," said Hasan. And he took the foods he had bought and went along home.

Now that the sister of the forty thieves had joined them, Hasan had two girls in his home. The next morning, he put his saddlebag on a mule and said to his mother, "Mother, mount my three-lira horse and go with this mule to the palace of the padishah. Say to him, 'My Hasan the broom maker has brought back the thirty thousand gold liras he was sent to the foreign state to get, but he no longer wishes to marry your daughter. My son says that you can also keep the mule on which the gold is loaded.' Give him the gold and the mule and then ride my three-lira horse back home."

His mother went to the padishah with the gold and the mule and spoke to the padishah exactly the words Hasan had given her. As for the padishah, he was so surprised to receive the gold that he did not even ask why Hasan no longer wanted to marry his daughter.

On the following day, Hasan bought a good piece of land and then he hired forty or fifty craftsmen and seventy laborers to build for him a mansion as fine as a palace. When it was finished, he took the two girls there to live. Inside, he had elegant carpets spread and *kilims* hung, and outside he had a beautiful garden made, one that was filled with flowers. He also had a stable built for the animals—the mules and Blackbird and his three-lira horse.

One morning the girl he had brought back from the foreign state arose and went outside to sweep the courtyard. An old woman who lived in a hut opposite their mansion saw her there. Now, word had gone all around the town that Hasan the broom maker no longer sought the padishah's daughter, so when the old woman saw the girl in the courtyard, she rushed to the palace. "*Aman, aman,* Allah! My padishah, I know now why Hasan the broom maker decided that he no longer wished to have your daughter. May this world and the next be my witness when I tell you that he brought back from that foreign state a girl who is suitable for you but not at all suitable for him. She is like all that is beautiful in the world."

"Hmmn!" said the padishah. "That is very interesting, but in truth I am beginning to be afraid of that young man. He brought back from a foreign state all the money I had been unable to recover myself. I do not feel that I can ask him for this girl."

"Do not worry, my padishah," said the old woman. "I shall bring such troubles down upon his head that he can never escape them. Then we shall be able to get this beautiful girl for you."

"Well, if you think such a matter can be managed, by all means do it," said the padishah.

The old woman spent all that night thinking what might be done to get Hasan out of the way. In the morning, she looked outside and there, sweeping the courtyard, was the other girl, the sister of the forty thieves. She was even more beautiful than the first girl. When the old woman saw her, she wrapped herself up hastily and rushed to the palace of the padishah. "Oh, my padishah," she said, "there is not just one girl. There are two! The girl I saw today is even more beautiful than the one I saw yesterday. They are both suitable for you and not at all suitable for that Hasan the broom maker. We should use all means to take those girls away from him."

Of course, the padishah agreed with the old woman. He moved down closer to her to hear what she planned to do. "My padishah," she said, "I have thought of something from which Hasan cannot possibly escape. There is a giant at such and such a place. You must act as if you are ill, and you must tell Hasan that you have a bad case of rheumatism in your legs. Tell him that the doctors have advised you to wrap around your legs the lungs of that giant from such and such a place. This, they said, is the only way in which your illness can be cured. Also tell him that he has the ability to accomplish this task. He will of course be killed by the giant, leaving both of the girls for you."

"That is a very good idea," said the padishah, and immediately he pretended to have unbearable pain in his legs. He called Hasan to him and said, "Hasan, my son, you are a good boy, and I have great confidence in your courage. Terrible pain has recently come to my legs. Doctors have examined me thoroughly and they have told me that I cannot get well unless I wrap around my legs the lungs of a giant that lives in such and such a place. You are the only one able to get these lungs for me."

What could Hasan do? He went home and spent a long while thinking about this. When she saw him so silent and thoughtful, the sister of the forty thieves said, "Hasan, what is troubling you?"

"The padishah has told me to get the lungs of a giant at such and such a place as a cure for his aching legs. That is what troubles me."

"If that is the case, then go to the marketplace and buy a sack of grapes. Carefully groom Blackbird, give her water to drink, and then pour before her the sackful of grapes. When Blackbird begins to eat the grapes, go and stand at her left side. She will look to her right as she is eating the grapes and she will see no one there. Then she will look to her left, and when she sees you there she will ask you what you want. At that time, tell her about your problem, and if there is a solution to it, she will tell you what it is."

"All right," Hasan said, and he went at once to buy a sack of grapes. He groomed Blackbird carefully, gave her water to drink, and poured before her the sackful of grapes. He went then and stood at her left side. As she was eating the grapes, Blackbird looked to her right and saw no one there. Then she looked to her left side and saw Hasan.

"What do you want?" she asked.

"The padishah has asked me to go and get the lungs of a giant living at such and such a place. I want to know how I can possibly complete this task."

"But, my son, why should you ask *me*? You killed the forty thieves and brought their sister and me to your *kaza*. I have no wish to help you." And she went on eating the grapes.

Hasan returned to the sister of the forty thieves. "Well, what happened?" she asked.

"She told me that she had no wish to help me."

Hearing that, the girl went and spoke to Blackbird herself. "See here!" she said. "This world is a place in which everyone pays for what he does. My brothers did evil things, and they have paid for their deeds. Now the padishah is doing this and that to take us away from Hasan. Therefore, if you can possibly do anything to help Hasan, do so. He is the one who will look after us, and he is the one who will take care of you, too!"

"I shall take him there, but I cannot bring him back," said the horse.

The girl heard what Blackbird said, but she did not fully understand it. Why *couldn't* Blackbird bring him back? Still, "All right," she said.

"Then he should be ready early tomorrow morning. Roast two large pieces of meat and a chicken for him to take."

"Very well," said the girl. And returning to the mansion, she roasted two large pieces of meat and a chicken.

The next morning, Hasan arose early and carefully groomed Blackbird. Then he mounted her, took the two roasted pieces of meat and the roasted chicken, and rode out of town.

After they were well away from the town, the horse said, "Close your eyes." Hasan closed his eyes. "Now open your eyes," said the horse. When Hasan opened his eyes, he saw that they had already arrived at the well in which the giant lived. He dismounted.

"Now listen carefully," said Blackbird. "If the northeast wind blows, you should move around to the southwest. On the other hand, if the southwest wind blows, you should move around to the northeast. The giant comes up out of the well with his mouth turned away from the wind. When the giant sticks his head out with his mouth open, shove the first piece of meat into his mouth. The next time, the giant will come up out of the well all the way to his waist, asking himself, "Where did that much good meat come from?" At that moment, shove the second piece of meat into his mouth. The third

124

125

time, he will come completely out of the well, asking himself, "Where did that much good meat come from?" Then you must shove the chicken into his mouth and immediately jump on his back, holding him firmly by his ears. If you do not jump on his back and hold him tightly by his ears, this giant will tear you into many pieces, and then you will not be able to return. The ears of the giant should be used as reins with which to direct him on your return home."

After saying these things, Blackbird flew back to the stable, and Hasan waited there for the giant. After some time, the giant started coming up out of the well. Since the northeast wind was blowing, Hasan quickly moved to the southwest side of the well. The moment the giant's head appeared above the edge of the well, Hasan shoved the first large piece of meat into his mouth. The next time, the giant came out of the well as far as his waist, asking himself, "Where did that much good meat come from?" At once, Hasan shoved the second big piece of meat into his mouth. The next time, the giant came completely out of the well, asking himself, "Where did that much good meat come from?" Immediately, Hasan shoved the chicken into his mouth and then jumped upon the giant's back and grabbed hold of his ears. After the giant had been captured in this way, he spoke to Hasan. "Ah, young man, if you had not jumped onto my back and held fast to my ears, I should have torn you into pieces."

"Do not talk so much, but move along," said Hasan. And using the ears as reins, he rode the giant to his own town.

Meanwhile, the padishah arose that morning and, still in his nightshirt, stood before the window yawning and stretching. When he saw Hasan bringing not only the lungs of the giant but the whole giant himself, *alive,* he shouted, "Close the gates of the town! Do not let that giant in! He will tear us to pieces!"

The guards closed and locked the gates, and when Hasan called, "Open the gates!" no one would open them. Hasan then steered the giant directly at the gates, and the giant rushed against them, smashing them open with his chest, and entered the town. *Lambır, lambır,* they went up the stairs of the padishah's palace and saw the padishah trying to hide in one of the corners.

"Oh, Hasan," said the padishah, "I have recovered, and I no longer need the lungs of that giant."

"My padishah," shouted Hasan, "shall I let the giant live or shall I kill him?"

"*Aman,* effendi! If you let him live, he will tear us all to pieces. Please kill him."

Hasan then cut the giant apart with the vineyard knife left by his father, and he gave the bloody lungs to the padishah, saying, "If you please, my padishah." Of course, the whole palace was smeared with the blood of the giant.

Soon after this, the old woman came to the palace and said, "My padishah, by now Hasan will have been torn to pieces by the giant and left there, so there is no possibility of his return."

"What do you mean, 'torn to pieces'? He brought the giant here alive and he then killed him here, giving me his bloody lungs. Now for your bad judgment you must carry all these parts of the giant outside and clean up every spot of blood from the palace."

The old woman cut the parts of the giant into smaller pieces and carried them out of the palace on her back. It took her three or five days to clean all the blood from the palace and three or five more days to wash all the carpets and whitewash the walls. All this work made the old woman so angry that she was determined to plan a task for Hasan that would get rid of him forever.

All the while she rested from her labors, she thought and plotted. Finally she had a plan that must surely work. She went to the palace and was admitted to the presence of the padishah. "Oh, my padishah, I have a plan now that will certainly cost Hasan his life," she said.

"He is a very brave young man," said the padishah. "I fear that if we do not get rid of him, he will take my kingdom away from me."

"There will be no way for him to escape this new difficulty," the old woman said. "There is a garden that belongs to the daughter of the padishah of fairies. This garden has red flowers that bloom on single stems, but you will ask him to bring to you from that garden a flower with three stems. Anyone who sets foot on the soil of that garden is immediately turned to stone."

"If you are sure that that will happen to Hasan, I shall ask him to get that red flower," said the padishah. And he called Hasan into his presence.

"Hasan, my son," he said, "you have brought back my thirty thousand gold liras from that foreign state and you have also brought back that giant alive. You are the only one who can bring back to me a certain three-stemmed red flower. At such and such a place there is a garden with three-stemmed red flowers that never grow pale or die. I want one of those flowers to put on my dining table. If you can bring me such a flower before forty days and forty nights have passed, then all will be well. If you cannot bring it to me by the end of that time, I shall give you over to my executioners on the forty-first day."

What could Hasan do? He went back to his mansion and started thinking about this task given to him by the padishah. Again, the sister of the forty thieves saw that he was troubled. "What are you thinking about so deeply?" she asked.

"Well, the padishah has set a new task for me. He wants a three-stemmed red flower that never grows pale or dies. How can I find such a flower?"

"Again you will go and groom Blackbird. Again you will water her and give her grapes to eat and stand at her left side. When she asks what you want, tell her about this flower, and if there is anything that can be done to get it, she will tell you."

So Hasan went to the market and bought a sackful of grapes. He groomed Blackbird thoroughly and watered her and placed the grapes before her. Then as Blackbird began to eat the grapes, he stood at her left side. The horse looked to her right and saw no one. When she looked to her left, there was Hasan. "What do you want now?" she asked.

"The padishah has ordered me to bring him a three-stemmed red flower from such and such a place. I need to know how I can get this flower for him. If I do not get it, he will take my life."

"Why do you ask *me?*" said Blackbird. "You took the lives of the forty thieves, and you brought their sister and me here to your *kaza*. I have no wish to help you."

Hasan returned to the sister of the forty thieves and told her what Blackbird had said. Again the girl went to the horse and said, "You know that the forty thieves paid with their lives for their evil deeds. You know, too, that this young hero who is now your master is taking good care of you and of me. If there is something that can be done to help him with this task, you must do it."

"Well," said the horse, "I shall take him there, but I cannot bring him back."

This time, the girl understood what Blackbird meant, and she said, "If he must be killed, let him be killed there and not here before my eyes. I cannot bear to see him killed here."

"All right," said the horse. "If this is the way it is, then tell him to take with him a whip and a cake of soap and a large needle. We shall leave early in the morning."

The next day soon after dawn, Hasan took the whip, the cake of soap, and the large needle to Blackbird's stall. He mounted the horse, and they set out on their way. When they came to a narrow pass between two mountains, the horse said to Hasan, "Oh, young man, once I was owned by the girl you are going to see, but the forty thieves stole me from her. From that day I became old, and I have never since returned to this place. This is the only route, and we must pass between these two mountains. All the fairies live here, and if they pull a certain rope while we are passing between these mountains, the mountains will come together and crush us. You will have to whip me in such a way that the first blow should penetrate the flesh, the second blow should cut to the bone, and the third blow should cause blood to gush forth from my whole body. The fairies will think that it is raining, and so they will pull the rope too late. This is the only way by which we can pass beyond these mountains. But do not feel any pity in whipping me."

Hasan whipped the horse as she had told him to do. With the first blow he penetrated her skin. With the second he cut through to the bone. And with the third he caused blood to gush forth from her whole body. Just as

128

they had reached the other end of the pass, the two mountains came together, and the tail of the horse was caught and broken off. When they were down on the ground again, Hasan saw that the tail of the horse had been broken off and he began to weep.

"Why are you crying?" asked Blackbird.

"I am crying because your tail was broken off."

But because she was herself a fairy, the horse simply licked the base of the tail, and the tail grew back again. "Now let me see you try to walk here," said Blackbird. When Hasan took one step forward, his feet turned to stone. When he took a second step, his legs turned into stone as far as his knees. "Now walk back to me," said the horse. And Hasan turned around and came back. As he returned, his legs and his feet became flesh and bone again.

"Pluck three hairs from my mane and three hairs from my tail," she said. Hasan did as Blackbird directed. "Take good care of those hairs, for you will need them to complete your task. You will place on the ground the first hair that you plucked from my tail and you will step on that hair. Then you will put on the ground the second hair that you plucked from my tail and you will step on that, too. And, finally, put the third hair there and step on that. Then you must take the first hair again and place it on the ground and step on it, and then the second again, and then the third. Continuing in this way, you will come at last to that building in the garden opposite the place where we are now standing. There you will find sitting on a chair an old grandfather who is very dirty and covered with worms and lice. You will pick him up from there and carry him to the side of the pool. That pool is enchanted, so you must then throw the hairs from my mane into the water; it will thus have no power over you. Next you will wash the old grandfather thoroughly with the cake of soap you brought, and you will pick all of the worms and lice from his body with your needle. From his room in that building you will take his clean clothes and dress him with them, and then you will take him back to his chair. He is the watchman at the gate. Then you must go and stand at his left side. After a while, his mind will grow clear again. He will look to his right side but will see no one. Then, looking to his left side, he will see you, and he will ask, 'Was it you who did such good deeds for me?' At that moment, do not hesitate to tell him that you were the one that did those things."

After saying all this, Blackbird flew back to her stable, and Hasan began to follow the directions she had given him. Hair by hair by hair by hair by hair he walked until at last he had reached the old grandfather. Picking him up, Hasan carried him to the pool. After he had thrown the three hairs from Blackbird's mane into the pool, Hasan bathed the old man thoroughly with that cake of soap. One by one by one by one with his needle he cleansed the old man's body of the worms and the lice. Leaving him by the pool, Hasan went into the building and found the old grandfather's clean clothes and took

129

them outside and dressed the old man with them. Then he carried him back to his chair and stood at his left side. After a while, the old grandfather's mind became clear again. Looking to his right side, he saw no one, but when he looked to his left side he saw Hasan there. "O young man," he said, "did you do these good things for me?"

"I did all those things, my grandfather."

And the old grandfather said, "You may request of me whatever you wish."

"Grandfather, I request of you a red flower with three stems," said Hasan.

"Ah, my son, those flowers are enchanted, and anyone who touches their leaves becomes stone. It is impossible for me to grant this request. But tonight you must stay as my guest, for a certain girl will come tomorrow. She comes only once a week. When she comes tomorrow to wash herself in that pool, you must steal her clothes and refuse to give them back to her when she comes looking for them. Ask for the ring on her hand in exchange for the clothes. That ring has miraculous power. Also, listen very carefully to what she will say to you."

So that night, Hasan stayed at the house of the old grandfather as his guest. In the morning, just as the old grandfather had said, the girl came with her forty female slaves, flying through the air and landing near the pool. The slaves ran away at once, shouting something that Hasan could not understand.

The girl removed her clothes and left them on the branch of a tree. Then she entered the pool to bathe. Hasan quietly left his hiding place, took her clothing, and hid himself again. When the girl had finished bathing, she discovered that her clothes were gone. She looked to this side and to that side, and at last she saw Hasan hiding behind a rosebush. "Young man, give me back my clothes," she said.

"I shall if you will first give me the ring from your finger."

"I shall give it to you," she said, throwing the ring toward him. "I know why you came here, and this ring will not help you in any way for that purpose. Tomorrow I shall wrestle with you, and if you can defeat me, then I shall give you one of those flowers."

After taking the ring, Hasan went back to the house of the old grandfather. The girl dressed and flew away with her forty female slaves.

"Well, what happened, my son?" asked the old man. And Hasan told him about the girl and her slaves and the clothes and the ring and exactly what the girl had said to him. "Tonight you must stay again with me as my guest," said the grandfather. "The wrestling ground is at such and such a place. You will need wrestling shorts, and I shall provide them for you. Do not be surprised if she appears in the form of a huge *Arap*, with one lip dragging on the ground and the other touching the sky. When she tries to squeeze you and win the wrestling match in that way, twist away from her hold and evade her every move. You will wrestle with her in that evasive way all morning. Then when the heat of noonday falls upon her head, her brains will become red hot. Then you will be able to lift her up and throw her to the ground."

Hasan stayed with the old grandfather that night. The next morning, he put on the wrestling shorts the old man gave him and went to the wrestling ground, saying to himself, "I look like a real wrestler. İnşallah, I shall throw that girl." All at once, someone hit him on the neck, but there was no one there.

"How amazing!" said Hasan. "I recovered the padishah's thirty thousand gold liras and nobody hit me like that. Where did the blow come from?"

Soon, Hasan received a second blow on the neck. "How amazing!" he said. "I was able to get the lungs of the giant that lives in such and such a place. That is the sort of man I am! Who can be striking me like this?"

After receiving a third blow of this kind, he saw the girl before him, with her forty slave girls all around them in a ring like spectators. "Come!" he said boldly. "Let us wrestle!"

"All right," said the girl.

And they began to wrestle. In order to grab hold of him, the girl dashed right at him, but Hasan ran first to this side and then to that side, avoiding her in this way the entire morning until noon. When the heat of the noonday sun fell upon the girl's brains, Hasan lifted her up and threw her to the ground. Since that wrestling ground was covered with sand, the girl was buried knee-deep in the sand by that first throw. Very angry, the girl rushed up out of the sand, grabbed Hasan, and threw him to the ground so that he was now knee-deep in the sand. Rushing up out of the sand, Hasan now threw her to the ground so hard that she was buried waist-high in the sand. The girl rushed out and likewise threw Hasan so hard to the ground that he likewise was buried waist-high in the sand. Finally, when Hasan threw her to the ground for the third time, the girl was buried in the sand clear to the top of her head. At that moment, the girl raised her arms and began clapping her hands, and her forty female slaves, seeing this, began clapping their hands and shouting, "Our eldest sister has found her match, found her match!" For she had taken an oath that whoever could defeat her in a wrestling match would marry her, but whomever she defeated would be beheaded.

Hasan took the girl by the hand and helped her out of the sand, and then they went directly to her palace. That night and for several weeks afterward they remained there, and then Hasan told her that the time had come for him to return to his own kaza. "Don't be concerned about that," said the girl. "We'll all go together." Then she said to her forty female slaves, "Take us—palace, garden, and all—and place us in the meadow behind the palace of the padishah."

When Hasan awoke the next morning, he was surprised to see that they had come—palace, garden, flowers, slaves, and all—to his own town. That same morning when the padishah got up, he looked toward the meadow and then rubbed his eyes, astonished, for it seemed to him that the meadow was all red. He called his viziers to him and said, "Is our back meadow burning? What has happened? Look! It is red all over!"

The vizier to his right looked and saw that it was indeed red. The vizier to his left also looked and he, too, saw that it was really red. He said, "My padishah, could this be the work of Hasan the broom maker? You sent him to get a red flower. It looks as if he has brought not only the flower but also the garden where they grow and the palace as well." They all looked again and saw that it was all indeed real.

Of course, when Hasan arose, he went at once and brought to the girl's palace the two other girls, his mother, and all of the other things he owned. Then the third girl said to him, "Hasan, now you must go and have a suit of clothes made. Buy also a hat and shoes, making sure that everything you get is better than what is worn by the padishah. Then, dressed in your fine new clothes, go to the coffeehouse where the padishah usually goes, and if he pays one lira for his coffee or tea, you pay five liras. If he leaves a tip of two and a half liras, you should leave one of ten liras. Do this so that everyone will notice that you are superior to the padishah."

"All right," said Hasan. He ordered an elegant suit, and when it was ready he bought the finest hat and the finest shoes in the town. Dressed in his new clothes, he then went to the coffeehouse where the padishah usually went. When the padishah laid out five liras for his coffee and left a tip of one lira for each of the attendants, Hasan took from his sash ten liras for his coffee, and he left a tip of five liras apiece for the attendants. After this had gone on for several days, the padishah began to look less wealthy and less distinguished than Hasan, and the whole town began to talk about it. One day the padishah approached Hasan in the coffeehouse. "Hasan," he asked, "where did you find all this wealth?"

"In the name of Allah, my padishah, if you will come and visit me and eat a poor man's soup with me, I shall tell you."

"This is all very well, Hasan," said the padishah, "but you have come here like an immigrant. You must therefore first come and visit me, and then I shall go to visit you."

"Let me consider the matter this evening," said Hasan, "and I shall give you my answer tomorrow at the coffeehouse." Hasan wanted to ask the third girl about the matter and get her opinion on it. After he had arrived home, he said to this girl, "The padishah asked me where I had found all my wealth, and I told him that I would tell him if he would come to visit me and have some poor man's soup with me. The padishah refused to come to me until I had first visited him, saying that I had come to this town after the padishah had and was therefore like an immigrant. I must therefore, he said, visit him

132

before he could visit me."

"Well," said the girl, "ask the padishah whether you should come with your soldiers or without them."

"All right," said Hasan, and the next evening he went as usual to the coffeehouse. Once again he gave ten liras for his coffee and five liras apiece for the attendants, in this way showing that he was superior to the padishah.

"What did you decide?" asked the padishah.

"In the name of Allah, my padishah, I must ask you whether you wish me to come with or without my soldiers."

The padishah said to himself, "By Allah! All of the soldiers here are mine, and I am the ruler of this whole land. Who are the soldiers of this Hasan the broom maker? Will he collect the lame and the blind and bring them along to be fed?" But to Hasan he said, "Come with your soldiers."

In the meantime, Blackbird had decided to surrender herself completely to Hasan, so he was able to ride her at any time he wished. Before he rode Blackbird to the padishah's palace, therefore, Hasan groomed her thoroughly and made ready to mount her. The girl who had brought him back from the land of the fairies—with the palace and the garden and all—then called for a certain horn, and that horn was brought. From the horn there came forth first a group of trumpeters followed by foot soldiers and artillery men. Hasan led them to the palace of the padishah, and the line was so long that one end was at the palace while the other end was still coming forth from the horn.

Seeing this huge crowd coming, the padishah ordered his cooks to prepare forty caldrons of rice and forty caldrons of boiled wheat with meat and forty caldrons of stewed fruit. As the soldiers continued to file into the palace, the padishah realized that he could never feed so many, and *still* they kept coming. "*Aman, aman,* Hasan Effendi," he said, "send some of your soldiers back." So Hasan ordered the ones outside the palace to return. But those who remained filled the whole palace.

After waiting for a while, one of the soldiers left the palace to relieve himself. As he passed the kitchen, he noticed that there would not be enough food for all of them, so he tipped up a caldron of rice and ate the rice all by himself. Then he ate a caldron of boiled wheat with meat and a caldron of stewed fruit. When he had relieved himself, he returned to his fellow soldiers and told one of them, "There will not be nearly enough food for all of us. Go out and eat something before it is all gone." One by one by one the friends of that soldier went to the kitchen and helped themselves, and soon every caldron had been emptied. Word went among the rest of the soldiers that the food had already been finished, and they began shouting, "We are hungry! We are hungry!" The padishah, who had invited his viziers and many other important people to come, was unable to supply food for the dinner, so the soldiers turned around and marched away.

Then the padishah said, "Hasan, I was unable to feed all those soldiers.

133

How do you manage to feed them?"

"My padishah, one who can bring back your thirty thousand gold liras from a foreign state as well as a live giant and a palace with its garden and its flowers and its slaves can surely feed his own soldiers! Perhaps you would like to have dinner with me tomorrow." And the padishah agreed to come.

But since the padishah had been disgraced by his failure to feed Hasan's troops, he sent criers throughout the entire town to invite everyone from seven to seventy—rich or poor, noble or not—to Hasan's palace for dinner the following day. Hasan, too, heard the criers and he hastened home to see that enough food was being prepared.

"Do not worry, Hasan Bey," said the girl from the land of the fairies. "Let them come, and you shall see." And though the whole town gathered there, it filled only one huge room of the palace. Suddenly there were elegant tables and chairs provided for their seating, and coffee was served to all of them in silver cups on silver saucers.

The padishah looked at his left vizier and his right vizier and said, "How is this? Here I am padishah of this whole country, and I could not serve coffee to even half of these people at one time. And in silver cups on silver saucers!"

Afterward, the three girls set out the horn, and all sorts of good foods came forth from it. The forty female slaves served all these different foods to the guests, bringing and bringing, until they were all completely satisfied. Then, after the meal was finished, the forty female slaves served all the guests unsweetened coffee, this time in golden cups on golden saucers. Each slave carried a tray with ten gold cups on it.

Now, when the padishah saw those golden cups and golden saucers, he said to himself, "Although I am the padishah of this land, I do not have even one golden cup and golden saucer in my palace. I shall drink my coffee and then hide my cup and saucer in my sash and take them along with me."

When the slave serving the padishah and his most important officers came to collect the cups and saucers, she could find only nine for her tray. "I beg your pardon," she said, "but I have only nine cups now and I came with ten. One of them is missing. Give me back my cup, for if you do not, my elder brother will be angry with me."

The padishah could not take the cup and saucer out of his sash because then everyone would know that he had stolen them. But when they searched the clothes of everyone present, they found the cup and saucer in the padishah's sash. Then the slave girl took all ten of her cups and saucers and left.

At that time, the girl whom Hasan had taken from the foreign state said to him, "Hasan, now the padishah will ask you where you got all of your wealth. All three of us girls will dress beautifully, and we'll hide in a closet with a chair in our midst. Tell the padishah that you will *show* him the source of your wealth, and just pull open the closet curtain and show us to him. Then

135

come and sit on the chair, saying that you found your wealth through us."

"All right," said Hasan. "And indeed it is true!"

A little later that evening, the padishah asked, "Hasan, where did you get all of this wealth? Won't you tell us?"

"My padishah," said Hasan, "I shall *show* you the source of my wealth."

The padishah, his viziers, and all of the other most important guests left their tables and followed Hasan. Hasan pulled back the closet curtain and revealed the three gorgeously dressed girls, each one more beautiful than the others, and he said, "I found all of my wealth through them." Then he went and sat on the chair in their midst.

As soon as the padishah and his viziers had seen those girls, each as beautiful as hyacinths and angels, they began to quarrel among themselves as to which one should have which girl. As the quarrel became more heated, they started to hit one another until each one had either a huge bump on his head or a damaged eye. The girl who had brought Hasan back to his *kaza*—palace, garden, flowers, slave girls, and all—then said to her slave girls, "Take all of these fighting fools under your arms and throw them into the Sea of Marmara. Let them look among the fish for the girls they deserve!"

Immediately, the slave girls did as they were ordered. Then that girl appeared before the people and said, "You have all seen the unworthiness of your former padishah. From now on, your padishah will be the hero Hasan. May he live long!"

Thus it was that Hasan the broom maker became padishah. In time, he married all three girls, holding for each of them a wedding that lasted for forty days and forty nights. They had their wish fulfilled. Let us go up and sit in their seats.

[*Onlar ermiş muradına; / Biz çıkalım kerevetine.*]

How the Devil Entered the Ark

M any hundreds of years ago all of the tribes were rebelling against their leaders. No one was able to control all of the problems that this caused. Allah finally decided to do something about this. He appeared to Noah in a dream.

"Noah," he said, "I want you to build an ark. I want you to build it such and such a length and such and such a width and such and such a height. After you have the ark ready, take aboard that ark a pair, male and female, of every kind of animal."

Noah listened. Because he was one of Allah's beloved creatures, he did

136

137

not ask any questions. He just started to work. While he worked, everyone laughed at him but one old woman. This old woman, too, was one of Allah's beloved. She came to Noah and said, "Noah, when the time comes for you to take all the other creatures aboard the ark, please take me." Each day while Noah was building the ark, she went to visit him, and each day she took him a jar of cow's milk. And Noah kept on working.

When the ark had been built and the time came to load it, a pair of every kind of animal—even the ants—filed into it. The Devil had also wanted to board the ark, but he had not been permitted to do so, for he had turned against Allah and refused to believe in Him. The Devil therefore decided to enter the ark in the body of one of the animals being loaded. He entered the body of one of the two donkeys.

As that donkey was being loaded onto the ark, it became balky. When it got near the edge of the ark, it drew itself back. It became stubborn and would not move forward any farther. Noah pulled him hard and said, "Get in there, cursed one!" It was in this way that the Devil got aboard with the donkey.

Later when Noah discovered that the Devil was aboard, he said to him, "I did not invite you aboard this ark because Allah would not have wanted me to do so. You failed to obey Allah's orders, and then you turned against Him. Therefore I do not want you aboard my ark. Get off!"

"No. You invited me here," said the Devil. "When you were loading the donkey you invited me to come too, for you said, 'Get in there, cursed one!' and I got in."

When the ark was all loaded and Noah wanted to launch it, it would not move. The people on the ark said, "We have some evil person among us. That is why it will not move."

Then it was discovered that Jonah, who had failed to govern his tribe well and did not have Allah's permission to enter the ark, had sneaked aboard unnoticed. Confronted by the other people, he held up his finger and said, "I am the guilty one."

"Throw him overboard!" everyone shouted.

They threw Jonah—may he rest in peace!—into the sea, where a fish swallowed him. After he had been there for a while, the angels pleaded with Allah, "O Allah, please rescue Jonah for our sakes."

Jonah, who was in the belly of the fish, prayed in a different way to Allah: "I am here because of the cruelty of people. Please forgive my fault."

In the meantime, Noah had been able to launch the ark. But after the ark had sailed only a short distance, Noah was unable to find among its residents that old woman whom he had promised to take. He turned the ark back and began searching for this woman. Gabriel guided him to where the old woman lived. There Noah asked her, "O woman, haven't you noticed that something very unusual is happening?"

"Well, I have noticed for several days now that there has been mud on my cows' feet when they came home at night. That is the only unusual thing that I have seen."

By then the whole world had become one large sea. I cannot remember how long that great flood lasted.

Paradise or Hell?: A Choice Made

There were once two close friends—only Allah knows how! One was a pious Muslim who revered Allah and believed in His Prophet, prayed five times daily, fasted during Ramazan, gave alms, and had made the holy pilgrimage. He was an unworldly man, one who trusted he would escape the problems of this world in the next life. His friend, on the other hand, was a pleasure seeker who lived a full and worldly life. He lived every day as if he would never die. Still, the two were very close friends.

As Allah would have it, both men died at exactly the same hour on exactly the same day. Of course, the good Muslim went to Paradise and the other one went to Hell. Let's consider now the one who went to Paradise.

As soon as he had arrived there, the guardian Gabriel said, "Here you can have anything you want. Just ask, and you will receive it." Well, the man went here and there, looking at everything and liking everything he saw. Still, he was not quite satisfied. Why was that? He missed his good friend, that worldly man. And in all his looking, he had not found his friend in Paradise.

"I know!" he said one day. "Gabriel told me I could have anything I asked for. I'll just ask to visit my friend, wherever he may be." So he went to see Gabriel. "Gabriel Effendi," he said, "you told me when I came here that I could have anything I asked for. Is that really true?"

"Of course, my good man," said Gabriel.

"Then I'd like to visit my friend, my closest friend during all the years I spent in the mortal world."

"Ah," said Gabriel. "That can be arranged. Let's see, now. Was your friend a good Muslim?"

The man thought for a moment. "Well, he was not exactly a *good* Muslim. At least, I have not been able to find him anywhere here in Paradise."

"Hmmnn," said Gabriel. "He must then have gone to Hell. Let me look in the directory for him. What was his name?"

"His name was Mustafa. He was the son of İbrahim and the grandson of Musa." So Gabriel looked in the directory very carefully, and then he looked again.

"I don't find his name here anywhere," said Gabriel at last. "Tell me. Exactly how good a Muslim *was* your friend?"

"Well, Gabriel Effendi, he wasn't a good Muslim at all. Still, he was my best friend, and I long to see him again."

"Ah! He must then have been sent to the lowest section of Hell, to Esfelüssafilin," Gabriel said, and he reached down for a dusty ledger at the very bottom of the pile of directories. He blew the dust from the ledger and then he opened it. As Allah would have it, Mustafa's name was the very first one on the very first page. "Yes. Here it is," he said. "Do you still want to visit him?"

"Oh, yes!" said the good one. "But how am I to get there? I do not know the way."

"I'll provide you with a round-trip ticket. Within a few hours, you will see your friend again." As he handed him the ticket, Gabriel wished him well on his journey.

True enough, in three or five hours the good man found himself outside a barroom in Esfelüssafilin. Pushing open the door, the man looked for his friend, and right away he saw Mustafa at the bar drinking *rakı*. Each saw the other at the same time, and they rushed to embrace one another in greeting. "Come and have some *rakı* while we talk," said Mustafa as he led him to the bar.

"*Rakı?* I never in the mortal world tasted *rakı*. Is it good?"

"Oh, indeed it is!" said Mustafa. "And I suppose you don't have such drinks where you are now. It's Paradise, I suppose. Do you like it there?"

"Yes, I like it all right," said the Muslim. "But how I miss the company of my best friend!"

"Then come," said Mustafa, "and let's drink to that friendship."

The Muslim hesitated. Then he remembered that he had already been accepted in Paradise and that this was only a visit. Surely he could celebrate their visit . . . So he slapped his hand on the bar, and when the barmaid came, he said, "I'll have some *rakı*, please."

"Well, then," said the barmaid, "where is your money?"

"Money?" said the Muslim. "Where I come from, we don't have to pay for anything."

"Ha! Down here, we pay for *everything*," she said, and she went on to serve another customer.

The Muslim was surprised and disappointed. "Come, my friend," Mustafa said. "We'll try the next barroom." And they walked along a bit to the next barroom and entered there, talking all the while, just as they had in the mortal world. When they reached the bar, the Muslim slapped his hand on the bar, and, "I'll have *rakı*, please," he said.

The barmaid came at once, but, "Where is your money?" she asked.

"Money? Where I come from, we don't have to pay for anything."

"Well," she said, "down here you pay for *everything*." And she moved on to the next customer.

141

"Never mind," said Mustafa. "We'll try the next barroom." And the two friends walked along the street to a third barroom, talking all the while as they went, just as they had in the mortal world. As soon as they had reached the bar, the Muslim slapped his hand on the bar and said, "I'll have some *rakı*."

"Oh?" said the barmaid. "Then where is your money?"

"Money?" said the Muslim. "Where I come from, we don't have to pay for anything."

"Ha! Down here, we pay for *everything*," she said, and she started to move along to another customer.

But, "Here. I'll pay for my friend's *rakı*," said Mustafa, and he laid the coins on the bar.

"You *know* that won't work down here!" the barmaid said. "Everyone here pays for his own!" And she turned away.

"Well, the chances of a Turk are three," said Mustafa. "We'll just have to celebrate by talking. It's too bad we can't have as much time to talk as we had in the mortal world."

Suddenly the Muslim smiled. "I have an idea," he said. "You go and stand outside the first barroom we visited. I liked that one best. Wait right there for me." And he hurried along the street, talking with one person and another until he had found the one he needed. Then he returned to that first barroom, where Mustafa was waiting for him. "Let's go inside. I'm ready for that *rakı* now, and for all the talking we could ever want."

The two friends walked inside and went directly to the bar. When the Muslim slapped his hand on the bar, that same barmaid came. "I'll have some *rakı*," he said, and he laid several coins on the bar.

Both the barmaid and Mustafa were surprised. "Where did you get the money?" asked Mustafa.

"Oh, it was easy," said the Muslim. "I sold my return ticket."

The Dragon-Prince and Banu

Once there was and once there wasn't an old woman who had three daughters. The two older daughters always stayed at home with their mother, but the youngest one, named Banu, used to go and work and bring food home to her mother and sisters.

One day as Banu was passing through the marketplace, she saw a crowd gathered around a man. She approached the group to see what the man might be selling. The man was saying, "I have a house to sell. You will regret it if you buy it; you will regret it if you do not buy it." Banu did not understand how both of these things could be true, but she was curious. She waited, but no one offered to buy the house.

Suddenly, "I'll buy the house!" Banu called. To her surprise, the man accepted the very low price Banu offered, and he sold the house to her. But in truth, the house was haunted. Whoever had bought that house would be found dead the following morning. The man who had sold the house to Banu had been the last owner, and his wife had been found dead that very morning. Of course, he did not tell Banu about that, but he took her directly to the house. It was an immense house, with forty rooms. In its garden were all kinds of flowers and fruits.

Banu was very happy. She ran back to her mother's old cottage and told her mother and her sisters all that had happened. Then she took her mother and her sisters to see the new house. On the way, they bought a loaf of bread and a jar of yogurt. When they arrived at the house, Banu said to her mother, "I want to see the rest of the house, so just put my share of bread and yogurt under the table. I'll eat them later."

Banu walked here and there through the house for two or three hours, and then she felt hungry, so she went to the kitchen. Both her share of the bread and her share of the yogurt were gone. But in the bottom of the yogurt jar was a big diamond! Banu could scarcely believe her eyes. She left the house with the diamond in her pocket, and returned to the cottage to her mother and sisters.

The next day, Banu went to the marketplace and sold the diamond for one thousand pieces of gold. With the gold, she bought for herself and her mother and her sisters new clothes and plenty of food. Still, she was puzzled about how this wonderful thing had happened.

That evening, she went again to the new house with bread and a jar of yogurt. She put the bread and the yogurt under the table. Then she hid herself behind a large water jar in the kitchen and waited. After midnight, she heard a noise. Suddenly the wall of the kitchen cracked, and a huge dragon walked in. He ate the bread and the yogurt. Then he dropped a diamond from his mouth into the empty yogurt jar.

As the dragon turned back and passed through the cracked wall, Banu followed him. After walking for hours, they came to a beautiful garden with fountains and roses. The dragon stood under one of the fountains, and as the water passed over him he changed into a very handsome prince. At that moment, Banu fell in love with him.

The prince walked toward a beautifully decorated bed, lay down there, and fell sound asleep. Then a very ugly woman came and stood beside the bed and said, "This is the punishment you get, young prince, for not marrying my daughter. You will stay like that forever unless someone takes that magic diamond ring from your finger. And no one in the world will be able to do that, since no one will see you." She disappeared, laughing.

Banu had, of course, hidden herself well, and she waited in her hiding place until she was sure no one would see her. Then she slowly approached the sleeping prince. She saw the beautiful diamond ring on his finger. Gently she lifted his hand and removed the ring. The prince awoke and saw Banu, as beautiful as the fourteenth of the moon.

"Who are you?" he asked. "And how did you come here?"

Banu told him the whole story. She told him, too, what she had heard the ugly old woman say as he lay sleeping. The prince said, "We must escape at once, before that ugly witch sees us."

They began to run, hand in hand, without looking back even once. They ran over mountains and through valleys until they had reached the palace of the young prince. There the prince's father prepared a wedding ceremony that lasted forty days and forty nights. But before Banu and the prince were married, they went together to the seashore and threw the diamond ring into the depths of the sea. Thus they were able to live safely and happily for the rest of their lives.

May we have a share of their good fortune!

Hasan Plucks Three Geese

In the days of the sultanate, many young men from Anatolia did their military service in İstanbul acting as guards of the property of the sultan of their time. A young man from Anatolia named Hasan was about to be discharged from the army after having served for three or five years. "But how can I convince the people of my village that I have actually spent all this time serving as a palace guard in İstanbul?" he asked himself. "I know what they will say to me: 'Hasan, you say that you served for three or five years at the palace of the sultan, but did you ever actually *see* our sultan?' " He decided that he must somehow manage to see the sultan before he left.

At first the attendants at the palace gate refused to admit him into the ruler's presence, but he insisted so long that they finally asked the sultan if he would admit this soldier into his presence. The sultan was willing, and Hasan was admitted.

"Why do you wish to see me?" asked the sultan.

"Sir, I have served at your door for three or five years. Now that I have completed my military duty, I am about to return to my village in Anatolia. If I tell the people there that I served at the palace of the sultan, they may think I am lying. They will probably say, 'You claim that you served at the palace of the sultan, but did you ever actually *see* our sultan?' The fact is, my sultan, that in all the years of service I performed, it was not until now that I ever saw you. That is why I wanted to see you."

"Well, have you seen me now, Hasan?"

"Yes, my sultan."

"Take a seat there while I ask you a question. If you can answer it, that will be fine, but if you cannot answer it, I shall have you arrested." Then the sultan asked, "What is the distance between day and night?"

After thinking about this question for a short while, Hasan answered, "My sultan, there is really no distance at all between day and night, for they are connected to each other."

"Here is my second question," said the sultan. "Hasan, are you able to pluck a goose?"

"Of course I can."

"Then sit over there at that side," said the sultan. He then ordered one of his servants, "Have my first and second and third viziers come in here." After these officials had entered the room and bowed before the sultan, he said to them, "I am going to ask you a question. If you can answer it, that will be fine. If you cannot answer it, I shall have you arrested, placed in prison, and given a week to discover the answer. If you still cannot give me the correct answer, I shall then have you executed." He then put to them the same question he had asked Hasan: "What is the distance between day and night?" When they could not answer this question, he ordered, "Take them away!" They were sent to a special prison, and Hasan was sent with them.

In prison the viziers thought and thought in an effort to calculate the distance between day and night while Hasan sat watching them. On the morning when their time was up and they were to return to the sultan with the correct answer, Hasan said to them, "Ağas, you have been thinking very deeply and intently. I may possibly be of some use to you. What is your problem?"

One of the viziers answered, "Hasan, we have been trying unsuccessfully to determine the distance between day and night."

"Oh, that is a very easy question to answer," said Hasan. "I can solve that problem for you quickly, but I shall charge you one hundred gold liras apiece to do so." The viziers ordered that one hundred gold liras be brought for each of them. When Hasan received this money, he said, "Ağas, there is no distance at all between day and night, for they are joined to one another."

The viziers found this answer entirely convincing. They then went to the palace, and Hasan went with them. When the proper time arrived, all four of them went upstairs to enter the presence of the sultan. He said to the viziers, "Well, have you solved the problem?"

"Yes, sir, we have. We found that there was no distance whatsoever between day and night. They are connected."

"All right. Be seated." Then turning to Hasan, he said, "I sent you three geese to be plucked. Did you pluck them, Hasan?"

145

"Yes, sir, I did."

"Where are the feathers?"

Taking from his sash the sack he had filled with the three hundred gold liras, Hasan said, "Right here, sir."

The three viziers were greatly embarrassed by all of this, but on the other hand, they were also very pleased to have saved their necks from the executioner.

What Would You Do Then?

One day two friends were walking through a forest. One of these friends, Hasan, was quite a coward. In order to feel a little safer in that dangerous place, he said to his friend, "Ahmet, suppose a bear should come along while we are going through this forest. What would you do?"

"I have my pistol with me," Ahmet answered. "I would just shoot him and kill him."

"That would be fine," said Hasan, greatly relieved for the moment. But soon he started worrying again, so he said, "Ahmet, suppose a bear should come along and you did not have your pistol. What would you do then?"

"Well, Hasan, I always carry my hunting knife. I would draw that knife and stab the bear to death."

"Ah, that would be good!" said Hasan, and again he was at ease for a little while. But as the forest became more dense, his fear returned, and again he questioned his friend. "Ahmet, suppose a bear should come along and you didn't have either your pistol or your hunting knife. What would you do then?"

Ahmet answered, "You see that I am carrying my pickax. If I didn't have my pistol or my knife, I would hit the bear on the head with this pickax and kill him."

"That would be the best thing to do," said Hasan, breathing more easily. He even forgot his fear of the bear for a few minutes, but then his anxiety returned. He said, "Ahmet, suppose a bear should come along and you didn't have your pistol or your hunting knife or your pickax. What would you do then?"

Quite annoyed by now, Ahmet shouted, "See here, Hasan. Let's get this straight. Are you on *my* side or on the *bear's* side?"

Nasreddin Hoca and the 999 Liras

One day Nasreddin Hoca prayed to Allah for one thousand liras, saying, "Allah, if there is one lira less than one thousand in the bag you send, I shall not accept it."

A neighbor of the Hoca's was standing outside the house listening through his chimney as the Hoca was praying. Now, this neighbor was known to be a miser, but he was also a practical joker, and he decided to play a trick on the Hoca.

He went home and put 999 liras into a bag and tied the bag tightly. Then he returned to Nasreddin Hoca's house, climbed up on the roof, and dropped the bag down through the chimney. When the Hoca saw the bag, he stared in amazement. Then, grabbing the bag, he untied it and began counting the coins. When he had counted the 999 liras, he opened his hands toward heaven and said, "O Almighty Allah! You have given me 999 liras today. I am sure that in the future you will give me the one lira that is missing." Then he tucked the bag with the 999 liras into his sash.

His stingy neighbor, who was listening through the chimney, regretted what he had done. He came down quickly from the roof, knocked at the door, and explained to the Hoca that it was he, not Allah, who had dropped the money down. "It was only a joke, Hoca Effendi. We shall laugh together over this many times, but now give me my money back and I shall go home."

Nasreddin Hoca would do nothing of the sort. He argued that Allah had sent him the money in answer to his prayer. Upon hearing this, the neighbor said, "If you do not return my money, I shall take my case to the *kadı*." He went, in fact, and complained to the *kadı* about Nasreddin Hoca, and the Hoca was summoned to appear before the *kadı*.

When he heard this, the Hoca said to his miserly neighbor, "I cannot go to court, for I have no suitable clothes to wear." The neighbor had never been known to *give* anything to anybody, but now he offered to lend the Hoca a suit of clothes and a turban so that he could appear in court to answer the charge against him.

"Thank you, neighbor," said the Hoca as he accepted the clothes. "Of course, I'll have to walk, since my donkey is lame, so I may be late for the hearing."

"You mustn't be late," said the neighbor. "I'll let you borrow my second donkey, and we can ride there together." The Hoca agreed, and then he went along to his house with the borrowed clothes and the borrowed turban and the borrowed donkey.

148

On the day of the hearing, he and his neighbor appeared before the *kadı* and the neighbor stated his complaint.

"Well, Hoca," said the *kadı*, "now I'll take your evidence. What is your defense against his claim?"

"Only that my neighbor is lying," said the Hoca, "and I think I can prove it. Before long, he will claim that even the suit I am wearing belongs to him."

The neighbor was astonished at this turn of affairs. "Why, it does!" exclaimed the neighbor. "Of course it is mine, and so is the turban that he is wearing."

"And of course the donkey on which I rode belongs to you?" said the Hoca, with his voice calm and his smile merry.

"Ah, yes, the donkey is mine, too," said the neighbor.

"You see what I mean," said the Hoca, not the least bit upset. "*Kadı* Effendi, he claims that the clothes I am wearing and even the donkey I rode belong to him. No wonder he claims that the money belongs to him, too." He then turned to his neighbor and said sternly, "From now on, don't you ever dare to interfere again in my affairs with Allah."

The *kadı* acquitted Nasreddin Hoca on this evidence.

The Farmer and the Bear

Once a bear and a farmer became friends. The bear used to steal things from here and there—especially honey and butter—and he would always bring some of these things to the farmer, saying, "Take these, but don't ever tell your wife where they came from, or I'll tear you limb from limb."

To find out whether the farmer was telling his wife or not, the bear used to listen through the chimney opening as they talked. Every day, the wife asked her husband, "Where are all these good things coming from?"

And every day, the farmer begged his wife just to enjoy the things he brought her but not to ask where they came from. "Eat the grapes, but do not ask from whose vineyard they come," he reminded her. But still she kept at him and *at* him, until finally the poor farmer's patience was exhausted, and he decided to tell his wife his secret. "I'll tell you," he said, "but don't ever tell it to anyone else. I have a bear friend who steals butter and honey and these other good things from the neighbors and shares them with me."

Now, the bear was listening to this conversation, and he became very angry. The next time he saw the farmer, he said, "Don't you remember what I told you? You'll get no more good things from me, and when you're out in your field I'll tear you limb from limb."

The farmer became very anxious about this, and he looked here and there the next day as he left his house to plow. As he was plowing, he kept one eye on the plow and the other on that matter of the bear. Suddenly a fox came along. "How are you doing, my old friend?" asked the fox.

"I am all right now, but I have a bear friend that is going to tear me limb from limb because I told my wife that he brought me good things that he stole from our neighbors."

Hearing this, the fox said to the farmer, "Will you give me one of your testicles to eat if I save you from the bear?"

The farmer thought about this for a while, and then he said, "All right. I'll give you one of my testicles to eat if you save me from the bear."

Then the fox explained his plan. "I shall tie to my tail some dry bushes, which I shall set afire and then run through the village shouting, 'The padishah of İstanbul wants a hundred bears. Ninety-nine of them have been found, but there is still one lacking.' If your bear friend looks frightened while I am shouting this, tell him to get into the big canvas sack that you have, and then you tie it shut while he is still inside." The fox looked and saw the bear coming, so he tied the bushes to his tail, set them afire, and started shouting as he ran to the village, "The padishah of İstanbul wants one hundred bears. Ninety-nine of them have been found, but there is still one lacking."

When the bear heard this, he was afraid, and he started looking for a place to hide. The farmer shouted to him, "Here! Here! Get in here!" And when the bear had gotten into the sack, the farmer tied it shut. Then the farmer gave the bear a good beating with his goad stick. When the fox returned, he told the farmer to go home and bring back a jug full of hot water. They poured hot water over the bear in the sack, and then they beat him again. They did this several times, with several jugs of hot water and several beatings, so that when they finally let the bear out of the sack, all his hair was gone and he was white all over.

As soon as the bear had escaped, he went to his bear friends and told them what had happened to him. He collected all his bear friends and led them to the village and right to the house of the farmer. Now, the farmer saw all those bears as they were approaching, and he became badly frightened. Seeking safety, he rushed to the minaret and climbed the winding stairs to the balcony. From there, he looked down at all those bears. The hairless bear saw him and pointed him out to the other bears.

The farmer had locked the door at the base of the minaret, but the hairless bear said to the others, "Now I shall stand at the foot of the minaret, and one of you will get up on my shoulders, and then the next one will get up on his shoulders, and so on until the one on top can reach the farmer."

The bears did this, and as the last bear was just about to reach for the farmer, that farmer shouted in a loud voice from the balcony of the minaret, "Bring me two jugs full of hot water!" When the hairless bear heard this, he panicked and started running away. All the bears that had been above him came tumbling down, and they were all killed. The farmer skinned all those bears and made much money from them. With some of the money, he bought a lamb for the fox and thus he was able to keep his testicle.

From Felek *to* Elek

Once a man from here had his camel stolen. He went north thirty kilometers to a man at Çerkeş who was known to be a thief and asked him, "Have you seen my camel?"

The man said nothing, but this thief's wife said as she was sifting flour through her *elek* [sieve],

"What came and what went through *felek!*
What a lot of flour went through *elek!*"

The fact was that he had taken the camel and sold it, considering the camel his destiny, or *felek*. With the money from the camel he had bought wheat and had it ground into the flour now being sifted by his wife through her *elek*.

The Mortality of a Caldron

One day back in those old days Nasreddin Hoca needed a big caldron. He looked everywhere in his own house but could not find there any caldron that was big enough. He therefore went to the home of a neighbor to see if he could borrow such a caldron. When the neighbor lent him one, the Hoca took it home and used it to accomplish the work he was doing.

A few days later the Hoca put a small caldron inside the large one and took them both to the home of the neighbor. When the neighbor opened the door to the Hoca's knocking, he was surprised to find the Hoca carrying two caldrons, one inside the other. "What is the meaning of this, Hoca?" he asked.

The Hoca said, "The big caldron is the one I borrowed from you and the little one is its child. It was born in my house, but of course it belongs to you." The neighbor was delighted with this news, and he accepted the new caldron with pleasure. The Hoca thanked him for the loan and then returned home.

After a while the Hoca again needed a large caldron. He went to the same neighbor and asked to borrow his caldron again. The neighbor gladly lent it to the Hoca, for he supposed that each time it was lent it would be returned with a little one.

Anyway, the Hoca got the caldron and carried it home. After three or five days, the neighbor was still waiting for the return of the caldron, but the Hoca did not bring it. Then when he couldn't wait any longer, the neighbor went to the Hoca's house and knocked on the door. As the Hoca opened the door, the neighbor said, "Hoca, you borrowed a caldron from me the other day but you have not returned it yet. Are you finished with it?"

"Yes, I am finished with it, but I forgot to tell you something sad about it. Your caldron has passed away, but may you live long."

"*Aman!* Do not say so!" said the neighbor, surprised. "How could a caldron die? What a nonsensical thing to say!"

The Hoca answered, "You accepted that a caldron could give birth to a small caldron. Why, then, can't you accept that a caldron can die?"

The Cock, the Fox, and the Renewed Ablutions

Once there was and once there wasn't a cock. This cock had gone to find food on a plain. It was close to sunset, and soon it began to grow dark. Afraid for his safety, the cock flew up to the branch of a tree to roost there for the night. Then he crowed.

A fox came running to the foot of the tree and said to the cock:

"Effendi!
I came with speed, you see.
You chanted the *ezan* for me."

Then the fox said, "Why don't you come down here so that we can worship together?"

"Very well," said the cock. But then he saw two hunters and a hound approaching, and he said, "Let us wait until those hunters and their hound arrive, so that we may have a larger congregation."

Thereupon, the fox, who was afraid of the hunters and the hound, said, "Pardon, friend, but I must go and renew my ablutions." So saying, he ran away.

It Can't Be Mine!

While Temel was working on a large construction site, the wooden scaffold on which he was standing collapsed, and Temel fell down. In the fall, unfortunately, one of his ears was torn off. He called to his friends, "Friends, my ear broke off! Come and help me look for it!"

His friends finally found the missing ear in the construction rubble and gave it to Temel. Temel took the ear in his hands, turned it over and over, and then said, "Friends, this ear is not mine."

His friends said to him, "Why isn't it yours, Temel? No one else's ear has been broken off except yours."

"I don't care about that. There was a pencil above mine!"

Seven Brothers and a Sister

Once there was and once there wasn't, in the old days, when the sieve was in the straw, when camels were barbers and the cock was a town crier—well, in such very old times, there was a man who had seven sons but no daughter. When these boys were attending school, one of their classmates was visited by his brother-in-law. Someone said to the seven brothers, "Look at that man. He is Hasan's brother-in-law. Wouldn't it be nice to have a brother-in-law? If only one of you had been a girl, then it would be possible for the rest of you to have had a brother-in-law."

That day as they returned from school, the seven brothers talked about this matter. "It *would* be nice to have a brother-in-law. Our mother is expecting another child. İnşallah, it will be a girl this time."

"Yes," said another. "Ali has a sister and Hasan has three sisters and Abdullah has two sisters. I want a sister, too!" So they made a plan.

When they arrived home, the oldest brother said, "Mother, today a classmate put us all to shame because we have no brother-in-law. This hurt us all badly. You are soon to have another baby. İnşallah, that baby will be a girl. We are all upset by what happened at school today, so upset that we are going to leave home and live by ourselves in the forest. We shall watch for a sign from you. If it has been written on our foreheads that we will have a sister this time, then as soon as the girl is born, hang a flour sieve on the oleander tree in front of our house so that we can know we have a sister. If you have another boy, hang a straw sieve there instead. We'll look now and then through our binoculars to see whether a flour sieve or a straw sieve is hanging there. If we see a flour sieve, we'll come home again to live. If it's a straw sieve we see, we'll leave you with that eighth boy and live our own lives apart from you."

After saying this, the oldest son and his brothers gathered their hunting equipment and this and that, and then they left. They went a little; they went far; they went for one autumn over hill and dale. They went and they went, but when they stopped to look back, they found that they had gone only the length of a grain of barley in their journey.

Finally they reached a forest, where they stopped and built a house for themselves. One day passed, five days passed, several more days passed, and they came time and again to the edge of the forest to look through their binoculars, but all that they saw hanging on the oleander tree was a straw sieve.

155

Now, it happened that a neighbor woman had been listening outside the chimney when the oldest son was talking to his mother. This neighbor had had no children at all, and she was envious of the mother with seven fine sons. When the sons' mother had had her baby—Allah be praised!—it was a girl! As soon as she could go outside, the mother hung a flour sieve on the oleander tree so that her seven sons would know the news and come home again. *Aman!* The envious neighbor took down the flour sieve and put a straw sieve in its place, and there it stayed.

Again and again the sons looked—even seven years and eight years and ten years later—but still there was only the straw sieve on the oleander tree. During all of this time, the brothers' house cat had made a visit each year to their mother's house. Now, the mother had had a daughter and that daughter grew and grew, to seven, to eight, to ten years of age. One day the girl said to her mother, "Mother, here is that cat again. It has been visiting us now for at least seven years. Whose cat is it?"

Her mother began to cry. "Daughter, you have seven brothers, and the cat belongs to them. He comes here once every year, but your brothers never come at all."

"I have *seven brothers?* Well, if they do not come to see us, then I shall go to see them. I shall follow that cat the next time it comes and in that way I shall find my brothers."

When the cat visited the next year, the girl was determined to follow it back in order to find her seven brothers. Before she left, her mother warned her, "My daughter, along its route this cat will pass over Boncuk Mountain. You had better not follow it. For if you do, you will be fascinated by the many kinds of beads there, stopping to pick up this bead and that bead, and then you may never return home to me."

"I'll be watchful, Mother. But I must go to find my brothers." Saying this, she left with the cat. But when they reached Boncuk Mountain, the girl started to pick up colorful beads here and there, and while she was busy doing this, the cat ran on ahead and out of sight. When she could not find the cat, the girl cried and cried, with her two eyes like two fountains. But crying helped her not at all, so she walked back the way she had come, and finally she reached her own home.

Again the next year the cat came for its visit, and once again the girl followed it when it left. This time, however, she tied a bandage over her eyes so she would not be tempted by the beads, and she kept her hand on the cat's back until they had descended on the other side of Boncuk Mountain. In this way, at last she reached the house her brothers had built. But they were away from home, hunting, and no one answered when she knocked—*Tak! Tak! Tak!* She tried the door and it was unlocked, so she went inside. She swept the house, put everything in order, cooked food, and then she hid herself before the brothers returned.

When the brothers arrived home, they discovered that the house had been cleaned and neatly arranged and that their dinner had been prepared. They said to the cat, "This does not look like your work. You have never cleaned the house or cooked meals. Who has been here to do these good things?"

But the cat told them nothing at all, and they wondered more and more about it, for each day when they came home they found the house cleaned and the meal cooked. After three or five days had gone by, the youngest brother said to the oldest one, "Oh, my oldest brother, why don't you remain here at home tomorrow and find out who it is who does all these things? This delicious food does not just come here by itself!"

The oldest brother accepted this suggestion, and the next day he stayed at home when the other six left for work. But because he was a hunting man who spent most of his time outdoors, he became very drowsy, and soon he fell asleep—*horol, horol*. While he slept, his sister came out from her hiding place and swept the floors, cooked the meal, carried the water, and then hid herself again. Thus the oldest brother did not discover anything at all.

The following day, the next brother remained at home to watch while the other six went hunting. But he, too, was not accustomed to being indoors all day, and he too fell sound asleep—*horol, horol*. While he slept, his sister swept the floors and cooked the meal and carried the water, and her brother never even saw her.

One by one by one, then, the first six brothers all failed to discover who it was who was doing these good things for them. On the seventh day, it was

the turn of the youngest brother. He looked here and there throughout the house to be certain that no one was there, and for a while he watched very diligently. Finally he, too, felt drowsy, and he lay down to rest, but he first took the broom and placed it beneath his head as a kind of pillow. "Before anyone can sweep the floors, I will be awakened," he said to himself.

After he had fallen asleep, the sister came out from her hiding place, cooked a meal, and carried some water, but when she reached for the broom, she found her brother lying on it. Gently, gently, she moved his head to get the broom from beneath it, but her brother awoke. When he looked at this young girl, he was amazed. "Are you a human being or a jinn?" he asked.

"I am a human being like yourself," she said, "a creature of the same great Allah who made you."

"But who *are* you?"

"I am your sister, a child of the same mother and father that you have."

"No. We have no sister. If we had a sister, we would be living at home instead of in this forest."

The girl had brought with her in her sash three or five apples from their family orchard. Taking out one apple, she showed it to her brother, saying, "See! This apple is from such and such a tree in our orchard."

Just as soon as the youngest brother saw the apple, he knew that it was indeed from a tree in their orchard, and he knew too that the girl was really his sister. "So we *were* destined to see the day when we would have a sister!" he said. They embraced one another, both crying for joy, and they spent the rest of the day talking.

The other six brothers spent the day hunting, and by the time they returned in the evening, the youngest brother had hidden their sister again. As soon as they arrived, they asked him, "What did you see? Did you find out who it was?"

"No. Like all the rest of you, I too failed to discover anyone here." But after they had eaten their good dinner, he asked, "What would you say if I told you that we really *do* have a sister and that she is the one who comes and cleans our house every day and cooks our meal?"

"We *can't* have a sister," said the oldest brother. "You remember how many times we went to look, and there was always a straw sieve hanging on the oleander tree."

"He's right," said the middle brother. "There was never a flour sieve hanging on that tree, so how could we have a sister?"

"If you saw our sister, would you believe me?" said the youngest brother. "I can call her here if you wish."

"Very well, then. Do so!"

"Come out, Sister!" the youngest one called.

She came out at once, and, oh, she seemed to her seven brothers the most beautiful girl in the world. They all talked at once because they were so happy. At last, they had the sister they had all wanted.

Before the seven brothers left the following morning, the oldest one said to his sister, "Today, since you are here, we shall leave our dog and our cat inside the house to keep you company while we are gone. But they are not accustomed to being inside. If the dog barks, feed him. If the cat meows, feed him *his* food. If you do not feed the dog, he will urinate in the fireplace and put out the fire, and you will be unable to make another fire. You will be unable to get coals for a new fire anywhere, for we live at a great distance from any other house. If you do not feed the cat, he will go and upset the lamp, and you will then have no way to light it again."

A few days passed without any difficulty. Then one day the girl remembered the beads she had picked up on Boncuk Mountain the year before. "I brought those beads in a sack inside my blouse," she said to herself. "Instead of just sitting here and doing nothing the rest of the day, I'll string my beads." She took the sack and a spool of thread from her blouse and began to string her beads.

While she was working on the beads, the dog barked, *"Hav! Hav! Hav!"* A moment later, the cat meowed, but the girl was so interested in stringing her beads that she forgot what her oldest brother had told her about feeding the animals. When the dog barked a second time and the cat meowed a second time, she remembered, and she said, "Wait just a minute. I have a few more beads to string, and then I'll feed you both."

But when the dog barked again and the cat meowed again and the girl *still* had not fed them, true enough, the dog urinated in the fireplace, putting out the fire, and the cat upset the lamp, leaving the room in darkness. *Then* the girl fed the dog and the cat, but there was no way of rekindling the fire or relighting the lamp. The girl began to cry. But would crying do any good? At last she went outside and climbed up on the roof to see what she could see.

Ah! There was smoke rising from a fire a great distance away. "I'll go there and get some coals to relight our fire," she told herself. She came down from the roof and got a bowl for the coals. And then she walked and walked and walked and walked and at last she came to the place from which the smoke was rising. There she saw a giant sleeping—*HOROL, HOROL*—on the ground, and there were seven women boiling bulgur. Approaching these women, she said, "Oh, sisters! I am a woman like you. I live by myself in a house on top of that mountain over there, and I have come to you to ask for some fire. Will you give me some?"

"Little sister, that giant over there has counted every one of these coals, and if he finds even one of them missing, he will eat all of us." But the women talked among themselves and finally decided to break off a small piece from each of the coals so that the giant could not know his loss. With tongs they broke little pieces of the coals into her earthenware bowl and they also put into her apron some bulgur that she could eat on the way home.

159

As the girl walked toward her brothers' house, carrying the coals very carefully and eating the bulgur, she kept looking behind her for fear of the giant. Suddenly she stumbled over a stone in the path and fell down. She saved the coals, but one of her toes began to bleed and the spool of thread she had used to string her beads fell on the ground and began to unwind. As she walked on, the thread trailed along behind her. Finally she reached home with the coals and relighted the fire and the lamp.

In the meantime, however, the giant had awakened. Arising, he sniffed to the left and he sniffed to the right, and he said, "Ah, there is here the scent of a rose that has not been touched by human hands."

"How you talk!" the women said. "Who would ever come into the presence of a giant like you?"

But the giant kept on sniffing, and then he began to look around here and there, examining the ground nearby. Seeing some faint footprints, he began to follow them, and he came at last to the place where the girl had fallen down. There he saw some drops of blood and a few grains of bulgur. Licking up the drops of blood, he found the end of the thread, and he followed, licking, licking, and rolling up the thread as he went along. Finally he came to the door of the brothers' house. "Open the door!" he shouted.

"No!"

"Open the door!"

"No!"

Finally the giant said to the girl, "All right, then, but stick your little finger out through the knothole in the door so that I can suck on it a bit."

Afraid of the giant, the girl put her little finger through the knothole, and the giant began to suck on it—*tsıts, tsıts, tsıts*. This sucking made the girl feel so weak that she sank to the floor.

When her brothers came home that night, they noticed at once how pale her face looked. "What happened, my sister?" asked the youngest brother.

But to that question and the others that followed, she gave no answer. "It is nothing, brothers. It is nothing."

The giant came day after day—three days, five days, and several days after that—and the girl's face grew more and more pale. Every day, her brothers pleaded with her, "Tell us, Sister. What has been happening to you? Please tell us. It would be a disgrace if we seven brothers should not be able to find a remedy for our sister's condition."

Finally the girl revealed to them all that had happened. "My oldest brother, I did not listen carefully enough to your advice," she said. "I let the dog put out the fire in the fireplace and the cat overturn the lamp. I walked and walked and walked to find some coals to rekindle the fire and relight the lamp. But the coals belonged to a giant, and he followed me here. Each day he sucks and sucks on my little finger—*tsıts, tsıts, tsıts*—and this leaves me very weak."

160

When the brothers heard this, were they angry! "How could any giant dare to come here to our house and do this to our sister?" After discussing the matter for some time, they said to the girl, "Sister, tomorrow when that giant comes, at first refuse to open the door. When he wants to suck your finger, refuse this too. Then when he again says to open the door, open it and leave the rest to us."

The seven brothers prepared their bows and arrows and their spears and then they hid themselves in various parts of the house. The next morning, the giant came again and shouted, "Open the door!"

"No!"

"Well, then put your little finger through the knothole!"

"No!"

"Open the door!"

This time the girl did open the door, and as soon as the giant came in, the brothers attacked him and killed him. Then they hauled his body away and cleaned up the blood where he had been killed, but from the ground into which his blood had flowed there sprang up at once onions and parsley. The seven brothers kept cutting these plants down at the roots, but by evening they would have grown again to the height of the roof. The brothers warned their sister about these plants. "Sister, do not ever put any of the onions or any of the parsley into our food, because if any of us eats even a little bit of those plants, he will go mad, leave home to live in the mountains, and there run wild."

One day passed, five days passed, and soon after that the girl was cooking a meal that required both onions and parsley. She remembered what her brothers had said. Still, she thought that if she took just two of the onions and only a few sprigs of parsley, that would surely not be enough to do her brothers any harm. But after her brothers had returned home that evening and had eaten their dinner, they all went completely mad and disappeared, running wild in the forest. The youngest brother, who had eaten most plentifully of the meal, also ran wild into the forest. There he found some water standing in the hoofprint of a deer. He drank this water, and he himself turned into a deer.

The girl was now left completely alone. Every day, she would climb onto the roof and sit there crying. One day the son of the padishah of that land happened to be hunting nearby. Seeing a beautiful young girl on the roof of that house, he dismounted and walked to the house and called, "Come down, my beauty!" When she came down, he asked, "Are you a human being or are you a jinn?"

"I am a creature of Allah, who made both you and me." Then, weeping again, she said, "I had seven brothers, but now they have all gone mad and are running wild in the forest."

"Would you marry me if I were to find your seven brothers for you?"

161

"If that is the destiny that Allah has written on my forehead, I would. I give you my word that if you find even one of my seven brothers, I shall marry you."

The prince then took the girl to his own palace, where he left her while he himself set out in search of her seven brothers. While he was wandering around in the forest, he came upon a place where deer were gathered, and among these deer he found the youngest brother and took him to the palace.

"Now, my dear," said the prince, "we shall be married." And so indeed they were. After they were married, the deer brother would lie every night at the foot of their bed. As he slept, he said in his sleep all night long, "This is my sister's leg. That is the leg of my brother-in-law."

Quite a while before this time, the prince had married an Arab girl, and almost immediately this Arab girl became jealous of the new bride. One day she gathered her laundry together and took it to the riverbank to wash it. The new bride and her deer brother went along too. After a while, the Arab girl suggested that it would be pleasant to walk along the riverbank for a little way. She walked on the inside of the path, and the new bride walked on the outside, close to the edge of the water. When they came to a very deep and swirling part of the river, the Arab girl pushed the new bride into the water. Just then a very large *alabalık* [trout] swam along there and swallowed the new bride. Her deer brother started saying, "Oh, Sister! The Arab girl has pushed you into the water and a trout has swallowed you!"

The Arab girl went back to where she had left her laundry, gathered it up, and took it back to the palace. There she put on one of the dresses of the new bride and went to the prince's chamber. They went to bed together, and the deer brother slept at the foot of the bed, saying, all night long, "This is the leg of the Arab girl, and that is the leg of my brother-in-law. This is the leg of the Arab girl, and that is the leg of my brother-in-law."

The prince felt that there was something strange about this, for before this the deer had repeated, "This is the leg of my sister. That is the leg of my brother-in-law." Why had he changed his chant?

When the Arab girl arose in the morning, she claimed that she was not well. She said to the prince, "If you will only kill that deer, I shall eat its heart and get well."

"No, I shall not kill that deer, but I shall go and hunt down another one for you."

"No. That would do no good. It must be this very one."

After some time had passed, the prince went deer hunting. The first deer that he encountered, however, was their own deer. He asked this pet deer, "What are you doing here?"

"The Arab girl pushed my sister into the water, and I have come here to be with her." The deer brother continually wandered through the forest and along the river singing this song:

"Oh, that Arab girl pushed my sister into the river,
And now the *alabalık* has swallowed her up!"

Now as he wandered along the riverbank, he heard a voice singing to him from the water:

"Brother, the Arab girl was the one who pushed me in,
And the *alabalık* did swallow me up,
But now a child with golden locks lies in my lap."

She had given birth to a child in the belly of the fish.

The prince said to the deer, "How can we believe that this is your sister? Your sister is home at the palace, sick in bed."

"Well, then, just listen to what the river says!" And the deer himself sang,

"Oh, Sister, whom the Arab girl pushed into the river,
And the *alabalık* has swallowed you up!"

From the water came the same voice as before, with the same song:

"Yes, my brother, the Arab girl did push me in,
And the *alabalık* did swallow me up,
But now a child with golden locks lies in my lap."

"Oh, prince, did you hear that?" asked the deer brother.

Now at last the prince realized what had happened. Taking the deer brother along with him, he set all of his soldiers and servants to work building a dam downstream in the river. When this was completed, they began to

cast nets in the river to catch the large trout containing the new bride and her new child. When the great trout was finally caught, its belly was cut open and the bride and her child were removed safely.

After they had returned to the palace, the prince asked the Arab girl, "Do you want forty swords or forty mules?"

"Oh, swords are suitable only for the necks of our enemies. Mules are better, because I might ride on them."

The prince selected two mules, one of which was thirsty and the other hungry. He tied one leg of the Arab girl to each mule and then whipped the mules. The thirsty mule pulled toward the water and the hungry mule pulled toward the pasture, and the Arab girl was torn in half.

Then the prince and the rescued bride had a wedding all over again, and the celebration lasted forty days and forty nights. They ate, drank, and had all of their wishes fulfilled.

Three apples fell from the sky: one for the teller of this tale, one for the listener, and one for anyone who might be offended if he did not receive one.

Timid Ali and the Giants

Once there was and once there wasn't a candy maker. This candy maker had an apprentice named Ali. Now, this apprentice was so timid that if he happened to see a mouse half a kilometer away, he would climb up on a chair and begin to shake with fear. The candy maker became disgusted with Ali because of his cowardice. "Go off and find another master, son," he said at last.

But everybody in the city made such fun of timid Ali that his mother finally said, "Son, go away from this house and do not come back until you have gained some courage."

Poor Ali put some bread and some cheese in his sack and left the house and the city weeping. He walked for three or five days and nights until at last he became so tired that he had to rest. He sat down under a fig tree and fell fast asleep. As he was sleeping, he dreamed that he heard a man shouting at him, "Wake up, Ali! Wake up! There is a snake ready to kill you!"

Ali opened one eye and reached for a stone and began to grip it tightly so that he might throw it at the snake when he saw it. But suddenly he realized that what he was squeezing in his hand was not a stone at all. It was something soft. It was the snake! Half asleep, he had squeezed the head of the snake in his hand, and the snake was now dead. Ali was surprised. Then he said to himself, "I didn't realize I was such a strong fellow! Why should I be a coward? If I use my wits and my strength, I can do many things that will show my friends I am no coward at all!"

He got up and continued on his way. In a cliff he saw an eagle's nest. He climbed up and looked, and there were eggs in the nest. "I'll just take these eggs along," Ali said, and he put them in his sack and climbed back down to the road. He walked along a little farther on the dusty road and then he bent over, scooped up some of the dust, and put it into his sack along with the eagle eggs.

As he went on and on along the way, he met a giant. The giant picked Ali up with his thumb and finger and said, "You will be my meat for dinner tonight." A few paces down the road, he took Ali into a cave where thirty-nine other giants were living.

But Ali said, "You can't eat me because I am stronger than you are. Let us have a contest to see which one is stronger."

The giant laughed and said, "All right. What is the contest?"

Ali said, "First, can you squeeze a piece of rock so hard that water will drop from it?"

The giant grabbed a small rock and squeezed and squeezed, but no water came out of the rock. While the giant was throwing the rock away, Ali reached into his sack and pulled out one of the eagle eggs, hiding it well in his hand. He squeezed just a little, and much liquid fell to the ground. All forty of the giants were amazed.

Then Ali said, "Can you hit that big rock at the mouth of the cave so hard that dust will fly out of it?"

The giant beat and beat and beat at the rock with his big fists, but nothing happened to the rock. It just stood there. While the giant was rubbing his hands together afterward to ease the soreness, Ali reached into his sack and scooped up a handful of dust and patted his hand against the rock. How the dust flew! Again, the giants were amazed. They said, "Indeed, you *are* stronger than we are."

"Of course," Ali said. "Now bring me forty trays of rice and forty roasted lambs and leave me alone to enjoy my meal, for I am hungry." The giants prepared this food and brought it to him and then they left him alone. Ali ate and ate until he was satisfied. Then he found a wide, deep crack in the stone floor of the cave and buried the rest of the food in it.

After an hour, Ali called the giants back and said, "Now I want you to take me back to my city." One of the giants bent down, and Ali climbed onto his shoulders. As soon as the giant felt how light Ali was, he said, "You lied to us, Ali. You are not really strong at all."

Ali thought very quickly. Then, raising one of his arms up high above the giant's head, Ali said, "Can't you see, you thankless giant? With one hand I am holding up the sky. Do you want me to let it go so that it can fall down on you and kill you?"

"No, no!" said the giant, and he began to walk with great strides down the dusty road toward the city.

"Come along, the rest of you!" said Ali. And the other thirty-nine giants came along behind him.

When Ali and the giants arrived in the city, the people could not believe their eyes. They were greatly frightened, and they began to beg, "Please don't kill us. Instead, we'll give you all the money that we have!"

Ali summoned everyone to the center of the city, including his mother and the candy maker. "You know now, my friends," he said, "how mistaken you were about me. You can see for yourselves that I am not a coward at all, but rather brave and clever. If I wished, my giants could destroy this whole city, but I will not ask them to do that. What's more, I forgive you all for making such fun of me. How could you know my strength and my courage?"

To the giant on whose shoulders he was riding, Ali said, "Set me down now, and go back to your cave." And that giant and the others did exactly that.

As for the people, they were so glad to see the giants leave that they held a great feast for forty days and forty nights. After that, Ali returned to his work with the candy maker. The last time I heard of him, he and the candy maker were partners in the shop. As for us, may we fare as well!

167

The Black Sheep and
Ahmet Ağa's Daughter

In the summertime the rich *ağa*s of the village used to send their sheep, cattle, and other livestock to the rich pastures nearby. Among them was a certain Ahmet *Ağa*, who was one of the richest. He was in the habit of taking his herds to the same pastures every year.

His daughter Ayşe was very beautiful, and all the men in the village, young and old, were in love with her. In order to win Ayşe's heart, the young men used to come and boast to her of their heroic deeds. "I killed so many lions and so many wolves," they would say. However, Ayşe would not pay any attention to them; she seemed to favor none of them.

One day the young men got together with the purpose of discussing Ayşe's lack of interest in them. They accused her of being insensitive to love and nicknamed her Insensitive Ayşe.

One day at dawn Ayşe came to her father and said, "Father, robbers are in the process of stealing our animals. You must do something about it."

Ahmet *Ağa* got his men together, and they went to the pastures. They succeeded in capturing the robbers. Ahmet *Ağa* was curious. He asked, "Ayşe, how did you find out about the robbery so early in the morning?"

"The shepherd informed me about it with his pipe," Ayşe answered.

Ahmet *Ağa* asked again, "How did he do it? What did he say?"

"The tune coming out of his pipe said that our flocks had been attacked by robbers, and he needed instant help," Ayşe explained.

Ahmet *Ağa* became suspicious and asked, "How could you interpret the message?"

Ayşe said, "There are roads between hearts."

Then Ahmet *Ağa* called the shepherd and questioned him. "Are you in love with my daughter?"

"Yes, sir," the shepherd answered.

It hurt Ahmet *Ağa's* pride that a lowly shepherd should love his daughter, and he decided to have him killed. He summoned the other *ağas* to a conference. They decided, "Let us put the shepherd to trial. We shall be justified in cutting his head off if he fails the test." These were the conditions of the trial: The shepherd was supposed to take a flock of lambs and sheep to a very dry and salty pasture and have them graze for three days and three nights. Then he was to lead the flock with his pipe to a watering place. He was to play his pipe in such a way that the flock would be dissuaded from drinking any water.

The shepherd was put to trial on a burning hot August day. After the flock grazed on the pasture with salty soil for three days and three nights, he herded the flock to the watering place. Then he started playing his pipe. The tune coming from the pipe begged the sheep not to drink any water from the spring. "Oh, my sheep, my sweet sheep, please don't drink any of the water. If you do, I'll lose my head. Then you will all be butchered. My Ayşe will become blind from crying for grief."

Two parties of men were formed by the spring: those who liked the shepherd and those who bitterly envied him. The executioner was waiting with a sword in his hand. He was ready to cut off the shepherd's head as soon as one of the sheep started drinking the water.

One after another, the sheep turned away from the water without drinking it. A black sheep came along last, and just as it was about to drink the water, the shepherd began playing a tune: "Dear black sheep, please don't drink the water. If you do, first I'll lose my head and then you'll lose yours. I took care of you when you were born. When you had lambs, I took care of them, too."

Those who loved the shepherd were begging the black sheep not to drink the water. Those who envied the shepherd encouraged the black sheep to drink the water: "Come on, black sheep. Drink the water. If you drink it, we promise to put gold bells around your neck." The two parties began competing with each other. One discouraged the sheep from drinking the water; the other encouraged it to drink the water.

The shepherd began playing his pipe again: "Dear black sheep, please don't drink the water. If you do, first I'll lose my head and then you'll lose

169

yours." Finally the black sheep went away from the water without drinking it. The victory was the shepherd's.

Then the men gathered around the shepherd and began questioning him. "We know you won the heart of the black sheep with the tune of your pipe. Why is it that the animal did not drink the water?"

The shepherd explained, "Gentlemen, on beautiful moonlit nights when Ayşe and I were dreaming of our love, my lips were burning with desire as the black sheep's lips were burning with thirst. But I never touched Ayşe. If I had kissed and violated her, the black sheep would have drunk the water. I owe this victory to my patience and suffering. It is why Ayşe and I still have a chance to be together."

In time, the shepherd wedded Ayşe. His strong willpower won him a beautiful wife and a victory fit for a padishah.

A Ticket to Trabzon

A Laz bought an airplane ticket for a flight from Ankara to Trabzon. When the time came to board the plane, this Temel walked along the aisle of the plane until he found a seat he liked, and he sat down.

As the other passengers came along one by one, a lady stopped at Temel's seat. She looked at her own ticket and said, "Sir, I believe you're sitting in my seat."

"Oh, no," said Temel. "This is my seat. I paid for a ticket, and I want to sit here."

While the lady was standing there talking with Temel, the stewardess came along. She looked at the lady's ticket and then at Temel's ticket and she said, "You are sitting in this lady's seat. Your seat is over there."

When Temel still did not move, another Laz came over. "Is there some sort of problem here?" he asked. "Maybe I can help."

The stewardess said, "This man is sitting in the wrong seat. This seat belongs to the lady."

"Let me look at your ticket," the Laz said to Temel. The Laz read the ticket. Then he handed it back to Temel. "You want to go from Ankara to Trabzon, don't you?" he said to Temel.

When Temel agreed, the Laz said, "Well, then, you have to take the seat with your number on it. *That* seat is the one that will take you to Trabzon!"

The Padishah's Three Daughters and the Spindle Seller

O nce there was and once there wasn't a padishah who had three daughters. Before the padishah left home on a journey, he warned his daughters, "While I am gone, do not go outside the house."

One day soon after that, while the padishah's daughters were spinning at home, an old man came along the street shouting, "I sell spindles! I sell spindles!"

The eldest daughter came out and said, "What did you say you were selling, grandfather?"

"I am selling *spindles,* my daughter," he said. "They are used for making yarn."

"Do you have some for me? I need spindles."

"There are none here in my basket that are good enough for a padishah's daughter," he said, "but I have better ones at home."

"Where is your home?"

"Not far," he said. "Just over there."

"Well, let us go then," said the eldest daughter.

They went a little; they went far. The old man kept saying, "It is quite near here," but all the while he was taking the girl farther and farther away.

Now, it was the habit of this old man to cut the throats of girls and hang them on the wall by their feet. When they arrived at his house, the eldest daughter was surprised to see this, and she asked, "Why did you hang those girls up there?"

"Don't talk too much," said the old man. "Just cut a piece of flesh from one of those corpses, and let us eat. I am hungry."

"I do not want to eat such flesh."

"If you do not," he said, "I shall kill you, too."

The girl cooked some human flesh, and then they sat down. The old man ate some of the flesh from the corpse, but the girl refused to do so. At once, the old man killed her, and he hung her body on the wall with the others. "She was of no use to me at all," he said.

After he had finished eating, the old man went out to sell more spindles. He went back to the village where the padishah lived. "I sell spindles!" he shouted. "I sell spindles."

This time, the middle daughter of the padishah came out to him. "Where is my sister?" she asked. "She came out to buy some spindles. I want to buy some spindles, too."

"There are none here in my basket that are good enough for a padishah's daughter," he said, "but I have better ones at home."

"Sir, where is my sister?" the middle daughter asked.

"She was going to my house to get spindles when she met the son of a padishah, and she ran away with him. She would not listen to me."

"Well, I shall go with you to get the spindles, then, for my young sister and I need them very much."

They went a little; they went far. The old man kept saying, "It is quite near here," but all the while he was taking the girl farther and farther away. Finally they reached his house.

As soon as they entered the house, the girl saw her sister's body hanging on the wall. She said to the old man, "Didn't you say that my sister had run away with the son of a padishah?"

"Don't talk too much," said the old man. "We are hungry now. Go and cut a piece of flesh from that body so that we can eat it."

"I cannot eat my sister's flesh."

"If you do not," he said, "I shall kill you, too."

With tears running down her cheeks, the middle daughter cut a piece of flesh from the body of her sister, cooked it, and served it to the old man. They sat down together, but the girl would not eat. Instead, she continued crying.

The old man said, "You are of no use to me." He then killed her, too, and hung her on the wall with her sister. The old man finished his food, rested that night, and then went out again the next day to sell spindles. He went back to the village where the padishah lived.

Passing the padishah's house, where now only the youngest daughter lived, he shouted, "I sell spindles! I sell spindles!"

The youngest daughter came out and said, "Grandfather, you took my two sisters. Where are they? What did you do with them?"

"My daughter, what *could* I do? The first one saw the son of a padishah and ran away with him. The second one saw an officer, and she just took his arm and went with him. She would not listen to me."

"Well, then, give me some spindles. I need them."

"There are none here in my basket that are good enough for a padishah's daughter," he said, "but I have better ones at home."

"Where is your home?"

"Not far," he said. "Just over there."

"Well, let us go, then, for I need some spindles."

They went a little; they went far. The old man kept saying, "It is quite near here," but all the while he was taking the girl farther and farther away.

Finally they reached his house. What should she see there but her two sisters hanging on the wall?

Now, the padishah had a little cat that was especially fond of this youngest daughter. It had followed the girl all the way to the old man's house.

When the girl saw her sisters hanging dead on the wall, she began to weep. "Stop that crying," said the old man. "Go and cut a piece of flesh from the body of your next-oldest sister and we shall eat. Her flesh should be quite tender."

The girl cut the flesh and cooked it, sobbing softly all the while. When the meat was ready, they sat down together, but the girl said, "I will not eat."

"If you do not," he said, "I shall kill you, too."

So the girl took a finger from her sister's flesh and pretended to eat it, but she gave it instead to the little cat, which was under the table. The old man then said, "Finger, where are you?"

It answered, "I am in a tiny little stomach." Of course, it was in the cat's stomach, but the old man thought that it was in the stomach of the youngest girl. From this he decided that the girl would be of some use to him there.

The next day, telling the girl to clean and sweep the house, the old man said that he was going out again to sell spindles. Before he left, he handed the girl a ring with forty keys on it, saying, "You may open all of the first thirty-nine doors and enjoy yourself, but *do not* open the fortieth door."

The girl opened three or five doors each day and she enjoyed herself in the rooms. One day, however, she became very curious about the fortieth room. "What is in that room that I cannot see?" she asked herself. She decided to open the door of that room, but then she realized that it was close to the time for the old man to return. She thought it would be better to wait to open that door until the next day.

173

As soon as the old man had left the next day, the girl went right away to open the door of the fortieth room. When she opened the door, what should she see but a young man alive and hanging by his hair from the ceiling? The room itself was filled with jewelry and all kinds of other precious things. The girl was surprised, and so was the young man. "Are you a human being or a jinn?" he asked.

"I am a human being, just like you," she said.

"Then will you please rescue me from this place?" asked the young man.

"Yes, but the old man will be coming home very soon for his lunch, and he will be hungry. As soon as he leaves tomorrow morning to sell his spindles, I'll come back and rescue you. Then we shall run away from here together."

She then went and started preparing food for the old man. They ate and drank. The next morning as soon as the old man had left, she went again to the fortieth room. She cut the hair that was holding him to the ceiling, and the young man fell to the floor. They gathered together everything in the room that was light in weight but heavy in value and escaped, taking all those treasures to the home of the padishah.

In the meantime, the padishah had returned from his journey to find no one there. His daughters had been gone for a week. "Where have you been, my daughter?" he asked as the girl came in. "I warned you all not to go out."

"Well, Father," she said, "an old spindle seller came along, and first my

174

eldest sister went with him to get some good spindles, and then my second sister went with him to get some good spindles. When they didn't come home, I went with him to get some good spindles. But, oh, my father, when I got to his house, I found my sisters dead and hanging from the wall. The old man made me cook their flesh as his meat, but I fed my share to your little cat, and the old man never knew about it. He kept me working there, and one day I found this young man in the fortieth room, hanging by his hair in the middle of all kinds of treasures. I cut him down and we ran away together, taking all the things that were light in weight but heavy in value. Now at last I am safe at home!"

After the padishah had heard all this, he said, "You did well, my daughter. Now, that old man will come this way again. When he comes, call me."

In three or five days, the old man did come again, and the padishah's men caught him. They built a huge fire and they threw the old man into it.

The padishah now had only one daughter left. He said to the young man, "My daughter seems to be your kismet. I have no son, and so you will be both my son and my son-in-law."

Then he gave them a wedding that lasted for forty days and forty nights. Of course, the tale ends here.

The Prophetic Dream

Once there was and twice there wasn't a family with three sons. These sons all attended a school where the reading of the Koran was taught. One day their *hoca* said, "When you have a dream at night, be sure not to tell it to anyone who does not first say, 'May it be auspicious!'"

Three or five weeks later, the *hoca* talked about dreams again, and then he asked the oldest son, "What did you dream about last night?" Immediately, the oldest son described his dream. The *hoca* then asked the middle son, "What did *you* dream?" The middle son told his dream. But when the *hoca* asked the youngest son what *he* had dreamed, the youngest son refused to tell him. The *hoca* beat the boy for this refusal.

When the youngest son returned home crying, his mother said, "What is the matter?"

"Mother, my *hoca* beat me."

"Why?"

"I refused to tell him about a dream I had last night, and so he beat me."

175

176

"Well, what was your dream?" But when he refused to tell her, his mother beat him, too.

The youngest son ran crying to his father, saying, "Both my *hoca* and my mother beat me."

"Why?"

"I refused to tell them a dream I had last night. That was why they beat me."

"Well, what *was* your dream? Surely you can tell your father." When the youngest son refused to tell his father about his dream, he received a third beating. The youngest son then ran away from home.

He went and went, until finally he passed the palace of the padishah. "What a remarkable dream that was!" he kept saying to himself. The padishah happened to be standing by an open window of the palace, and he heard what the youngest son was saying.

"Son, what was so remarkable about your dream?" he said.

When the youngest son refused to tell him about his dream, the padishah said, "How dare you defy the padishah?" Immediately he called his executioner and ordered him to kill that boy.

Now, the daughter of the padishah had a small palace of her own that was near the execution grounds. When she looked out of her window that day, she saw a handsome young man being led to the execution grounds by her father's executioner. When the princess interrupted the executioner and his assistant, they refused to listen to her, saying, "No, no! We are supposed to execute this one because of his rudeness to the padishah. If we do not kill him and take back his bloody shirt as evidence, then your father will kill us."

"Take this bag of gold and divide it," said the princess. "Then kill a dog and dip this young man's shirt in the blood of that dog. Take the bloody shirt to my father and leave the young man with me." They took the gold and did as the princess had directed, and thus the padishah was satisfied. As for the princess, she took the youngest son and hid him in her palace.

Now, at that time the padishah had received an ultimatum from a European country. The padishah of that country had sent him a complicated machine with these instructions: "Take this machine completely apart, with not one piece joined to another, and then put it back together so that there are no parts missing and no parts left over. If you can do this, we shall add a European city to your territory; if you cannot, we shall declare war against you."

The padishah and his viziers took the machine apart, piece by piece, until not one part was fastened to another, but when they put it back together, there was one screw left over. *Aman!* They took it apart and put it together again, piece by piece, but this time there was a screw missing. None of the mechanics in his whole territory could puzzle out the answer to this problem. The padishah became so worried about this task that he was unable to sleep at night. When the youngest son heard that the padishah was pacing

177

the floor instead of sleeping, he said to the princess, "I think that your father is in trouble of some kind. Go and find out what is troubling him."

Going to the padishah's palace, the princess discovered that her father was greatly concerned about putting that machine together. The padishah and his viziers and mechanics from here and there had been working at it constantly and with no success at all. The princess returned to her own palace and told the youngest son that her father was greatly upset because neither he nor his men could put the machine together properly.

"Go and fetch that machine. *İnşallah,* I shall put it together for him myself."

When the princess returned to her father and asked him to let her take it to her palace and put it together correctly, he laughed and asked, "What do you know about machines? Are you a mechanic?"

She paid no attention to his questions, however, and while he was engaged in other business she picked up all the pieces of the machine and took them back to her own palace. The next morning, the youngest son rolled up his sleeves and set to work on the machine. By working very hard for a short time, he managed to put it together correctly, with no parts missing and no parts left over. Then the princess took the machine to the padishah, and he sent it at once to the padishah of the European country. There it was examined and declared to be put together perfectly. Thus war was avoided, and the padishah had a European city added to his territory.

In three or five weeks, the padishah of that same European country sent another ultimatum: "We are sending you a painted stick. You are to examine it carefully and determine which part of this stick came from the root end of the tree trunk and which part came from the branch end of the tree trunk. If you can solve this puzzle correctly, we shall add a second European city to your territory; if you cannot solve it, we shall declare war against you."

The padishah gathered together at the palace his viziers and all the carpenters of the land to work on this problem. Some said, "This part came from the root end, and that part came from the branch end." Others said, "No, no! *That* part came from the root end, and *this* part came from the branch end." No matter how long they discussed it, they could come to no agreement. Again the padishah paced the floor instead of sleeping. After three or five days, the youngest son said to the princess, "I believe that something is upsetting your father again. Go and see what it is."

Going to the padishah's palace, the princess asked, "Father, what is the matter?"

"This is what is the matter," he said, and he held out the painted stick. "This painted stick was sent to us by the padishah of that same European country with a message: 'You are to determine which part of this stick came from the root end of the tree trunk and which part came from the branch end. If you can tell us that, we shall add another European city to your territory; if you cannot, then we shall declare war against you.'"

When the princess heard this, she said, "Father, let me take the stick for a while, and I shall then bring you the correct answer."

"What will *you* do with it? Are you a carpenter?"

"Never mind, Father. Just let me try." She then took the stick and carried it to her own palace and showed it to the youngest son. After she had told him about the ultimatum, she handed the stick to the youngest son and he examined it carefully.

Then he said, "Take this stick back to your father's palace and tell him to have his carpenters make a trough that is as long as this stick. After filling this trough with water, he must put this stick into the water and watch it carefully. The part that rests lower in the water will be the one that came from the root end of the tree trunk; the other part will be the one that came from the branch end."

When the princess returned to her father's palace with the painted stick, the padishah and his viziers followed the directions exactly. They marked each part of the stick according to what the test had shown—the root end and the branch end—and then the padishah sent it back to the padishah of that European country. The answer was correct, so the Turkish padishah had not only avoided a war but had added a second European city to his territory.

Three or five weeks later, the padishah of that same European country sent a third ultimatum: "We are sending you three horses, all three the same

179

color and the same size. You are to determine which of these three horses is the mother, which is the daughter, and which is the granddaughter. If you can do this, we shall add another European city to your territory; if you cannot, then we shall declare war against you."

The padishah at once summoned his viziers and all of the veterinarians in his territory to assemble at his palace. When they were all there, they were told to examine all three of the horses to determine which was the mother, which the daughter, and which the granddaughter. Some said one thing and some said another—about the teeth, the hoofs, the mane, the eyes—but there was no agreement. After three or five days of discussion, the youngest son said to the princess, "I think that your father must be in trouble again. Go and find out what it is that is upsetting him so."

Going to her father's palace, the princess asked, "Father, what is worrying you so much?"

"Well, Daughter, that same European padishah has sent me another puzzle. He has sent three horses, all the same color, all the same height, and all seemingly the same age. With them came this message: 'You are to determine which of these horses is the mother, which the daughter, and which the granddaughter. If you can do this, another European city will be added to your territory; if you cannot, then we shall declare war against you.'"

When the youngest son heard about this third puzzle, he thought for a few minutes and then he said, "Tell them to feed all three of those horses

with barley for three days without allowing them to have even a drop of water. Then, after the third day, take them to a stream and watch them carefully. The one that drinks and leaves first will be the mother, the one that leaves next will be the daughter, and the one that leaves last will be the granddaughter."

The princess carried this message to the palace of the padishah, and the padishah's veterinarians followed these directions exactly. On each horse they placed a tag telling which one was the mother, which the daughter, and which the granddaughter. Then the Turkish padishah returned the three horses to the padishah of that European country. In that other country, the answers were judged correct. Furthermore, the people there asked to see the man who was so clever that he could solve the three puzzles sent to the Turkish padishah.

Of course, the padishah supposed that his wise daughter had solved the puzzles, so he called the princess into his presence. He said, "Daughter, we have been asked to send for a visit to that European court the person who has solved the puzzles. I am therefore going to send you to that European court with an escort of five hundred soldiers."

"Father," the princess said, "I was not the one who knew the correct answers to those puzzles. It was such and such a young man who gave me the answers to give to you."

"Well, my daughter, bring him here."

When the youngest son was brought to the presence of the padishah, the Turkish ruler said, "Here, my son, are five hundred soldiers to accompany you. I want you to go to such and such a European court for a visit."

The youngest son said, "My padishah, I do not want to be accompanied by any soldiers at all."

"Why is that?"

"I need no soldiers." After saying this, the youngest son set out at once on his journey to the European court. On the way, he came upon a man who was holding his ear to the earth and listening. He said, "*Selâmünaleyküm*, O Listener to the Ground!"

"*Aleykümselâm*, O Solver of Three Great Puzzles!"

"How did you know that I am the Solver of Three Great Puzzles?"

"By listening to the ground."

The youngest son then said, "I am going to such and such a European court. Will you become my companion on that journey?"

"Yes, I shall." So he joined the youngest son in his walking.

After walking for a while together, they came to a river where they saw a large man sucking up the water with his mouth so fast that none flowed past him. "*Selâmünaleyküm*, O Water Drawer!" said the youngest son.

"*Aleykümselâm*, O Solver of Three Great Puzzles!"

"How did you know that I am the Solver of Three Great Puzzles?"

"By drawing in this water."

"I am on my way to such and such a European court. Will you become my companion on that journey?"

"Yes, I shall." So now they were three companions.

As the three walked along and walked along, they came upon a man who kept tossing huge trees this way and that way. Some of them he tossed great distances, as far as from here to Çarşamba or even Samsun. The youngest son called to this man, "*Selâmünaleyküm,* O Tosser of Trees!"

"*Aleykümselâm,* O Solver of Three Great Puzzles!"

"How did you know that I am the Solver of Three Great Puzzles?"

"By tossing these trees."

"I am on my way to such and such a European court. Will you become my companion on that journey?"

"Yes, I shall." So now they were four companions.

As the four walked along and walked along, they saw a man a great distance ahead of them, but that man reached them in two mighty leaps. The youngest son called to this man, "*Selâmünaleyküm,* O Mighty Leaper!"

"*Aleykümselâm,* O Solver of Three Great Puzzles!"

"How did you know that I am the Solver of Three Great Puzzles?"

"By leaping."

"I am on my way to such and such a European court. Will you become my companion on that journey?"

"Yes, I shall." So now they were five companions.

They walked along and walked along, and after a while they reached that European country. Soon they came to five hundred Europeans stationed along the way to welcome them. Those people were surprised to see only five Turks arriving instead of the five hundred they had expected would accompany the Solver of Three Great Puzzles. The leader of the European group said, "This shouldn't be. Our padishah went to great expense to arrange for at least five hundred people to be our guests, but only five of you have come."

"Do not worry," said the youngest son. "We shall accept the provisions for five hundred people."

"If you do, young man, that will be fine, but if you do not, we shall cut you all to pieces."

"Very well," said the youngest son.

For dinner, food had been prepared for five hundred people, and the Turks were required to consume it all. Four of the Turks—all except Water Drawer—sat down at the table, but the fifth one stood apart, not eating at first. All of the Europeans stared at him. As for the four seated Turks, they ate and ate until they were full and they left the table. Then Water Drawer started in on the food. He just sucked up whatever was being brought in in large kettles and then tossed the empty kettles aside. After he had consumed five caldrons of food in this way, the Europeans were satisfied. "All right," they said. "That is enough."

When they were resting in their quarters, the Solver of Three Great Puzzles said to Listener to the Ground, "Listen and discover what the Europeans are saying about us."

After keeping his ear to the ground for a short while, Listener to the Ground said, "These Europeans have a girl whom they will race against us tomorrow. If we fail to beat her in a footrace, they will kill all of us."

Then the Solver of Three Great Puzzles said to Mighty Leaper, "You will be on duty tomorrow."

Mighty Leaper said, "Go and find a nice cold drink for me. I'll get the girl to sit in the shade of a tree, drink some of that liquid, and fall asleep."

But the next day as the race was about to begin, the youngest son looked in vain for any sign of Mighty Leaper. When the girl started to run, the youngest one asked Listener to the Ground to find out what Mighty Leaper was doing. Listener to the Ground reported, "Mighty Leaper is sitting asleep beneath a tree." Tosser of Trees threw a tree at Mighty Leaper and awakened him just barely in time for him to win the race.

That evening when they were resting in their quarters, the youngest son said to Listener to the Ground, "Listen and find out what they plan to do tomorrow."

Placing his ear to the ground for a few minutes, Listener to the Ground said, "They are sprinkling gasoline everywhere for the purpose of burning us up."

"Listen again and find out if there are any rivers nearby."

After a moment Listener to the Ground reported, "Yes, there is a river located in such and such a place."

The youngest son then sent Water Drawer to that river to draw up a large quantity of water. In the morning when the flames began to rise, the five companions were unconcerned. They lay still in the house where they were staying. As the flames approached that house, Water Drawer emptied the water of that river over them and put the fire out.

Finally the padishah of that European country called the youngest son to his presence. "You have not only solved the three puzzles I sent to your padishah, but you have completed the three tasks I set for you here. I now give you my only daughter as your bride."

Accepting the daughter of this European padishah, the youngest son took her—with all of her things that were light in weight but heavy in value—and his four companions, and they started back toward Turkey. They traveled and traveled and traveled until they came to the place where Mighty Leaper had joined them. "I'll stop here," said Mighty Leaper, and so he did, with the rest going on without him, traveling and traveling.

When they came to the place where the youngest son had found Tosser of Trees, that companion said, "I'll stop here," and so he did. The rest went on without him, traveling and traveling.

When they came to the place where the youngest son had found the large man drinking a river dry, Water Drawer said, "I'll stop here," and so he did. The rest went on without him, traveling and traveling.

When they came to the place where the youngest son had found the man with his ear to the earth, Listener to the Ground said, "I'll stop here," and so he did. The youngest son and the daughter of the European padishah went on without him, traveling and traveling, until finally they arrived in the presence of his own padishah.

"Well," said the padishah, "I see that you have gone and come back again. What happened to you in your travels?"

The youngest son told the padishah everything that had happened, from first to last, leaving out not a single detail. "And now," he said, "I have this beautiful girl who is to be my bride."

"Ah, yes," said the padishah. "Now, young man, aren't you the one I ordered to be executed because you would not tell me your dream?"

"I am, my padishah."

"Tell me, then, your dream. And may it be auspicious!"

"My padishah, I dreamed that I held a cross in my left hand and a crescent in my right hand. Here in the princess of that European country I have the cross I dreamed about. As for the crescent, I do not know."

"But I know," said the padishah, "for I am going to give my daughter to you as your bride. She will be the crescent in your right hand, just as the European princess is the cross in your left hand. Your dream was indeed auspicious!"

In good time, then, two weddings were celebrated, each for forty days and forty nights, one for the youngest son and the European princess and the other for the youngest son and the Turkish princess. They had their wishes fulfilled. Let's go up and sit in their seats!

The Snake and Prophet Mohammed

Six hundred years before the time of the Prophet Mohammed, a snake spoke to Prophet Jesus. The snake said, "There are places called Mecca and Medina, and I want to know where those places are. Can you tell me about these places?"

Prophet Jesus asked the snake, "What would you do with such information?"

The snake answered, "I have heard of a person named Mohammed. I shall go there and look for Mohammed."

"But there will be six hundred years between you and Prophet Mohammed when he comes," said Prophet Jesus.

But the snake was determined. He said, "I don't care. I shall go there and await him, whether it takes six hundred years or a thousand years."

Prophet Jesus then explained to the snake how he should go in order to reach Mecca and Medina. The snake then crawled to Saman Mountain and waited six hundred years in a cave in that mountain for the coming of Prophet Mohammed. He had been told that Prophet Mohammed would come to that very cave.

While Prophet Mohammed was fleeing to Medina, accompanied by Caliph Ebu Bekir and Caliph Ali, Ali often slept in Mohammed's bedroll. He did this so that anyone who tried to kill the Prophet would be deceived and kill him instead. When Allah observed this, He said to His angels, "Would you give up your life for someone else?"

"No, we could not do that," they said.

"Go and watch my Caliph Ali," said Allah. "He puts himself in the bed of the Prophet Mohammed, saying, 'If they want to kill someone, they can kill me.'"

But Allah had been watching them even before they had fled Mecca. On the evening they were to leave, Allah had appeared to Prophet Mohammed and said, "Recite the ninth verse of the thirty-sixth sura of the Koran, and then take a handful of soil and sprinkle it on the main street of Mecca. Everyone will then fall asleep, and you will be able to escape unnoticed." It was thus that Prophet Mohammed and Caliph Ebu Bekir and Caliph Ali were able to run away. And then they went to the cave in the side of Saman Mountain.

After they had entered the cave, Allah caused a great sandstorm to arise. It drifted sand that closed the mouth of the cave. Then a black bush sprang up before the mouth of that cave. A pigeon built a nest in that bush and hatched her eggs there. A spider spun a strong web across the mouth of the cave, and that spider said to the pigeon, "No one in the entire world can break my web!"

The snake that had been waiting for six hundred years for the arrival of the Prophet Mohammed made seventy holes through one of the inner walls of the cave. He said, "I have made seventy holes so that I will be sure to be able to see the holy face of the Prophet Mohammed. Even if they seal many of these holes, there will surely be one left through which I can see his face."

When the three men arrived at the cave, Caliph Ebu Bekir was worried that poisonous insects might come from those holes and sting the Prophet. He therefore took off his clerical gown, tore it into strips, and stuffed those strips into the holes to plug them. Since he had only sixty-nine strips, one hole remained unplugged.

When they lay down to sleep, Ebu Bekir placed his heel over that one unplugged hole in order to seal it off. But the snake was desperate to see the holy face of Mohammed, and to do so now, it bit Ebu Bekir's heel. It bit out a piece the size of a bird's egg. Prophet Mohammed's head was lying on the lap of the older Ebu Bekir as they slept. When the snake bit Ebu Bekir's heel, the Caliph did not want to move lest he awaken the sleeping Mohammed, but the pain in his heel was so great that tears flowed from his eyes.

When some of these tears dripped on the face of the sleeping Mohammed, he awoke. Seeing Caliph Ebu Bekir weeping silently, he asked, "Why are you crying?"

"That snake bit my heel," Ebu Bekir answered.

When Prophet Mohammed rubbed the bleeding heel with spittle, the wound was healed at once. He then asked the snake, "Why did you bite the heel of Ebu Bekir?"

"My dear Prophet," said the snake, "I was told six hundred years ago that someday I would see your holy face here, and that is the reason I came to this cave. I waited six hundred years to see your holy face, but Caliph Ebu Bekir plugged all of the holes I had made for observing you. The only hole that I could open was the one covered by his heel, and that is the only reason I bit his heel. I did not mean to hurt him. I wanted only to see your face clearly."

Prophet Mohammed then stroked the snake's back, and the snake began to smell clean and fragrant. They say that there are still certain kinds of snakes at Medina that have a very fragrant smell.

186

The Learned Turban

A man came to Nasreddin Hoca with a letter in his hand, and he wanted the Hoca to read it for him.

When the Hoca opened the letter, he saw that it was not written in Turkish. It was in Arabic, and the Hoca did not know any Arabic. He handed the letter back, saying, "I cannot read this letter."

The man said, "Why can't you read the letter?"

"Because it is not in Turkish," said the Hoca.

The man did not understand why the Hoca could not read what was written in Arabic, and he said, "Oh, Hoca, aren't you ashamed of yourself? If you aren't ashamed before me, aren't you ashamed of the turban you wear on your head?"

The Hoca smiled, and immediately took his turban off his head. He put that learned turban on the head of the man and said, "All right. You have the turban on your head. *You* read the letter!"

187

The Stepdaughter Who Married the Dervish

Once there was and once there wasn't a woman who had three daughters. Two of these daughters were her own, but the eldest was her stepdaughter. All three of the girls were very good tailors. She used to buy all sorts of things for her own daughters. But she bought nothing for the stepdaughter, and for this reason the stepdaughter was unhappy and used to cry secretly.

When the mother was sewing by the window one day, a dervish was passing by the house. The woman invited the dervish to come and tell her the fortunes of her daughters. "Open the luck of my daughters!" said the woman.

"How many daughters have you?" said the dervish.

"I have two," said the woman. But the dervish had already seen the stepdaughter weeping by another window. He brought out an apple and gave

it to the woman, saying, "Cut this apple into two halves, and let each of your daughters eat one half of it. This will open their luck."

The stepdaughter was listening to this conversation from upstairs. When the dervish was going away, she was watching him from where she sat, and the dervish wondered why she had not come down. Was she perhaps the daughter of a neighbor?

When the dervish was walking past the house the next morning, this same girl was alone in the house because her stepmother and sisters had gone out. The dervish knocked at the door—*Tak! Tak! Tak!*—and when the girl opened it for him, he said, "Are you the woman to whom I gave the apple?" This woman looked, of course, like all other women, for women in those days were veiled.

"Oh, no," she said. "I am only a stepdaughter. The apple that you gave was eaten by my two stepsisters. My stepmother and my stepsisters do not like me, and they treat me very badly."

The dervish brought forth a pear and gave it to her. "You will eat a bite of this pear each night for seven nights, and then seven days later a very important man will ask you to marry him. Your stepmother may try everything to prevent your marrying that man, and she will try to make your marriage unhappy afterwards. But do not throw away the stem of the pear. You must guard it carefully."

Fortune began to smile on the faces of the daughters. They each married what appeared to be a fine husband. An old man came along after the fourteen days had passed and asked for the hand of the eldest. When the stepdaughter saw this, she was greatly disappointed and cried for hours. Seeing her stepdaughter's unhappiness, the stepmother decided to marry her to him. When her husband opened her bridal veil and she looked at his face, she was amazed to see that he was a very handsome man. "Was it you who wanted to marry me? The one who wanted to marry me was an old, old man," she said.

"Do you remember the dervish who gave you the pear? Well, I am that dervish," said her husband.

The men that the other two sisters married were very cruel to them. They beat them almost every day. As for the stepdaughter, she was very happy in her marriage. One day she decided to visit her stepmother, so she put on her finest clothes and rode in a splendid horse-drawn carriage. She took with her many gifts for her stepmother. The stepmother greeted her with amazement. "Why are you so well dressed?" she asked. "The man whom you married looked like a very poor man."

"Oh, no," said the stepdaughter. "My husband is a very rich man. I have a very fine house and many maids and cooks, as well."

"There must be some mistake in this. The man that wanted to marry you was a poor old man. I am sure that you must have married a different man from the one to whom we agreed to give you."

"Well, you remember that you took me to him. This is the man that I saw when my veil was lifted."

"No, it can't be," said the stepmother. "You must have married a different man." From pure jealousy, the stepmother was very angry with her stepdaughter. She tied her hands and carried her down to the cellar and locked her up there. Each day, she gave her only a pitcher of water to drink and a piece of bread to eat. The only comfort the girl had was the stem of the pear that the dervish—now her husband—had given her. She looked at that stem hour by hour and wept for the loss of her happiness.

Meanwhile, the husband of the stepdaughter waited for her for a long time, and when she did not return he became quite worried about her. He walked over to his mother-in-law's house and asked, "Have you seen my wife? She was going to visit you today and bring you some gifts. Has she been here?"

"No. I haven't seen your wife," said the stepmother. "She didn't come here today at all."

They looked all over the town for her. They had town criers go about the streets announcing her disappearance.

Finally the stepmother decided to go down and take a look at her stepdaughter in the cellar. Because of that pear stem, all of the tears that had fallen from the girl's eyes had turned into pearls. When the stepmother unlocked the door of the cellar and entered, she could not believe her eyes, for the place was full of beautiful pearls. "Where did you get all of these pearls?" she asked. And without even waiting for an answer, she took as many pearls as she could carry and she went to the market to sell them. For those pearls, she received a great amount of money.

A little later, the dervish went to the market, and as he walked around he noticed that the pearls in all of the jewelry stores looked alike. He took up one of the pearls, which was a magic pearl, and looked at it closely, and he was able to see in it the place where his wife had been locked away. He asked the price of the pearl, paid the price that was asked, and took it with him. By looking at the pearl steadily as he walked, he was guided to the house where the girl was imprisoned. When he came to the entrance of the cellar, he heard his wife crying, "Save me! Save me!" The dervish tied the hands of his mother-in-law, broke down the cellar door, and took his wife away with him. Later, they went together to another country.

Now let us go back and see about the two stepsisters and what they are doing. The middle sister had become blind, and the youngest one had lost her wits entirely. The dervish asked his wife what he should do to punish the stepmother and the stepsisters who had been so cruel to her. "Do whatever you like to my stepmother," she said, "but do not be too cruel to my sisters. They have already suffered enough."

Then, by use of magic, the dervish transformed the stepmother into a

190

badly deformed hunchback. She became so ugly that when her husband came home that evening he could hardly recognize her. One day, still puzzled about this strange change in his wife, the father-in-law took one of the pearls in his hand, looked at it closely, and saw in it the image of the dervish. He put it down, saying, "Oh, these are magic pearls. Now I understand why you have become deformed like this. The dervish must have punished you because of your injustice to my daughter, your stepdaughter."

When his wife took up several of the pearls and looked into them, she too saw the image of the dervish in them, with his long beard and his gown. "There is nothing to do, then, but to find the dervish and ask his forgiveness," she said. "*İnşallah,* he will have a kind of mercy on me that I did not show to your daughter."

The two of them sought here and there until they found the dervish. They threw themselves at his feet, asking him to forgive them. As for the dervish, he said, "I have forgiven you." At that moment, the stepmother returned to her former condition.

And there ends our tale.

The Last Word

A Muslim, a Christian, and a Jew were arguing. The Muslim finally became angry and said, "I pray that five thousand Christians will die!"

The Christian responded furiously, "I pray that ten thousand Muslims will perish!"

During this exchange of curses, the Jew had remained silent. The Muslim and the Christian asked the Jew, "Well, don't you have anything to say?"

"What should I say?" the Jew answered. "I ask only that Jehovah will answer both of your prayers."

The Boy Who Would Not Become a Decent Individual

Once there was and once there wasn't a man who had one son. This son always did the opposite of what his father asked him to do. He was lazy, too, and cared about nothing at all. His father used to say to him, "You will never become a decent individual." Still, the boy did not change his careless and obstinate ways.

Time came, time went, and the son left his father's home. He began to work here and there. At last he became a vizier of the country. When he had achieved that position, he remembered his father's words: "You will never become a decent individual." So he sent servants to his father's house and invited him to come to the palace.

The father went to see his son. When the vizier saw his father, he began to laugh. "Father," he said, "you always used to say that I would never become a decent individual. Now, look and see. I have become a vizier, praise Allah! You were wrong to think the way you did."

The father smiled. "My son," he said, "I did not say that you could never become a vizier. I said you would not become a decent individual, and I still say the same thing."

"Why, Father?" asked the son.

"Well, after you had become the vizier, you ordered your father to come to your feet. You are my son, and I am your father, even though you are the vizier. Would a decent individual treat his father the way you treated me by making me come to you?"

The Youngest Princess and Her Donkey-skull Husband

Once there was and once there wasn't a padishah who had three daughters, each one more beautiful than the others. When these girls had all reached the age for marriage, he sent town criers everywhere in his land, shouting, "On such and such a day everyone is to assemble before the palace. My daughters on that day will seek their marital destiny. I shall give each of my daughters an apple. Each one will throw her apple at the crowd of people, and whatever unmarried man her apple hits will become her husband."

On such and such a day all of the people gathered before the palace. The oldest daughter came to the balcony of the palace and threw her apple. It struck the son of the padishah of Egypt. When the second sister came and threw her apple, it hit the son of the padishah of Iran. Then it was the turn of the youngest daughter. She came and threw her apple from the balcony, and it fell upon a donkey skull that was rolling along in the street.

"No, no! That can't be! Throw it again!" everyone shouted.

They brought the apple back to the girl, and she threw it again. Just as it had done before, the apple landed on the donkey skull.

Again the crowd shouted, "No, no! That can't be! Throw it again!"

She threw the apple a third time, and again it struck the donkey skull. "Well," the people said, "the chances of a Turk are three. It must be her kismet to have the donkey skull!"

There was a large wedding shortly after that in which all three of the padishah's daughters were married. (This is a tale, you know.) On the night of the final day of the wedding ceremonies, the brides were taken to the nuptial chambers of their husbands. When the youngest daughter went to the nuptial chamber, she noticed that the donkey skull was beginning to change. In less than a minute it had changed into the form of a handsome young man of eighteen.

The youngest daughter was delighted with this change. Her husband gave her a warning, however. "You must never tell anyone about me. If I hear that you have told anyone of my present form, I shall leave, and you will never be able to find me, even if you wear out an iron cane and a pair of iron shoes in your travels."

In those days many Turkish women used to go to the public bath on whatever days were reserved for them. The first time that the youngest daughter went to the bath after her marriage, the other women there talked among themselves about her. When they saw her entering the bath, they said to one another, "Look! The wife of the donkey skull is coming." During the time she was there, many such remarks were made, and, of course, some of these reached her ears. This made her angry, but she could not tell any of the other women the truth about her husband.

"This must be kept secret," she kept reminding herself. She knew well that if she revealed the truth, she would lose her husband.

This annoying situation happened one day in the bath. It happened two days in the bath. It happened three days. At last she could bear their gossip no longer, their saying, "There is the wife of the donkey skull. Look at her!"

One day when she had heard still more gossip of that kind, she burst out, "Oh, the donkey's skull or something else's skull! My husband is really a young man who is like a ball of heavenly light. He is like a lion!"

"What? Is that so?" the other women asked.

This was exactly what the young man had feared. He had climbed onto the dome of the bath and was listening to their conversation. When he heard her reveal the secret of his transformation, he descended and knocked on the door of the bath—*Tak! Tak! Tak!* When his wife came to the door, he said to her, "Now you have lost me forever! You will never be able to find me again, even if you should wear out an iron cane and a pair of iron shoes. Because you disobeyed my instruction to keep our secret, I must now say farewell." Saying this, he disappeared, and the winds blew in his place.

As soon as she had finished at the bath, the youngest daughter went directly to her padishah father and said, "My dear father, my husband was not really a donkey skull but a ball of heavenly light, truly a lion of a man!"

"Is that so?"

"Yes, but I have lost him by revealing this secret. I could not stand having the women at the bath make fun of me any longer, and so I told them of his real nature. He has gone, but I shall seek him and find him somehow."

Her father bought her an iron walking stick and a pair of iron shoes, and she set out at once on her search. She went a little; she went far. She climbed mountain after mountain in her journey. After going for a very great distance, she came to a fountain. She sat there to rest for a bit. In a little while she saw a girl approaching that same fountain, and the princess asked that other girl, "What is the name of this place?"

"This is Pearl Fountain."

The princess said,

"You wear pearls in your hair.
You wear pearl-studded clogs.
You come to this fountain for water—*tıpış, tıpış.*
Has my sweetheart passed this way?
Where, then, is my sweetheart today?"

The Pearl Maiden said, "He has gone to that other mountain, the one over there." And she pointed the way.

The princess picked up her iron walking stick again and traveled toward that other mountain, far, far away. As she walked along the base of that mountain, she came to a fountain. When another girl came to that fountain to get water, the princess called to her, "What is the name of this place?"

"This is Gold Fountain," the girl said.

Then the princess said to her,

"You wear a golden dress,
And clogs of gold are on your feet.
You come to this fountain for water—*tıpış, tıpış.*
Has my sweetheart passed this way?
Where, then, is my sweetheart today?"

The Golden Maiden answered, pointing off in such and such a direction, "He is on that mountain over there."

Again the princess began to walk, walking and walking, toward that mountain far, far away, over mountain, over hill, over plain. As she approached the mountain to which the Golden Maiden had directed her, she came to a fountain. When another girl came with a diamond-covered pitcher to get water, she asked that other girl, "What is the name of this place?"

195

"This place is called Diamond Fountain."
Then the princess said to her,

"You wear a diamond dress,
And diamond-studded clogs upon your feet.
You come to this fountain for water—*tıpış, tıpış.*
Has my sweetheart passed this way?
Where, then, is my sweetheart today?"

The Diamond Maiden said, "Your sweetheart is in the mansion on that high, high mountain over there." The princess followed the directions the girl had given to that mountain, and as she approached it, she saw a huge mansion on its lower level. Coming closer to that mansion, she saw her husband looking out of one of its windows at her.

When he recognized her, her husband rushed out in disbelief to meet her, saying, "My girl, how did you ever get here? What courage you must have had!"

"I have been looking for you from this place to that place," she said, "and now I have found you." She began to tell him some of the things that had happened along the way, how she had gone from mountain to mountain, how she had stopped at three different fountains and taken directions from three different girls.

"Very well done," he said, "but come inside quickly!" Taking her inside the mansion, he said, "My mother, who is a giant, will be returning here very soon. If she should see you here, she would become terribly angry and punish you." Since he was not just an ordinary person but had magic powers, he slapped her once, and the princess became a broom.

Very soon after that, his mother arrived. She entered the mansion saying, "*Öf! Öf!* I smell a human girl here. She smells as if she could be the daughter of a padishah."

"Nonsense, Mother! There is no such thing!"

"Something smells bad. It smells! In my nose is the odor of the daughter of a padishah!"

"No, Mother. For fear of you, no one comes near this mansion. How could a daughter of a padishah do such a thing?"

They argued this way until they went to bed. The mother of this boy was indeed a giant. She was the owner of all the mountains through which the princess had traveled to get there.

When morning came, they arose, and the mother prepared to go out to oversee her mountains. The boy said, "Mother, I am curious. If the daughter of a padishah *should* happen to come this way, would you eat her? I am just asking."

"No, I wouldn't eat her if she should come, but, in fact, none has ever come. If one ever should, however, I promise not to eat her."

Having received her promise, her son slapped the broom, and his wife reappeared. She could now live there with them. Before the giant woman left for her mountains, she said to her new daughter-in-law, "Girl, while I am gone, sweep or do not sweep the house. It is up to you." Saying this, she left.

When his mother had gone, the young man went outside and took a short walk. When he returned to the mansion, he found his wife in tears. "Princess, why are you crying?" he asked.

"Why shouldn't I be crying? When your mother left, she said to me, 'Girl, while I am gone, sweep or do not sweep the house. It is up to you.' What can she mean by that?"

"Princess, there is nothing to wonder about in that. Sweep half of the house and leave the other half unswept. That is the meaning of my mother's words."

The princess swept half of the mansion and left the other half unswept. In the evening the giant woman returned with a great roaring noise. When she looked at the work done by her daughter-in-law, she asked, "Girl, did my son teach you how to do this?"

"No, my dear mother. I just did the work you told me to do."

"Very well, then." Saying this, the giant sat down and started picking from her teeth the remains of animals which she had hunted and eaten that day. As she picked her teeth, she also gave orders to the girl to do this and do that and do something else. She did not, of course, want the girl in the house. But the evening passed and then the night.

In the morning the giant woman called the princess to her again and said, "Girl, while I am gone today, I want you to do something. Do you see these forty caldrons?"

"Yes, I do."

"Well, I want you to weep enough during the day to fill these forty caldrons with your tears."

"*Aman!* How can I ever fill up these forty caldrons by weeping? Why, that is impossible!"

"Well, if you do not fill them by the time I have returned this evening, I shall eat you!"

Her husband did not hear this order, for he was outside the mansion in the garden at that time. The girl wept and wept and wept. When her husband came inside and found her, he asked, "Princess, why are you crying?"

"Why shouldn't I be crying? Before your mother left, she ordered me to fill these forty caldrons with my tears before she returned this evening. How could anyone do that?"

"What can be easier than that? Don't cry about it. We can manage that matter very easily." Searching quickly around the kitchen of the mansion, they found a box of salt and poured a small amount of it into each of the forty caldrons. Then they filled the caldrons with water and made a mixture

197

of salty water that tasted just like tears.

In the evening the giant woman came riding a large earthenware urn that roared—*v-u-u-u-v*—as it came through the air.

"Oh! Your mother is coming!" said the bride.

"Don't worry! Let her come!"

When the giant woman entered the mansion, the first thing that she did was to go to the forty caldrons. She dipped her finger into the first caldron and tasted its contents. The liquid tasted like tears. Then she went to the second, the third, the fourth, and all the rest of the caldrons, tasting their contents in that way. They were all filled with something that tasted like tears. "Aha!" she said. "My son taught you again how to do this, didn't he?"

"No, my dear mother. I have filled them by weeping hard all day."

In the morning the giant woman called, "Girl, come here." When the princess went to her, she said, "At the very peak of this mountain, there is another mansion. In that mansion on a shelf there is a closed box. You will go there, get that box, and bring it to me." After giving these orders, the giant woman left.

The princess began at once to cry, confused and discouraged. To herself she said, "A mansion at the very peak of this mountain . . . difficult to reach . . . that box, a closed box . . . how can I bring it?" And she cried and cried and cried.

The young man came to her right away. He had magic powers, of course. He asked, "Now why are you crying, princess?"

"Today your mother gave me some difficult work again."

"What did she say to you?"

"She said, 'There is another mansion on the very peak of this mountain. In that mansion on a shelf there is a box, a closed box. You will get that box and bring it to me. If you do not, I shall eat you.' That is what she said to me."

"Don't worry; don't worry, but listen carefully now to what I tell you. On your way to that other mansion you will come to a fountain. The water from one of its faucets is sweet; that from the other faucet is bitter. You will drink some of the water from the bitter faucet and say,

> '*Aman,* O Fountain!
> My soul, O Fountain!
> What delicious water you have!'

"Pass along quickly then, and you will soon come to a pear tree. Its fruit is sour—oh, much too sour to eat. But you will take a bite from one of these pears and hold it in your mouth, saying,

> '*Aman,* O Pear Tree!
> My soul, O Pear Tree!
> What sweet fruit you have!'

"Then pass along quickly. You will come to the mansion next, and you will see that it has double doors in front, one of which stands open and the other closed. Close the open door and open the closed door.

"Then when you enter the mansion, you will find two animals guarding the inner hallway, a lion on one side and a horse on the other. Before the lion you will find a trough of grass, and before the horse you will find a trough of meat. Take the grass and place it before the horse; then take the meat and place it before the lion.

"Go immediately then to the shelf and take the closed box. Run away with it, without looking back and being sure to keep it closed all of the time."

The princess set out at once and soon came to the fountain that had sweet water flowing from one faucet and bitter water from the other. Taking a drink of the bitter water, she said,

"Aman, O Fountain!
My soul, O Fountain!
What delicious water you have!"

Passing on quickly, she soon came to a pear tree whose fruit was very sour. Taking a bite of one of the pears and holding it in her mouth, she said,

"Aman, O Pear Tree!
My soul, O Pear Tree!
What sweet fruit you have!"

Moving along quickly, she then came to the mansion with double doors in front, one of which was open and the other closed. She opened the closed door and closed the open door.

Inside these doors she found a lion standing guard on one side and a horse on the other. There was a trough of grass before the lion and a trough of meat before the horse. She exchanged these troughs so that the grass was in front of the horse and the meat in front of the lion.

She went then to the shelf, took the closed box, and started to run away with it, never once looking back. As she ran, she heard a loud voice say, "Catch her, lion! Stop her, horse!"

But the lion said, "Not I! I suffered for years trying to eat the grass placed before me, but she came and gave me meat!"

"Not I!" said the horse. "I went hungry for years trying to eat the meat placed before me, but she came and gave me grass!"

As she came to the front doors of that mansion, the voice shouted, "Stop her, closed door! Stop her, open door!"

"Not I!" said the closed door. "I stood open for years, but when she came along she closed me."

"Not I!" said the open door. "I stood closed for years, but she came and opened me."

She ran out of the mansion and started along the path down the mountain. Behind her she heard the voice shout, "Block her path, pear tree! Block her path!"

"Not I!" said the pear tree. "For many years no one would eat my fruit, but she took a bite of one of my pears and said,

> 'Aman, O Pear Tree!
> My soul, O Pear Tree!
> What sweet fruit you have!'

No, I'll not block her path!"

As she ran on, she approached the fountain, one of whose faucets poured out sweet water, and the other bitter water. She heard the voice behind her call, "Stop her, fountain! Flood her pathway and make it impassable!"

But the fountain said, "Not I! For years, one of my faucets went unused, but she came along and drank water from that faucet, saying,

> 'Aman, O Fountain!
> My soul, O Fountain!
> What delicious water you have!'

No, I'll not stop her!"

As she ran along toward the mansion of the giant woman, the princess opened the lid of the box a little to see what it contained. She had forgotten that her husband had warned her to keep it shut at all times. Immediately there flowed out of the box wild music—songs and exciting dance tunes. The princess began to dance uncontrollably, and everything around her also began to dance. Unable to stop dancing and unable to stop the music, she began to cry loudly.

When her husband heard the wild music, he ran to her and pushed the button that closed the box. "If I had not come, you would have died here," he said. "But now place the box where my mother will find it when she comes home."

When the giant woman returned and found the box, she was very suspicious about how it got there. She asked the princess, "Didn't my son teach you how to get this box?"

She answered, "No, no, my dear mother. I found a way to bring it here myself."

The giant woman was greatly upset by this. She decided to eat the girl the next day without giving her any more difficult tasks to accomplish. But her son, who had magic power, was able to understand what was going on in her mind. When he went to bed that night, he said to his wife, "Let us leave this place."

"How can we do that?" she asked.

"Later tonight, when we are sure that my mother is asleep, we shall flee

201

from this mansion." At midnight they arose, and they went and went and went and went.

When the giant woman woke up, she saw that the boy and the girl had disappeared. She mounted her earthenware urn, and—*v-u-u-u-v!*—she flew after them. When the princess looked back, she said, "*Aman,* your mother is coming!" But the boy had magic power. He slapped the princess once, and she became a mosque. He slapped himself and became a minaret.

When his mother reached the spot where they had disappeared, she looked around and saw nothing but a mosque and a minaret. "They are not here," she said.

They abandoned their magic forms as soon as she had flown away, and they continued to flee as they had before.

The uncle of the giant woman said to her, "Let me go and look for them this time." He went after them, but a short time later he returned without having seen them at all.

The giant woman's aunt then said, "Let me try now."

Looking behind them, the princess said, "*Aman,* your mother's aunt is now pursuing us!" This time when the young man slapped his wife, she became a flock of sheep, and he became a shepherd.

The aunt came along and called, "Ho, shepherd! Have a girl and a boy passed this way?"

He said, "The road goes in this direction as well as in the other direction. You can go either way on it."

"Damn you! I didn't ask about the road. Did a boy and a girl pass this way?"

"Well, the road goes in this direction as well as in the other direction."

"Damn you again!" she said, returning to the mansion with no more success than the uncle had had.

Then the giant woman said, "I'll go after them again. My son is doing all this! That flock of sheep is the girl, and that shepherd is my son." Mounting her earthenware urn, she flew with great speed toward them—*v-u-u-u-v!*

Looking back, the daughter of the padishah said, "Your mother is coming again!"

When he heard this, her husband said, "There is only one thing now to do." He slapped the girl again, and this time she became a poplar tree. He slapped himself and became a terrible snake, a monstrous snake poised to strike from atop the poplar tree.

When the boy's mother reached them, she said, "The poplar tree is the girl, and the snake is you, my son."

The snake now spoke, saying, "Now that you have caught us, Mother, let me kiss you for the last time." But he was deceiving her, for as he was kissing her, he opened his lips and the deadly snake venom entered her body. She died right there without even struggling.

He then slapped both himself and the girl to restore them to their normal forms. They began now to travel toward the home of her padishah father. As they approached the town where he lived, everyone along the road, on both sides, began shouting, "The youngest daughter of our padishah is coming! The youngest daughter of our padishah is coming!"

The padishah became almost delirious with delight at the return of his daughter. He assembled all of the people and had his daughter married all over again in a ceremony that lasted for forty days and forty nights, and they lived very happily after that.

İfrit, His Uncle, and the Ağa

Once there was and once there wasn't, time in time, when the sieve was in the hay—well, in those times, there was a padishah who had three sons and a daughter. This padishah said to his children, "When I die, load my body on our white camel and let him go. Follow him, and wherever he kneels down to rest, bury me there. Moreover, when you come to visit my grave, be sure that you never take the right-hand road; always take the left-hand road."

Shortly after that, the padishah died, and his sons put his body on a white camel and let it go where it would. They followed it and followed it until finally it knelt to rest. But what was this? The camel had knelt by the side of a coal cellar! "We have no choice," said the eldest. "It was our father's will that he be buried where the white camel knelt, so we must bury him here." And so they did.

Some time after the father had been buried, his sons decided to go and pray at their father's grave. The eldest son went first, but he did not return. Puzzled, the middle son set out for his father's grave, but he did not return, either.

Finally the youngest son set out for his father's grave, and after praying, he fell asleep beside the grave. As he slept there, his father spoke to him from the grave. "My son," he said, "your elder brothers have been at my grave and have prayed for me, and then they have proceeded on down the road and have taken the first left-hand turn that they saw. I want you to do the same thing. When you take that left-hand turn, you will meet a dervish with a big fur coat. He will ask you to come and sit on his fur coat, but you must say, 'It would not be proper for me to sit on your fur coat instead of you, for you are older.' Then the dervish will sit on the coat himself."

After hearing this, the youngest son woke up and started walking along the road until he came to the junction. Then he took the left-hand turn and after a while he saw a dervish sitting at the foot of a tree. The dervish asked the young man, "Will you come and sit on my fur coat?"

"No, thank you," said the youngest son. "It would not be proper for me to sit on it while you sit on the ground."

When the young man refused to sit on the fur coat, the dervish sat on it himself, and as he did so, he suddenly fell down into a well over which the fur coat had been spread. This was the fur coat on which the two older brothers had sat, disregarding the directions given to them by their dead father.

The dervish had a large palace nearby, and now that the dervish had fallen down into the well, the youngest son appropriated this palace. A few days after he began living there, he returned to his father's palace and told his sister that he had come to possess a palace that was even finer than that of the padishah, and he invited her to come and live with him there. She agreed to do this, and the two of them went to live in this new palace.

One day the youngest son went hunting to shoot two good birds. His sister would eat one of them, and he himself would eat the other one. Now on that same day, his sister had been walking in the palace garden while her brother was away hunting. As she walked through the garden, she heard a voice coming from the bottom of the well. "There is a certain staff in one of the highest rooms of the palace. If you will bring that metal staff here and touch it to the stone at the top of the well, it will enable me to get out of this place." The girl was greatly surprised at hearing this voice, but she searched through the upper rooms of the palace, finally found the metal staff, and returned to the well with it. She touched the staff on the stone rim of the well, and a few minutes later the dervish came to the surface.

At first sight, the girl fell in love with the dervish, and she hid him in the palace. That day, her brother shot three birds instead of two, and he brought all three of them home. By the end of the day, all three birds were eaten. The brother noticed this, but he did not say anything about it.

Every day the brother went hunting, and every day he managed to shoot three birds and bring them home. Each day, all three of the birds were eaten. This curious business went on for about six months. At the end of that time, the brother noticed that his sister began to act rather strangely. He asked her if she were ill. "No," she said. "I am not exactly ill."

This strange behavior of his sister went on for another three months, and then one day the brother found that four birds came close enough to him so that he could shoot them. He shot the four birds and took them home, and when he arrived there, he found that a son had been born to his sister.

When he saw the baby, he asked, "What is this, Sister?"

"Well, this was my 'illness,' Brother."

"Well," said her brother, "it is better that it should be revealed. I am glad that you have a son. May you have great joy of him."

When the brother and the sister were considering what name they should give to the infant, the child miraculously began to talk. He said, "Call me İfrit." The brother and sister therefore decided to name him İfrit.

Four or five more months passed during which the dervish continued to live in hiding in the palace. He and the sister were very much in love with each other. One day the dervish said to his wife, "This arrangement cannot go on like this forever. Let us kill your brother."

"How shall we do that?" asked the girl.

"I shall become a snake," said the dervish, "and I shall hide on the transom of the door. When your brother enters the room, I shall spring on him and sting him to death."

The dervish's wife agreed to this, and the dervish became a snake and lay along the transom of the door, waiting for the brother to return from hunting and enter the room. But it so happened that his son, İfrit, was playing in front of the door. When the dervish's brother-in-law came home, he reached down and picked İfrit up and set him on his shoulder, for he was very fond of the child. When the dervish saw that his own son was being brought toward the door on his brother-in-law's shoulder, he changed his mind about killing the man, because in doing this he might kill his own son, too. So the brother-in-law was saved this time from death.

Now the dervish made a plan to kill his brother-in-law in another way. He said to his wife, "I shall turn into a scorpion and hide in your brother's boot. Then when he puts his boot on, I shall sting him to death through the sole of his foot."

As the padishah's son prepared to go hunting the next day, he looked

for his boot. His young nephew was with him, and the boy said, "Will you let me wear your boots, Uncle? I would like to walk around in them before you go."

"Of course you may try them on," said his uncle. Before İfrit put on his uncle's boots, he turned them upside down, and the scorpion fell out. The child thus again saved his uncle's life.

Well, for the second time, the padishah's son had escaped, and the dervish was determined to destroy him on the next attempt. This time, he decided to turn into a poisonous bird and fly across the hunter's path. Since the brother-in-law hunted only birds, this would certainly be a way in which the dervish could reach him. He knew that if the brother-in-law shot and ate the poisonous bird, he must surely die. Moreover, the dervish knew that because he himself had magical powers, he could return to life after the deed had been done.

As usual, the padishah's son went hunting that day, and on the way home he saw flying across his path the most beautiful bird he had ever seen. He aimed at it and shot it dead. He brought it home in the evening and said to his sister, "Pluck the feathers of this bird, but don't throw them away. They are so beautiful that we can make a cushion from them for İfrit." This was exactly what the dervish had hoped he would say because it would keep his feathers from being scattered about, and as long as there was some part of him left, he could be restored to life.

The dervish's wife cooked the bird and placed it before her brother. Just before the dinner, İfrit shouted, "Uncle, Uncle! I see a big crowd coming, just like a wedding party. It is approaching our palace!"

His mother said, "İfrit, sit down and be quiet!"

But, "Come and see for yourself!" said İfrit.

When his mother and his uncle went to the window to see the crowd, İfrit changed the plates, putting the plate of the poisonous bird before his mother and an ordinary bird before his uncle. When they returned to the table and sat down, they began to eat the food.

The padishah's daughter said, "My dish is tastier than yours," but she was dead before she had finished her sentence. Her brother began to cry.

İfrit said, "Why are you crying, Uncle? Don't you know what they have tried to do to us? Bring those feathers here. They belong to a devil who is trying to kill you." İfrit took the feathers and burned them.

Now that the sister was dead, there were only two of them left, the padishah's youngest son and İfrit. After they had lived for some time in the palace, İfrit said to his uncle, "Do you see that fire in the distance? I'm going to walk over there and get some fire and bring it here so that we can light a fire of our own."

İfrit reached the place in a single jump even though the fire was as far away as Cyprus is from here. He reached it and found there above the fire a caldron that was boiling. He took an egg out of the caldron and a piece of burning ember from the fire and ran back with them to his uncle. Now, the padishah of the area where the fire was burning had a daughter who suffered from a grave illness. This girl, however, suddenly became well. İfrit said to his uncle, "Why don't you go there and say to the padishah, 'I cured your daughter'?"

"How could I prove that I had cured the padishah's daughter?" asked his uncle.

"My uncle, it was because of this egg," said İfrit. "We can prove that, too." They took the egg and had the Koran read over it by a *hoca*, and then they started to boil the egg again. As they boiled the egg, the girl became sick again. The more they boiled the egg, the more ill she became. They reported this to the padishah and told him that they could cure his daughter by removing the egg from the boiling water. He offered them a reward if they could cure her in any way whatever. When they stopped boiling the egg, the girl recovered again. The youngest son was thus able to persuade the padishah that he had cured his daughter, and he therefore received the reward.

İfrit and his uncle lived together for a long while and then one day İfrit said to his uncle, "This arrangement of ours cannot go on forever. It would be better for you to go one way and for me to go another." Before they parted, İfrit pulled two hairs from his head and gave them to his uncle. "Uncle," he said, "whenever you are in distress, rub these hairs together and I shall be there to help you."

İfrit went to the west and his uncle went to the east. After a long journey, the uncle came to a village. He found the *ağa* of that village and asked him for a job on his farm. The *ağa* agreed to give the young man a job and to provide his food, but he set certain conditions. "I shall provide your food," he said, "but you must promise that you will never tear the edges of the *yufka*. Also, you must not break the skin of cream from the top of the yogurt. Furthermore, you must never say, 'I am hungry.' If you do say that you are hungry, I shall take enough skin off your back to make a pair of shoes. On the other hand, if you can upset me and make me angry, then you will take enough skin from my back to make a pair of shoes."

The young man agreed to this, and several days passed as he worked on the *ağa*'s farm. Every day he became more hungry, however, for he could not eat. He could not eat the yogurt without breaking the skin of cream on the top, and he could not eat the *yufka* without breaking its edges. As a result, he began to starve to death. Three days and five days passed in this manner with the young man's not eating anything at all. At last, he became so weak and so ill that he just lay there without getting up at all. The *ağa* came and asked him, "Well, young man, are you angry with me?"

"No, I am not angry with you," said the young man, "but I am truly hungry."

"Ah! You say you are hungry," said the *ağa*. "You remember our bargain.

208

Lie right there while I take from your back enough skin to make a pair of shoes." And at once the *ağa* removed the skin that he required.

In deep pain, weeping from the sore place on his back, the young man put his hand in his sash, took out the two hairs that İfrit had given him, and rubbed them together. Immediately, İfrit appeared and asked, "What is the matter, Uncle?"

"Well, I bargained to work for this *ağa* for my food. I was unable, however, to fulfill the terms of the agreement, and as a result, he cut a piece of my skin off my back." Then the uncle explained to İfrit exactly what had happened, leaving out not a single detail.

"Where is this *ağa*?" asked İfrit.

"He lives over there in that large house," said the uncle.

İfrit went to the *ağa* and asked whether he might be hired to work as a farmhand.

"All right," said the *ağa*, "I shall hire you, but I have certain conditions under which you must work."

"What are they?" asked İfrit.

"You must not break the cream on the top of the yogurt that I give you to eat, and you must not break the edges of the *yufka*. Also, you must never say, 'I am hungry.' If you break any of these conditions, I shall cut a piece of hide from your back large enough to make a pair of shoes. On the other hand, if you can make me admit that I am angry, then you will cut a piece of hide from my back large enough to make a pair of shoes."

İfrit at once began to work for the *ağa*. He ate the *yufka* by cutting a large piece from the center of it with his knife and leaving the edges intact. He ate the yogurt by breaking a hole in the bottom of the jar and sucking the yogurt out in that way. The skin of cream was left whole in the jar. By these means, he managed to eat as much as he wanted.

One day, İfrit made a large fire in a field. He put many skewers in the fire, and when they were red hot, he took them and stuck them into the bellies of the flock of sheep. In that way, he killed five or six hundred sheep. When the *ağa* came and looked at the pasture where hundreds of sheep were lying dead, he said, "What is the matter with them?"

"*Ağa*, they are tired and they are resting," said İfrit. "Are you annoyed at me?"

"No. Why should I be?" The *ağa* then asked İfrit, "Do you know how to garden?"

"There is nothing that I know better," said İfrit. The *ağa* gave İfrit a forty-acre orchard to tend, but during the first night İfrit cut down all the trees in the orchard. When the *ağa* came to inspect the orchard in the morning, he was amazed at what he saw. He asked İfrit, "What is all this?"

"Well, *Ağa*," said İfrit, "do you sleep standing up or lying down?"

"I sleep lying down!"

209

"Well, the trees are doing the same thing," said İfrit. "They are tired. When they have had enough sleep, they will wake up and stand up again."

The *ağa* was deeply concerned with what he saw. He wondered what İfrit might do next, and that evening he suggested to his wife that they leave for somewhere else as soon as possible, because he realized that İfrit was a very dangerous person. İfrit overheard the conversation between the *ağa* and his wife, and he turned himself into a grain of millet and hid in a corner of the *ağa*'s saddlebag. As the *ağa* and his family were leaving that village, they were attacked by three dogs. The *ağa* said, "I wish İfrit were here to chase these dogs away."

When İfrit heard this, he jumped out of the saddlebag. "Here I am, Ağa." He then killed the three dogs and traveled along with the *ağa* and his family in his usual form.

At last they came to the bank of a river where they were going to spend the night, and they pitched their tent there. The *ağa* and his wife, talking quietly, decided to get rid of İfrit by throwing him into the river after he had fallen asleep.

While they were all sitting around the fire before bedtime, one of the *ağa*'s sons said, "Mother, I have to urinate."

The *ağa*'s wife said, 'İfrit, take him somewhere to urinate."

İfrit took the boy a short distance away from the campsite and said to him, "Son, if you urinate even a drop, I shall kill you!" He then took the boy back to the campfire.

After a little while, the child again said, "Mother, I have to urinate."

Again the mother said, "İfrit, take the child away so that he can relieve himself."

This time, İfrit said to the boy, "If you dare to urinate even one drop, I shall slit your throat!" Then he took the boy back again to the family.

Once again, the child complained that he had to urinate, and once again İfrit was asked to care for him. "Take him and burst him, İfrit," said the *ağa*'s wife.

Doing exactly as the woman had instructed, İfrit took the boy into the nearby woods, dropped a large rock on his belly, and actually burst him. He returned without the boy and told the *ağa*'s wife that he had done what she had ordered him to do. While the *ağa* and his wife went to look for the child, İfrit took from their bundle one of the wife's gowns. After everyone else had fallen asleep, İfrit got up and put on the wife's gown. Then he carefully lifted the wife over to his bed and he crawled into bed alongside the *ağa*. Around midnight, İfrit whispered in a woman's voice, "Come. Let us throw İfrit into the river before he wakes up."

They went to the bed where the *ağa*'s wife was sleeping. They lifted the whole bed by grasping the canvas sheet on which it was made. They swung it back and forth three times, and then they heaved it far out into the river.

The *ağa* said, "There! We have at last gotten rid of İfrit!"

İfrit answered, in his own voice now, "At last we have gotten rid of your wife." When the *ağa* realized what had happened, he began to weep. "Why are you weeping?" asked İfrit. "Are you annoyed or angry at me, *Ağa?*"

"Of course I am angry with you," answered the *ağa*. "You have ruined first my flock and then my orchard and now my family. You have killed both my wife and my son."

When İfrit heard the *ağa* say this, he said, "Aha! You have become angry and have therefore failed to meet the condition of our agreement. Take off your shirt and lie down so that I can cut from your back enough hide to make a pair of shoes."

When İfrit had removed sufficient skin from the *ağa's* back, he made a pair of shoes with it and put the shoes on his own feet. Wearing these shoes, he walked back to the farm for his uncle, and then the two of them left that land.

As for me, I walked here to tell you this tale.

It's So Simple, My Friend!

One evening Nasreddin Hoca's neighbor looked out of his window and saw the Hoca digging and digging in the garden in the bright moonlight near his doorstep. Curious, the neighbor went next door to see what the Hoca was doing with all that digging.

"Hoca Effendi," he said, "are you looking for something?"

"Yes, yes!" said the Hoca, not stopping his digging as he spoke. "I've lost my signet ring, and I'm trying to find it."

The neighbor, eager to help, fell to his knees and began digging, too, looking for the Hoca's ring. But no matter how deeply their hands turned up the earth, they could find no ring. At last, the neighbor stopped his digging and settled back on his heels. "Hoca Effendi, are you *sure* you lost your ring out here?"

"Out here?" said the Hoca. "No, no, my friend. I lost it in my coal cellar."

"In your *coal cellar!*" exclaimed the neighbor. "Then why, Hoca Effendi, are you looking for it out here in your garden?"

The Hoca, too, squatted on his heels and spread out his arms as he spoke. "But it's so simple, my friend! The *light* is better out here!"

The Bilingual Boars of Sinop Province

There was a young Turk of Georgian ancestry who returned to this village late one summer after having completed his military service. When he arrived there, all of the peasants were worried about their corn crop, for now that it was ripening, boars were beginning to feast on it. These boars came under the cover of darkness and ate the corn. Although the farmers kept watch at night for them, it was often too dark to see them.

The young soldier who had just come home decided to watch in his family's cornfield one night when there was fairly clear moonlight. As he was watching, he heard the grunting kind of sound peculiar to pigs, and soon he saw a couple of these animals approaching him.

Unfortunately, he had neglected to bring his gun with him, and of course he wanted to shoot those boars. "I am afraid that if I go back to the house to get my gun, the boars will become frightened and run away. I'll just call to my wife and have her bring my gun," he decided. "Since these are Turkish boars, they will not understand Georgian, so I'll call in Georgian." At once he shouted, "*Gogo saçma çaçvi, keni topi meydani Dranga,*" which means, "Lady, bring my gun loaded with buckshot to the field." While he waited for his gun, he thought, "I'll fire at those boars and at least knock them down."

Of course, when the boars heard him shouting to his wife, they became frightened and ran away. Seeing them leave, the young man exclaimed, "By Allah, those are very intelligent boars! They understand Georgian as well as Turkish!"

The Prince and Pomegranate Seed

Once there was and once there wasn't, when Allah had many creatures and to talk too much was a sin, when camels were salesmen and fleas were shepherds, when I was rocking my father's cradle *tıngır mıngır*—well, in those times, in a certain country there was an old woman called the fairy mother.

One day with the other women of the village, the fairy mother took her old water pitcher and went to the spring outside the padishah's palace to draw water. That day, the prince had nothing better to do, so he sat at his window watching those who came to the spring. To amuse himself, he threw a precious stone—sometimes a diamond, sometimes a pearl—at each person who drew water. And of course he threw a gem at the old woman, that fairy mother. But the gem hit the pitcher instead. And the pitcher broke in her hand, and the water spilled all over the ground. She looked to her left and to her right, but she saw no one. Then she looked up, and there sat the prince at his window laughing. The fairy mother was very angry. She tossed her head, saying, "Son of the padishah, may you burn with desire for Pomegranate Seed!" Without another word, she left.

Suddenly the prince began to burn inside, and nothing would ease the burning. Sick with desire, he neither ate nor slept, day after day. The servants reported this strange illness to the padishah, and the padishah told his wife, and the prince's mother came at once to see him. When she heard him moaning, "Pomegranate Seed!" she said, "Oh, what could be easier?" and she had baskets and baskets of pomegranates sent to his room. But the prince didn't even look at them. "I burn!" he cried. "I am burning!"

Doctor after doctor was called, but none could discover the cause for the prince's pain. And if no cause is known, how can a cure be found? Finally, the only doctors left were İdi and Bidi. İdi came and looked at the prince. Then he said, "Only Bidi can tell what the illness is." As for Bidi, he, too, looked at the prince. Then he said, "Only İdi can tell what the illness is." From İdi to Bidi, from Bidi to İdi, and neither was willing to give an answer.

In truth, both İdi and Bidi knew that the prince burned with longing for Pomegranate Seed, but neither one dared to tell the padishah. And both İdi and Bidi knew that the fairy mother would not take back the curse she had laid on the prince.

The padishah sent his spies to the place where İdi and Bidi came to talk.

213

And when they talked of the prince's illness, the spies hurried back to the padishah with the news. At once, the padishah sent for the old woman, but she refused to come, either for the padishah's servants or for his viziers. "If the padishah wants to know about this matter, he must come here and ask me himself," she said.

That night, the padishah and his grand vizier disguised themselves in shabby clothes and went to the home of the fairy mother. Of course, she knew them, and how she laughed! But she had them sit down, and then she told the whole story of the prince's breaking her old pitcher—the pitcher she had had from her mother and her grandmother—and of his laughing and of the prince's burning love for Pomegranate Seed because of her curse. "Now," she said, "he will either burn forever for love of Pomegranate Seed or he will seek her and gain nothing but grief."

The padishah, remembering his son's cry "I am burning! I am burning!" wept as he begged the fairy mother to grant the prince the Pomegranate Seed he burned for. At last she said, "Your son cannot put the pieces of my jar together and recover the water that was spilled. He must, then, for seven days and nights carry water from one spring to another for me. If he can do that, I shall tell him how he can find Pomegranate Seed."

Carrying the fairy mother's two big jars to the prince, the padishah said, "My son, there is no way of breaking the fairy mother's curse. You must either gather up the water you spilled or you must carry water for her in these jars for seven days and seven nights."

What could the prince do? He burned for Pomegranate Seed! So he carried water, carried water, day and night for seven days, until his strength was almost finished. At the end of that time, the fairy mother called him to her. "This you must do," she said. "Pass seven mountains beyond Kaf Mountain. Cross seven seas. Then you will see seven roads; choose one and walk along it for seven years and seven months. Then you will find yourself in the land of Pomegranate Seed. The rest is up to you. If you are lucky, you will win Pomegranate Seed."

The prince begged for mercy; he pleaded for a helper in the task. He even asked, "Who *is* Pomegranate Seed?" But he could get no further help.

"You must do this thing yourself, since the trouble is of your own making. But watch and listen carefully the whole time," she warned.

There was no choice: he must go by himself to seek Pomegranate Seed. So he went home. From his father he got a pair of iron shoes and an iron staff; from his mother he got an old robe and food for seven years. And he said neither yes nor no, though his father beat his knees and begged him to stay and his mother asked him to forget this mad quest. He just kissed their hands and left.

He went over hills and across rivers. He went a little distance; he went far; and when he turned to look, he found he had gone only the length of a barley grain. "I am burning! I am burning!" he cried. Suddenly he saw a beautiful fish on the road at his feet, flopping in the dust. The prince stopped, remembering that the fairy mother had told him, "But watch and listen carefully the whole time."

He listened, and the fish spoke. "Seven seas have thrown me out onto dry land, and I shall die without water. Son, O son, if you are human, take me to a sea before I perish."

Pitying the fish, the prince murmured, "May this bring me good luck," and he picked up the fish and started walking. In the closing and opening of an eye, he saw the sea, and he threw the fish into it.

In a moment, the grateful fish lifted his head above the water and said, "Son, O son, you helped me by returning me to the sea. Now I can help you. Come. I'll carry you to the other side of the sea on my back." And he carried the prince to a land just *filled* with roses. "Here, my son," he said. "You are on dry land again. But someday you may need help. Take three scales from my back and keep them safe. If you are ever in trouble, burn one of those scales and I will come at once."

The prince took the scales and tucked them safely inside his sash. Then the fish sank into the water again, and the prince went on his way. He walked and walked and walked. As he walked, he saw a bird caught in a bush, with its wing all bloody. The bird said, "Son, O son, hear my trouble, and help me if you can. My wing is torn, and I cannot fly until it has been mended. If you

215

are human, mend my wing so that I can fly."

Pitying the bird, the prince freed him from the bush and tied the broken wing and waited there until the bird could fly again. The bird flew a little way, and then he returned. "Son, O son," he said, "you have helped me. Now I can help you. I'll carry you on my back across Kaf Mountain." And he carried the prince over Kaf Mountain and set him down in the valley beyond. "You are here," he said, "but you may someday need help. Take three feathers from my mended wing and keep them safe. If you are ever in trouble, burn one of the feathers and I will come at once."

The bird flew away as soon as the prince had plucked the feathers and put them safely in his sash. Then the prince walked on and walked on and walked on, all the while shouting, "I am burning! I am burning!" As he walked, he came to a stone on which a sick ant was lying. Since the fairy mother had told him, "But watch and listen carefully the whole time," he stopped. "Son, O son!" the ant cried. "Hear my story, and help me if you can. Today both my son and my daughter are being married. There will be two weddings at my house. But I have burned my feet and I cannot go any farther. Please, if you are human, take me to my home before the weddings have been finished."

Pitying the ant, the prince took the ant gently in his hand and climbed over one mountain after another until at last he came to a valley. There he found a nest for the ant.

But the ant said, "This is my valley, but this is not my nest—this is not my home. In the middle of this valley there is a city; in the middle of the city there is a palace; in the middle of the palace there is a garden; in the middle of the garden there is a small nest. That nest is my home. And—don't you know?—the valley is called Pomegranate Valley; the city is called Pomegranate City; the palace is called Pomegranate Palace; the garden is called Pomegranate Garden. And who walks in this garden? Pomegranate Seed, the most beautiful girl in the world, walks in this garden. Her lips are redder than the pomegranate, and her skin is whiter than snow. But who can enjoy her beauty? Her two executioners stand at the door to kill whoever speaks of her beauty if she says, 'Kill, my men. Kill.' If you value your life, do not enter the gate of that palace! Come. Follow me, and I will show you the way through the side door of the palace."

The prince eagerly followed the ant to the side door. There the ant said, "You helped me when I could not help myself, and now I have helped you. But someday you may have trouble. If you will, take three hairs from my foreleg and save them. When you are in trouble, burn one of those hairs, and I will come at once." The prince took three hairs from the ant's foreleg and put them carefully into his sash. Then he carried the ant through the door into the garden.

In the garden, hundreds and hundreds and hundreds of ants were milling about on the ground, seeking the lost parent of the two who were to

216

celebrate their weddings. With great rejoicing at the return of their lost one, they went back to their nests.

That day, Pomegranate Seed had come to the garden as the ants were gathering. Just as she was wondering what this strange invasion of ants might mean, the ants scattered again. Then she noticed a stranger beside the door. "Get him," she said to her slaves. "Blindfold him and bring him to me." And immediately they did as she had commanded.

As the prince was led forward blindfolded, he heard a beautiful voice asking, "Who are you? Tell us, so that we may help you." Yes, it was the voice of Pomegranate Seed.

"My lady, I am the prince of Kemlik country," the prince answered. "Because of what I did to the fairy mother's pitcher, I began to burn with desire for Pomegranate Seed. To find that Pomegranate Seed I have walked for seven years and seven months. Along the way, I saw none but a fish and a bird and an ant. I helped them, and they helped me, and now I have come to your garden. I want Pomegranate Seed—nothing more."

Pomegranate Seed said to her forty serving girls, "Pick a pomegranate, each of you, and give it to this young man."

But when the pomegranates were offered to him, the prince said, "Girls, keep those pomegranates for yourselves. I want Pomegranate Seed, the untouched beauty."

Pomegranate Seed smiled and said, "If he wants an untouched Pomegranate Seed, he must do something to win it. My bird sister gave me a ruby, but I lost it in the desert. If he finds it, he will have Pomegranate Seed; if not, he will have as many troubles as there are seeds in a pomegranate."

The forty girls with one voice repeated to the prince what Pomegranate Seed had said. Then, with one voice, they added, "Many have tried to win Pomegranate Seed, and all have failed. If you are sure that you can succeed, then try; if not, leave while you are still alive."

"Have I come so far without risk?" asked the prince. "I'll not go back. Wherever the ruby is—İnşallah!—I shall find it." And he left the garden.

He wandered here and there in the desert beyond the valley. How could he find a ruby in such a place, and with his eyes blindfolded? "If only I had my eyes!" he cried. "I am burning!" Suddenly he remembered the bird, and the bird's feathers. He felt carefully in his sash and pulled out a feather and burned it. Then, *prrrt*, there came the bird. "O bird," the prince cried, "I am truly in trouble. I have found Pomegranate Seed, but now I must find a ruby that she dropped in the desert. How can I find a ruby in such a place and without eyes to see? Please help me."

Without answering, the bird flew away and away and away. Then, *prrrt*, back came the bird with the ruby.

The prince tucked the ruby safely in his sash and at last found his way back to the palace. "Girls, girls!" he called. "I have found the ruby, and here

217

it is. Please tell Pomegranate Seed that I have come to claim the reward she promised." He handed the ruby to the servants.

Pomegranate Seed looked at the ruby. "Yes, it is my ruby, girls," she said. "But what is a ruby to me? I have lost in a lake the pearl ring my fish sister gave me. Tell him to find it and bring it back."

With one voice, the girls repeated to the prince what Pomegranate Seed had said. The prince answered, "If I was able to find a ruby in a desert, İnşallah!, I will find the pearl ring, too." And he left.

But as he walked along and walked along, blindfolded, slowly, slowly, toward the lake, he said, "How can this be? Can one without eyes find a pearl ring in what is surely a bottomless lake? Oh, I am burning! I am burning!" Suddenly he remembered the fish, and the fish's scales. He felt carefully in his sash and pulled out a scale and burned it. At once, he heard a splash in the water at his feet. "O fish, fish," said the prince, "I am truly in trouble. I have found Pomegranate Seed, and with the help of a bird I have found the ruby Pomegranate Seed asked of me. But now she wants her pearl ring from this lake. Please help me."

Without answering, the fish dived deep into the lake and swam and swam. Then, with a splash, the fish came up to the shore and laid the ring at the prince's feet.

The prince tucked the pearl ring safely in his sash and at last found his way back to the palace. "Girls, girls!" he called. "I have found the pearl ring. Please tell Pomegranate Seed."

Pomegranate Seed looked at the ring. "Yes, this is my pearl ring, girls," she said. "But what is a pearl ring to me? I have dropped into the ashes the diamond earring my ant mother gave to me. If he can find it and bring it back, he can have his Pomegranate Seed."

With one voice, the girls repeated to the prince what Pomegranate Seed had said. The prince answered, "Without eyes I found a ruby in a desert and a pearl ring in a bottomless lake. İnşallah!, I shall find the diamond earring, too." And he left.

But as the prince walked along and walked along, not able to see, not even knowing where the ashes were, he thought, "How can I ever find a diamond earring in the ashes? I cannot even find the ashes with my eyes all blind! I am burning! I am burning!"

Suddenly he remembered the ant, and the hairs on the ant's foreleg. He felt carefully in his sash and pulled out one of the hairs and burned it. At once, the ant was at his feet. "O ant, ant!" he cried. "I am now truly in trouble. I have found Pomegranate Seed, and with the help of a bird I found the ruby she asked of me. With the help of a fish, I found the pearl ring that Pomegranate Seed asked of me. But now she has asked for the diamond earring she dropped in the ashes. Please help me."

Without answering, the ant searched the ashes here and there, and

brought the earring to the prince. The prince tucked the earring safely into his sash and at last found his way back to the palace. "Girls, girls!" he called. "I have found the diamond earring, and here it is. Please tell Pomegranate Seed that I have come to claim my Pomegranate Seed, the untouched beauty!"

When Pomegranate Seed saw the earring, she said, "Oh, girls, this prince must truly be my kismet. Prepare now for our wedding."

In time, there was a wedding at Pomegranate Palace that lasted for forty days and forty nights. Then the prince and Pomegranate Seed went home to Kemlik country. They had their wish fulfilled. Let's go up and sit in their seats.

The Merchant's Youngest Daughter

Time in time, when the sieve was in the straw—well, in that time a rich merchant lived in a certain country. The merchant had three daughters, but the youngest daughter was quite different from the other two. Because she was interested, the merchant sent her to the *hoca* to learn to read the Koran. The two older daughters spent their time sewing,

219

doing handicrafts, and helping their mother in her housework, while the youngest one spent her time in praying, reading the Koran, and learning from the *hoca*.

Each time the merchant sold all of the goods he had on hand, he went to a large city in another country to purchase new goods. Before leaving for that city, he always asked his wife and his daughters what they would like to have him bring them from the city. The merchant's wife and his two older daughters always wanted pearls, other beads, silk and satin fabrics, and such things. But the youngest daughter asked for a prayer rug or prayer beads or a prayer cloth or something else that would help her in her worship, and each time her father would bring her exactly what she had asked for, just as he did for his wife and his other daughters.

One day the *hoca* asked the youngest daughter, "Will your father be traveling to the city again soon?"

"Yes, he will go soon," she said.

"Every time your father has asked you what you want him to bring you, you have always asked for the same kinds of things. This time, you must ask for something different," the *hoca* said. "Ask him this time to bring you İnci."

Because the *hoca* was her teacher, the girl said, "All right." And when her father was ready to leave on his journey, he was surprised when his youngest daughter asked this time for İnci.

"İnci?" her father said.

"Just İnci," his youngest daughter answered.

"Very well, my daughter," said the merchant. But still he was puzzled. As he bought, one by one, the things that he needed for his business and, then, as he bought for his wife and his two older daughters the things they had asked for, he kept saying to himself, "İnci. İnci. Does my daughter really mean that she wants a *pearl*?"

He asked here and there throughout that other country for İnci, but no one seemed to have the İnci that his youngest daughter wanted. Finally he asked a jeweler in the large city where he had always done his buying, "What about İnci? My youngest daughter has asked for İnci, and no one seems to have it. I have always done business with you. Surely you can help me."

"*İnci* is not the same as the pearl that you may be thinking of," said the jeweler. "In this country, the name of the son of the padishah is İnci. I think that he is the İnci your daughter is seeking."

"Oh, no," said the merchant. "You do not know my daughter. She would not ask in that way for the son of a padishah."

"Still," said the jeweler, "this İnci that she seeks is not the kind we have sold you for your older daughters. Try this: Go to the palace and tell the son of the padishah that your youngest daughter wants to marry him."

The merchant said to himself, "How can I tell him such a thing? I can't." But he loved his youngest daughter very much. At last he said, "For the sake of my daughter, I will go and talk to the padishah's son."

The merchant went to the palace of the padishah. He looked until he found the son of the padishah. "O son of the padishah," he said, "I am a merchant from such and such a country. My youngest daughter wishes to marry you."

The son of the padishah listened quietly. "It is possible," he said finally. "But I have a certain condition that must be met. When you reach home, you will build a nice house for me, a house suitable for the son of a padishah, and you will furnish it and decorate it. It will belong to your daughter and me. Here are two feathers. One is white, and the other is black. After you have finished preparing the house, have your youngest daughter rub these feathers against each other. I will then become a bird and fly there. When I reach your daughter, I will again become a man," said the son of the padishah.

The merchant was puzzled to hear this, but, "All right," he said. "What you have said will be done. For the sake of my youngest daughter, I will endure any kind of difficulty." Then he took the feathers and put them safely in his sash and went along home with his caravan. The things he had brought for his wife and his two older daughters he gave to them. To his youngest daughter, he said, "My daughter, I want to talk with you alone."

"Yes, my father. What is it that you wish to say?"

"The İnci that you asked for is the son of the padishah of that other country. I talked with him, and he has asked me to build a house and furnish it elegantly. He sent with me these two feathers. When I have finished and furnished the house, you are to rub these two feathers together, and he will come to you as a bird." And the merchant handed his daughter the feathers.

The youngest daughter looked at the feathers. What could the prince mean by his coming as a bird? Still, since her father had found the İnci her *hoca* had told her to ask for, she was happy.

Immediately, the merchant began to build the house, a house fine enough for the son of a padishah. When the construction was finished, he furnished the house and decorated it delicately. His youngest daughter prepared herself for the coming of her prince, and then she rubbed the two feathers together. In the winking of an eye, she saw a bird flying toward the house, and she opened the windows. When the bird had flown inside, he shook himself and became a young man as handsome as the moon itself. As soon as she saw him, she loved him, and they were married and lived happily together. Each morning, he became a bird and flew away, and each evening he flew to the girl and there became a man. This way of life continued for them for a long time. Then one morning before he flew away, the youngest daughter said to her husband, "My dear, today I will go to the public bath with my mother and my sisters. Could you give me some money for my entrance fee?"

The prince said, "My dear, aren't you making our bed every morning?"

"No. My older sister makes our bed each morning," she answered. "Why do you ask?"

"Haa! Every morning before leaving, I place a bag of gold under your pillow," he said.

"Oh? I didn't know about the gold."

"Trust me. Look under your pillow right now," he said.

She lifted up the pillow, and truly there *was* a bag of gold beneath it. "*Aman!* My older sister has taken all the other bags of gold, then, and she never said anything to me about them. From now on, I shall make up our bed myself." And she began to care for their bed herself.

After the prince had flown away that morning, the older sister came into the room and found that the bed had already been made. "I have been doing this work for you, my sister," she said. "Why don't you let me do it now?"

"It is no problem for me to make our bed," said the youngest one. "I want to do it myself from this time on."

The oldest sister understood then that her young sister had learned about the gold, and her jealousy of the youngest one began to burn even more deeply. "What can I do that will hurt her the most?" she asked herself. And she began to make an evil plan. When her mother and her two sisters were ready to go to the *hamam*, the oldest one said, "I don't want to go with you, after all. Instead, I shall stay at home and sleep."

"All right," they said, and they left to spend the day at the *hamam*. As soon as they had gone, the oldest sister dressed and went out to find a boy who would serve her purpose.

To this boy she said, "Take this piece of gold and buy with it many needles, many skewers, and many nails. The rest of the money will be yours."

The boy ran to the market and bought everything that she had asked for and brought these things to her. Without being seen by anyone, she went up to her youngest sister's bedroom, opened the window, and arranged all of the needles, the skewers, and the nails on the windowsill. Then she closed the window and went to her own room, well satisfied.

When the mother and the other two daughters returned home from the *hamam*, the family had dinner together. Then the youngest daughter hurried to her room and rubbed the two feathers together, but no bird came. Again she rubbed the feathers together, and still no bird came. Again and again and again she rubbed the two feathers together—but no bird came.

Oh, but she was worried about her husband! In the morning, she told her father, "I rubbed the feathers together again and again and again, but my husband did not come."

"Perhaps he had something that he had to do in his own country," her father said. "Surely he will come tonight."

The second night, the youngest daughter rubbed the two feathers together again and again—but no bird came. The third night, she rubbed the two feathers together again and again and again—but no bird came. At last, she lost hope entirely and stayed all the time in her room. She could not eat; she could not drink; she had no taste for anything in this life. Not only her merchant father but her whole family became greatly worried about her.

One day her room became so tiresome to her that she went to the window and opened it wide. As soon as she had opened it, she saw that all sides of the window were covered with the points of needles and skewers and nails, and all of those points were bloody. When she saw this, she went in anger to her mother. "Mother," she cried, "who could do this cruel thing? My husband *did* come, but he was wounded and he returned to his own country."

Then to her father she said, "Father, I will go to that country and I will find him."

"Oh, my daughter, don't do it!" said her father. "How can you go there? Don't even *try!*"

But, "Father, I will go. I need one pair of iron shoes and an iron staff, one pair of nylon shoes and a nylon staff, and one pair of leather shoes and a leather staff. Please get them for me," said the youngest one.

So her father got her the things that she asked for. "Here they are, my daughter," he said. The youngest daughter then put some food in a saddlebag and set off to find her wounded husband.

After walking and walking and walking, she came to a fountain and sat there to rest and refresh herself. Then she got up again and went on her way, walking, walking, walking. From time to time, when she felt she could walk no longer, she rested by a fountain to eat and to drink the cool water and to

gain strength to go on.

One day as she was lying down beside a fountain after having eaten her bread and drunk her fill, she closed her eyes to sleep. But sleep would not come, because she was so worried about her husband. As she lay there, exhausted, two pigeons perched on a branch near the fountain and began to talk to one another.

One pigeon said to the other, "Do you know what a terrible trouble that girl has?"

"No, I don't," said the other.

"Well, while she was living a happy life with her husband, her oldest sister was very jealous of her. In her jealousy she placed some needles and skewers and nails on the windowsill of this girl's room. When the youngest one's husband came, he was badly wounded by the needles and skewers and nails, and he returned to his own home. Now he is very ill from those wounds, and he is unable to leave his bed. Didn't you know that?"

The girl understood what the pigeons were saying, but she lay there without moving, and continued to listen. Perhaps from them she could learn how to help her husband.

"What should she do now?" said the second pigeon.

"Well, if she only knew, she could kill us with her iron staff. We could be sacrifices for her. She could put the blood from one of us into a bottle and take the flesh of the other one of us as meat. Then when she finds her husband, she could take him to the *hamam* and wash him with this blood and at the same time feed him our meat that she had cooked. Her husband would thus completely recover," said the first pigeon.

"Really? Is that possible?" said the second one.

"Yes. It is the only way in which that illness can be cured."

"*Aman!*" said the second one. "If only she could know . . ."

At that moment, the girl arose and killed both pigeons with her iron staff. She put the blood of one in a bottle, and packed the other one's flesh as salted meat. Then, forgetting her weariness, she set out again to find her husband, walking more and more quickly with this new hope in her heart.

She went and went and went until she came to another country, but she did not know what country it was. She asked the first person she met, "Is this such and such a country?"

"Yes, it is that country."

"Could you show me where the padishah's palace is?" said the girl.

"Yes. Come with me and I will show you," said that person, and he walked with her to the palace. "There it is," he said.

As the girl entered the courtyard, she saw that there were great crowds of people both outside and inside the palace. One of the padishah's daughters was in the garden, tearing her hair because of grief at her brother's illness.

The youngest daughter of the merchant began to shout, "I am a doctor, an unknown doctor! I'm a good doctor!" And she shouted this same message over and over.

When the padishah's daughter heard this, she became greatly excited and ran at once to her parents. "Father! Mother! There is a new girl outside, a stranger here, who is shouting, 'I am a doctor, an unknown doctor! I'm a good doctor!' Perhaps she can help my brother."

The padishah said, "There is no hope of a cure, my daughter. We have had all of the most famous doctors of the world come here. And they have given him the best treatments, but they have been unable to help. Our son is going to die, and we all know that. Don't you remember, my daughter? Besides all of the best doctors, we have called magicians and healing *hocas*, and not even they could heal him. We have done all that we can. There is no hope."

But the prince's sister begged, "Mother, at least one time let her see my brother. Mother! Mother! That girl might be able to help. Why don't you come outside and talk with her?"

At last the padishah and his wife came out into the courtyard. "Who are you?" they asked the merchant's youngest daughter.

"I am a stranger in your country, but I may be of help to your son," said the girl.

"What is your treatment?" asked the padishah.

"Don't worry about that," said the merchant's youngest daughter. "Just

225

226

take this meat and boil it, and prepare the *hamam*. Those two things are all that I need. Oh, and this, too: no one must be present during the treatment except your son and me."

"All right," said the padishah. "We can at least *try* the treatment you plan." He called his servants and had the *hamam* prepared and the meat boiled and brought to the *hamam* door. Then two servants carried the prince to the *hamam* and left him there with the youngest daughter of the merchant.

The girl kept the prince in the hottest part of the *hamam* until he was well covered with sweat. Then she massaged his battered body thoroughly with the pigeon's blood. While she was still massaging his wounds, she called to the servants waiting at the door, "Please bring me the meat now!"

At the sound of her voice, the prince opened his eyes and said, "Where am I? And why am I here?"

"Do not say a single word," said the girl. "Just open your mouth and eat this meat." And she placed in his mouth the meat that the servants had brought. As he slowly chewed the meat, she continued to massage his punctured skin.

When the last of the meat had been swallowed and the last of the pigeon blood had been used, the prince came to himself and he found to his amazement that his wife was there beside him. "You are here!" he cried. "What happened to me?"

"Don't say anything now," said the girl. "We'll talk later about all that has happened. Wait here for me." And she ran to the door of the *hamam* and sent the servants to call the padishah. "Tell him that his son is well now. He can come to see for himself!"

When the padishah heard this, his heart almost burst with joy, and he ran straight to the *hamam*. "You are right, my girl!" he cried. "My son has recovered completely! Wish from me whatever you want: my land, my title as padishah. You have saved the life of my son, and for that you may have anything that is within my power to give."

"Your Majesty," the girl said, "I want nothing but your son."

The padishah was amazed. "How can that be?" he said. "We do not even know who you are!"

"I am your daughter-in-law, your son's wife. My older sister tried to destroy our life together, but Allah made it possible for us to be reunited."

The padishah looked long and longer at this young woman who had saved his son's life, and the longer he looked, the more satisfied he was with her as his daughter-in-law. To add to their joy, he arranged another wedding celebration that lasted for forty days and forty nights. From that time on, she and the prince lived happily in his home country, and as far as I know, they are living there still.

Mişon's Debt

M işon was in debt to his friend Salamon for a loan of sixty-six golden liras. When his debt came due, Mişon was unable to pay it, and this made him very uncomfortable.

The night before the day the debt was due to be paid, Mişon went to bed, but he could not sleep. His restlessness soon began to bother his wife, Raşal. When Raşal was unable to stand her husband's continuous tossing any longer, she asked, "My dear husband, what is the matter with you? What has happened? Tell me. Are you sick? I can call a doctor."

"No, no, my Raşal," said Mişon, "I am not sick. I am just fine."

But Raşal did not believe that, and so she persisted in trying to discover Mişon's difficulty. "No, my dear. You should tell me. I am begging you to tell me. If you love your God, then you should tell me." She pleaded in this way, but in spite of all her pleading, Mişon refused to tell her anything.

The night passed very, very slowly. Finally it became two o'clock in the morning, and then after a long while, three o'clock. Mişon was still tossing about on the bed, unable to sleep. Finally he said, "All right, Raşal, I shall tell you what my trouble is. Tomorrow I am supposed to repay Salamon sixty-six golden liras that I borrowed from him some time ago. I have not been able to pay it up to this time, and I shall not be able to pay it tomorrow. I have been worrying and worrying about this, for it makes me very uncomfortable that I shall not be able to pay my debt tomorrow."

Greatly relieved, Raşal said, "Oh, my dear Mişon, is that your problem? Oh, thank God that that is all that is bothering you! Now listen to how I am going to take this burden off your back."

Mişon and Raşal lived just a few doors from Salamon on the same street. Raşal opened the window and began shouting, "Salamon! Salamon!" Everyone in the neighborhood woke up.

Salamon came to his window and asked, in a very concerned tone, "Oh, my dear Raşal, what has happened? Is there something wrong?"

Raşal answered, "Oh, no, Salamon, nothing has happened, but I want to tell you something. As you know, my Mişon owes you sixty-six golden liras, and the debt is due to be paid tomorrow. He will be unable to pay you tomorrow, and he has been worrying a great deal about that. He simply won't be able to pay it, and now it is your turn to worry and remain sleepless. That is all that I want to tell you!"

After that, she shut the window, and she and Mişon went back to bed and slept very comfortably.

The Donkey, the Dog, the Cat, and the Cock

Once there was and twice there wasn't, when Allah had many creatures, and to talk too much was a sin—well, in those times there was a woodcutter. This woodcutter had a donkey on whose back he loaded the wood he cut to sell in the marketplace. As time passed, the donkey got old and lame. "This donkey is of no use to me any more," said the woodcutter, and he turned the donkey out to go wherever he chose.

The donkey wandered here and there, hungry. He went and went, and finally he came to a dog. "How are you doing, Brother Dog?" asked the donkey.

"Ah, Brother Donkey, I have been doing well until now. For many years I was a faithful sheep dog for a certain shepherd, protecting his sheep from wolves. When I became too old to be of use to the shepherd, he turned me loose to go wherever I chose. But now I am hungry, and where shall I go for food?"

"I, too, am hungry," said the donkey. "Come, Brother Dog. Let us go together to search for food."

They went and went, two together, until after a long time they came to a lean and lonely cat. "How are you doing, Brother Cat?" they asked.

"Ah, Brother Donkey and Brother Dog, I have been doing well until now. For many years I had an owner, and I protected his cocks from foxes. But now that I have become old, he has turned me out to look after myself. See! I have been three or five days without food, and I am hungry," said the cat.

"We, too, are hungry," said Brother Donkey and Brother Dog. "And we need a place to live. Come with us, Brother Cat. Together we may find both food and shelter."

They went and went, three together, until after a long time they came to a cock. "How are you doing, Brother Cock?" they asked.

"Ah, Brother Donkey and Brother Dog and Brother Cat, until a few days ago I had an owner. My owner had chicks and chickens, and I was protecting them from other cocks, the cocks belonging to his neighbors. But now that I am old, he thinks I am no longer useful, so he has turned me out to look after myself. Still, I am lonely, and, oh, but I am hungry!" said the cock.

"Well, then," said Brother Donkey, Brother Dog, and Brother Cat, "come

along with us. We, too, are old and lonely and hungry, and we need shelter from the weather. As four companions, perhaps we can make new lives for ourselves together."

They went and went, four together, until far ahead they saw a light. "Let's go toward that light," said Brother Dog. "That may be lighting just the house that we need."

"You are right," said Brother Donkey. "Come, now, all of you, and climb up on my back. It is strong enough to carry my friends, and we can reach the house more quickly that way."

So the dog got up on the donkey's back, the cat got up on the dog's back, and the cock got up on the cat's back. "I'll watch," said the cock, "since I am up where I can see well." And along they went until they came to that house.

As they stood by a window of the house, Brother Dog said, "What do you see inside, Brother Cock?"

"Ah!" said Brother Cock. "I see a long table just *filled* with good foods. But hear this, my brothers: around that table there are forty thieves!"

Still, all that the four companions could think about was that good food, and in one voice Brother Donkey brayed loudly, Brother Dog barked loudly, Brother Cat meowed loudly, and Brother Cock crowed as if the sun were rising. As for those forty thieves, their lice ran down to their feet, they were so startled at this strange noise. "Gendarmes!" shouted the leader. "Run for your lives!" And the forty thieves never looked around. They just ran!

As soon as the last thief had disappeared from sight, Brother Donkey trotted into the house with his three friends on his back, and they all settled down to feast at the table. When they had eaten all that they could hold, Brother Cock flew up to perch on the rafter, Brother Cat curled up in front of the fireplace, Brother Dog lay down next to the doorsill, and Brother Donkey

found a comfortable corner. Then, how they slept!

Off in the forest, the thieves talked among themselves. "*Was* that noise the gendarmes coming after us?" said one.

"I don't know," said the bravest one, "but I am going to go and look. I am not afraid of anything, gendarmes or not." And off he went toward the house.

As the thief entered, there was no noise at all. He laughed. "I'll just light my cigarette here by the fire and then go to tell the rest." He bent down to light his cigarette, but the glowing coal he saw was not a coal at all, but the eye of Brother Cat. "*Miav! Miavvv!*" Brother Cat screeched, and scratched the thief's face with his sharp claws.

Hearing this, Brother Dog awoke and bit the thief. "*Hav! Hav!*" he barked. "Brothers, here is a thief!"

Brother Donkey got up from his place in the corner and gave the thief's hip a tremendous kick. And from the rafter Brother Cock called, "Leave some for me! Leave some for me! *Üh-üh-üh-üh-üh-h-h!*" Then he flew down and pecked at the thief's eyes.

No longer brave, the thief ran back to his friends in the forest and told them what had happened. "This cave in the forest is much safer for us than that house!" he said. "Let's stay right here!" And so they did.

The next morning, Brother Donkey, Brother Dog, Brother Cat, and Brother Cock went to the nearest village and reported to the gendarmes, "We have found the forty thieves. Please come to our house and get the stolen goods they have hidden there." The gendarmes came and recovered the stolen goods and then, following the forty thieves' footprints, they captured the forty thieves themselves.

A fine reward was given to the four friends for the help they had given, a reward large enough to let them eat in comfort for the rest of their lives.

Azrail and the Forty-day Furlough

There was once a young man who had one great fear throughout his life, and that was the fear of death. One day he said to his mother, "Mother, I am going to the Immortal Village." He then went out of his room—and out of the world, in one sense.

As he was traveling along, he saw approaching him a man on a white horse. The horse kicked up a great cloud of dust as it came. The horseman was Azrail. Blessed Azrail called out to him, "Where are you going?"

"I am seeking the Immortal Village."

"The Immortal Village is where I live," said the horseman. "I am Azrail. If you stand by me, you will live. Otherwise, you will die."

The young man went with Azrail and worked for him for seven years. Azrail paid him seven *akçes* at the end of that period, one for each year's work. The young man then said, "Blessed Azrail, I want to return to my home village, but I need to ask you a very important question first. When shall I die? When will you come to take my life away?"

Azrail took his notebook from his sash and looked at a certain page in it. Then he said, "When you were in your mother's womb, your destiny was written down. You will live until you enter the nuptial chamber. If you marry and enter the nuptial chamber, I shall come for you."

"Very well, then," said the young man, "I shall never get married, and then you will never have occasion to come for me."

The young man put the seven *akçes* into his sash, and then he left the Immortal Village. He went little; he went far. He went through rivers, over hills, and across plains. One evening he came to a village where he was accepted in a large house as the guest of Allah.

At that house there was a young woman who was very ill. As her parents were giving her water, Azrail entered through the doorway. No one saw him except the young traveler. This young man immediately arose and showed respect to Azrail. Since the young man had served Azrail for seven years, he knew very well why the angel had come. The owners of the house, however, knew none of this, and they scolded the young man for disturbing the grieving relatives. "Why did you rise and distract us from caring for our patient?" they asked. "Our sick woman here needs all the peace that she can get."

"Azrail has come to take the young woman's life," said the young man.

He had no sooner said that than Azrail moved to the foot of the patient's bed and took her life. The family was amazed that this young stranger had known what was happening. They asked him, "Are you Hızır or Hazır? How did you know that Azrail had come?"

"I served Azrail for seven years, and that is why I could detect his presence." The family members then apologized to him for having scolded him. Dinner was served shortly after that, and soon the young traveler was shown to his room for the night. After breakfast the following morning, the young man asked his host's permission to leave and then continued to travel toward his own village.

When he reached home, he was welcomed back after his long absence. "What kinds of experiences did you have in your search for the Immortal Village?" his neighbors asked.

He explained to them everything that had happened. "I also discovered something about my own life and death," he added. "Azrail told me that as long as I remain single, he will not come to take away my life."

"That is just an old tale," said one of the women. And the rest agreed

233

that it was certainly unnatural for a young man not to marry.

The young man decided to settle down again in his native village. First he had a fine house built. When it was finished, the neighbors talked this way and that about which young woman he should marry, and finally he became engaged to a girl. After a year's time, the couple were married in a wedding ceremony that lasted for forty days and forty nights. When the final day of festivities had ended, the couple went to the bridal chamber, but as they entered that room, the bridegroom said, "He will be here at any time now, yes, any time. He told me that he would take my life on my nuptial night."

They had no sooner entered the nuptial chamber, hand in hand, when there was a knock on the door. Azrail entered and said, "Get up, Ali *Ağa*. I have come to take your life."

"Wait for me," Ali *Ağa* said, "and I'll explain the situation to you in a minute."

But the girl said, "Now look here! People doing military duty get a few days off every two or three months. You served Azrail for seven whole years, and yet you never had a single day of furlough. Ask permission to have a furlough now."

Going to the Angel of Death, the young man said, "O Azrail, I served you steadily for seven years, and during that time you never gave me a single day off duty. In the military service, men are allowed to have a few days' furlough occasionally. Can't you give me a few days of furlough now?"

While this conversation was going on at the entrance to the room, the girl was inside the room praying to Allah to grant her wish and give her husband a few days more of life. Allah accepted her prayer and sent Blessed Gabriel to intervene. Allah said to Gabriel, "Tell Azrail that I have given forty more days of life to Ali *Ağa* and that he should therefore not take the young man's life."

After he had received this message from Gabriel, Azrail turned to the young man and said, "Allah has granted you forty more days of life." And so it was that the wishes of Ali *Ağa* and his bride were fulfilled.

Nimrod, Abraham, and the Camel from the Rock

Nimrod the pharaoh once said to Hâlil Abraham, "You say that you are a prophet. Well, if you really are a prophet, then call out from that rock over there a camel with curly hair and eyes tinged with kohl. Furthermore, let it come out with feet of ruby, and have it foal the same way that birds do."

Hâlil Abraham prayed to Allah. The rock split in half, and out came a camel of the kind requested. There before them, the camel foaled as a bird does. People ran to catch this unusual camel. But the camel stepped back into the rock, and the rock closed again.

Prophet Hâlil Abraham said, "O my Allah, did You create that camel in response to my prayer?"

Allah answered, "No, my Hâlil. I created it many thousands of years ago, knowing that they would want to have exactly that creature produced by you. It has been waiting there in the rock all that time."

The Girl Rescued by Three Suitors

Once there was and once there wasn't—there was a merchant in the city of Kabul who had a beautiful daughter named Zöhre. When this girl was of marriageable age, she said, "I am going to put the man I marry to a certain test. Whoever can win the test will have my hand in marriage."

Criers went throughout the country announcing the suitor test, and many men came to try for her hand but none succeeded. One day three fellows came together, one a carpenter, one a dervish, and one a warrior who was a good horseman and swordsman. They had heard of the test, and they had come and submitted their applications. The girl's father said, "You arrived too late for the test today. You will take it in the morning—İnşallah!—and the one who wins will marry my daughter."

They went to sleep, and during the night, the girl disappeared from her room. Her father had a search made for her, but they could not find her anywhere. He finally went to the three companions and said, "The girl you applied to marry is missing. I had her searched for everywhere and I cannot find her. I have come to hear what you will say about her disappearance."

The dervish said, "The girl is imprisoned in the home of a giant on an island in the Indian Ocean, but it is a difficult thing to bring her back from there."

The carpenter, who was able to make a horse that would go on both land and sea, said, "I can make a magic horse, but someone has to ride it."

The warrior said, "If you make the horse, I'll ride it and go and get that girl and bring her back."

The carpenter made a horse of wood. The warrior rode it and brought the girl back. Now, the girl had returned, but a dispute arose among the companions as to which should get her as his bride.

The dervish said, "I discovered where the girl was; therefore, the girl is mine. If I hadn't found her, how would you have been able to bring her back?"

The carpenter said, "Yes, you discovered where the girl was. But I made the horse that brought her back. How would the girl have returned if I had not made the horse?"

Then the warrior said, "You, my dervish friend, discovered where the girl was, and *you,* my carpenter friend, made the horse. But who would have brought the girl back if I hadn't ridden there? Therefore, the girl is mine."

How would you solve this dilemma if you were a judge? To whom did the girl belong?

[After heated discussion among the listeners, with each of the three suitors strongly supported by one or more from the audience, Abdurrahman Erkaya said, "She belongs to the one who brought her back," and the narrator, İbrahim Gürsoy, said, "Yes. That's right. She is his."]

Nasreddin Hoca and Tamerlane Go Hunting

One day Tamerlane was planning to go hunting on the big mountain near Akşehir. He sent word to Nasreddin Hoca asking if he wished to come along on the hunt. Hoca replied, "Indeed I would." Tamerlane had the puniest horse in his stable prepared for the Hoca, and they all went hunting.

All of a sudden there was a great downpour, as it happens nowadays. The Hoca did not own a change of clothes, so he quickly stripped off his clothes and tucked them under his horse's saddle. He found a trail around the mountain and reached his house in Akşehir. The rain had stopped by then, and he therefore slipped his clothes back on.

Tamerlane sent one of his men to see if the Hoca had arrived safely. He was told that the Hoca had not even gotten wet. He asked to see the Hoca, and when Hoca came to him, Tamerlane asked what had happened. Hoca told him that when the downpour started, the horse that Tamerlane had given him, being far superior to that of the Prophet Ali, had sped like lightning and had gotten him home safely. Tamerlane was totally baffled to hear this story.

The next week, when he was about to go hunting again, Tamerlane asked his men to prepare that particular horse for him. Once again there was a storm while they were out on the mountain. This time, the Hoca had been given a decent horse, and he was able to return safely and quickly without getting very wet. But Tamerlane had a very hard time with the horse. He prodded and goaded the horse to go faster but with no success, and he returned to camp thoroughly soaked and disgusted. He asked his men to go fetch the Hoca. He said that the Hoca had mocked him and that he would have him executed.

They brought the Hoca to his presence. "Hoca," said Tamerlane, "how did you dare to make fun of a conqueror like me?"

Hoca replied promptly, "I did not make fun of you. You just are not as quick-witted as I am—that's all. You should have known that horse was slow and you should have done as I did. You should have taken all your clothes off, tucked them under the saddle, and ridden through the forest. Then you should have put your clothes back on before you got to the village center."

Tamerlane acknowledged the wisdom of what Hoca had said, and they resumed their friendship.

Mohammed Protects Man from Satan

While our Prophet was once at the mosque door, Satan passed by carrying three bowls. One of these bowls was full of water, one was full of honey, and the third was full of soil. Our Prophet asked Satan, "Where are you going?"

Satan answered, "There is a battle going on nearby at such and such a place. I am going there."

Our Prophet asked, "Why are you going there?"

Satan said, "I shall put some honey in the mouths of the fighters in order to make them even more ferocious."

Prophet Mohammed then asked, "Of what use is the bowl of soil?"

Satan answered, "Whenever I sprinkle this soil on the worshipers in a mosque, they begin to feel very sleepy. After a while they fall asleep, and they cannot then listen to what the *hoca* is preaching about."

Prophet Mohammed then asked another question: "And what is the use of the water in the third bowl?"

Satan said, "That is not exactly water, but I pretend that it is. In that bowl I put whatever spittle I find and all the slimy materials from latrines. I take this bowl to the deathbeds of people who have but a few minutes to live. I say to such dying people, "Give me your soul, and in exchange I shall give you a drink of this water." They usually turn their heads to the other side, but then I go quickly around to that side, too, and there repeat my question. The family and attendants think that the patient is dying at that very moment and that that is his reason for rolling his head back and forth. But that is not the reason the patient is doing this. The reason is my presence. He is trying to avoid me. If the person gives his soul to me, then he dies as an infidel."

Prophet Mohammed was greatly concerned about the salvation of people. He advised them, "Whenever a person is dying, be certain to have plenty of water at hand to give to him if he seems to be at all thirsty."

Prophet Mohammed then prayed to Allah. He said, "O my beloved Allah, if Satan does such evil things even while I am here on earth to thwart him whenever I can, what may he do to people after my death? I ask that You make him invisible so that he will not be able to appeal to people so easily." (As you know, Satan once walked about everywhere, just like any other creature, and could be seen by everyone.)

Allah accepted the prayer of Prophet Mohammed and made Satan invisible, and that is the way he has remained ever since that time.

Nimrod and the Prophet Abraham

Nimrod the pharaoh said to the prophet Hâlil Abraham, "O Abraham, have you understood the last Judgment Day so well that you could stand up in the middle of a crowd and explain what will occur then? First, you would have to state what sign will indicate the coming of Judgment Day, and then you would have to explain what will happen."

Nimrod then took a piece of chalk, crushed it in his hand, and blew away the dust. He then said, "The person who dies will become dust and will be blown away like this. There is no such thing as Judgment Day!"

When he was alone after that, Hâlil Abraham prayed. He said, "My Allah, what shall I say if this infidel asks me again about Judgment Day? Show me what it will be like."

Allah said, "O my Hâlil, bring me four birds." Hâlil Abraham brought four birds. One was a pigeon, one was a peacock, one was a rooster, and one was a crow.

Allah then said, "Now cut off their heads and lay the heads aside." Abraham cut off their heads and laid them out together.

Allah then said, "Now grind up the bodies of these birds so fine that you can mix them all together in a paste." After this had been done, Allah said, "Now divide this mixture up into four parts." When Abraham had finished this step, Allah said, "Now place a rock on top of each part." And this too was done by Abraham.

After the bodies of the birds had been treated in this way, Allah said, "Now take the birds' heads to the top of that mountain over there, and call the birds."

Abraham took the birds' heads to the top of the mountain, and there he called out, "Come here, birds!" The birds came, and the flesh and the feathers of each were separated from the rest, and each bird, trembling, attached itself to its own head. There stood the four birds just as they had been originally.

Allah then said, "This is how it will be on Judgment Day. I shall separate and mix but still keep everything recoverable. Tell Nimrod this if he asks again."

Ishmael as Intended Sacrifice

After Abraham had had no children by his first wife, he married a second wife. He also prayed to Allah, "O my Allah, if You will give me a son, I shall sacrifice him to You." Allah accepted his prayer, and Abraham's second wife bore him a son whom he named Ishmael.

Abraham's two wives were so jealous of each other that they could not get along very well together. Therefore, Abraham took his second wife, whose name was Hacerullah, to a plot of ground near Mecca. From time to time he took food and other provisions to them there. But for one brief period Abraham was unable to go there, and so Hacerullah and her son went hungry. Hacerullah left Ishmael on the sand and went out in search of food. When she returned, she saw a splendid man standing near the baby. This puzzled her, and she was not certain what she should do. But the man spoke, saying, "O Hacerullah, be not afraid of me! I am Gabriel."

Before Gabriel had come there, Hacerullah had spun around on her heel and gouged out a place in the ground. From that place, water had begun to flow. Using her hands, she had made retaining walls of mud to contain the water that flowed from that spot. When Gabriel saw this, he said, "If you had not made those retaining walls, the whole earth would have become a sea." That is the place from which the Zemzem Spring flows.

And so Ishmael survived and grew up to become a healthy boy. One night, however, Abraham had a dream that involved the boy. In the dream a voice said to Abraham, "You once vowed to make a sacrifice to Allah, but you have not carried out your promise."

On the following day Abraham said to Ishmael's mother, "Have Ishmael take a bath, and see to it that he is clean. I shall take him with me to show him around." Hacerullah did as Abraham had directed, and then Abraham and Ishmael left home.

They began to walk toward the Mine Mountains. Ishmael ran ahead of his father, playing along the way, jumping, and singing. Abraham was so sorrowful about what he was preparing to do that he could not bear to watch the boy. He said, "Ishmael, you come along behind me." After that, Ishmael followed his father as they walked along. When they reached the place where the sacrifice was to be made, Abraham said, "O my Ishmael, come here. We must consider something together. I once made a vow to Allah that if He gave me a son, I would sacrifice that son here." Then he laid Ishmael upon the ground to slaughter him.

Ishmael said, "Oh, Father, tie my hands and arms before you sacrifice me. If you don't do that, I may try to protect myself."

Abraham tied his son's hands and arms and covered his face with a handkerchief. He then tried to cut the boy's throat, but the knife would not cut it. He tried a second time to cut his throat, and again the knife had no effect. The third time the knife failed to cut Ishmael's flesh, Abraham threw it to the ground, where it cut in half a stone that it struck.

At that same moment Allah said to Gabriel, "O Gabriel, take this sacrificial animal to Abraham, and tell him to sacrifice this creature for me. Go quickly!" Thus a sacrifice was sent from the sky, and Ishmael's life was saved.

If that knife had cut Ishmael's flesh, then all sacrifices from that day onward would have been human beings.

Osman Kalkan and the Twice-shared Lemons

One day we were in Erzurum and we were getting ready to come back here to Tercan. In those days transportation was not as good as it is today with all those buses going back and forth. We traveled by train then. All the people from Tercan got on together, and there were seven or eight of us at least. As we were waiting on the platform at the train station, Osman Kalkan said, "Two of you get into the train and get a compartment for us. We are eight or ten, and one compartment should be big enough to hold us."

Zeynel Effendi and I went aboard the train and got a compartment. We took the baggage that our friends handed us through the window. By the time they all joined us there, it was pretty crowded. Osman Effendi had brought a crate of lemons, and we put that in the compartment, too.

A little later the conductor came along. When he started to check our tickets, he asked, "Whose lemons are those?"

"They are mine," said Osman Effendi.

The conductor said, "Uncle, that will also require a ticket. Give me ten liras, and I shall give you a receipt for that amount. When you get into Tercan, you can go and get your change with that receipt. Lemons are a kind of fruit, and so you will have to pay the delivery charge for fruit."

"All right," said Osman Effendi to the conductor. To me he said, "Hand me down that crate of lemons." As soon as I gave him the crate, he began to share the lemons with all of us in the compartment, giving several to each person until the crate was empty. When the conductor returned, Osman Effendi said, "The lemons are all gone. You may have the crate, if you want it."

The conductor laughed and said, "How did you do it?"

When he had gone, Osman Effendi told us to put the lemons back in the crate. "We shall share them again in Tercan," he said.

Osman Effendi
and the Train Ticket

One day it was the turn of Osman Kalkan to go to Sivas with some friends to buy and bring back many things that people in this town had ordered. They went there and picked out all of the merchandise wanted, but there was some time left before the return train to Tercan. During that time, Osman Effendi drank quite a bit and forgot all about buying a ticket for the return trip.

When they boarded the train to go home, all his friends had tickets, but Osman Effendi did not. When the control man [conductor] started coming through the cars to check everyone's ticket, Osman Effendi immediately arose and started saying his prayers. As a result of that, the control man could not ask him anything. Throughout the whole trip he could never approach Osman Effendi because he continued saying prayers whenever the control man was near.

When they reached the Erzincan border, the train crew changed, and there was a new control man. The control man who was leaving said to this new one, "I could never check the ticket of that fellow over there, because every time I went near him, he was praying. Will you please do that for me?"

Just before you reach Tercan coming from Sivas, you pass through the village of Kargın. When the train came to Kargın, the new control man went and stood right alongside of Osman Effendi until he had finished his prayers. Then, before he could start praying again, he asked Osman Effendi for his ticket.

Osman Effendi reached down into his bag and took out a cake he had there. Handing this cake to the control man, he said, "Control man, although I prayed for all of your family, I still could not get away from you. I'm going to get off at Tercan and shall not go any farther."

The control man laughed and let him go.

The Hoca *and the* Dessert

One evening a *hoca* and a *Bektaşi* were invited to dinner at the home of a friend. After the main part of the meal was finished, the host brought the dessert and placed it in the middle of the dining tray.

Looking closely at the dessert, the *hoca* said to his host and the *Bektaşi*, "My friends, that dessert seems rather small for three people. If we divide it into three equal portions, none of us will have more than a taste. I have a suggestion. Let's not eat it tonight but save it until tomorrow. Then the one who has had the most interesting dream tonight will be given the whole dessert to eat."

The other two agreed to this suggestion, and the dessert was placed on a shelf. The three men talked together hour after hour. And then since it was so late, the host rolled out sleeping mats for his guests for the night. At last they all retired.

In the middle of the night, however, the *hoca* awakened and felt somewhat hungry. He went quietly to the shelf, found the dessert, and ate the whole dishful himself.

When they arose in the morning and were seated at breakfast, the host said, "Let us now tell our dreams to see who will get the dessert from last night's dinner. *Hoca*, you tell your dream first."

"No," said the *hoca*, "I'd rather tell mine last. You and the *Bektaşi* tell your dreams first."

The *Bektaşi* said, "I dreamed last night that I was somehow down under the surface of the earth. I kept going down and down and down into the underworld until at last I reached the seventh level below the surface. There I saw such and such." And the *Bektaşi* told them all about what he had seen there.

The host then told his dream. "Last night I dreamed that I could fly. I flew higher and higher and higher into the air until I had reached the seventh level of heaven. There I saw such and such." He then proceeded to tell his friends what he had felt and what he had seen up there.

Now it was the *hoca*'s turn to tell his dream. He said, "It's curious, but last night in my dream I saw my *Bektaşi* friend seven levels below the earth and my host seven levels above the earth. You were both so very far away from this world that I supposed neither of you would ever return. I therefore got up and ate that dessert myself."

246

Separation Born of Suffering

There were once an old couple and their only child, a son. They were very poor, and they had no livestock except a cow to support them. One day while he was grazing his cow at the edge of the forest, the father came upon a large hollow rock that was partly filled with water. Somewhat tired by then, the man sat down in the shade of that rock and fell asleep.

When he awoke, he saw a large snake drinking water from the hollow rock. It drank and drank and drank, and licked up the last drops from the surface. "How very thirsty that snake must be!" said the man. "I'll help him." After the snake had crawled away from the rock, the man poured into the hollow the milk that he had brought along for his own lunch. He watched as the snake returned to the rock and drank every drop of the milk. When it had finished, it spat a gold coin into the hollow and left.

Very pleased, the old man picked up the gold coin, tucked it into his sash, and went along home with the cow. "See, my wife," he said, and he showed her the coin.

"Where did you get that gold coin?" she asked, amazed.

"I got it from a snake."

"From a *snake?*"

"Yes. I saw a large snake drinking water thirstily from a hollow rock at the edge of the forest. After it had drunk all of the water, I poured my lunch milk into the hollow rock, and the snake drank the milk too. Then it spat up this gold coin and left." The old man decided to return to the hollow rock the next day, and as the sun rose high above, he poured his lunch milk into the hollow in the rock. Once again, the snake came and drank the milk thirstily. Then, after finishing the milk, it spat up a gold coin into the hollow and went away. Since gold coins were very valuable, the old man decided to continue this fine exchange. Each day he took a container of milk for the snake, and each day the snake spat up a gold coin into the hollow for him.

This same exchange went on for five years. Then one day the father became ill and was unable to go to the edge of the forest to get the daily gold coin. He sent his son, instead, giving the young man careful instructions about what he should do. Following these instructions, the young man went to the edge of the forest and, true enough, returned with a gold coin.

Because his father's illness continued for some time, the son had to

247

repeat this visit to the forest day after day. He grew tired of it after a while and decided to kill the snake and extract from its body all of the gold at one time. He went to the rock and poured the usual container of milk into the hollow. But when the snake started to drink the milk, the son took out his knife and attempted to cut the snake in half. Instead, he succeeded only in cutting off the snake's tail. Enraged by this attack, the snake sprang upon the boy, coiled itself about his neck, and strangled him.

The boy did not return home that night, nor did he return for several nights after that. When five days had passed, the father was so worried about the welfare of his son that he decided to seek him in the forest despite his own illness. When he reached the hollow rock, he found his dead son, swollen and decayed, lying beside it. Looking around, he saw the tail of the snake lying on the ground.

The snake then came from its hole and spoke to the old man: "Mehmet *Ağa*, do not bring me milk anymore. If you do, it will not be good for either of us. Your son injured me, and I killed him. As a result, you are now my enemy, and I am yours."

"I do not think of it in that way," said the man. "If he had not injured you, you would not have killed him."

"No, please don't bring me milk anymore. As long as I remember the pain of my lost tail and you remember the pain of your lost son, we two cannot get along with each other."

The Chastity Wager on a Faithful Wife

Bekri Mustafa made a living by extorting money from the people of İstanbul. He had a brother who owned a coffeehouse. Bekri Mustafa slept on top of his brother's coffeehouse when he wanted to, he drank when he wanted to, and he worked when he wanted to.

At that same time there was a widow living in İstanbul who had a single son. This son was a very handsome and strong boy, but he upset his mother very much because he would not take an interest in any girl she recommended to him as a likely bride. After a while she grew tired of trying.

One day when she was standing on a street corner, she was thinking about this problem, and she was thinking so hard that she drew the attention of an old man who happened to be passing by. He realized that she was deeply troubled, and he asked her, "Lady, what is wrong?" When she told him what was bothering her, the old man thought for a moment and then he said to her, "The sultan, who lives in that palace over there, has a beautiful and well-mannered daughter of about twenty. She does not know İstanbul at all, but you could never find a girl that was her equal. Your son might well like her. And if he does, you might have the two of them married."

"Oh, but we are poor," the woman said, "and she is in the sultan's family."

The old man told her not to worry about that. "I do not think that that would have to be a problem."

Thinking that she had nothing to lose by trying, the woman finally went to the palace and knocked on the front door. Female slaves opened the door and asked her, "Lady, what do you want?"

"I want to talk with the sultan, if you will permit me to do so."

When the slaves reported this to the sultan, he told them to let the woman come in. When the sultan asked her what she wanted, the woman told him that she had a son of marriageable age. "He wants a girl who is beautiful, religious, and who has not known or been known by İstanbul society. But my son, alas, is poor."

"His poverty would present no difficulty. If my daughter likes him, they may marry. But she cannot go anywhere with you outside the palace. He will have to come here."

The woman was very pleased with this response, and she said that she would bring her son there in about an hour. "He can walk about in your palace, and you will have an opportunity to look him over. If you like him, we can make all of the necessary arrangements for their marriage."

She went home and told her son everything that had happened. He got dressed, went to the palace, met the sultan, and then walked about the royal quarters. Both the sultan and the sultan's daughter liked him very much, and afterward the sultan told the boy's mother that he was entirely satisfactory.

It was not long after this that they were married in a big wedding that lasted for forty days and forty nights. The newly wedded couple went on a honeymoon and seemed to be very happy together. Of course, sometimes being completely satisfied can itself be disturbing to people. They need some kind of action. The young man said to his wife, Fitnat, "In our family it has been a tradition for a man not to live on his wife's money. I am going somewhere to work so that I shall have money of my own."

His wife said, "But, Mehmet, where will you go? Almost everyone comes to İstanbul when he wishes to make money. Why would you want to go away?"

"I would go any place I had to go."

His wife pleaded with him for some time, but the young man was very stubborn. In the end, all that she could say was, "All right."

Taking his gun and a small amount of money, the young man mounted his horse and set out on a journey to seek his fortune. He went little; he went far. He crossed streams and went over hills. He went for six months and an autumn, but when he looked back, he saw that he had gone only the distance of the length of a grain of barley. Anyway, he finally reached İzmir, which was then the second-largest city in Turkey after İstanbul. He went to an inn in İzmir, and after he was settled there, he asked if the innkeeper could recommend a good coffeehouse to him. The innkeeper said, "There is one at Karşıyaka called Gâvur *Hacı* Coffeehouse."

Mehmet went to that coffeehouse, sat down, and ordered a cup of coffee. When he paid for his coffee with a golden lira, everybody stared at him. Just at that moment there was a stir in the coffeehouse, a sudden movement of people. Mehmet asked, "What is happening?"

One of the other customers there said, "You must be a stranger here. Gâvur *Hacı* is coming. Be careful around that man. He will become very angry with anyone who does not stand up when he enters the room."

When Gâvur *Hacı* entered the coffeehouse, everyone immediately stood up except Mehmet. He remained seated, just as he had been before. Gâvur *Hacı* noticed this and said to him, "What bad manners you have, young man! Why don't you stand up?"

The young man answered, "Go away! Who do you think you are, anyway?"

Gâvur *Hacı* was angry by now. He said, "Let me ask you that question. Who do you think *you* are?"

"I am the son-in-law of Sultan Mecid the First. I am the husband of the sultan's daughter, Fitnat."

Gâvur *Hacı* said, "Is that the same Fitnat that I once loved?"

Now the young man became angry. He said, "I spent years looking for a girl like her. How can you make the claim that you know her? If you once knew her, show me a memento, something which once belonged to her."

"Give me three days," said Gâvur *Hacı*, "and I shall bring such a thing to you." He then left his coffeehouse, went to the docks, and took ship for İstanbul. There he found a witch and explained the situation to her. He then said, "You must somehow get me into the palace."

"All right. Here is what I need in order to do that. You must have constructed a large wooden box that can be locked from the outside but that can also be locked and unlocked from the inside. You will have one key and I shall have the other."

Gâvur *Hacı* left and had the box built and then transported to the witch. She put him inside the box at once and hired porters to carry the box to the palace. When the slaves came to the door and asked her what she wanted, the witch said to them, "My son is going away on military service. I am taking him some food, but now that it has grown dark, how can I manage this heavy box? I should like to leave this box here on the porch and pick

250

it up in the morning."

The slaves went to Fitnat and asked her for her permission to allow the box to be left on the porch overnight. The permission was granted, and the box remained on the porch.

Inside the box Gâvur *Hacı* had with him a flashlight, a watch, and a gun. At one o'clock in the morning he opened the box with his key and entered the palace. He found a beautiful woman in bed in the room he knew to be Fitnat's room. He found her to be so beautiful that he changed his mind about his purpose for entering the room and desired only to get into bed with her.

When he tried to pull back the quilt near the top of the bed, he received a sound slap. He said to himself, "I tried this from the top of the bed and failed. Let me try it now from the bottom." But when he tried to pull back the quilt from the bottom, he received another sound slap. He then said to himself, "Since it seems impossible to get into this bed with her, let me do what I originally intended and get some memento from this room to take back and show to her husband." He took a golden cup, a golden comb, and a golden pot and then returned to the wooden box.

When Fitnat awakened in the morning, she noticed that the candles in the room had been blown out. She asked her slave girls who had come into her room during the night, but they said that they knew nothing of anyone's having entered her room. She then told them to go and see what was inside the wooden box that lay on the porch. They reported that they could not get into the box because it was locked securely.

Later in the morning the witch returned and claimed her box. She had porters carry it back to her house, where Gâvur *Hacı* unlocked it from the inside and stepped out. Giving the old woman a handful of gold, he took ship back to İzmir. As soon as he arrived there, he took the three objects stolen from Fitnat's room and delivered them to her husband.

As soon as Mehmet saw the golden cup, the golden comb, and the golden pot, he recognized them as Fitnat's property, and he said to Gâvur *Hacı*, "You win the bet!" To the customers in the coffeehouse he shouted, waving a glass, "Who would like to drink for the sake of this bad woman?"

Back in İstanbul Fitnat grew more and more worried. She was greatly concerned about the welfare of her husband, from whom she had heard nothing since he had left.

Her husband was suffering from many unpleasant feelings. He was very sad. He was dejected and hopeless. He was also angry. He sat down at last and wrote a letter to his wife in which he said this: "I looked for seven years for a girl from a good family. Then I found you. Now I know that you are even worse than a bad woman. I am selling water here in İzmir, and I shall continue that, for I never want to see you again."

When Fitnat received that letter, she called her slaves and said to them,

"There was something very strange about that wooden box that we kept overnight on the porch." Then, after thinking for a moment, she asked them, "Do you know any reliable old man whom I might trust to do some work for me?"

One of them said, "There is an old man named Ahmet who would be reliable."

"Bring him here at once." When Ahmet arrived, she said to him, "Please take this money and buy me a nice suit of man's clothing and a pair of man's shoes. Whatever money is left is yours."

After Ahmet had returned with the things she had ordered, Fitnat dressed up as a man. She said to her slave girls, "No matter how long I may be gone, do not open the door to anyone but me."

Fitnat left the palace, but since this was the first time she had ever been outside by herself, she did not know where she should go. She just started walking, and after a while she came to the coffeehouse where Bekri Mustafa lived. She sat down there and ordered a cup of coffee. Everyone else in the coffeehouse looked at her, for here, they thought, was a very handsome young man. Some, however, said that there was something very unusual about this person. The owner of the coffeehouse asked her, "Are you a resident of İstanbul?"

"Yes."

"Do you need help of any kind?"

"Yes, I do. I need a reliable man to do some work for me. If this man already has a job that pays him ten liras, I shall pay him one hundred. If he does not have any job right now, I shall pay him two hundred liras."

The coffeehouse owner was surprised to hear this. He asked, "What is your name?"

"My name is Yellow *Ağa*."

"Well, Yellow *Ağa*, I have a brother whose name is Bekri Mustafa. He makes a living by extorting money from the people of İstanbul."

"All right. I'll take him."

"Bekri, come here!" his brother called. "You have a job. Yellow *Ağa* wants you to work for him."

After Bekri had accepted this offer, Fitnat gave him some money and said, "Go and buy for each of us a horse, a whip, a bag, a gun, and a knife." After these purchases had been made, Fitnat and Bekri mounted their horses and rode to İzmir. When they arrived in that city, one of the first places they came to was the coffeehouse of Gâvur *Hacı*. They decided to stop there and drink some coffee.

While they were sitting there in Gâvur *Hacı's* coffeehouse drinking coffee, Mehmet came along selling water. Fitnat called him over and ordered a cup of water. After she had drunk this water, she paid for it with a gold lira, and she said to Mehmet, "Go and get a shave! Don't you have a family? Why do you go about looking this way?"

Of course, Mehmet did not know that this was his wife talking to him. He went and got a shave. Three days later when he was passing that way again, he called out, "Water! Water! Who wants to drink water?"

Fitnat called him over and ordered a cup of water. When she had finished drinking it, she gave him ten liras and told him to return to İstanbul.

Right at that moment Gâvur *Hacı* entered the coffeehouse, and as he did so, everyone but Fitnat stood up. Very angry at her behavior, Gâvur *Hacı* asked her, "Why didn't you stand up?"

"Why should I stand up? Who do you think you are?"

"This man over here said that to me a short while ago, and now he is selling water for me. The same kind of thing will happen to you, too!"

Fitnat called Bekri and said to him, "Show him who we are!" Bekri threw down Gâvur *Hacı* and beat him soundly. Bekri then asked everyone present, "Who wishes to side with him and help him?"

Nobody answered, and Gâvur *Hacı* said, "I have had enough!" The *hacı* felt that he had encountered some very troublesome people, but he decided to invite them for dinner and try to become friends of theirs.

That evening they went to Gâvur *Hacı*'s house. He had a big table full of food and plenty of strong *rakı*. But Fitnat had with her some even stronger *rakı*, and she told Bekri to serve that stronger *rakı* to Gâvur *Hacı*. She did not drink any.

When the drinking started, Bekri always served Gâvur *Hacı* İstanbul *rakı*, and it was not long before Gâvur *Hacı* was very drunk. Fitnat then said to Bekri, "Pull his trousers down." When Bekri did this, she heated her father's imperial seal and branded Gâvur *Hacı* on one buttock with it.

The following morning they returned to the Gâvur *Hacı* Coffeehouse, but Gâvur *Hacı* was not yet there. He had still not recovered from his drinking of the night before. When he finally arrived there, Fitnat said to him, "What has happened to you amounts to nothing. We shall do much worse yet."

After she left the coffeehouse, Fitnat wrote a letter to the local judge. This is what she said in that letter: "When I was very little my father died, and my uncle became the sultan. The man now called Gâvur *Hacı* grew up in our household. When my father was dying, he was worried about this man, and in his will he warned us against him. My father was justified in believing him a bad man, for when this man left, he took many of the expensive things from our palace. He moved here and bought a business and became a rich man. Now that we have discovered him, we want to get our possessions back."

When they went to see the judge, he said, "I understand your claim against this man, but my men would not dare bring him into court."

Fitnat said, "Very well, but my man Bekri can do so."

As a matter of fact, all that Bekri had to do was to go to the coffeehouse and say to Gâvur *Hacı*, "Come with me!" and he followed Bekri back to the

253

judge's office. When he arrived there, the judge read aloud to him the accusation made against him.

Gâvur *Hacı* denied what it said. "No, no, Your Honor. I am a native of this city, and what wealth I have I earned entirely by myself."

Fitnat said to the judge, "Of course he is going to deny it."

The judge then asked her, "How can you definitely prove the truth of your accusation?"

She said, "Your Honor, my father was a sultan. These are his signet rings. This man has these letters and the symbols of these signet rings marked upon one of his buttocks."

The judge ordered Gâvur *Hacı* to expose his buttocks, and when he saw the signet markings, he ordered that the accused man be beaten. The court confiscated all of Gâvur *Hacı*'s property and distributed it among the poor. He now had nothing, and when Fitnat and Bekri Mustafa were returning to İstanbul, they asked him to go along with them as a servant.

Mehmet had already returned to İstanbul. As soon as he arrived there, he went to the palace to see his wife, but he was unable to find her anywhere. When Fitnat got back, she took off her male clothing and called her husband. When he came to her, she asked, "How could you ever have believed anything that that man said about me? He is here now in such and such a room. You must stay here and talk with him. Ask him about his lies about me!"

While Mehmet waited, Fitnat changed back into her male clothes. She then said to Bekri Mustafa, "Bring Gâvur *Hacı* here."

When Gâvur *Hacı* was brought to them, they ordered him to tell the truth about how he had deceived Mehmet concerning his wife's chastity. He told them everything.

They had him tied to the tails of forty horses and then whipped those horses. When the horses ran away, he was killed immediately.

Bekri Mustafa was given a place to live in the palace. And after that, Mehmet and Fitnat lived happily together. Their hearthstone coal burned bright; / May ours not lose its light. [*Onlara kömür; / Bizlere ömür.*]

Guide to Pronunciation of the Turkish Alphabet

Turkish Alphabet: *a, â, b, c, ç, d, e, f, g, ğ, h, ı, i, j, k, l, m, n, o, ö, p, r, s, ş, t, u, ü, v, y, z*

Sounded as in English: *b, d, f, l, m, n, p, t, v, z*

Not used at all: *q, w, x*

Difficult sound to make: ğ. Suggestion: Lengthen the sound of the vowel that immediately precedes it (example: *ağa*) and give the ğ no sound at all.

Turkish Alphabet	*Example*
a as *u* in *puddle*	*hamam* (Turkish bathhouse)
â as *ya* in *kayak*	*helâl* (religiously approved action, item, or relationship; without obligation)
c as *j* in *judge*	*hoca* (Muslim preacher and/or teacher)
ç as *ch* in *cheese*	*akçe* (small silver coin now out of use)
e as *e* in *get*	*ezan* (Muslim call to worship)
g as *g* in *goat*	*Giresun* (a Turkish province)
h as *h* in *happiness*	*hacı* (Muslim who has completed the pilgrimage to Mecca)
ı as *u* in *rub*	*kadı* (Muslim judge in pre-Republican Turkey)
i as *i* in *ridge*	*imam* (Muslim prayer leader)
j as *s* in *treasure*	*ejder* (dragon)
k as *k* in *kettle*	*rakı* (Turkish alcoholic beverage)
o as *o* in *rope*	*sofra* (short-legged dining table or tray)
ö as *ir* in *shirt*	*Köroğlu* (name of Turkish Robin Hood)
r as *r* in *race*	*Ramazan* (Muslim fasting period)
s as *s* in *sacred*	*köse* (beardless man, villain in tales)
ş as *sh* in *sheep*	*Bektaşi* (member of a Muslim sect noted for flaunting standard Muslim practice)
u as *u* in *full*	*Dursun* (name frequently used among the Laz people along the Black Sea coast)
ü as *ew* in *new*	*üh-üh-üh-üh-üh-h-h* (sound of rooster crowing)
y as *y* in *year*	*yatsı* (Muslim evening prayer performed two hours after sunset)

Glossary of Turkish Terms
and Folk Elements

Turkish words or words derived from the Turkish are rendered in the Turkish alphabet.

ABLUTIONS Required ritual washing by Muslims preparatory to prayer; subsequent to various other acts

AĞA Landowner accorded leadership and/or respect because of holdings; also, honorific often attached to personal name as a mark of respect

AKÇE Small silver coin used during Ottoman period

ALEYKÜMSELÂM! Response of Muslim to another Muslim's greeting (*Selâmün-aleyküm!*); meaning: "And peace to you, too!"

ALLAH The Muslim term for God

AMAN! Expression used when surprised, distressed, or dismayed; stronger forms: *Aman, aman!* and *Aman, aman,* Allah!

ARAP Narrators' version of "Arab"; an enormously large supernatural jinnlike creature represented as having somewhat Negroid features and often described as black, though Arabs not black; performs tasks ordered by one summoning him

ATATÜRK Turkey's national hero; military leader effecting independence of Turkey following World War I and founder of present-day Republic of Turkey

AZRAİL In Muslim belief system, the Angel of Death

BAGGY TROUSERS (Turkish: *şalvar*) Traditional rural dress, warm in winter and cool in summer; trousers gathered at waist, baggy in seat, low in crotch, and narrow at ankles; men's *şalvar* typically wool and solid black, gray, or brown; women's *şalvar* typically bright-colored cotton print

BATMAN Premetric unit of weight varying through time from 2.5 to 10 kilograms

BAYRAM Feast day or days, especially those following end of Ramazan; includes both religious and government holidays

BEAT THE KNEES Traditional way for both men and women to express deep grief

BEKRİ MUSTAFA Uninhibited bully boy and notorious drunkard of early seventeenth-century Ottoman Empire; subject of many tales and anecdotes

BEKTAŞİ Member of an order of Muslim dervishes

BEY Formerly a title inferior to "pasha" and superior to "*ağa*"; used as term of respect following a name (as Ahmet Bey) or as term signifying "gentleman" or "chief"

BİSMİLLÂH! Meaning: "in the name of Allah"; used by Muslims when beginning any task or undertaking

BREAST OF FEMALE GIANT In Turkish tales, female giants' breasts flung over shoulders when kneading bread; hero's nursing undetected from breast essential to afford hero status as "milk child" and protection from and by giantess

BURST Turkish euphemism for taking child aside to urinate (not intended literally)

CHIMNEY OPENING Listening point at which eavesdropper can readily overhear conversation of those within Turkish home

CHOICE BY APPLE-THROWING Method used to determine groom; one hit with apple thrown by princess becomes her groom

CİRİT Game played by men on horseback similar to polo but requiring skill in throwing javelin-like sticks

CLOG Shoe with three- or four-inch wooden sole with strap for support worn usually in Turkish bathhouse but occasionally outdoors as well; usually beautifully decorated

COFFEEHOUSE Place restricted to men for drinking of tea and coffee (usually tea) and socializing; part of coffeehouse often extends outdoors; forerunner of European sidewalk cafés

CURSE When uttered, especially by parents or by offended or injured individuals, invariably effective; in tales, often requires difficult quest by hero or heroine

ÇARŞAF Garment covering Muslim woman from head to foot, revealing only eyes and one hand; traditional outdoor wear among some social classes during Ottoman period

ÇÜŞ! Turkish equivalent for "Whoa!"

DERVİSH Member of any of various Muslim religious orders dedicated to a life of poverty and chastity

DONKEYS AND SONS OF DONKEYS! An offensive epithet among Turks; even use of word *donkey* occasion for apology by speaker

EFFENDİ Term of respect added to a personal name (as Ahmet Effendi) or, as more recently debased, used in addressing children and servants

EYVAH! Turkish expression of distress; meaning: "Alas!"

EZAN The five-times-daily call to prayer from the minaret

FAT TAIL Representative of ultimate in luxurious living; derived from taste for tail of fat-tailed sheep, considered a delicacy

FATHER Term of respect used by younger person to older male not member of family; other similar terms of address to unrelated individuals: aunt, daughter, grandfather, grandmother, uncle, son

FORTIETH ROOM In many Turkish tales, the forbidden room, one not to be opened or entered

FOUNTAIN Any public source of water, most often supplied through a faucet or faucets

GÂVUR *HACI* Name, translated "Infidel Pilgrim," signal of character from whom only the worst to be expected

GENDARME Officer assigned to maintain order in village, area of countryside, or neighborhood; now, member of army forces designated to serve Ministry of Interior

HACI One who has completed the pilgrimage to Mecca, one of five basic tenets of Islamic faith

HAMAM Public bathhouse to which people go not only to bathe but to enjoy social gathering; certain sections for men and others for women, or certain days for men and others for women; no mixing of sexes at *hamam*

HANIM Title of respect, meaning "lady," used when addressing a woman; example: Ayşe *Hanım*

HARAM Forbidden food, item, or act in Muslim canon law; unless made *helâl* (acceptable), punishable on Judgment Day; example: removal of corpse from grave

HELÂL Acceptable food, item, or act in Muslim canon law; free of obligation on Judgment Day

HELVA A dessert or candy made from sesame oil, farina or flour, and syrup; occasionally, nuts and spices added

HIZIR Most frequently mentioned Muslim saint; guardian of the virtuous and deserving; last-minute rescuer in time of danger; usually represented as an old man with white hair and long white beard; his blessings and curses always effective

HOCA Muslim preacher or teacher; in anecdotes, often viewed as somewhat greedy

İBRİK Water pitcher with long, curved spout; used to pour water for guests or older family members or for self for washing of hands and other parts of body

İFRİT Creature with supernatural powers; sometimes helpful, sometimes harmful; can have special insight into character and intentions of others

İMAM Prayer leader in mosque; also, a religious leader in Islamic faith

İNŞALLAH! Term meaning "if Allah wills"; said when one states a plan or expresses a desire for something

IRON SHOES AND AN IRON STAFF Traditional equipment provided to hero or heroine for use in quest of lost sweetheart or spouse

KADI Judge of Muslim canonical law in pre-Republican Turkey; in folktales, any judge, religious or secular, past or contemporary

KAF Location of the Mountains of Kaf, part of Muslim mythology, and thought to form the rim of the world around the edges of the Circumambient Ocean

KAYSERİ City and province in central Turkey; residents reputed to be excep-

258

tionally clever

KAZA Political subdivision of a province in Turkey; equivalent of "county" in the United States

KELOĞLAN A boy or man bald from a scalp disease; in folktales, degraded but clever and lucky; next to Nasreddin Hoca the most popular folk hero

KIRAT Name usually given to the powerful magic steed of the folk hero Köroğlu (translation: Gray Horse)

KISKAÇ Hinged tool with metal teeth at open ends; used to grip broomstraws in place while cord or wire being bound around straws to form broom

KISSA Moral fable using people and not animals as characters; intended to guide behavior of people in power

KİSMET Fate, or fortune

KÖROĞLU The Turkish Robin Hood, subject of many tales and ballads; meaning of name: son of the blind one (father blinded at order of cruel Bey of Bolu); leader of many others wronged by Bolu Bey

KURUŞ A small copper coin; in earlier times, 100 kuruş equal to one lira; with lira now greatly devalued, kuruş worthless

KÜP A huge pottery urn or jar, normally used for storage of water or oil; also, ridden through air by witch as means of transportation to achieve evil ends

LAZ Resident of region along Black Sea coast; butt of jokes told by Turks elsewhere; falsely reputed to be stupid

MILITARY SERVICE Now mandatory in Turkey for all males between 18 and 40, with average service two years; preceding establishment of Republic (1923), males expected to serve in military as needed

MILK BROTHER One nursed even briefly by other than own mother, thereby becoming milk brother or milk sister of other woman's child or children; milk siblings expected to help and protect one another

MİNARET Tall, slender tower attached to a mosque and encircled by one or more balconies, from one of which the *ezan* chanted; encloses a narrow, winding staircase usually without handrail

MOSQUE Muslim house of worship attended by men for both daily and Friday (Muslim Sabbath) services; women secluded if present; *hoca* preacher there, and imam prayer leader

MUHTAR Local administrator of village, small town, or ward of city; only elected official many rural Turks ever see in person

NAMAZ Turkish term for Muslim religious service

NASREDDİN HOCA Best-known Turkish folk character; believed to have lived in time of Tamerlane, but Hoca anecdotes universally appropriate; sometimes wise, sometimes foolish, but always entirely human; subject of thousands of anecdotes; served as preacher, teacher, and occasionally village judge

NOOSES OF ROPES OILED In preparation for execution by hanging, nooses of ropes oiled to ensure snug fit; when nooses oiled, execution imminent

259

NÜKTE Anecdote dependent for effect on terminal word play; difficult to communicate in language other than Turkish

ÖF! Turkish equivalent of "Ugh!"

ÖLÜSÜ KANDİLLİ! (translation: candle-lighted corpse) A scornful and insulting oath

PADİSHAH Ruler or king of a country or of a class of subjects (padishah of birds, padishah of fairies, padishah of snakes); has power of life and death over his subjects

PERMISSION TO LEAVE Custom of a guest's asking his host's permission to leave still strong in Turkey and in tales; a mark of courtesy and good breeding

PİLAV A rice dish, often including pine nuts and dried currants, and sometimes bits of meat; staple in Turkish diet

PLUCK A GOOSE Euphemism for "cheat a fool" or "elicit money or goods from a fool"; similar: "fleece" the unwary

RAKI A strong alcoholic beverage made from rice, molasses, or grain and having an anise flavor; when mixed with water, turns cloudy or milky, thus often called "lion's milk"

RAMAZAN The thirty-day fasting period observed each year by faithful Muslims; during daylight hours, absolutely nothing eaten or drunk or smoked; nighttime hours spent in eating, socializing, and storytelling

SALT IN A CUT OR WOUND Device used by hero or heroine to keep self awake to detect a dragon, an intruder, or one performing service secretly

SASH A cummerbund; a long, wide strip of cloth wound several times around the waist of a man or woman, both to carry valuables and to provide abdominal support while doing heavy work

SEAL Item embossed with insignia of royal family; often mounted on a ring; pressed into wax, used to seal letters or chests containing costly items; when heated, used for branding

SELÂMÜNALEYKÜM! Greeting given by one Muslim to another when meeting as strangers; meaning: "Peace to you!"; designed to show intent to be cordial

SHERBET In Turkey, a cold sweet fruit drink served at festivals, used to announce a birth or some other happy event, and enjoyed during outings at Turkish bath

STATE BIRD Upon death of heirless padishah, padishah's dove (the state bird) set free to fly over gathered crowd to select new padishah; one on whose head the bird alights named padishah

SULTAN A Muslim ruler having the power of life and death over his subjects; tends to govern more territory than a padishah

TALISMAN Object associated with safety or life force of person; when object destroyed, person destroyed; if person endangered or dying, talisman rusty or bloody

TEKERLEME Nonsensical rhymed beginning formula of a folktale catching listeners' attention and preparing them to hear a tale; unlikely and/or impossible situations described; removes listeners from everyday life, ready to enter the world of the tale; sometimes used as separate tale when plot complete and conflict resolved

TEMEL Name frequently found among Laz males, and now almost a generic term for "Laz"; other names commonly found: Dursun, Hızır, and İdris

TESTIMONIAL STATEMENT Basic statement of belief made by one accepting Islam as faith: "Allah is one, and Mohammed is His Prophet"

VİZİER A high officer during the Ottoman Empire, serving as advisor to a sultan or a padishah

WAR OF INDEPENDENCE War led to victory of Turks against Greek and other Allied invaders following World War I; leader: Atatürk

WELL In tales, rarely only a source of water; often a deep, dry pit serving as entrance to underworld

WITCH Person who may or may not have supernatural powers; often simply a meddling or malicious old woman serving as accomplice of villain; witch's transportation: a flying *küp*

YUFKA Flat sheet of unleavened bread baked on slightly convex metal *saç* or *sac*; sheets stored until needed; moistened to soften before use

ZEMZEM SPRING Spring visited by those on pilgrimage to Mecca, with containers of sacred water taken home to share

Index of Tales by Title